DEREK LANDY

ALSO BY
DEREK LANDY

NOVELS

DEREK LANDY

HarperCollins*Publishers*

First published in hardback in Great Britain by HarperCollins *Children's Books* 2014*

HarperCollins *Children's Books* is a division of

HarperCollins*Publishers* Ltd

77-85 Fulham Palace Road, Hammersmith, London W6 8JB

Visit us on the web at www.harpercollins.co.uk

Visit Skulduggery Pleasant at
www.skulduggerypleasant.co.uk

Derek Landy blogs under duress at
www.dereklandy.blogspot.com

1

HB ISBN: 978-0-00-755953-4
TPB ISBN: 978-0-00-756211-4

Typeset by Palimpsest Book Production Limited, Falkirk, Stirlingshire

Printed and bound in England by Clays Ltd, St Ives plc

* *The Lost Art of World Domination*, first published in *Skulduggery Pleasant*, 2012 Down-under Tour Edition; *Gold, Babies and the Brothers Muldoon*, first published in *Playing with Fire*, 2012 Down-under Tour Edition; *The Slightly Ignominious End to the Legend of Black Annis*, first published in *The Faceless Ones*, 2012 Down-under Tour Edition; *Myosotis Terra*, first published in *Mortal Coil*, 2012 Down-under Tour Edition; *The Wonderful Adventures of Geoffrey Scrutinous*, first published in *Mortal Coil*, 2012 Down-under Tour Edition; *Just Another Friday Night*, first published in *The End of the World*, 2012 Australian Edition; *The End of the World*, first published in 2012; *Trick or Treat* and *The Button*, first published on www.dereklandy.blogspot.com

This book is dedicated to my brand new nephew, Cameron.

Cameron, I'm sure you'll grow taller as you get older, but right now you're simply way too short. You also can't talk or stand up, and I have yet to see you read a book. None of this is entirely your own fault, however – I blame the parents – so I hope my words don't upset you too much.

The problem is, you're surrounded by a formidable sister and some formidable cousins, so you're going to have to grow up to be an exceptional person. I'll do what I can to help, but the rest is up to you.

THE TIMELINE

INTRODUCTION

I've always loved Introductions.

They remind me of when I was a kid, wandering through second-hand bookstores, pulling battered old horror paperbacks from the shelves. Those wrinkled covers, those dog-eared pages, that wonderful, slightly stale smell of stories... Those books pulled you into their own history, made you a part of it, and if you were lucky – like, *really* lucky – right before the story started you'd find the Author's Introduction.

This, to a kid who wanted nothing more than to be a writer, was a portal into imagination. I couldn't Google a writer's name and read his blog or watch every interview he'd ever done on YouTube (and I hereby wave to some reader way off in the future who's just read that and is now getting information about "Google" "Blog" and "Youtube" downloaded directly into his brain), so I had to make do with what brief glimpses I was afforded. It was in the Introductions that authors talked about their work and their process, and I scoured these words, searching for the secret to writing, hunting for the Big Clue that would lead me to Where Stories Come From.

I found glimpses of the Big Clue in the words of Stephen King and other masters of the genre, but nothing definite. Still, in many ways it was enough. These glimpses brought with them their own kind of inspiration, and when I was a kid, when I was a teenager, that's all I needed. My early stories dripped with blood. They were soaked in it. Drenched. I had yet to learn concepts such as subtlety or restraint, and there is definitely a place for subtlety and restraint – but it was not a place that held any interest for me. I was all about the blood, the rawness, the viscera. I was reading King and Clive Barker and James Herbert and Michael Slade and Skipp and Spector and Shaun Hutson and dear GOD the list goes on. My life was blood-soaked books, horror movies and heavy metal.

Ah, youth...

And yet, dig a little deeper and you reveal a love of film noir and craggy detectives in rumpled suits and cool hats. Dig a little more and you uncover a love of westerns inherited from a father, a love of screwball comedies inherited from a mother (and for a kid who has stammered all of his life, to find these movies where everyone talks really really fast was beyond exhilarating), and a love of science fiction and adventure that blossomed in the eighties because of people like Spielberg and Lucas and shows like *Knight Rider* and *Airwolf* and *The Six Million Dollar Man*...

Taking all this into account, I am the sum of my obsessions. I am every movie I've ever seen and every book I've ever read. I am every song I've ever listened to. I am every comic I've ever bought. I am entire collections by Joseph Wambaugh and Elmore Leonard and Joe R Lansdale and I am *His Dark Materials* and I am *Harry Potter*.

And in all of these things, I have glimpsed the Big Clue. And these glimpses were enough to open my eyes to the ideas swimming naturally through the soup of my mind. It was from that soup that I plucked Skulduggery Pleasant himself, back in the summer of 2005, and he brought with him every genre I've ever loved.

He is a detective (crime) who is also a skeleton (horror) who takes on a partner (screwball) and they fight monsters (fantasy) and they save the world (adventure). With a little bit of sci-fi thrown in, to stop things from getting boring.

The stories in this collection – arranged here in chronological order for your reading pleasure – are but fragments of the world that Skulduggery has opened up for me. It is because of him that I am able to write a western and sit it comfortably beside a novella about a middle-aged man revisiting the horrors of his childhood. It is because of him that the tones of these stories shift so radically between one and the next. It is because of him that I have the freedom to write the kind of stories I loved, and continue to love, to read.

And if there is a fledgling writer out there who is searching through this Introduction in an effort to find the Big Clue – the secret to writing that I, along with all the other writers, share only amongst ourselves – I am afraid I must disappoint you. This is something you must find out for yourself, fledgling writer, as the Author's Code expressly forbids me from speaking of it in public.

I may already have said too much...

Derek Landy,

Dublin

Saint Patrick's Day, 2014

ACROSS A DARK PLAIN

ACROSS A DARK PLAIN

t was the year of Our Lord eighteen hundred and sixty-one, and it was up west of the Missouri River in South Dakota, and the Dead Men were riding again.

This was still years before that damn fool Custer stumbled across all that gold in the Black Hills, years before Wounded Knee and the massacre that took place there. This was back before the territory was admitted into the union, back before Deadwood, back even before that pitiful Treaty of Laramie promised the region to the Lakota people, a treaty that, if ever that was one, was drawn up just to be burned.

It was a time of gunfighters and outlaws and hard living and easy dying and, of course, it was a time of mean-spirited, blood-slicked magic.

The Dead Men had travelled east from Wyoming, tracking their quarry, who'd led them a merry dance. But the longer they tracked, the easier it got. This was on account of the fact that their quarry had taken up with a Necromancer named Noche, who was developing a habit of leaving dead folk in his wake. Not regular dead folk, neither, but the kind that jumped up and ran around and had a madness in their dull eyes and a terrible, terrible hunger that could only be sated by human flesh. The kind only fire or a bullet to the brainpan could put down. Thankfully, fire and bullets were what the Dead Men specialised in.

Seven of them, all Irish, some of their accents a little muddied due to all the travelling and the living they'd done. There was Saracen Rue, all easy charm and easy smiles, like a man trying to convince himself he's nicer than he is. Beside him rode Dexter Vex, one of the more thoughtful of the group, though he wasn't one to show it. The quiet one with the week's worth of stubble was Anton Shudder, and a scarier man was hard to find, even in this forsaken land. There was Erskine Ravel, recently returned from his sojourn to lands even more foreign and forsaken than this one, and Hopeless, a man of one name and many faces.

Riding in the lead was the scarred man, Ghastly Bespoke, and beside him the living skeleton, the one who looked like the Grim Reaper himself, the first of the Four Horsemen written about in the Bible and shouted about from pulpits up and down this wounded and pockmarked country.

And I looked, and behold a pale horse: and his name that sat on him was Death, and Hell followed with him. And power was given unto them over the fourth part of the earth, to kill with sword, and with hunger, and with death, and with the beasts of the earth.

Skulduggery Pleasant's clothes were scuffed and faded, and his coat was long and may have been black once upon a time. Among normal folk, what these men called 'mortals', he'd take that kerchief from around his neck there and tie it over all those teeth that were fixed in that permanent grin, and he'd pull that hat down low over those empty eye sockets. He had two pistol belts, criss-crossing low and held in place with tie-downs, and in those holsters he had guns with pearl handles and long barrels. Colt Walkers, they were. Guns built for stopping men.

They'd been riding for days and their horses were tired and thirsty, and the riders with flesh were chafed and sore. They came upon the town of Forbidden, and didn't think much of it. A town of three streets and dirty people who bathed not often or well. There was a mangy dog lying in the middle of the street, who looked at them with mild indifference as they passed. When they were safely gone, the dog offered up a feeble growl, then lay back down and went to sleep or died. Didn't make much difference to anyone which one it was.

They found the livery down the other end of town and the owner, an ungrateful piece of work called Sully, limped out into the sun, scratching himself in places soap hadn't touched in a long, long time.

"Yeah?" he said with a mouth full of spit. "What the hell d'you want?"

The Dead Men dismounted. Pleasant and Bespoke stayed at the back, them being the most likely to draw attention, and Rue and Vex looked at the proprietor and frowned.

"What the hell do you think we want?" Vex said. "We want our horses fed and watered. You own this place, don't you?"

The piece of work Sully looked at these men, saw the steel in their eyes and the steel on their hips, and he lost some of his scowl and swallowed some of his spit.

"I do," he said. "Proud owner of Sullivan's Livery. If the paint hadn't peeled off years ago, you could see my name on the sign up there, even though it was spelled wrong and the 'y' was missing from Livery. I blame myself, not being able to read, and I blame the fella I hired to make the sign, him not being able to write. But regrets are what regrets are – we all have 'em, and those who don't have 'em don't miss 'em. Fed and watered, you say. You can depend on me, provided you have coin enough to pay for such a service."

Vex tapped Rue's arm. "Show the man some coin, Saracen." He went to join the others, who were walking down the wide patch of dirt called Main Street towards the saloon. The townspeople gave them a decent berth, watched them with wary eyes and waited till they were out of earshot to start whispering. Men with guns were never a good sign. Men who looked like they knew how to use those guns even less so.

Bespoke was first through the doors into the saloon. Inside were a few uneven tables, a solid bar and a cracked mirror. There was a small piano nobody played and the floor was dried mud and sawdust. As far as patrons went, there weren't many here, but all heads turned, and all mouths dropped open. To see a man of Bespoke's scarring was not something you're ever likely to see again, and most people seemed to realise that, so they made sure to stare extra hard when they first met him.

Bespoke tipped his hat to the room and walked up to the bar.

The other Dead Men followed, filing in one at a time. Pleasant came last, found a table in the corner to sit, watching the room from beneath the brim of his hat.

"Good day to you, barkeep," said Bespoke. "What sort of drinks do you serve here?"

The barkeep, a man who'd seen a lot and heard more, had never been one to allow ugliness to get in the way of making money. There was a time he'd even served a leper who had wandered through town, though he served him out back, away from the eyes of his regulars. Money was money, he figured, and it didn't matter a whole lot how many stumps for fingers a hand had if what it was holding could add to the coffers.

Fact is, the barkeep hadn't even washed the mug the leper had used all that much. So the barkeep told the scarred man what was on offer and the scarred man asked for six drinks. Saracen Rue came in as the sixth was poured, and they all drank like thirsty men. Except for Pleasant, of course.

"Now that," said Ravel, "was a long time coming. And it was

welcome." He smiled at the barkeep. "We're looking for a friend of ours. Two friends, actually, would've just passed through here. Maybe you saw them. Maybe you served them two of these delicious and refreshing beers."

The barkeep said nothing.

"Our first friend," said Vex, "is like us – he's Irish. Tall and dark-haired and kinda pale, though in this sun he's probably reddened up a little. Wears a glove on his right hand. The other fella wears black and carries a staff with him wherever he goes, the height of a man."

The barkeep looked at the Dead Men and still said nothing.

"It is very important that we catch up to our friends as soon as possible," Rue said. "We have news from home that requires their immediate and direct attention. Tragic news. Time is of the essence."

"Haven't seen anyone," said the barkeep.

"You're sure? Our first friend, he has green eyes. Normally eye colour means very little when talking about a man, but if you'd ever looked into those eyes, you'd remember them. Like a snake's. And the second, as I said, carries a big old staff. That's something to stick in the memory, isn't it?"

The barkeep shook his head. "Can't help you, fellas."

"Well," said Ravel, "that is a shame."

Bespoke turned to the dusty, dirty patrons. "How about the rest of you? Seen anyone like the men we just described?"

A few people kept staring at Bespoke's face. Others looked down at their beers. One or two, and this caught the attention of the Dead Men, flickered their gaze to a man who sat alone with his eyes fixed on his hands. He was so knotted up, he was shaking. The long silence that followed grew heavy and seemed to weigh down on his narrow shoulders. It grew so heavy he evidently couldn't take it any more and he jumped to his feet and went for his gun all at the same time. He made a mess of both, went stumbling and fumbling and panicking, and Hopeless crossed to him so quick no one knew quite what was happening till the man hit the floor with a broken nose and no gun in his hand.

Hopeless walked back to the bar, put down the man's gun and picked up his drink, finished it just as the man realised he was bleeding.

"What did you do that for?" he said. He had a peculiar accent, German or Dutch or some such.

"You were going to shoot us," said Vex.

"I was not," said the man, though there wasn't a person there who believed him.

"People try to shoot me all the time," Rue told him. "Usually because of a wife or a daughter or a sister or a mother. The point is, I'm used to having people shoot at me. We all are. But we generally know why we're being shot at."

The man got to his feet, blood running freely through the fingers that cupped his nose. "I wasn't going to shoot you."

"I'm having a hard time believing you," Ravel said, "seeing as how you were going for your gun at the time."

The man didn't have much to say about that.

"What's your name, friend?" said Rue.

"Joost," said the man.

"Joost? What kind of name is that?"

"Dutch," said Joost.

Rue nodded. It figured. From the accent and all, and anyway, half the world had come west to search for gold.

This was when Anton Shudder stepped forward, and the five other Dead Men at the bar seemed to step back, even though no actual steps were taken. Shudder looked at Joost, and to the poor, panicking Dutchman it seemed like the world was narrowing to a very tight space.

"Tell us what the man with the green eyes said to you," Shudder said in his quiet voice.

"Church," Joost managed. "He said something about going to church."

The church, such as it was, stood on a hill a few miles south. A ramshackle place where not much worshipping went on – and when it did, half of it was half-remembered and most of it was made up. It catered to three different townships, of which Forbidden was one. Its roof sagged and let in water when it rained, its walls groaned and let in wind when it blew, and its doors creaked and let in hypocrites when it suited.

There were two sides of narrow pews and a narrow aisle in between, and there was a table for an altar and the pulpit was a box to stand on. It had once been a barn, and it had never got rid of the comforting smell of cow dung.

In town, there'd lived a man named Wooley, a quick wit who always found amusing, if sometimes crude, names for people and places. He'd come up with a name for this falling-down church-barn that smelled of dung, and it was quite a clever and funny name, but he died of dysentery before he could tell anyone. Mighty unlucky man, that Wooley.

The Dead Men walked up from the bottom of the hill towards this sad-looking church with a single candle burning in its window. It was night, and a warm one at that, and they followed the winding trail between all those graves. They walked single file, with Pleasant in the lead, the moonlight making his skull shine beneath his hat. At the top of the hill the trail widened out, and it was at this point that the Dead Men stood abreast of each other, observing the double doors with the window on one side.

"Nefarian Serpine," Pleasant called, "if you're in there, come out. Come get what's coming to you."

The candle flickered behind the thin, cracked glass. The doors banged gently in the hesitant breeze. Pleasant looked at Rue, who shook his head. No one was in that church.

Pleasant made to step forward, then stopped. The other Dead Men watched him as he turned slowly. They started to turn, too.

Corpses lunged up from the graves all around them, pushing aside packed dirt and overturning markers of wood and stone. They burrowed out from six feet under and less, moaning and groaning and uttering sounds that whistled through dried-up throats. They clambered to their feet and staggered and lurched and shambled, all going straight towards the seven sorcerers who were slowly backing away from them.

More and more crawled to the surface, breaking through to add their sounds to the growing chorus of the dead. Hundreds of graves, going back sixty years. Some of the dead, zombies they were called, were fresh enough, and some were little more than skeletons. Skulduggery Pleasant might've felt right at home at that moment. If he did, he didn't show it.

"Start shooting," he said.

Guns cleared leather and immediately the night was shaking to the thunder of gunfire. The Dead Men stood in a line and fired calmly, making every bullet count. Shots to the legs to slow them down, to the chests to drive them back, and to the heads to give them a death they wouldn't be walking away from. Bullets were easier than magic when it came to zombies. Quicker, too. Even the skeletons, those without a brain, went down when a bullet shattered their skulls.

Bone fragments flew. Rotten flesh burst. Soon enough the Dead Men were standing in a cloud of acrid gunsmoke, and still the zombies came.

"Reloading," Vex said, taking one step back. The other Dead Men closed in, filling the gap. When his guns were ready, Vex said, "Firing," and stepped into the space that was immediately made for him.

That's how they went, the Dead Men, doing this dance, covering for their partners. Guns got hot and fingers got singed, and still they fired and reloaded and fired, and still the zombies came.

Three zombies from the back pushed forward. Fresher corpses, these. They ran at Bespoke and he blasted one of them in the face and one in the throat. The bullet passed right through the spinal cord and the head flopped backwards, tearing decaying skin, then fell off. The third zombie he punched with a column of air that lifted it off its feet. He fired at it as it hurtled backwards, hit it in the back of the head.

The zombies were surrounding them now. The Dead Men moved into a tight circle, constantly turning, a spinning top of death. Empty cartridges fell. New ones slid into chambers. Hammers pulled back and struck down and powder lit and lead flew. Faces, heads and bodies disintegrated. The spinning circle of Dead Men spun its way halfway down the trail. The slower-moving zombies had to adjust their lumbering course a few times just to get within snarling distance.

Pleasant slipped into the middle of the circle and Ravel covered his back while he holstered his empty Colts. He held up his hands, gripping the air. It wasn't easy to do what he was doing. The rifles and shotguns that had stayed behind with the horses lifted from their holsters and packs, and he brought them up the hill, over the heads of the foul-tempered dead.

"I'm out," said Hopeless, returning his pistols to his belt. His rifle, a Sharps, fell into his waiting hands and he brought it to his shoulder and resumed firing.

Rue was next, and he made his Winchester sing, using the butt whenever a corpse got too eager. Shudder had the shotgun, a double-barrelled monstrosity he liked to call Daisy. He fired that from the hip, blowing apart any zombie dumb enough to go up against him. The others all had Henrys, except for Pleasant himself, who favoured the Spencer. They dug in their pockets for shells, reloading as fast as they were able, but it was clear there were more zombies than there were bullets.

A big zombie, a man who'd died scarcely two weeks before, charged into the circle and the circle split apart. Any rational mind watching might think that this'd be the moment to panic, but the Dead Men went about their business, hurried but calm, knowing that one mistake, one fumble or misfire, could lead to being swarmed and torn apart. They dodged among the grasping hands, firing and lashing out, reloading whenever they had a moment.

One by one, rifles were dropped and balls of fire flew. Coloured streams of light burst from Vex's hands, sizzled right through necrotic flesh. Rue went to work with his bowie knife and Hopeless took out that machete of his. Only Shudder was still firing, his pockets providing a seemingly endless supply of shells.

"To the church," Pleasant shouted when it became clear they were about to be overrun, and each of them started making their way back up the hill.

A wave of his hand opened the double doors and they grouped together once more, backing into the shelter of the Lord. But the Lord must've been busy that night, or else He was sleeping on the job, because there was no respite in here. The carnivorous corpses kept coming, clambering over the pews, and the Dead Men kept backing up, shoulder to shoulder. They slowed their retreat some, only stopping when they had to, when the sheer numbers forced them to.

Bespoke gestured behind them and the makeshift altar and the pulpit slid to the side, out of their way. By the time they reached the single door at the other end of the church, every zombie still moving was packed inside.

At Pleasant's signal, Hopeless kicked open the door, held it for his friends, and the Dead Men turned and got the hell out of there. Shudder was last, but instead of running, he turned in the doorway and pulled open his shirt. Pleasant, Bespoke and Ravel held out their hands, forming a wall of solid air, keeping the zombies from getting at their friend. They dropped the wall when Shudder nodded. The zombies rushed forward.

There are types of magic that are easy, relatively speaking, that take no particular toll on the sorcerer using them. They'll get tired, sure. They'll get worn out, and drained. That's what happens when magic is used. Same as anything a body does.

But then there are types of magic that demand a price. Anton Shudder's magic was one such. The risk he took every time he used it, the pain and anguish it caused him, were immense. Few people ever mastered that discipline of magic. There were those who said it could never *be* mastered. Shudder himself was one such person.

His gist burst from his chest – a screaming, squawking, nightmarish version of Shudder himself. It was made up of every bad thought and feeling the man possessed, and by the look of the fangs and the claws and the madness, those bad thoughts were many, and resourceful. Attached to Shudder by a twisting stream of light and dark, it went at the zombies like they were the things it hated most in the world. Which, at that moment, they were. It went through them and over them and back again, that stream looping over itself like an ever-growing snake. The zombies, with no room to duck even if they'd had a mind to, were reduced to tatters.

Shudder's knees gave out and Rue and Vex each grabbed one of his arms, held him up. With the last of his strength, Shudder called the gist back to him. It hollered and screeched and fought, but the thread between them shortened, and shortened again, and then the gist was sucked back into Shudder's chest, and the night was silent apart from the low moaning of the zombie remains.

Rue and Vex helped Shudder walk away, and Pleasant, Bespoke and Ravel clicked their fingers and filled their hands with flames. They tossed those flames through the door, manipulated them a little, and within seconds the whole church was burning, taking the last of the zombies with it.

The Dead Men headed back down to their tired horses, where Hopeless was waiting for them. He'd collected their fallen rifles and had picked up something extra along the way. A man in black, unconscious, with blood running from his nose and his hands in shackles. Beside him, as he lay in the dirt, was his staff.

* * *

They rode back into town, found an empty corner in Sullivan's Livery and dumped the Necromancer in there while the Dead Men took rooms for the night. Only Pleasant stayed to guard him – true dead men never needing sleep. Pleasant stood, arms folded, looking at Noche. Not saying anything. Not moving – not even to breathe.

A few minutes past eight the next morning, the rest of the Dead Men turned up, rested and fed. A bucket of water woke the Necromancer, who sat up with a lunging breath and then rolled over into a series of coughing fits. When he was done with all the spluttering, he looked up at his captors.

"What'll we do with him?" asked Bespoke.

"I think we should kill him," Rue said. "I don't like him. Look at his eyebrows. They're odd. He's got odd eyebrows, and I think they might be magical. He's trying to hypnotise me with his odd, magical eyebrows."

"Nobody is trying to hypnotise you," Shudder said.

"We should shave them from his face and experiment on them."

"I think the stress has finally got to our dear friend Saracen Rue," said Ravel sadly. "He was a good man while he lasted. Annoying at times, perhaps, but a good man nonetheless."

"I will be missed," Rue nodded.

Noche frowned up at them. "You're all insane."

"You should have the measure of insanity," said Vex, "what with all the palling around you've been doing with Nefarian Serpine.

Why are you associating with the likes of him anyway? The Necromancers have been staying out of the war. Are you really going to join the losing side right before it ends?"

"My brothers and sisters remain neutral."

"So it's just you, then," said Pleasant. "A rogue Necromancer teaming up with the last of Mevolent's Three Generals. Why? To aid him in his escape? He's been running from us for months, and we're closer to him now than ever. It's only a matter of time before we have him."

Noche smiled, the smile adopting a certain smug quality. "But time isn't on your side, is it? You're absolutely right – Mevolent's dead, Vengeous is in shackles, and the war is coming to an end. Last I heard, your Sanctuaries were talking of an amnesty. So long as the war is ended soon, and not allowed to drag out, they'll be offering forgiveness to all of Mevolent's followers who aren't yet imprisoned. That's why you're so eager to get to Serpine – because you know that time is ticking away. If you don't get him before the amnesties are granted, you'll lose your chance to have your revenge. Won't you, skeleton?"

Pleasant tilted his head in that way of his. "You're working with him. I really don't care why. Maybe he has something on you. Maybe you owe him. Maybe you're just a glutton for punishment. I don't care about you or your motives. All I want is a question answered."

"You'll not get any information out of me," Noche sneered.

"We just want to know one little bit of information," said Rue.

"It's barely worth mentioning, really. Barely worth the breath that would carry the words from my lips."

"Just one tiny bit of information," said Vex, "and then we'll let you go. You can run off and we won't tell anyone you helped us."

"We'll swear to it," said Bespoke.

"Our word is our bond," said Rue.

"Serpine," Ravel said. "Where is he headed?"

Noche glared. "I'll never tell."

"Please?" said Ravel. Another glare, and Ravel straightened up. "Right, well. You are of no use to us whatsoever, are you? I don't even see why you went to the trouble of being captured, I really don't. What's the point of being a prisoner if you're not going to divulge secret plans to your captors?"

"Defeats the purpose," Vex grumbled.

"It does indeed, Dexter," Ravel said. "What do you have to say for yourself? Are you suitably ashamed? You should be. If I were you, I'd have a good long think about what a disappointment you've been to us. We had high hopes."

"The highest."

"That's right, Saracen, the highest. See? You've upset Saracen."

"I just have something in my eye," said Rue.

"I have never seen Saracen Rue weep," Ravel said, "since this morning, but you've made him weep like a little child. I hope you're proud of yourself."

Noche looked at them warily. "You *are* all insane."

Anton Shudder walked forward. "Tell us where Serpine is going. I don't play games like my friends. They're saying all this to confuse you and frighten you. I prefer to simply ask, and I expect a simple answer."

"I would rather die," said Noche, a touch less convincingly.

"Do you know my chosen discipline, little man?"

"You're a... You have a gist."

"That's right. And when I let it out there are times when I just cannot control it. And it's a sight to behold. Terrifying. Ferocious. Merciless. Tell us what we want to know or I shall release it, and believe you me you will garner its full attention."

Noche swallowed like he'd something sharp stuck in his craw. "Serpine... he mentioned Lancaster County, in Nebraska, as somewhere he'd be safe. Sounded like that's where he's headed."

Rue peered at him. "Are you lying?"

"No."

"I don't trust him."

Ravel nodded. "I don't trust him, either."

"I trust him," said Vex happily. "And I've changed my mind about his eyebrows, too. Skulduggery, can we keep him?"

Pleasant tilted his head at the Necromancer. "You're lying."

"No, I—"

Pleasant splayed his hand and Noche flew off the ground, hit the wall, his feet kicking at air.

The Dead Men fell silent, lost their smiles and looks of good humour.

"My friend Anton will kill you," said Pleasant, "but I will kill you worse. Why are you with Serpine?"

"Please, I..."

"You have one chance. If you lie to me, I will start killing you."

Something changed in Noche's eyes, something dripped away. His melting resolve, most likely.

"He's heading for the Temple," he said. "I was to meet him, take him back to it."

"The Necromancers are going to hide him?"

"Y-yes. I don't know why. He has an... an agreement, of sorts. Made long ago."

"He left you here to delay us," said Pleasant, "and went on to the Temple without you. How far is it?"

"Three days' ride," Noche said.

Pleasant curled his fingers, and the Necromancer gasped for breath. "Tell us where it is."

They rode.

On the second day they had grass under their horses' hooves.

The third day they found Serpine's horse. It had snapped its leg in a gulley and Serpine hadn't even had the decency to put it out of its misery. Hopeless laid his hand on its neck and put a bullet in its head, and it was a kindness, and then he remounted and they carried on.

They made good time. Serpine's tracks got fresher. They reached the top of a hill, looked down across the valley and saw a man running and falling, making his way to a rocky outcrop of curiously shaped stones and boulders. Standing outside the opening to what looked like a cave were a dozen figures in black, all in a line, watching Serpine approach.

The Dead Men tore down that hill like the devil's own demon dogs. They got close enough so that when Serpine glanced back they could see the fear and exhaustion painted across his dirty, sweating face.

Then he stumbled through the line of black, and disappeared into the cave behind them.

Pleasant leaped from the saddle, using his magic to propel himself through the air like he'd been shot from a cannon. He landed a couple of strides from the line of Necromancers.

"Move," he said.

The Necromancers, being the contrary lot that they were, showed no intention of budging an inch. The one in the middle, the one who'd stepped aside to allow Serpine pass, gave Pleasant a smile.

"Welcome to our Temple," he said. "Ours is a place of peace and learning. Do you have business here?"

"Move," Pleasant said again. His voice, usually so smooth, was coarse as the sand they'd travelled across to get here. The Dead Men dismounted behind him, walked slowly up till they formed a wedge at his back. They kept their hands close to their guns.

"Nefarian Serpine is a guest," said the talkative Necromancer. "He has provided us a service in the past, and so he is under our protection. I'm afraid I can't let you through."

"If you side with our enemy," said Pleasant, "you become our enemy."

To his credit, the Necromancer didn't seem all that intimidated by a walking skeleton with guns on his hips. He gave Pleasant another smile. "That's a rather simplistic view of things, isn't it? There's really not much room for manoeuvring around that little philosophy. I prefer, personally, to take each moment as it comes, and to treat every obstacle as an opportunity to do something different. It makes life interesting."

His patience worn to a frayed thread already, conversing with a smiling flannel-mouth such as this one was enough to snap it clean. Pleasant went to push by, and suddenly there was a wall of shadows looming over their heads. The Dead Men went for their guns, but froze before drawing. Once those guns cleared leather, death would come flying and there'd be no turning back.

"You think you scare us?" the Necromancer asked. "They call you the Dead Men, but it is my brothers, my sisters and I who wield the true death magic. You think we're afraid to die? Really?"

"I think you talk big," said Pleasant. "I think you talk about death like it's your friend. But if you really want to get acquainted, we can help you with that."

"Then kill us," the Necromancer said. "But be warned. We stand at the mouth of a Temple. Beneath our feet, there are more of us than you can imagine. They'll tear you to pieces and you still won't be any closer to your quarry."

"Then we'll wait," Bespoke said. "We'll make camp right here and we'll wait."

"As much as I would enjoy seeing you waste your time in such a fashion," the Necromancer replied, "our Temple has hidden entrances and exits leading far and wide. You're just going to have to accept the fact that Serpine is out of your reach, get on your horses, and trot away."

"We don't give up that easily," said Ravel.

"Then you should start," said the Necromancer. "Because you've lost this little game. The skeleton knows it. That's why he's gone so quiet. All this time, all this effort, all this building of hatred and anger... all for nothing. You were a few seconds too late, gentlemen. That can't be easy for you. You have my commiserations. But the game is done. It's over. You can pick it up again in another country, maybe. But in a few months or a few years there's going to be a treaty, and an amnesty, and then Mr Serpine will be able to walk free without a care in the world, and there won't be a single thing you can do about it."

The Dead Men took their hands from their guns. They'd been alive long enough to know when they were beaten, and they had enough wisdom between them to know there was no shame in it. Sometimes the cards flipped right, and sometimes they didn't.

At Pleasant's nod, they got back on their horses. The Necromancers began to file into the cave, and the wall of shadows became little more than black smoke in the wind. Finally, there were just Pleasant and the Necromancer left standing there.

"What's your name?" Pleasant asked.

That smile again. "Cleric Solomon Wreath, at your service," said the Necromancer. He even gave a little bow.

"Mr Wreath, today you have prevented me from doing my duty."

"On the contrary, I have prevented you from exacting your revenge."

"Which amounts to the same thing. I won't forget this."

"I don't expect you to," said Wreath, but Pleasant had already turned his back on him.

That night they rested their horses by a stream and didn't talk a whole lot.

Pleasant sat by himself, looking out into the darkness. To say he had a peculiar anger would of course be something of an understatement, but a peculiar anger it was, as it wasn't the sort any normal folk could understand. It was a slow-burning heat, capable of firing up at a whim, but never in any danger of puttering out. It kept him. It sustained him. Maybe there was even a part of him that was glad Serpine had wormed his way free.

As long as the man who'd killed him and his family was alive, somewhere out there across the dark plain, Pleasant had a reason to fight, a reason to keep putting one foot in front of the other. But kill the killer, and what was left? Something cold and uncertain. Could be he hung on to what he had – his hate, his anger, his job – because hanging on was all he had. The war was coming to an end. His time as a soldier was coming to an end.

What then? Was there something else out there, something he had yet to discover, that could keep him going when he'd used up everything else? Some thing or some person that would give him a purpose again, that would light a different kind of fire within him?

Most likely, he didn't know. He probably didn't care to think that far ahead.

The Dead Men slept. But not Skulduggery Pleasant.

No, Skulduggery Pleasant just hung on, waiting.

Because it was all he had.

THE HORROR WRITERS' HALLOWEEN BALL

THE HORROR WRITERS' HALLOWEEN BALL

"Hell may well be other people," Gordon Edgley muttered as they entered the ballroom, "but if you're looking for an everlasting purgatory of snide remarks and bitter snipes, look no further than other writers."

The costumed guests mingled and laughed, sipped champagne and wine and plucked tasty but pointless canapés from the trays of passing waiters. A string quartet played from the darkened gallery, as if they'd been shunted to one side to make room in the light for the chosen few. And the chosen few they really were; invitations to Sebastian Fawkes's parties were rarer than an honest coin in a politician's pocket.

That wasn't a bad line, actually, Gordon realised. Needed work, but it had potential.

"Invitations to these parties are rarer than an honest coin in a politician's pocket," Gordon said to his companion, and waited for the response. When none came, he frowned, stored the line away and vowed to play around with it later.

He recognised a few of the faces – the moustachioed face, for instance, of R. Samuel Keen, an American whose every book had to have either an unnaturally wise child or a psychic dog. His latest one, which Gordon had tried to listen to as a book on tape before the cassette unspooled in his car, had both. It hadn't been very good.

He saw Adrian Sykes, a soft-spoken Geordie whose work was fantastically gory and outrageously imaginative. The theme of the party was, as usual, horror, and Sykes had come dressed as one of Clive Barker's Cenobites, all black leather and hooks. Gordon had met him only once before, and had come away thinking of him as a thoroughly decent person. It was occasionally true to say that the writers of the most disturbing horror stories were among the nicest people you could possibly meet.

There were exceptions, of course. For instance, the gentleman Sykes was chatting to, Edgar Looms, another American, was a man of singular vulgarity. Gordon had first met him ten years earlier, just after Gordon's first book was published, and since then he had developed quite an abhorrence of the man. Tonight Looms was one of many who had come dressed as Frankenstein's monster – from the James Whale movie, not the book.

For his first time here, Gordon himself had come as the Creature from the Black Lagoon – a costume he'd had specially created at no little cost. It was worth it, though, even if the flippers made it difficult to walk and the mask made it difficult to see, hear or breathe. It also made it difficult to be heard, which may have explained why his companion hadn't responded to his politician line.

Gordon leaned in closer, careful not to topple over in his costume, and said, quite loudly and clearly, "Invitations to these parties are rarer than an honest coin in a politician's pocket."

His companion, dressed as he was in a 1930s suit and tie, his head covered in bandages exactly like Claude Rains from *The Invisible Man*, turned slightly, so that Gordon could see his own costume's reflection in those sunglasses.

"Are you having a stroke?" Skulduggery Pleasant asked. "You keep repeating the same phrase. Is it hot in there? It looks hot."

"It is," Gordon admitted. "But I'm not having a stroke. I'm too young. I'm only thirty-five, for God's sake. Though I may start hallucinating, and thirst will likely become an issue before too long."

"How do you take the mask off?"

"I'm not entirely sure. It took two people to get me into this thing. They probably told me how to take it off, but the mask makes it hard to hear properly."

Skulduggery said something.

Gordon leaned in again. "What?"

"I said what about toilet breaks?"

"I hadn't thought of that. Can you see a zip anywhere?"

"It looks rather seamless."

"Damn it. And now I want to pee. I didn't before you brought it up, but now I can feel how full my bladder is. Oh dear God. If I wet myself in front of all these writers, they'll never let me live it down."

Skulduggery nodded. "Writers are small-minded like that."

A waiter came over. Gordon went to wave him away, but his huge flipper hand caught the edge of the serving tray and sent glasses of champagne flying. Even before they'd crashed to the ground, Gordon was spinning on his heels and lurching awkwardly away.

Skulduggery fell easily into pace beside him. "It's hard to look innocent when you're the Creature from the Black Lagoon."

"I suppose that's the one advantage of this mask," Gordon responded. "Nobody knows who I am."

"Gordon Edgley!"

Gordon had to turn his whole body to look round at whoever had called his name. She came out of the crowd like a bespoiled vision in mint green – 1960s skirt and sweater, her blonde hair tied up, scratches all over her face, and attached to her jacket half a dozen plastic birds.

"Tippi Hedren," Gordon said at once, smiling even though she couldn't see it.

"What gave it away?" Susan said, standing on tiptoes to kiss both cheeks of his mask. "It was either this or Grace Jones from *Vamp*, which would have raised a lot more eyebrows, believe me. Who's your friend?"

Susan was a typical upstate New Yorker – talking a mile a minute.

"This is my associate, Mr Pleasant," Gordon said. "Mr Pleasant, may I introduce Susan DeWick, author of the *Chronicles of the Dead* series."

"Mr Pleasant," Susan said, shaking Skulduggery's gloved hand. "How delightfully formal we suddenly are."

"Miss DeWick, it is a genuine pleasure to meet you," Skulduggery responded, his voice beginning to work on her already. "I've been a fan ever since Gordon recommended you. Your latest book is one of your best."

"Oh, you're just saying that because it's true," Susan said, and laughed. She looked back to Gordon. "So, Fishface, is this your first time here? I've been waiting years for an invitation. When it finally came, I have to admit, I squealed a little. Just a little, mind you, for I am a horror writer, and so I comport myself with absolute solemnity at all times."

"Oh, naturally," Gordon said, really wishing he wasn't wearing a stupid mask. "When did you get to London?"

"Wednesday," she said. "I thought travelling all this way for a silly costume party would have appalled my dear late mother, but my dad insists that even she had heard of Sebastian Fawkes and the extravagant bashes he throws. The who's who of the horror elite, all in one place. Kind of gives you an illicit little thrill, doesn't it? Mr Pleasant, are you a writer also? I'm afraid I'm not familiar with the name..."

"I am a mere reader," Skulduggery said. "Gordon allows me to help him with his research and in return I live out my writer fantasies vicariously through him."

"Oh, I like a man with writer fantasies," Susan said, flashing him a smile.

Gordon felt the sudden need to step between them, but doubted he could manage it dressed like a big fish-monster.

A heavily bearded Wolfman swooped upon Susan, nuzzling her neck, and she laughed and allowed herself to be dragged away. She looked back before vanishing into the crowd, but Gordon didn't know if she was looking at him, or Skulduggery.

"She's nice," Skulduggery said.

Gordon made a noise that sounded like agreement.

"She looks a little like Grace Kelly."

"Now listen here," Gordon said, "I didn't invite you to this thing so that you could sweep Susan DeWick off her feet. If anyone is going to be sweeping her off her feet, it'll be me, in a fitting homage to the Gill-man and Julie Adams. Admittedly, it won't be easy. Co-ordination is not what this suit was designed for, and I do have a bad back, and all this heat is making me feel quite weak so I may pass out and drop her, but just the same—"

"No sweeping her off her feet," Skulduggery said, clearly amused. "You have my word. Besides, why would I antagonise a friend who has taken me to the first party I've been to in years?"

"You have the Requiem Ball, don't you?"

"Full of sorcerers talking about Sanctuary business," Skulduggery said, dismissing it with a wave of his hand. "It's an evening of

46

carefully chosen words and awkward silences, where nobody wants to mention the name Nefarian Serpine in case I suddenly get it into my head to kick down his door and kill him. As if that thought isn't constantly swirling through my head as it is. No, Gordon, you have brought me to a proper party, of mortals. Of mortal *writers*, no less. This is beyond wonderful. This is just what I've been looking for."

"Well, I'm glad," said Gordon. "We weren't supposed to bring guests, but I did suspect that you might appreciate it. And if Fawkes finds out and banishes me to the horror wilderness for the rest of my career, it will have been worth it to pay you back, in some small way, for everything you've done for me."

"Why, Gordon, I never noticed this before, but you are such a sentimental fool."

Gordon laughed. "Indeed I am, my friend, and proud of it."

The lights suddenly dimmed and the string quartet stopped playing as a spotlight fell upon a balcony high above, on which stood their host for the evening. Sebastian Fawkes was tall and thin with high, narrow cheekbones. His black hair was shot through with startling streaks of silver, as was his goatee beard. Even his eyebrows, arched to perfection, each had a slash of silver. Apart from the Dracula costume he wore, he looked, Gordon realised, exactly like his author photo from twenty years ago. The crowd fell into a deep and respectful hush.

"Horror," Fawkes said, casting his gaze down upon the room. He had a deep, musical quality to his voice that made him sound like an English Vincent Price. "Fear. Dread. These are the commodities in which we trade. In return for the devotion of our readers, we conjure for them the stuff of nightmares."

He paused, allowing his words to permeate the air. A tad melodramatic, but Gordon didn't mind melodrama every now and then – just as long as it didn't get too pretentious.

"We are the dark guardians of the soul," Fawkes continued. "The new millennium is a mere twelve years away, and we stand between Scylla and Charybdis to hold back the tide of apathy and indifference that threatens, even now, to engulf us all. We offer glimpses into madness, we bring their hands close to the black fires of terror... and then we guide them, safely, back to the light. Ours is a noble calling.

"Where once we would have sat round the campfire telling our stories, now we sit at our typewriters or our word processors. The world is our campfire now – but while you may think we have banished our demons with our modern technologies, with our VCRs and our CD players and our MTV, they still lurk, out there, in the dark. And we are their hunters."

He bowed his head and the ballroom erupted in applause. Gordon clapped his webbed hands along with everyone else, glad that he was wearing a fish-mask so no one could see him cringe.

Fawkes motioned for silence. "And here we are, gathered together on this most special of nights. A lot of you have been here before. A lot of you already stand within the inner circle. You know the secrets. You have reaped the rewards."

A low murmur rippled through Fawkes's audience. People were nodding and smiling softly.

"But others are here tonight for the very first time," Fawkes continued. "They stand on the cusp of enlightenment. They stand on the edge of wonder. We have seven uninitiated writers among us, writers who have proven their worth, who are ready to be welcomed into our... family."

Fawkes chuckled at the word, and the guests laughed along with him. Gordon didn't know what the hell he was talking about any more.

"But all that is still to be revealed," said Fawkes. "For now, eat, drink, talk, laugh... be merry. And give me a hip hip hooray for horror. Hip hip..."

"Hooray!"

They did that three times in all, and Gordon could only blink at the sudden shift in tone.

Fawkes gave a wave, everyone clapped, and the lights came back on. A few moments later, Fawkes made his entrance into the ballroom and the string quartet started up again.

Skulduggery looked at Gordon. "The man's an idiot."

Gordon nodded. "He does seem to be idiotic."

"I never liked his books. Maybe he's improved with age, but his early work is derivative with definite signs of pretention. And look, he's coming this way. This will be a wonderful opportunity for me to make like the character I've come as, and disappear."

Skulduggery moved backwards into the crowd, and by the time Gordon shifted his position to look around, he was gone.

The mask was ridiculous. He seized it with both hands, squeezed and pulled, and only managed to shift the eyeholes around to his ear. Now he couldn't see anything.

"Help," he said. He reached out and heard a crash. *Another tray of drinks bites the dust.* He stepped back, bumped into someone, heard the unmistakable intake of breath that accompanies a well-dressed lady spilling wine down the front of her dress. "Terribly sorry," Gordon said, spinning quickly, hitting someone else and getting a muffled curse in response.

Suddenly there was a steadying grip on his arms, and he heard Susan DeWick say, "Hold on there, Fishface. You're leaving a trail of destruction in your wake."

"My head's on sideways," he explained.

"I can see that. Want me to take it off?"

"If you wouldn't mind," said Gordon. "Thank you."

He felt her hands take hold of the mask. She twisted and pulled and fiddled, and just when Gordon's claustrophobia was closing in on him, she yanked the Creature's head off. Air rushed in, cooling the sweat on his forehead, and he gasped, laughed and ignored the glares he was getting from the people around him.

"You're a lifesaver," he said, and Susan laughed and handed him back the mask.

"I couldn't watch you flail about any longer," she said. "It was funny, sure, but also kind of sad and pathetic."

"Sad and pathetic are two of my most charming traits."

Susan smiled, a wicked look in her eye, but her response was curtailed by the arrival of Sebastian Fawkes.

"Susan," Fawkes said, kissing her hand, "it is so good to see you again. I'm sure it's been said already tonight by men more charming than I, but you look simply ravishing. Tippi Hedren, yes?"

"Got it in one," Susan replied. "Thank you so much for the invitation, by the way. I was just telling Gordon here how much of an honour it is to be at one of your Halloween parties."

"Ah, yes, Gordon Edgley," said Fawkes, shifting his gaze and holding out his hand. "Very good to meet you."

"Likewise," said Gordon, smiling broadly as he removed one of his gloves. The handshake that followed was unsatisfying and dry. "I've loved your books since I was old enough to read," he said. "I don't wish to embarrass you, but you've been a huge influence on my own work."

"Have I?" Fawkes said. "I haven't read your books so I wouldn't know if I'm supposed to be flattered or insulted." He laughed. Susan laughed, too, but it was hesitant and accompanied by a frown. "And how are your sales, Gordon? Robust, I hope?"

"I can't complain."

"Well, you could," said Fawkes, "but who would listen, eh? Sales can always be better, can't they? It still astonishes me, even to this day, the kind of tripe that sells. Are you one of these exponents of splatterpunk that I've been hearing about lately? Writers who value vulgar gore over genuine chills?"

"I wouldn't count myself as such, no."

"Dreadful stuff. No finesse to their writing. Violence and bloodshed in graphic detail. Where's the character? Where's the theme? Where's the nuance? Cheap shocks, cheap thrills. Blood spills, cheap thrills, eh?" He chuckled at his rhyme. "I'm sure you're successful enough, Gordon. You wouldn't be here otherwise."

"Oh? There's a sales criterion, is there?"

"Oh, absolutely," said Fawkes. "My associates go through the numbers, pick out the writers who are currently in vogue, like you, writers who sell enough books, and their names go on the list."

"I feel so special."

Fawkes's smile faded a little. "I'm sorry, Gordon? I didn't quite catch that."

"I didn't quite throw it."

Now Fawkes's smile was looking decidedly strained. He took a small spiral-bound notebook from his inside pocket, and flipped through it. "Edgley, Edgley... here we are. Gordon Edgley. Writer of, among others, *Caterpillars*. Oh, dear... was that the book about the killer caterpillars?"

Gordon reddened. "That's it."

"The killer caterpillars who eat people?"

"When they swarm, yes."

"I'm interested – are caterpillars known to swarm?"

"I took... liberties with the science."

"I can see that," said Fawkes.

"They're a mutant strain of caterpillar that feasts on human flesh."

"Oh dear Lord."

"I wrote it when I was nineteen," said Gordon, a touch aggrieved. "It was my first published book."

"You're hugely fortunate it wasn't your last, dear boy. Carnivorous caterpillars, eh? Have you written the sequel yet? *Butterflies?* Or the prequel? *Larvae?*"

Gordon ground his teeth. "They're in the pipeline."

Fawkes roared with laughter. "Oh, that is brilliant! That is wonderful!"

"*Caterpillars* is actually an excellent debut," said Susan, "and it follows in a glorious tradition. You have Herbert's *The Rats*, Hutson's *Slugs*, Guy N. Smith's *Night of the Crabs*, Halkin's *Blood Worm...* *Caterpillars* stacks right up there with the best of them."

"I'm sure it is esteemed company indeed. I apologise, Gordon, I didn't wish to insult or belittle you. I'm sure you have enough critics belittling you without me judging you by my own standards."

Gordon frowned. "That's an apology?"

"It is nevertheless a pleasure to meet you," said Fawkes, smiling again, "and thank you for coming. Stick around – I have a feeling it will be a memorable night for you both. If you'll excuse me...?"

He walked away.

"You're excused," Gordon muttered.

Susan looked at him. "Wow."

"Yes."

"Wow."

"So that was Sebastian Fawkes, eh?"

Susan gave a small shrug. "If it's any consolation, whenever I meet him, he's lovely to me. Always calls me ravishing."

"He didn't call me ravishing."

"I noticed that."

"Maybe he has something against Irish people."

"He probably just hates you," said Susan.

"I think he's racist."

"Are Irish people a race?"

Gordon frowned. "Aren't we?"

"Don't think so."

"Damn. Maybe he just hates me, then. It's probably because I'm better looking than him."

"Oh, I don't know," said Susan.

"What? You seriously think he's better looking than me? He's old!"

"He looks great."

"He's been around forever!"

"Doesn't look a day over fifty."

"Fifty is old," said Gordon sullenly.

"You won't be saying that when you're fifty."

Gordon peered at her, making sure she was telling the truth. "You really think he's good-looking?"

"I really do."

"So why does he hate me?"

"I don't know. Did you sleep with his wife?"

Gordon looked around. "Which one's his wife?"

Susan laughed. "Hey, I think you're a great writer, and I loved the hell out of *Caterpillars*, and every book since just gets better and better, and I'm a ravishing young lady. So who are you going to believe – me or him?"

"Well," Gordon said, "you *do* have better taste."

"See? Now quit your bellyaching and dance with me, you subaquatic fool."

Gordon stopped drinking halfway through the night. He had a longstanding policy – never drink too much in front of rivals and colleagues. Also never drink too much when you don't know where the zip is on your costume. That was an important policy, too, but it was a new one, with limited applicability. Still, what these policies allowed him was the chance to stand back and watch as fellow authors got drunk, and the drunker they got, the funnier it all became. Petty jealousies reared their heads. Comments got snippier. Compliments became barbed. There were many backs behind which many things were said. It was all highly amusing.

He started to notice the crowd being thinned. Very slightly at first, with certain people – all at the low end of the pecking order – being escorted into another room. When it was done, the guests had been split into two groups, with Gordon staying in the main ballroom. Walking with his mask tucked under his arm, he searched for Skulduggery, whom he had glimpsed charming various people throughout the night. Surely Skulduggery would not have allowed himself to be escorted away.

Gordon noticed that the music had stopped and, in fact, the string quartet had left. He was about to ask somebody the time when he saw the waiters and waitresses leaving the ballroom, stepping out as if synchronised, and closing the doors behind them.

The conversation died, and all attention was turned to Sebastian Fawkes, standing where the quartet had been playing. He waited for absolute, solemn silence.

"My fellow writers," Fawkes said, "and here I speak only to the uninitiated... welcome to the darkest of secrets."

Gordon stifled a groan.

"As writers, it is our solemn duty to take our readers by the hand and lead them down a barely lit path, on either side of which lie perils, waiting in the shadows. This we do out of a sense of duty. Someone has to shine a light into the dark, after all."

Gordon examined his mask, wondering if he could put it back on by himself. Then maybe he could look as bored as he felt.

"I was approached, years ago, by a being," Fawkes continued, "an... entity. A man, but... something more than a man. And this being, this magnificent presence, showed me a way to use my talents and be rewarded... not just financially, but also spiritually. Physically. He showed me a way to draw life energy – anguish and pain and emotional suffering – from the hearts and minds of my readers, and to use that energy to keep me successful, young and virile. Behold, Argento."

OK, now Gordon was deciding he should be paying attention. Had Fawkes just talked about how virile he was? How was *that* appropriate ballroom conversation? He became aware of someone moving through the crowd. An excited thrill rippled by, utterly failing to thrill Gordon himself. He stood on his tiptoes, but all he saw were the guests parting before a man in a white toga. He was pale and heavily muscled, and brightness seemed to spill out of him, although that may just have been the spotlight that followed his every step.

Fawkes continued talking as the big man in the toga moved gracefully through the room like a body-building angel. "He showed me the symbols to hide in the words on the page, in the arrangement of the letters, the order of the sentences, of the paragraphs. These mystical symbols not only act upon the readers' subconscious, convincing them to buy multiple copies of my books, but they also draw forth energy, which then flows into me and keeps me young..."

Fawkes smiled beatifically at the people around him. "Fifteen per cent of which goes to Argento, naturally, with twenty per cent for foreign territories."

Gordon had gone cold inside his Creature from the Black Lagoon costume. Fawkes was talking here about magic. Real, actual, supposed-to-be-kept-secret-from-mortals magic.

"I know what you're thinking," Fawkes said. "I thought it, too. I asked the same questions you're asking. We all did. Is this right? Is this fair? But don't we deserve this, after all we sacrifice for them? As writers? We hold a mirror to the face of society, a scalpel to its dark underbelly... Don't we deserve a little extra for the depths to which we must plunge?"

Gordon spotted Susan in the crowd, looking mystified.

"You have been invited here tonight so that you may become one of us. So that you may become family. We will share with you the secrets, the symbols you need to put in your books. You will learn the different types of pain, the particular strain of anguish that is most effective. You will be shown how to get your readers to care about your characters so much that when those characters die the readers are traumatised far past the point of tears. You will be instructed on the best way to bombard your readers with emotions, with feelings."

Susan stepped forward. "So you make your readers suffer, and you draw strength from that?"

"Their pain makes me strong," said Fawkes, smiling. "And your readers' pain can make you strong."

"And you actually believe everything you're saying?"

"You will believe, too, my dear."

"Uh-huh," said Susan. "You said something about draining their life energy. Isn't that, like, bad?"

"No, not necessarily. Is it exploitative? Yes. But fatalities are few."

"Fatalities? Are you saying you've killed your readers?"

"It is regrettable, obviously. We don't want to hurt anyone. We're refining the process even now. Argento is supplying me with new, safer symbols. We want our readers living a long life... so they can keep buying our books!" He chuckled.

Susan looked around. "I don't get what's going on here. Are you all this stupid?"

"There's always one," Fawkes said, his smile growing sad. "Always one who needs convincing."

The crowd parted and a gap opened between Susan and Argento.

"I can feel your doubt," Argento said, his voice soft yet piercing.

"Yeah, no kidding," Susan replied.

"Doubt, uncertainty... these are feelings laced with a bitter aftertaste. Powerful, in their own way, and made all the more so by the fear that always follows."

"Uh-huh," said Susan.

Argento held out his hand. "I will drink from you now."

Susan gasped, her body sagging, and Gordon tried to push through the tightly packed guests.

Argento's hand glowed and he closed his eyes. "Delicious," he said. "Doubt turns to realisation... to the truth... and the truth is a scary thing. Let me taste your fear."

Susan had gone ashen-white, and still Gordon fought to get to her, and then suddenly there was a cry from above and everyone turned, looked up at the balcony from which Skulduggery had just thrown the spotlight operator. He stood there, looking down at them all.

"Terribly sorry," he said, "but I'm going to have to bring an end to tonight's festivities. It's just... I'm disappointed. I wanted tonight to be special. I'm here with my friend, I'm surrounded by writers and I wanted to talk about books and stories and creativity and I wanted to overhear conversations about social responsibilities and the writer as outcast, but... but instead I get this.

"I get an empathy vampire and a group of idiots who are working with him. And he looks ridiculous. I mean we're all here dressed up in costumes, I understand that, but he wants you to think that this is how he dresses normally. It's not. No one dresses like that normally. Why would they? I met a vampire once, an ordinary vampire, who dressed like Lestat. I told him what I'm telling this one – stop reading books about vampires."

Fawkes cleared his throat and looked at Argento, who stepped forward with a dramatic swish of his toga.

"You talk like you know my kind," Argento said. "You, who are nothing to me but an insect, would dare stand upon that balcony and attempt to wound me with insults. I am made of sturdier stuff, my friend. I cannot be hurt by words, nor by blade, nor by bullet. I am eternal. I am the night. I am the day. I am forever. And who are you?"

Skulduggery let his sunglasses fall, then clicked his fingers and set fire to the bandages around his head. They went up in a blaze that died as suddenly as it began, revealing the skull beneath. "I'm Skulduggery Pleasant."

"Oh, hell," said Argento.

"And you're under arrest."

Argento spun on his heels and sprinted away. Skulduggery leaped high into the air, using his magic to boost himself halfway across the ballroom. He landed and gave chase. Argento shrieked.

There was a moment of stunned silence. Then somebody screamed, and the guests surged to the doors, yelling and shouting and tripping over each other. Gordon pushed his way through, catching Susan as she fell. He checked her pulse and her eyes fluttered open.

"That was weird," she said, sounding drunk. "Did that happen?"

"It did," said Gordon, making sure she could stand on her own. "Are you OK? Will you be OK here?"

Susan frowned at him. "Where're you going?"

"I'm going after Fawkes."

Susan grinned. "I'm fine. You go get him, tiger."

He nodded, left his mask with her, and ran as fast as his costume would allow. He got to the door, emerged into a narrow corridor. He followed it to an empty kitchen with three doors leading out from it. He chose one at random, ran the length of it, and found Sebastian Fawkes trying to get out of a window.

"You're going nowhere," Gordon said.

Fawkes turned. "Edgley," he said. "What the hell are you doing here? Go away. There are forces at work you cannot possibly fathom."

"I know all about magic," Gordon said. "I know about the Sanctuaries and the sorcerers. You're not the holder of dark secrets. You're an idiot, and you're not going to get away with what you've done."

Fawkes stopped trying to get away, and regarded Gordon with new eyes. "I don't understand why you're against this. It's power. It's success. It's wealth. And it's a longer life to enjoy all that. Why won't you just go along with it?"

"Because you're hurting your readers," said Gordon.

"Writers hurt their readers all the time! And the readers love it!"

"This is different. This is torture."

"Nonsense! How can it be torture, how can it be cruel, if they don't even know it's happening? We give them stories, they give us longer life. It's a fair trade."

Gordon approached. "So what about the readers who've died reading your books? What do you call them?"

Fawkes shrugged. "The learning curve."

"No. This will not continue."

Colour rose in Fawkes's cheeks. "Who are you to stand up to me? I am Sebastian Fawkes! The *Telegraph* called me the world's greatest living horror novelist. The *New York Times* said my work was artfully sublime. My last novel was heralded as a humane, heartbreaking journey through a nightmare landscape and a triumph in form. What awards have you won? What accolades have you gathered? You're a flavour of the month, easily dismissed, easily forgotten. I am a literary horror novelist. What the hell are you?"

Gordon took a last step towards him. "I'm a storyteller, you pretentious buffoon," he said and he pushed Fawkes.

Fawkes stared at him, his eyes wide. He pushed Gordon back.

Gordon lost his temper, gave Fawkes an extra-hard push to teach him a lesson.

Fawkes let out a roar and charged. Gordon tried to keep him away, but he was too slow. They collided, and stood there, wrestling. Every so often, they'd move their feet slightly. There was a lot of grunting.

Fawkes got a hand against Gordon's face. Gordon squeezed his eyes shut. Fawkes's palm was crushing Gordon's lips painfully. Gordon stuck out his tongue and Fawkes snapped his hand away, yelling in disgust. Gordon tried to press his advantage, but the Creature of the Black Lagoon suit was making it difficult. Fawkes stumbled and flailed, and his elbow whacked against Gordon's chin. Gordon cried out and dropped to his knees, cradling his face. Fawkes stood over him, too out of breath to say anything. Ignoring the pain in his chin, Gordon lunged at Fawkes's leg, wrapping his hands round the left knee.

Gordon held on as Fawkes cursed and staggered back. He weathered the storm of slaps that fell upon his head. One of them clipped his ear – it really hurt – but he didn't let go. Fawkes turned, tried to pull his leg free. Gordon's grip slipped a little, but his fingers tightened again like a vice round Fawkes's ankle. He was dragged a few centimetres across the floor every time Fawkes took a step.

"Let go of me!" Fawkes screeched.

"No," Gordon gasped.

Fawkes overbalanced and fell and, like a ninja, except slower and with less co-ordination, Gordon crawled on top of him. He was sweating badly now. The suit was way too hot to fight in. Fawkes struggled, tried to turn over on to his back to push him off, but Gordon let his body go limp, and he lay on top of him.

Fawkes's breath came in ragged wheezes. "You may..." *wheeze, wheeze,* "think you've..." *wheeze,* "won, but..." *wheeze,* "you'll never," *really long wheeze,* "escape."

Gordon focused all his attention on staying as heavy as possible, and gasped. "Your time is..." *gasp,* "over, you..." *gasp,* "you utter..." *gasp,* "utter nutball."

"Ar..." *wheeze*, "...gento will..." *wheeze*, "tear your soul into..." *wheeze*, "tiny little bits."

"Your friend is..." gasped Gordon, "already in handcuffs..." *gasp*, "and your reign of..." *gasp*, "terror is at an..." *gasp*, "end."

Fawkes shook his head fiercely. Gordon nodded insistently. They lay there like that for some time.

When Skulduggery Pleasant and Susan DeWick found them eight minutes later, Gordon was sitting astride Fawkes like an oddly dressed cowboy riding an exhausted and flattened-out horse.

The Cleavers arrived to take Argento into custody, and a pair of Sensitives talked to the main body of guests, convincing them they'd had a nice, if slightly boring, night, and that nothing unusual had happened.

The writers who knew the intricate details of Fawkes's deal could not be dealt with in the same manner, so they were instead threatened with terrible and gruesome deaths if they spoke a word of this to anyone. According to Skulduggery, threats worked just as well as psychics.

Sebastian Fawkes was released, since an unexplained disappearance would not have gone unnoticed in the mainstream media. His next book, however, failed to reach a receptive audience. The follow-up barely punctured the Top Twenty Bestseller list. After he appeared, uninvited and drunk, on *Wogan*, a light-entertainment talk show broadcast by the BBC, his publishers quietly dropped him, and nobody much cared.

Gordon asked that Susan DeWick's memory of the night be left intact. Skulduggery granted this request. Gordon and Susan were entangled romantically for three months afterwards before she fell for a struggling young actor and he fell for a supermodel. They remained close friends until Gordon's sudden and unexpected death years later. Her book *Stirrings at Norfolk*, the first true horror novel to win the Booker Prize, was dedicated to him. It said, simply, *To Fishface*.

Gordon was to go on to document, in his way, the darker realities of life of which the normal person is not aware. He wrote stories to shock, entertain, thrill and traumatise, and he regretted not one moment of it. His participation in real-life adventures was not quite so prolific (that role would, of course, eventually go to his niece), but he did accompany Skulduggery Pleasant on at least one more case, solving the mystery of the Phantom Killer at Darkenholme House. But that... is another story.

It's also not very interesting. The butler did it.

THE LOST
ART OF
WORLD
DOMINATION

THE LOST ART OF
WORLD DOMINATION

With the shadows wrapped around him and the sliver of light falling dramatically over his eyes, the evil sorcerer Scaramouch Van Dreg stood in the dungeon and watched his captive with predatory amusement.

The dungeon was dark and damp and dank, and the chains that bound the skeleton detective were big and thick and heavy. They shackled the bones of his wrists to the stone floor, forcing him to kneel.

Scaramouch liked that. The great detective, the living skeleton who had foiled plan after plan, scheme after scheme, was now forced to look *up* at Scaramouch. Like he had always been meant to. Like *everyone* had always been meant to.

The detective, his dark blue suit burnt and torn and muddy, hadn't said anything for almost an hour. In fact, he hadn't *moved* for almost an hour. Scaramouch had been standing in the shadows, gloating, for a little over fifteen minutes, but he wasn't entirely sure that his captive had noticed.

He shifted his weight noisily, but the detective still did not acknowledge his presence.

Scaramouch frowned. There was very little point in going through all this if his efforts weren't rewarded with due and proper attention.

He brought himself up to his full height, which wasn't very high, and sucked in his belly, which was substantial. He gathered his cloak and stepped forward, gazing down at the top of the detective's skull with the pitiless gaze he had practised for hours.

"Skulduggery Pleasant," he sneered. "Finally, you are within my grasp."

The detective shifted slightly, and muttered something.

Good God. Was he *asleep*?

Scaramouch cleared his throat and gave the detective a little kick. The detective jerked awake and looked around for a moment, then looked up with those empty eye sockets.

"Oh," he said, like he had just met a casual acquaintance on the street, "hello."

Unsure how to counter this unexpected approach to being a captive, Scaramouch decided to replay the sneer.

"Skulduggery Pleasant," he repeated. "Finally, you are within my grasp."

"It does appear so," Pleasant agreed, nodding. "And in a dungeon, no less. How brilliantly postmodern of you."

"You have interfered in my plans for the last time," Scaramouch continued. "Unfortunately for you, you will not live to regret your mistake."

Pleasant tilted his head curiously. "Scaramouch? Scaramouch Van Dreg? Is that you?"

Scaramouch smiled nastily. "Oh, yes. You have fallen into the clutches of your deadliest enemy."

"What are *you* doing here?"

Scaramouch's smile faltered. "What?"

"How are you mixed up in all this?"

"How am I...? What do you mean? This is *my* plot."

"*You're* plotting to use the Crystal of the Saints to bring the Faceless Ones back into our reality?"

Scaramouch frowned. "What? No. What do the Faceless Ones have to do with this? I don't want the Faceless Ones back, I don't even worship them. No, this plot is for *me*, to gain absolute power."

"Then... you're not in league with Rancid Fines or Christophe Nocturnal?"

"I've never even *met* Rancid Fines," Scaramouch said, "and I *hate* Christophe Nocturnal."

Pleasant absorbed this information with a nod. "In that case, I'm afraid there's been a bit of a misunderstanding."

Scaramouch felt like he'd been punched in the gut. All the breath left him, and his shoulders slumped. "You mean, you're not here for me?"

"Dreadfully sorry," Pleasant said.

"But... but you arrived at the hotel. You and your partner, the girl. You were asking all those questions."

"We were looking for Fines and Nocturnal. We didn't even know you were in the country. To be honest, and I don't mean to offend you or anything, but I thought you had passed away some time ago."

Scaramouch gaped. "I just took a little break..."

Pleasant shrugged. "Well, at least now I know. So what are you up to these days?"

"I'm... I have plans," Scaramouch said, dejected.

"The absolute power thing you mentioned?"

Scaramouch nodded.

"And how's that going?"

"It's going OK, I suppose. I mean, you know, everything's on schedule and proceeding apace..."

"Well, that's good. We all need something to get us up in the mornings, am I right? We all need goals."

"Yeah." An unwelcome thought seeped into Scaramouch's mind and lingered there. He tried ignoring it but it flickered and swam, and finally he had to ask, "You don't view me as your deadliest enemy, do you?"

Pleasant hesitated. His skull remained as impassive as ever, but this hesitation spoke volumes. "I view you as *a* deadly enemy," he said helpfully.

"How deadly?"

"I don't know... relatively?"

"Relatively deadly? That's all? I thought we were arch-enemies."

"Oh," Pleasant said. "No, I wouldn't call us *arch*-enemies. Nefarian Serpine was an arch-enemy. Mevolent, obviously. A few others."

"But not us?"

"Not really..."

"Why? Is it because I'm not powerful enough?"

"No, not exactly."

"Then why? What's so different between me and, say, Serpine?"

"Well," said Pleasant, "Serpine had options. He was adaptable. Remember, the deadliest enemies are not necessarily the strongest, they're the smartest."

"So it's because I'm not *smart* enough? But I *am* smart! I am highly intelligent!"

"OK," Pleasant said in an understanding voice.

"Don't patronise me!" Scaramouch snapped. "I have *you* as a prisoner, don't I? You fell into my trap without even a hint of a suspicion!"

"It *was* a clever trap."

"And those chains that bind your powers – you think that's easy to do? You think *that* doesn't require intelligence?"

"No, no," Pleasant said, "I have to admit, you got me fair and square."

"You're damn right I did," Scaramouch sneered. "And you don't even know about my plot yet, do you? You don't even know how intelligent *that* is."

"Well, like I said, I've been busy—"

"Busy with Fines, and with Nocturnal, busy with the threat of the Faceless Ones – but you haven't been busy with the *real* threat, have you?"

"I suppose not," Pleasant said, and then added, "You mean you, don't you?"

"Of course I mean me! I've been smart enough to fool you all into thinking I was dead. I've been smart enough to work under your radar, to set in motion events that will grant me absolute power, which will lead to my total dominion over this world! Now *that*, detective, *that* is smart!"

"Total dominion?"

"Oh, yes, skeleton. How does it feel to know that an opponent such as I, an adversary you would have classified as merely 'relatively deadly', will soon rule this planet with a will of iron, and a fist of..." He faltered. "...iron."

"Um..."

"What?"

"I was just going to say, have you really thought this through?"

"What do you mean?"

"You're talking about ruling the world, right?"

"Yes."

"Not bringing back old gods, not turning the world into some new version of hell, not remaking it as you see fit..."

"Well, no."

"You're just talking about ruling it, then?"

"Yes. With a will of iron and a fist of iron."

"Yes. And again, I'm compelled to ask – have you really thought this through?"

Scaramouch pinched the bridge of his nose with his thumb and forefinger. He was getting a headache. He could feel it coming on. "What do you mean? What is so wrong with planning to rule the world?"

"Well, for a start, think of all the work."

"I'll have minions," Scaramouch said dismissively.

"But they'll still need orders. They'll need you to tell them what to do. You'll be inundated with reports, with documents, with briefings. There won't be enough hours in the day to go over them all, let alone make any decisions."

"Then I'll just order that the days be longer," Scaramouch said. "I will decree that a day stops and starts when *I* decide, not the sun or the moon."

"And how will you cope with warring nations?"

Scaramouch laughed. "When I am ruler, there will be no wars. Everyone will do what I tell them."

"There are billions of people in the world, all with their own viewpoints, all with their own rights. It won't be as simple as telling them to just *stop*. What about famine?"

"What about it?"

"What will you do about it?"

"I'm not sure I understand."

"If famine strikes a country, what will you do?"

Scaramouch smiled evilly. "Maybe I will do nothing. Maybe I will let the country die."

"In which case, you will have an entire country rise against you, because they have nothing left to lose."

"Then I will destroy them."

"And you'll have to deal with the neighbouring countries squabbling over the remains."

"Then I'll destroy them – no, I'll order them to... they'll do what I tell them, all right?"

"And the media?"

Scaramouch sighed. "What about them?"

"How will you cope with the media questioning your policies?"

"There will no questions. This won't be a democracy, it will be a dictatorship."

"There will always be dissent."

"What did I say? I'll have minions, I told you. *They'll* take care of any rebels."

"You'll have a secret police?"

"Of course!"

"You'll assign minions to levels of power?"

"Naturally!"

"And when these minions get ambitions of their own, and they go to overthrow you?"

"Then I'll kill them!" Scaramouch said, exasperated. "I'll have absolute power, remember?"

"And how do you plan to attain this absolute power?"

"It's all in my plan!" Scaramouch yelled, pacing to the wall of the dungeon.

"What about sorcerers?"

Scaramouch tore the cloak from around his neck. It was heavy, and too warm, and when he paced it was annoying. "What about the bloody sorcerers?"

Pleasant's chains jangled slightly as he shrugged. "You don't really think they'll just stand back and let this happen, do you? I realise I'll be dead, so that's one less you'll have to worry about, but there are plenty more."

"There won't be," Scaramouch said, stepping back into the shadows for dramatic affect. "When my plan is complete, I will be the only one capable of wielding magic."

"So you're going to kill them all?"

"I won't have to. They will be left as ordinary mortals, while I will be filled with their powers."

"Ah," Pleasant said. "OK."

"Now do you appreciate my vast and superior intelligence?"

Pleasant thought for a moment. "Yes," he decided.

"Excellent. I'm sorry we can't talk further, detective, but my Hour of Glory is at hand, and your death will be—"

"One more question."

Scaramouch's chin dropped to his chest. "What?" he asked bleakly.

"On the surface, this plot is fine. Drain the magic from others, and then use this magic to become all-powerful and unstoppable and take over the world. I can't see anything wrong with that plot – in theory. But my question, Scaramouch, is how exactly are you going to achieve all this?"

Scaramouch picked his cloak off the ground, felt through it until he came to the cleverly concealed pocket. From this pocket he withdrew a small wooden box with a metal clasp.

He held the box for Pleasant to see. "Recognise this?"

Pleasant peered closer, examining the etchings in the wood. "Ohhh," he said, impressed.

"Exactly. This container, enchanted with twenty-three spells from twenty-three mages, is one of the fabled Lost Artifacts. I have spent the last fifteen months tracking it down – and tonight, it is finally mine."

"So it's true, then?"

"Of course it's true. Why wouldn't it be?"

Pleasant's head jerked up sharply. "You mean you haven't checked it?"

Scaramouch suddenly felt a little foolish. "I... I don't have to," he said. "Everyone knows—"

"Oh, Scaramouch," Pleasant said, disappointment in his voice.

"I just got it!" Scaramouch said defensively. "Literally, I just got it three hours ago!"

"And you haven't checked it?"

"I didn't have *time*. I had to capture *you*."

Pleasant looked back at the box, and his head tilted thoughtfully. "If that *is* the box from the Lost Artifacts, and it certainly does *look* like it might be authentic, then it contains an insect with the power to drain magic at a bite."

"Exactly."

"Providing that insect is still inside."

Scaramouch looked at the box. "There are no holes in it."

"It's been lost for three hundred years."

"But the insect's meant to live forever, right? It doesn't need food or anything?"

"Well, that's the legend. Can you hear it? You should be able to hear it buzzing around in there."

Scaramouch shook the box, and held it up to his ear. "Nothing," he said.

"Well, it's a thick box," Pleasant said. "You probably wouldn't be able to hear it anyway."

Scaramouch shook it again, then listened for any buzzing. Even a single buzz. Anything.

"Did you pay much for it?" Pleasant asked.

"The guy who found it, he needed to mount expeditions and things. It wasn't cheap."

"How much did he charge?"

"I, uh, I gave him everything I had."

The detective went quiet.

"But I'm going to be ruler of the world!" Scaramouch explained. "What difference does it make to me?"

"He made an awful lot of money by just handing over a box, without even verifying that it contained what you hope it contains."

"How will I know?"

"There's only one way. You have to open it."

"But the insect will fly away!"

"Let it out near me," the skeleton suggested. "You're going to kill me anyway, right? So what do I care if it drains my powers before I die?"

Scaramouch narrowed his eyes. "Why would you make this offer?"

"Because I'm *curious*. Scaramouch, I'm a detective. I solve mysteries. If my final act in this world is to establish whether or not a mythological insect could still be contained in one of the Lost Artifacts, then that, to me, would be a good death."

Scaramouch looked at him, and nodded. "OK."

"Put it on the ground, open it, and stand back. When it's finished draining me, it'll be sluggish. That's when you recapture it."

Scaramouch nodded. He licked his lips nervously, and placed the box on the floor. He undid the metal clasp, felt his heart pound in his chest, and he opened the lid.

He scampered back into the shadows.

The detective gazed down into the box.

"Well?" Scaramouch asked from the corner.

"Can't see anything," Pleasant said. "It's a little dark... wait."

"Yes? What?"

And then, the most beautiful sound Scaramouch had ever heard – a buzzing.

"Amazing," Pleasant said in a whisper.

Something rose from the box, rising into the air after centuries of being trapped. It was unsteady, and weak, but it flew. It *lived*.

"One little insect," Pleasant was saying. "The legends say it rose from the carcass of a slain demon. An insect borne of evil, and wickedness, the demon's last attempt to destroy its enemies." The insect flew up, dancing in a shaft of light. "One little insect, and it could be responsible for bringing this world to its knees."

"Wonderful," Scaramouch breathed.

The insect landed on the ground in front of its box, its prison for all those years. Pleasant looked down at it, then moved slightly and knelt on the insect and squished it.

Scaramouch screamed and the door burst open and Valkyrie Cain stepped into the dungeon.

"What the hell is going on here?" she asked.

Scaramouch charged at her and the girl closed her eyes and flexed her fingers. Her eyes and hand snapped open and the air around her rippled. Scaramouch was hurled back off his feet. He crashed into the far wall, hitting his head and collapsing with a groan. He heard the girl and the detective talking, and he heard the chains being unlocked. Moaning, he turned over and looked up at them.

"It was a trick," he said. "You really *were* here to stop me, weren't you? You really *were* here to foil my plan. This is the last time, you hear me? I will escape whatever prison you send me to, and the next time we meet you will pay for—"

"Who's this?" Valkyrie Cain asked.

Scaramouch paled. "What? What do you mean, who am I?"

"His name's Scaramouch Van Dreg," Pleasant told her.

"She knows who I am!" Scaramouch shrieked. "I am your deadliest enemy!"

Cain raised an eyebrow but ignored him. "Has he got anything to do with Fines and Nocturnal?"

"Nope."

"Then why are we wasting our time? Come on, we've got real bad guys to stop."

Cain walked out. Skulduggery Pleasant looked down at Scaramouch and shrugged.

"I'll just chain you up for the moment, but the Cleavers will be around soon to take you into custody. Is that all right with you?"

Scaramouch started crying.

"Good man. Don't let this get you down, though. We all need goals, and I fully expect to do battle with you again, OK?"

Scaramouch wailed.

"We need more villains like you, you know that? We need more bad guys who want to take over the world. There aren't enough of them. The others think it's just, you know... *silly.*"

Scaramouch felt the shackles on his wrists. He had to look up to watch Skulduggery Pleasant leave the dungeon.

Gold, Babies and the Brothers Muldoon

GOLD, BABIES AND THE BROTHERS MULDOON

The cemetery was cold and dark, and the dead man was standing on his grave, watching her as she approached.

"Hello," she said.

The clothes he had been buried in were torn and musty, his shoes caked with mud. He stood with a slight stoop and he had, for the most part, skin and hair. The middle of his face had rotted, however, robbing him of lips and nose and eyelids.

"You're late," he grumbled. "Midnight has come and gone."

"Sorry about that."

"Lives hang in the balance. You're lucky I stayed."

"Yes, I am."

"You are Valkyrie Cain."

"That's right."

"Thirteen years old, Elemental by power, partner of the skeleton detective, and late."

"I suppose."

"You're lucky I stayed."

"So you said."

"I could have left, you know. One minute past midnight, when you weren't here, I could have walked away. I didn't have to wait here for you. I was under no obligation. But I stayed, because I have no wish to see innocent lives taken."

"You're a corpse," Valkyrie said. "Where were you going to go?"

He glared at her, but didn't answer.

He started walking, shuffling off his grave, up towards the ruined church. She followed.

"I thought the skeleton would be with you," the dead man said as they walked.

"We're quite busy at the moment, so Skulduggery had to stay behind. I said I'd take care of this one on my own."

He looked back, and she was thankful the moon was only a sliver, for his face was mostly hidden. "Maybe you underestimate what awaits."

"No, I think I've got it. Three babies snatched from their cots, being held by a family of goblins who want to exchange them for gold. Fairly straightforward."

"If you fully realised the danger you are walking into, you would not be so calm."

"Ah, I'm sure I would. They're goblins, you know? How bad can they be?"

"They were not always goblins," the dead man said, irritation in his voice. "The Muldoons were sorcerers, descended from a long line of the most powerful mages the world had ever seen. They were rumoured to be descended from the Ancients themselves."

"That was disproved," Valkyrie said.

"What?"

"I asked Skulduggery about that. He said the Muldoons reinvented their own family tree in a sad attempt to appear threatening, and then they actually started to believe their own lies."

"If you know so much," the dead man scowled, "then why are you asking *me*?"

"Oh, right, sorry. Please go on."

The corpse muttered something under his breath, then resumed. "The father died, and the mother went insane, but the children maintained the belief that, because of their heritage, they should be the rulers of the world. They believed in the inherent superiority of those who wield magic, and they despised the mortals, whom they saw as pedestrian and drab."

"Why *are* they called mortals?" asked Valkyrie.

"What?"

"I've been wondering that. Non-magical people, I mean, why are they called mortals? Sorcerers are mortal, too."

"Sorcerers don't claim any different."

"But by calling non-magical people mortal, it's like they're implying that they themselves are *im*mortal. And they're not – magic just makes them live longer."

The dead man stopped suddenly and turned. His brows were furrowed across his unblinking eyes. "Do you want to hear the story of the Muldoons or not?" he asked.

"Sure. Sorry."

He grunted, then turned and carried on towards the church. The breeze caught the mustiness of his clothes and brought it down to her. "The Council of Elders identified the Muldoons as the sorcerers behind a spate of attacks on mortals. In an effort to keep the mortals safe, and to keep the magical communities hidden, the Muldoons were ambushed, and although they escaped, they were not unharmed."

"This is my favourite bit," Valkyrie said. "This is when they get turned into goblins, right?"

"Correct. Over the years they have amassed a collection of gold, for gold is the only thing that could return them to human form, but it has not been enough."

"So they started stealing babies."

"Yes."

They arrived at the ruined church. The dead man looked at her "My role is almost fulfilled. I agreed to make the introductions and witness that both parties keep their side of the bargain. There are innocent lives at stake."

"So you keep saying."

"Earlier, I was with the goblins, and I saw that the three babies were safe and well. Thus far, they have kept their word. And you, Valkyrie Cain, are you here with gold?"

"Yes, I am."

"May I see it?" the dead man asked.

"No, you may not."

"And why not?"

"Because it's not for you to see."

The dead man looked at her, and he gave the slightest of nods. "Very well."

He turned to the open door of the church, and spoke loudly. "It is I, and I stand with the girl, the Elemental and the partner of the skeleton detective, and although she is late she is here, which is the important thing, and we are moving on. I ask that the exchange take place, the three innocent lives for the gold she claims to possess, though as of yet I have not seen it. If it makes a difference, she has an honest face, although her eyes are as dark as her hair. Will you bid her enter?"

Torches flared in wall brackets inside the ruin, beating the darkness back. The dead man stepped away.

"You may enter," he said.

"You're not coming?"

"No."

"You wouldn't be letting me walk into a trap, would you?" asked Valkyrie.

"Why would I do that? I'm dead. What do I have to gain?

I can't leave this graveyard. There is nothing that brings me joy any more, there is no pleasure to be had, there is nothing I can use so there is nothing that I want. I am empty. My existence is a shallow thing of coldness and—"

"OK," Valkyrie interrupted, "I get it. You're miserable, fine. I'll go in now."

The dead man shrugged. Valkyrie left him there and stepped into the church.

Part of the roof had caved in, and her boots brushed rubble as she walked. Her boots, like the trousers she wore, and the tunic and the coat, were made of impenetrable materials that had saved her life on numerous occasions. Everything she wore was black, and it was a black that melted into the shadows and hid her from unsuspecting eyes. It wasn't hiding her *tonight*, however. Every move she made was being watched. She could feel eyes on her.

There were a few broken pews in the church, but no altar, and no decoration. The flickering torches reflected off wet patches on the stone walls where the rain had fallen.

Valkyrie stopped walking.

"Hello?" she called. "Goblins?"

"Gold," came the voice from behind her.

She turned slowly, making no sudden moves.

The goblin was maybe up to her shoulder, short and squat and distressingly ugly. He had large bulbous eyes and a long bulbous nose, and his nostril hair mingled with a moustache in a way that was far from appealing. His green skin looked unhealthy in the torchlight, afflicted as it was with sores and boils. He wore a filthy grey suit that had lost all the buttons from the jacket. His belly protruded. Hair sprouted from his belly button.

"Give us the gold," he said.

"Give me the babies," she told him. "Then you get your gold."

He shook his head. "Give us the gold, then you get the babies."

"How do I know the babies are here? I can't hear them crying."

"Maybe they're happy."

"Then show me them smiling."

The goblin scratched his belly thoughtfully. "Compromise," he said.

"OK."

"We'll give you half now, you give us the gold, and then we give you the other half."

"There are three babies. How do you give me half?"

He shrugged. "Chop a baby in two."

"You know, even for a goblin, that's disturbed. Bring the kids out, right now, or I walk away with the gold."

The goblin growled in displeasure. "Colm," he said, "Fintan, bring them out."

From behind him, two more goblins emerged. Valkyrie was amazed to realise that the first goblin was the handsome one of the family. His brothers wore rags, torn and dirty, and they carried the babies between them. The babies had dummies jammed in their mouths.

"See?" the first goblin said. "Alive, uneaten, and not chopped or anything. Now, the gold."

Valkyrie reached into her coat and brought out a bag that jangled in her grip.

The goblins stared at the bag, practically drooling.

"Put the kids down," she said. "Just place them on the ground over here, very gently, and step away. Then I'll give you the gold and we'll say goodbye."

One of the goblins, she didn't know which one he was, so she decided that he should be Colm, grunted. "How do we know there's gold in that bag?"

"Because I tell you there is."

"We don't know you. Liam, we can't trust this girl."

The first goblin, Liam, scratched his belly. "We were expecting the skeleton. Where is he?"

"He couldn't make it."

"He sent you instead?"

"Yes, he did," said Valkyrie

"You're his assistant, then?"

"Partner."

"You're a child."

"You're a goblin."

"Only on the outside."

"And on the inside you steal babies. Looks *and* personality."

"I don't like you."

"You just have to get to know me," she said. "Are we going to stand around talking all night, or are we going to do this ransom thing?"

"The skeleton should be here," the third goblin, Fintan, mumbled.

"Shut up," Liam barked. "We'll settle that later. Right now, give her the brats. I want to see that gold."

Colm and Fintan walked forward, bringing with them an interesting aroma of dried sweat and boiled cabbage. They put the babies on the ground, close to Valkyrie, and the babies gurgled and made baby noises.

The goblins stepped back, rejoined their brother.

"Now," Liam said with a snaggle-toothed smile, "give us our payment."

"And then you'll let us go?"

"Of course."

"Why don't I believe you?"

Liam shrugged. "A deal's a deal – we held up our part, now you have to do the same."

If things turned nasty, Valkyrie would only be able to scoop up one of the kids before the goblins were on her. The goblins didn't look very fast, so she'd probably be able to beat them to the door, but it would mean leaving two babies here. She didn't see any alternative, however, and the goblins' patience was running out.

She tossed the bag, and Liam caught it and yanked open the drawstring. He let the gold coins spill out into his hand.

Fintan licked his lips. "They real? Liam, they real?"

Liam put one of the coins in his mouth and sucked on it a moment, then reached his grimy fingers between his lips to retrieve it. "It's gold," he said happily. His wide eyes glinted.

"Pleasure doing business," Valkyrie said, hunkering down to the kids.

"You're not leaving," said Liam.

Valkyrie sighed. "Is this a double-cross?"

"That's what this is. It'd be better if the skeleton was here instead of you, but when we send him your head, wrapped up in a pretty bow, he'll come looking for us and we'll get him then."

"You have issues with Skulduggery?"

"We hate him," Fintan snarled. "He's the one responsible for turning us into creatures of slime and bad breath."

"I see," said Valkyrie. "Before you kill me, can I ask you a question?"

Liam laughed. "Go ahead."

"Thank you. My question is, what makes you think I came alone?"

Liam's smile faded. "What?"

"You know Skulduggery, right? You've gone up against him before. You know how smart he is."

"Not *that* smart," Colm grumbled.

"And he knows you," Valkyrie continued. "He knows how treacherous you are, and he's told me how you never keep your side of a bargain, and how you always double-cross..."

Liam frowned. "So?"

"So smile, goblin. Skulduggery Pleasant has been here all along, and tonight's the night when he gets to kick your green and wrinkly little—"

There was a crash on the roof above them and the rotten wood splintered and gave, and Skulduggery fell through and hit the ground with his face.

"Oh my God," he muttered as he lay there. "Oh my God, that hurt."

Valkyrie hesitated. No one made a move, and no one made a sound. Even the babies had stopped gurgling. The goblins grinned. Valkyrie chewed her lip.

"This is... slightly unexpected," she said.

Skulduggery Pleasant, the skeleton detective, his blue suit ripped and streaked with dirt, rolled on to his back and groaned. If his skull had features, they would surely be twisted in pain. "Don't move," he managed to say. "You're all under arrest."

The goblins laughed.

"You think you're the only one with back-up?" Liam grinned at Valkyrie. "You think you're the only one with a surprise?"

Valkyrie glared at him. "So who've you got out there? More of your little buddies? Some assassins? Couple of monsters, maybe? Because I have to tell you, we've faced them all, and we keep winning."

"No assassins," Liam said. "No monsters. Just Peg."

"Who's Peg?"

Liam sneered. "Oh, of course, you haven't met our sister, have you? Peg'll be the one who threw your friend there through the roof. *Peg!*"

A massive shape filled the doorway, and Peg the Ugly Goblin stepped in. She was twice Valkyrie's height, and had legs as wide as tree trunks, and arms as wide as her legs. Her body was a solid slab of meat, clothed in what appeared to be a half dozen grimy wedding dresses sewn together, and her hair hung long and lank over her face.

Skulduggery got unsteadily to his feet. "Don't worry," he told Valkyrie. "I have her on the ropes now."

"She threw you over a church," Valkyrie pointed out.

For a moment he was silent. And then he said, "Not *all* the way over."

"Skuluggy," Peg moaned. "Oo uv me."

Valkyrie frowned. "Did she just say what I think she said?"

Skulduggery shook his head quickly. "No."

Peg took another few steps inside. Her brothers cackled and let her pass.

"Skuluggy," Peg moaned again. "I uv oo."

Skulduggery glanced at Valkyrie. "OK. She *may* have a thing for me."

"She *loves* you?"

"Well, yes, but I assure you, it's very unrequited."

Liam grinned. "Weren't expecting *this*, were you, Mr Detective? Probably thought, once a mountain fell on her, you'd seen the last of our sister, eh?"

"To be honest," Skulduggery said, "yes."

"She's tougher than she looks," Fintan said.

"Now *that's* an achievement," Skulduggery murmured.

Peg stood there, a wall in a wedding dress, and held her arms out. A swollen tongue dragged itself over her cracked lips, and she struggled to form her next word.

"Kiss," she said.

Valkyrie arched an eyebrow. Skulduggery nodded, more to himself than anybody else.

"I'm going to have to let her down gently," he said, and ran forward and leaped, slamming both feet into Peg's belly. She roared in anger and swiped at him and he dodged, kicking at the back of her knee. She barely noticed.

The three brothers were coming for Valkyrie. She clicked the fingers of her right hand and made a spark, then caught the spark and cultivated it into a flame that burned in her hand.

Fintan was closest. She reached out with her left hand, feeling the air against her skin. He ran at her and she felt the space between them, felt how it connected, and when she found the right spot she splayed her hand and snapped her palm and the air rippled and hit Fintan like a truck. He flew back and smacked into the church wall.

The fire in her other hand was burning fiercely and she threw it. The fireball hit Colm's ragged coat and he shrieked and stumbled back, tearing it off. He raised his head to see her running straight at him, but couldn't do anything to stop the elbow that smashed into his jaw. He spun around, then tipped over backwards and didn't get up.

Liam rushed her and she tried to move but she wasn't fast enough. She was taken off her feet and slammed into the ground, Liam's hands at her throat, trying to throttle her.

Behind him, she saw Peg strike Skulduggery. He hurtled into the shadows.

Valkyrie tried breaking Liam's grip, but his fingers were short and thick and she couldn't pry them loose. She grabbed his wrist and twisted, but he was too strong. His fingers dug into her throat and black spots flashed in her vision, her head swimming. She brought her hands in, felt the air between herself and the goblin, but Liam scuttled up, knelt on her left hand and pinned it to the ground. He took one hand from her throat and held her right wrist away from him.

"Try your little tricks *now*," he snarled, his foul breath hot on her cheek.

Blood pulsed through her temples. Her lungs burned, and although her struggles were getting more frantic, she could feel herself growing weaker.

Spittle dripped from Liam's lips on to her face. Her muscles ached and her body was tired, and darkness seeped into her vision. She couldn't hear anything over the beating of her own heart.

Liam was kneeling on her left hand. His right knee was pressed into her belly, leaving her legs to kick uselessly behind him.

She brought her legs in, bent them, the soles of her boots flat to the ground. With the last ounce of her strength, Valkyrie lifted her backside off the church floor. Liam lurched forward a little and laughed.

"Think that'll do it? I've tamed wild horses, little girl, and they buck a lot harder than you."

Valkyrie took her right foot off the ground. She could feel the air on her face, on her hands, on her exposed skin. Now she struggled to feel the air through her boot. It was possible. She knew it was.

And as her consciousness ebbed, she thought she felt it, a slight resistance, and that's all she needed. She stepped on the air and it shimmered, and Valkyrie's body flipped over backwards, and the goblin screeched as he was catapulted away.

Valkyrie landed on her belly and gasped, sucked in breath hungrily. Tears had sprung to her eyes and she wiped them away, in time to see Skulduggery reach out a hand. A large piece of rubble lifted off the ground. Skulduggery made circular motions and the piece of rubble started to move. Faster and faster it went, in an ever-increasing circle.

The piece of rubble slammed into Peg's jaw and before she could even growl, it had made its way around and slammed into her jaw again. It struck her repeatedly until Skulduggery's hand stiffened, and the piece of rubble hurtled into Peg's face and shattered.

Peg fell back to a sitting position. She held a huge hand to the side of her face and moaned.

Valkyrie stood, and saw Liam. He was on his feet and sneaking towards the babies.

She ran at him and he snarled. She ducked under a punch and he twisted to get at her again. His fist swung and she blocked but her block wasn't strong enough, and his knuckles hit the side of her face and she staggered. He grinned and she smacked him, and goblin blood, the colour of mucus, sprayed from his lip.

In the middle of the church, Peg had Skulduggery wrapped up in a bear hug. He was trying to hit her with a section of a broken pew.

Liam ran at Valkyrie, yelling out a war cry. She clicked her fingers and he stopped and cowered, expecting the fireball. But instead she moved in, stiffened the fingers of her other hand and jabbed into his neck. His head swung around, offering up the perfect target. Her elbow connected with the hinge of his jaw, and Liam the goblin crumpled to the ground.

"You don't really love me," she heard Skulduggery say.

Peg was sitting against a wall, Skulduggery standing over her, the remains of the broken pew in his hands.

"I'm flattered," he continued, "really I am. I'm sure you're a lovely girl."

Peg moaned.

"But the truth is, we don't know each other. Not really. I don't know what your favourite song is, or what flower you like most, or what you like to do on long summer evenings. And what do you really know about me?"

"I uv oo, Skuluggy."

"No, you don't, Peg. This isn't real love. This isn't true love. You deserve someone who can give you true love."

"Oo?"

"No, not me."

"Moh."

"I'm sorry. I didn't want to hurt your feelings."

Peg sniffled.

"He's out there, you know. Your Mister Right. And I'm sure he's looking for you."

She looked up. "Eally?"

"Really. You just have to find him."

Peg nodded, then nodded again, with renewed determination. Skulduggery stepped back as she stood up and brushed some of the dust off her wedding dress.

"Stay away from your brothers, OK? They're not a very good influence on you."

She nodded, and marched for the church door. Before she stepped out, she stopped, and looked back tearfully. "I awah ink awoo, Skuluggy."

"And I'll always think of you, too," Skulduggery replied.

And then Peg was gone.

Valkyrie stood beside Skulduggery. "Anything you want to tell me?"

"No," he said. "Not really. Are all the babies safe?"

"Safe and unharmed. Their folks will be glad to have them back. Are you sure there's nothing you want to tell me? To share?"

"Relatively positive, yes."

"She seems nice. Peg, I mean."

He looked at her. "It's going to take you a while to stop teasing me about this, isn't it?"

She grinned. "Oh, yes."

He sighed. "Then you may as well get started."

THE SLIGHTLY IGNOMINIOUS END TO THE LEGEND OF BLACK ANNIS

THE SLIGHTLY IGNOMINIOUS END TO THE LEGEND OF BLACK ANNIS

Black Annis didn't like living in a ditch, but times were changing, and the England she had known as a child was long gone. She narrowed her eyes – left eye blue, right eye green – and tried to remember what she had been like as a child. It had been so long ago she had quite forgotten.

Had she laughed and played, like other girls? Had she giggled and joked, and run through the meadows and the fields of Leicester, letting the sunshine warm her skin? Highly unlikely. The more she thought about it, the more she remembered. She couldn't recall any friends, nor could she recall any giggling or joking. She seemed to remember a lot of screaming, though. Oh, yes, a whole lot of screaming.

Annis walked to the cave mouth, her feet crunching on bones and human remains. It was almost morning. She hated mornings. She hated the morning, the noon, the early afternoon, the late afternoon, and bright evenings. She hated a lot of things.

What had she been thinking about? Oh, yes, her childhood. Now *that* was a time of her life that had outstayed its welcome. Her parents had been terrified of her. Her father had thought she was the spawn of the devil, but she'd always taken that as a compliment. Whenever she got angry her fingernails would grow long and pointed, and her teeth became jagged and her skin turned blue. She'd never really understood why her skin turned blue, or what purpose it served, but her parents used it as an early-warning system. Annis's temper was not a pretty sight.

All in all, it had probably surprised no one when she started eating people. Her parents' friends had probably nodded when they'd heard, maybe shrugged, saying something like, "Aye, doesn't surprise me one bit, her eatin' people. Always had that look about her, didn't she?" Black Annis didn't mind. By the time she was twenty she'd eaten everyone in her village, parents and all.

That had been... how long ago? Two hundred years, maybe. Now she had streaks of grey in her black matted hair, and her face was lined and she wore her age like an ugly shawl. This was her life – living in a cave that opened into a ditch, kept awake during the day by the tractors that ploughed the field above.

A rat scampered in from the ditch outside and she snatched it up. It was thin and mangy and squirmed in her grip, but she hadn't eaten in a week, so she bit down and the rat squealed and its warm blood ran down her throat.

She munched through it, not bothering with the tail, which was always too chewy, and dropped the remains at her feet. She coughed up a hairball and spat it out, then wandered back to the fire at the centre of the cave.

She heard Scrannel returning, heard the clanging of his armour, and she allowed a spark of hope to permeate her usual dour humour. He was hurrying. Maybe that meant he'd been successful. Maybe he was struggling with someone. She heard him lose his footing and splash and crash into the ditch. She didn't care who he'd brought with him – child, adult, old person, she genuinely didn't care. She was regretting eating the rat now – she should have held off a little longer. She heard Scrannel hiss in pain – either the meal had struck him, or he'd become tangled in the thorns again. Black Annis licked her lips, picturing a plump child, maybe ten years old. She was *starving*.

But when Scrannel appeared at the cave mouth, he was alone. Disappointment became a weight in the pit of Annis's stomach.

"Hullo," Scrannel said, his armour dripping with ditch water. "I'm back." It wasn't real armour, of course. He had made it from an assortment of tin products and segments of corrugated iron. It was held together by nuts and bolts and pieces of frayed string. It clanked when he walked. It clanked when he *didn't* walk. It just *clanked*.

"Where's my dinner?" Black Annis asked, even though the answer didn't interest her. The only thing that mattered was that she wasn't going to eat. Again.

"No one's about," Scrannel said, giving an apologetic shrug that kicked up quite a racket. "Everyone's asleep."

"Of course everyone's asleep," Annis snapped. "It's night. You were supposed to sneak into a house and grab someone."

"I tried," Scrannel claimed, eyes wide with earnestness. "But every time I got close to a door or window, the lights would come on and I'd have to run away. I don't know how they knew I was there. It happened six or seven times."

Annis crossed her arms. Her dress was shapeless and made of sackcloth. "Do you think," she said, her voice quiet and filled with barely restrained rage, "that maybe they hear that stupid armour you insist on wearing?"

Scrannel frowned. "They hear *this*? I don't think that's very likely, Annis. They're probably all psychics. That's what *I* think."

She resisted the urge to tear him limb from bloody limb. Scrannel was, for lack of a better word, a pet. His mother was a troll, to whom his father was nothing more than a drunken blur one dark and stormy night, and so Scrannel himself was a crossbreed, a mongrel, an *oddity*. He had milky-white eyes that were set too far apart, he had no nose to speak of and a mouth wide enough to swallow a decent-sized rock. He had tiny teeth and high cheekbones and only the barest hint of a chin, upon which he was trying to grow a beard. He had been trying to grow this beard for the past three years. His chin looked vaguely fluffy, but that was as far as it had got.

Scrannel was an idiot of a creature, who actually enjoyed living in a ditch, and the only reason Annis had not eaten him was because he tasted dreadful. The first time they had met she'd torn off a chunk of his leg, chewed it for a few moments before spitting it out. She'd spent the rest of the night being sick in a stream, and Scrannel had stuck around, eventually offering to hold her hair back while she vomited.

That had been twelve years ago, and he still hadn't left.

"I have a bit of news," he said, trying to sound casual. "I think I was followed."

She stared at him. "What?"

"I can't be sure now," he said hurriedly. "But there was a woman, and she had blonde hair and a long coat, and I've never seen her before, and she looked, you know, out of place."

"And why do you think she was following you?"

"Because when I ran away, she ran after me."

Annis could feel her skin starting to turn blue.

Scrannel spoke quickly. "I might be mistaken, of course. Could just be coincidence. She might be a jogger, or something."

"A jogger?" Annis growled. "In a long coat? At night?"

"Carrying a sword."

"*What?*"

"I'm fairly certain she was carrying a sword."

Annis felt her fingernails grow long. "That doesn't sound like a jogger, now, does it?"

Scrannel pondered, then shook his head. "To be honest, no, it doesn't. And now that I think about it, I don't think she was even wearing jogging shoes. What kind of jogger doesn't wear jogging shoes?"

"You're an idiot," Annis snarled.

His armour clanked when he nodded.

There was movement at the cave mouth. Scrannel scuttled away, and a young woman with tousled blonde hair, wearing a long coat over brown leather trousers and a brown leather tunic, stepped into the cave holding a sword in her right hand.

"That's her," Scrannel said unhelpfully.

The woman was holding a coil of thick rope in her other hand, which she let drop into the human remains at her feet.

"Nice place," she muttered, almost to herself. She had a London accent. Annis liked Londoners. They tasted great.

Scrannel let out a battle cry, then he ran forward. The young woman didn't use her sword, as Annis expected. Instead, she swayed to one side and slapped Scrannel on the back as he hurtled by. He ran into the cave wall.

Annis could feel her teeth start to lengthen in her mouth. "Who are you?"

"Tanith," the young woman said. "Tanith Low."

Scrannel charged at her again and she kicked out, slamming her boot heel into the piece of tin wrapped around his knee. He hit the ground with his insignificant chin.

Tanith ignored him as he rolled around in pain. "And I'm just guessing here, so don't be offended if I get this wrong, but you must be Black Annis. I've heard an awful lot about you."

"Is that so?"

"Yes indeedy. The blue skin, the nails, the cave littered with the bones of your victims. It's all very impressive."

Annis's jaw dislocated with a loud pop, and her mouth hung open – impossibly wide – to accommodate her growing, jagged teeth.

"Why, granny," Tanith said with a smile, "what big teeth you have."

"You don't know *everything* about me," Annis said. "If you did, you wouldn't have dared set foot in my home."

Tanith shrugged. "I know that you're under arrest, and I know you really shouldn't resist."

Black Annis laughed.

Scrannel forced himself to his feet and threw a punch, but Tanith struck his forearm with the hilt of her sword. The piece of tin that covered that section of arm now had a large dent in it. She kicked him and the corrugated iron that made up his chest-plate rattled as he fell back.

Tanith looked over at Annis. "I know enough. I know that sunlight turns you to stone for all eternity. I know that you've killed and eaten hundreds of people over the years."

"Thousands," Annis corrected.

"Well, in that case, you are doubly under arrest."

"You shouldn't have come here alone."

Scrannel ran to the dark corner of the cave where he kept his stuff, and grabbed the wooden spear he'd been working on for weeks. He ran back towards Tanith and when he was close enough so there was no way he could miss, he hurled the spear and missed. It sailed past her, right out through the cave mouth. She didn't even have to duck.

Tanith jumped and spun, a leg snapping out from nowhere and hitting Scrannel in the jaw. He whirled and clanked and fell and clanked and hit the ground and clanked, and then he lay still and didn't clank any more.

Annis bent her knees, ready to spring. "Any last requests?"

Tanith shrugged. "Fall over and go to sleep?"

Tanith dodged the first swipe of the nails, but only just. Annis pressed the attack, forcing the intruder to retreat. Tanith, panic showing in her eyes, blocked with the sword, but Annis had both hands working, which was the equivalent to ten long knives slashing through the air.

A boot found Annis's knee and she stumbled back and hissed. Tanith came forward, thrusting the sword high then sweeping it low, but Annis had anticipated the feint and the nails of her left hand connected with the blade and forced it down, while her right hand went to carve up Tanith's pretty face.

At the last moment Tanith raised an elbow, striking Annis's arm and making her miss, but the move meant that she had taken one hand off her sword. Annis flicked her left hand and tore the sword from Tanith's grip. It fell between them, then Annis stepped over it, hands flashing.

Tanith stumbled back, desperately trying to dodge another few swipes. Annis's nails struck the cave wall repeatedly, but she was grinning now, looking forward to the meal that was about to come.

Tanith kept moving, however, swaying just far enough so that the nails would miss and hit the wall. Annis was growing impatient, and Tanith moved in, punched her right on the nose, before moving away again.

Annis could see, by the skin of her hands, that she was at her bluest. She felt the anger build, and she let out a roar and her attack became a frenzy of slashing claws that hit nothing but cave wall. She rushed at Tanith, who leaped to the wall and ran sideways along it. Annis howled her rage and tried to reach her. But now Tanith was upside down, above her, and as Annis whirled Tanith jumped and flipped, landed beside her sword, snatching it up.

They went at it, sword against nails, and now Annis could see something new in Tanith's eyes. The panic was gone, the desperation was gone, and Annis suddenly realised it had never been there in the first place. She knew, instinctively, that this had all been planned. But why? What could Tanith possibly have to gain by simply defending, and dodging attacks?

Tanith ducked under another swipe and dropped to the ground. She swung her foot out, hitting Annis in the back of the leg. Annis fell, tried to get up, but Tanith smashed a boot heel into her jaw.

Dazed, Annis swiped at where Tanith had just been, and her nails found nothing but air. She felt something tighten around her ankle, and looked up.

"What're you doing?" she asked dully.

Tanith had tied the thick rope to Annis's leg, and for the first time Annis realised that the other end of the rope trailed out of the cave. Tanith gave the rope a little tug, then stood up and stepped back.

"It's morning," Tanith said. "See outside? That's sunlight, that is."

Annis shook her head to clear it. "So?"

"So," Tanith continued, "there's a farmer out there on a tractor, and the other end of this rope is tied to that tractor, and his instructions are, when he feels a tug on this rope, he is to start driving, very slowly, away."

Annis frowned. The rope was beginning to tighten. After a moment, it was taut, and Annis felt herself begin to move towards the cave mouth.

"You'll turn to stone," Tanith said, "for all eternity. You don't want that, do you?"

Annis, her odd-coloured eyes wide, sat up and slashed at the thick rope with her nails.

"You've gone a bit blunt, I'm afraid," Tanith said. "Striking my sword was bad enough, but that cave wall? That's what did it."

Annis squealed as she was slowly dragged towards the sunlight. She slashed again and again at the rope.

"There's no way you're going to cut through that in time," Tanith said. She took a pair of wrist irons from her coat, and tossed them on the ground. "Put those on."

"Never!" Annis screamed.

"OK."

Annis attacked the rope with renewed vigour. She cut through one strand. By the looks of it, only another two hundred to go. She twisted around.

"Scrannel! Scrannel wake up!" Scrannel didn't move. He snored gently.

Annis glared at Tanith. "You can't do this! You can't!"

"You eat people," Tanith said. "I pretty much can, unless you put those shackles on and let me take you in."

The sunlight was mere inches away.

"Fine!" Annis screeched. Tanith kicked the shackles over to her and Annis clicked them on around her wrists, the chain dangling. Immediately she felt her powers fade. Her skin began to lose its blue tint, and her teeth and nails shortened and her jaw relocated.

"I hate you," Annis said.

Tanith nodded. "A lot of people in shackles do."

"If I ever get out..."

"You'll come after me? Tear me apart? Cut off my head? I've heard it all before, Annis. It doesn't impress me."

"If I ever get out of prison," Annis said, ignoring her, "I'll find you and eat you."

Tanith smiled. "Well, OK then. Haven't heard that one in a while." She took hold of Annis's arm and pulled her to her feet.

"I've got a sack outside," she said. "I'm afraid you'll have to wear it until I get you to the van, just to keep the sunlight off. Hope you understand."

Annis perked up. "Is it a nice sack?"

"It's pretty stylish, as sacks go."

On their way out, they passed Scrannel, who was snoring peacefully in the dirt. Annis gave him an affectionate kick, and he mumbled something and went back to snoring.

"Boyfriend?" Tanith asked.

"Pet," Annis answered.

Tanith nodded. "All the best ones are."

FRIDAY NIGHT FIGHTS

FRIDAY NIGHT FIGHTS

She was food, she was told as they dragged her to the cell. She was lunch. She was little more than a snack, thrown to the beast to reward it for blood spilled. The men were strong, and she kicked at them and they hit her, but still she kicked. She would not go gently to her death. Not her. Not Valkyrie Cain.

Her knees scraped over rough stones and rubble and bled through her jeans. The cold shackles dug into her wrists. Her struggles echoed down through the concrete corridor, as wide as the school running track. The sunlight was too far behind to throw shadows. The darkness was too close in front.

The man holding her arm let go, and keys jangled as he went to the cell door. He slid open a hatch before he unlocked it, to check on the beast. She felt the other man tense, and for a moment his attention was away from her. She twisted from his grip. The light was too far away, so she ran into the darkness. Laughter followed her.

She ran fast. Her tennis shoes splashed in dark pools of stagnant water, and the uneven ground threatened to cut short her escape. She kept her shackled arms up, like a boxer, to protect her head should she run into a wall or a low-hanging pipe. Her eyes were adjusting to the world of shadows, and she couldn't risk a backwards glance.

There was a break in the solid mass to her left, and she veered into a branching corridor. The cold registered on her bare arms, but she didn't feel it. She wouldn't feel anything until the adrenaline faded.

Their voices came, calling for her. Cell doors, iron and old, blurred by on either side. There were people in some of those cells. She could hear them, reacting to the mocking calls of the men. In other cells, there were beasts. They snarled and snapped and hurled themselves against the iron, excited and bloodthirsty, adding to the cacophony.

Concrete steps led upwards to a faint yellow light. Valkyrie left the darkness and took the steps three at a time. The staircase spiralled and the light grew stronger. Another corridor, long and thin, the sunlight streaming through the narrow windows on one side. At the end of the corridor, a wooden door. She ran past the narrow windows and through them saw a small stadium, basic stone seating curving round a lowered arena.

Where the hell had they taken her?

The wooden door opened before she got to it. The man with the keys smiled. Oddly, for someone so dirty and brutal, he had a nice smile. Behind her, the other man was blocking her retreat.

"You'd better be coming along now, girl," the man with the keys said.

Valkyrie went to a window, turned sideways, and squeezed the upper half of her body through. There was an open space of flat concrete twelve metres below, just before the seating started. She managed to get her hips through, but a hand grabbed her leg as she fell. She swung into the wall and did her best to loosen the grip. The man with the keys could barely get his head through the window. His fingers were tight on her ankle.

"Go down and catch her," he said to his friend.

Coins fell from Valkyrie's pocket as she dug into her jeans with her shackled hands, searching for something to break his hold. Something sharp. She unbuckled her belt and pulled it free, held the buckle in her palm with the prong sticking up through her index and middle fingers, and closed her fist. She curled her body upwards, stabbing the prong repeatedly into the back of his hand. It was a crude dagger, and limited. He cursed and yelled and gritted his teeth, but didn't let go.

The muscles in her abdomen were burning. She had to break his hold *now*. She wouldn't get another chance.

Valkyrie released his forearm and grabbed his hand, doing her best to prise a finger loose. She could raise his fingertip off her leg, but that was it. She heard him laugh at her efforts.

Her muscles screaming at her, she dug the buckle prong beneath his fingernail. He cried out for his friend to hurry up. She squirmed the prong deeper and he cursed at her, the pitch of his voice rising with the pain. Finally his nail lifted and she fell with his screeches, turned her body and tucked her chin to her chest. She hit the concrete with her shoulder and tried to absorb the impact through her side. She knew how to fall. She'd been taught how to fall.

But she'd never fallen from this height.

She lay on her back and tried to breathe but couldn't. She tried to move but couldn't. Her arms wouldn't push her up and her legs wouldn't bend.

She made a sound, a long involuntary groan. Her lungs were trying to inflate. Her stomach muscles were bunching up and she had to fight the urge to curl into a ball. When the first bit of control returned to her, she arched her back and groaned again.

A sliver of breath, in through her lips.

Valkyrie turned over, got up, saw the other man running for her. She stumbled away from him, still trying to breathe. He was fast and he was gaining. Her legs struggled to find a rhythm, but at least she was running again. Valkyrie jumped on to the stone seating, leaping from seat to seat, moving diagonally down to the arched tunnel that led out of the stadium. He was behind her all the way.

Her breathing was ragged, but back under her control as she dropped from the last seat. The tunnel lay ahead, opening out on the other side to a view of magnificent green countryside. She ran for it. She could lose him in the fields, or the trees, or even swim a river to get away. She could flag down a car on the road. She could pick up a rock and smash his brains in. Once she got through that tunnel, she could do a lot of things.

She was halfway through when there was a rattle and a rumble, and a gate began to lower. It was one of those old latticed gates, the kind that protected medieval castles. It was waist-height as Valkyrie neared, and she had to throw herself down and roll beneath it, springing up immediately on the other side.

Her pursuer shot his arm through the gate, but she was well out of reach.

She looked round, hands behind her head, sucking in air and gearing up for the next run. She was standing in a large makeshift car park that pushed back the countryside as far as it would go. Hills of green rolled like frozen waves towards the horizon. To her left was a forest that spread unchecked, enveloping everything within reach, and to her right were houses in the distance. She counted seven, isolated from each other on the sides of the hills. But for all Valkyrie knew there was a town beyond that clump of trees, or a village hidden by that hedgerow.

"Don't go too far," the man behind her said. "We'll get you soon enough."

She took off at a quick jog, following the trail that led away from the car park. She could hear Skulduggery's voice in her head, telling her to stay off the path, telling her that was making herself an easy target. But the trail would lead to a road, Valkyrie knew, and a road would mean cars, and other people.

She took the trail downhill, where it evened out and became a small road. She turned the jog into a run. The road joined another, and as she approached a tractor passed. She waved but the driver didn't see her, and it was round the next bend before she reached the junction. She took off after it, wishing she had something with which to tie her hair back. She didn't like running with it loose.

The tractor was ahead of her, trundling on its way. It was old and, by the look of it, ran primarily on rust. It didn't have any wing mirrors, so Valkyrie's frantic waves were going unnoticed. She had to slow, she had to, and she glared at the tractor as it trundled on.

She heard another engine, a car or a van, coming from behind, and had visions of the van the men had been driving when they'd grabbed her. She was about to jump into the ditch when a blue sedan came round the corner and stopped sharply. The woman behind the wheel stared at her, then opened the door and stepped out.

"Are you OK?" the woman asked. She was about sixty, with short grey hair.

"Two men are chasing me. I need to get away."

The woman waved her hand at the passenger side. "Get in."

Valkyrie did as she was told, and buckled up as the woman put the car in gear.

"What happened?" the woman asked as they overtook the tractor and sped on. "Who's chasing you?"

What was Valkyrie going to say? Was she going to tell the truth?

Of course not. "Bad men," she said. "They kidnapped me, brought me here. I got away, but they're chasing me. I have to get back to my friends. They'll be able to help."

"What's your name?"

"Valkyrie," she said without thinking.

"Valkyrie... what an unusual name. I'm Grace. I'm not from around here, so you're going to have to tell me where to go."

"I don't even know where we are."

"I think we're in Kildare. I'm so sorry, I'm kind of lost."

"Do you have a phone? They took mine."

Grace winced apologetically. "I have, but the battery's run out, and I left the car charger at home. I think the best thing we can do is just head for the nearest town." She took a right turn. "I passed one about five minutes ago."

Valkyrie frowned. "We're going back?"

"Not the same way. I think this road loops around."

"I really think we should be getting as far away from here as possible."

"You don't have to be afraid. There's no one about."

"I don't think you're getting how serious this is. They're not going to just let me *escape*." Valkyrie frowned. "Are you sure we're not headed back on the exact same road we were on? This looks familiar."

"Oh, no," said Grace, "I'm quite sure. Why are you looking at me like that? You seem almost... Oh, my. You think I know those men, don't you? You think I'm bringing you back to them?"

"Let me out," said Valkyrie. "Let me out right—"

The van reared up at Grace's window and swerved into them, and there was a crunch of metal and the world spun and Grace was screaming. The car dipped sickeningly and hit something and the air bags rushed out, knocking Valkyrie's head back.

Suddenly it was still. The engine was running, but they weren't moving.

Valkyrie opened her eyes. She heard Grace moan, and started to push the air bag down. They were in a ditch. Her thumb clicked the seat-belt release catch, and she reached for the door, but it wouldn't open. She moved her head, looking back at Grace. There was movement outside. Someone was opening the driver-side door.

"Help," Grace said softly.

The man reached in and took hold of Grace's head, and he twisted until her neck broke. Then he looked over at Valkyrie.

"Told you we'd get you," he said.

They dragged her to the cell and this time they didn't take their attention off her. The man with the keys opened the iron door and his companion threw her inside.

Valkyrie stumbled in. Her foot hit something and she fell. The door shut and darkness swarmed. She stayed very still, on her hands and knees, and listened for the beast, but she could only hear her own breathing.

Moving slowly, she tracked her hand back to whatever she'd tripped over. There was a cold metal ring bolted to the middle of the floor, and a thick chain led from it and snaked towards the far right corner of the cell.

Valkyrie moved backwards, wincing every time she made a sound. She got to the door, her foot loud against the iron. After waiting a moment to make sure this hadn't roused the beast to attack, she crawled sideways to her left, sat back into the corner, and pulled her knees into her chest.

She held her hand in front of her face and couldn't even see movement. The ground was smooth, with no rocks to use as weapons.

She still couldn't hear the beast. Had they been lying? Toying with her? She thought of Grace and the sound her neck had made, and she folded her arms across her chest and brought her knees in closer. She was starting to shake. It was freezing in here and the adrenaline had worn off. She felt the panic rise, from her belly to her throat, and bit her lip. She wasn't going to cry. They could have a camera on her right now, and she wasn't going to cry. She did her best to close down her mind, but one thought slipped through, and that was all it took.

I wish Skulduggery were here.

Her face crumpled and tears came, and she lowered her head and cried.

When there were no more tears to fall, Valkyrie wiped her eyes. She was fairly certain she was alone in the cell. Anything that hadn't been woken when she'd been thrown in would surely have stirred since then. So they'd been playing little games with her. She wasn't food for anything. So what, then? Was she to be used as leverage against the Sanctuary? She doubted Grand Mage Thurid Guild would negotiate too much over her fate.

"Hello," said a voice.

Valkyrie cursed in fright and pressed herself back into the corner, widening her eyes to try and distinguish shapes in the dark.

"I'm not going to hurt you," the voice assured her. It sounded like the voice of a young man. "Probably."

"Who are you?" Valkyrie asked, her voice loud and harsh.

The voice was smooth and quiet. "I'm Caelan. This is my cell. You're sitting in my favourite corner, you know. Switching corners every few days is the only thing that makes life bearable in this place. Keeps things fresh."

She frowned. "Sorry."

"It's OK. You can have it."

"What's happening?"

"They haven't told you? Usually, they tell people."

"They just said I was going to be food."

She could almost sense him nodding.

"So they *have* told you. But technically you wouldn't be food. You'd be drink."

Valkyrie went cold. "You're a vampire."

"Aha," he said slowly. "You must be a sorcerer, then? Don't suppose you could use your magic to get us out of here?"

She held her hands up in the dark. "These shackles are bound. I can't use magic."

"Ah. It was a nice idea while it lasted. What's your name?"

"Valkyrie. Valkyrie Cain."

"You say it like that name is supposed to mean something to me."

"I work with Skulduggery Pleasant."

"The Skeleton Detective," Caelan said. "Now, him I *have* heard about. I heard he was gone, though. Sucked into another dimension or something equally stupid."

"He is. I'm going to get him back."

There was a moment's silence. "And you're doing a wonderful job of that."

She glared at the darkness. "So what about you? What are you doing here?"

"Right now? Right now I'm on hunger strike."

"Since when?"

"Since this morning. It's going pretty well so far, but I always falter around dinnertime..."

"What are you striking about?" asked Valkyrie.

"I don't want to play their game any more. Have you seen the arena? The pit?"

"Yes."

"Every Friday night," said Caelan, "we're taken to the pit and we're made to fight each other."

"*We?*"

"The others like me, in the other cells."

"Vampire pit fights?"

"Not just vampires. All sorts of creatures. It draws a crowd. Of course, I'm not allowed to change fully. The beast I'd become would rip apart anything it faced, and where's the fun in that? So they give me a half-dose of serum to trap me halfway through the change. For the sport. If I win, I'm taken back here and before my next fight I'm thrown a morsel to keep my strength up. You are said morsel. If I lose, I'm dead. Real dead, not just vampire dead."

"So you're not drinking my blood because...?"

"They want me strong when they put me into the pit. That's the only way the crowd will be satisfied. Who wants to pay to see a starving vampire flail at a zombie or a bridge troll? If I don't eat, they won't put me in the pit. I've been here three months, and I'm not going to do it any more."

"That doesn't make any sense," said Valkyrie.

"You really don't want to be talking me out of this, you know. I've been draining every person they throw in here. You're lucky today's the day I've changed my mind."

"Who are they? The men who do this?"

"You mean are they sorcerers?" asked Caelan. "They are not. They're mortals who know more than they should. Those shackles binding your power are just one of the things they've picked up over the years. Everything they have is scavenged. The big one's Bruno. I don't know the name of the smaller one.

"As far as I can tell, the whole thing is run by a man who calls himself the Promoter. And the audience that gathers every week? Mortals, also. They keep all this a secret from the press to prevent the Sanctuary from noticing them and sorting them out. I've come to the conclusion that mortals are far worse than any vampire or sorcerer."

"What'll happen when they realise I'm still alive?"

"If I don't feed on you, they're going to give you to someone who will. What day is it today?"

"Thursday."

"Then you'll be dead by tomorrow night."

Valkyrie didn't say anything to that.

She didn't have anything to say for the next four hours, either. She was cold, and getting colder, and she was hungry, and she had other needs.

"I have to pee," she called out.

For a moment there was just darkness and silence.

"Well," Caelan said slowly, "that's a little awkward."

Embarrassment made her angry. "So what do I do? Knock on the door, or what?"

"I'm really not sure. No other meal has survived long enough to want to go to the bathroom. You're going to have to just go in here."

Valkyrie got up, felt her way to the door, and banged her fist against it. "Hey!" she shouted.

She heard the voices from the other cells shouting "Hey!" back.

She kicked the door. "I have to use the toilet!"

The responses she got to *that* one were predictably disgusting.

And then a new voice, clearer than the others. "Shut up in there!" It wasn't a voice she recognised.

Most of the other prisoners quietened down, and those that didn't got a sharp rap on their iron door as a warning. Valkyrie waited until she could be heard.

"Hello?" she called. "I need to go to the bathroom. Hello?"

She heard striding footsteps getting louder, and then the door rattled and the viewing hatch slid open. The beam of a torch blinded her and she immediately looked away.

"What's going on?" the man demanded. "Why isn't she dead?"

"I need to use the toilet," she told him, blinking her vision back.

The man ignored her and repeated his question. "Why isn't she dead?"

"I'm on hunger strike," Caelan said.

The man shoved the torch through the hatch in an attempt to see into Caelan's corner, and Valkyrie reached out and grabbed it, wrenching it out of his grip.

"Give that back!" the man roared.

"You let me go to the bathroom and I'll give it back."

"You're supposed to be dead!"

"Well, I'm alive and I need to pee."

"Keep the bloody thing!" he snarled, and slammed the hatch shut. She heard him striding away.

"I won't look," Caelan said, "I promise." Angrily, Valkyrie swung the torch to the sound of his voice.

The beam fell upon a boy around her age, maybe a bit older.

He languished with his back to the corner, one long leg stretched out straight along the floor, the other pulled in. His boots were scuffed and his jeans dirty and torn. His torso was bare, the light flowing over the lean muscles of his arms. But it was his face that caught her attention – black hair falling to his brow, and a smile so wicked and cheekbones so sharp. He had one hand up, shading his eyes.

"I won't even tell anyone about it," he continued. "Your dignity is safe with me, I swear."

She let the torch beam drift down to his torso again, and allowed herself a moment to marvel at the way the light caught his abdomen.

"Excuse me?" he said. "I'm starting to feel just a little bit objectified here."

"Don't flatter yourself," she retorted, but still the beam lingered. "You're kind of good-looking, in your own way, but you're really not my type."

She was, of course, lying.

She swept the beam to his outstretched leg, to the shackle that was attached to the heavy chain. She scanned the walls, looking for cameras or windows, but there were none.

She pointed the torch at one of the free corners. "I'm going to go here."

"I'm not looking."

Valkyrie went to the corner and kept the torch on him, to blind him if he did look. But it appeared that he was going to keep his word. His face was turned away and his eyes were closed.

She hesitated, then undid her jeans and hunkered down.

"Talk," she ordered.

"What?"

"Talk to me, but do it loudly. I don't want you to hear me."

That smile again, playing with the corners of his mouth. "What would you like to talk about?"

"I don't care."

"Very well. Your friend, the skeleton. How do you plan on rescuing him from this other dimension?"

"It's a long story," said Valkyrie. "It's complicated. I'm almost there, though. I just have one more thing I need to get and that's it."

"And what is this one more thing?"

"The Murder Skull."

"I'm afraid I'm not familiar with it."

"You don't have to be. I've been trying to find it for ages now, trying to find out who has it. That's what got me in trouble, actually. The guy who has it is a man called Chabon. In my efforts to get in touch with him, I've been mixing with a bad crowd."

"What a nice way of putting it."

"Thank you. The bad crowd led me to the big guy... What did you say his name was?"

"Bruno."

"Bruno, who figured out I was a sorcerer and thought I was coming to arrest him or set him on fire or something... I turn away for one second and *bam*. I wake up in a van with my wrists shackled."

"Just when you'd got within arm's reach of your goal."

"I'm a little more than arm's reach away. I don't know anything about this Chabon guy."

"He's a criminal," said Caelan. "Thames Chabon, an information broker-slash-lowlife from London."

"You know him?"

"I know some people who can get in touch with him."

"Can you help me?"

Caelan laughed softly. "Sure. We'll just explain to the Promoter that we've got stuff to do and he'll let us walk out of here."

"If I can get you out, will you set up a meeting?"

"You're chained up in a cell, about to be fed to whichever monster isn't picky about its food. You're not getting anyone out."

"But if I do?"

He sighed. "If you get me out, I'll owe you a favour, I suppose."

Valkyrie stood, doing up her jeans. "Good." She walked to her corner, but didn't sit. Instead, she leaned back against the wall and turned off the torch. "How long have you been a vampire?"

"Longer than some," he said. "Not as long as others."

"How did it happen?"

In the dark, there was silence, and then he spoke. "I was in love. Her name was Anna. Our parents wouldn't allow us to be together, they said we were too young, so we planned to run away and get married."

His voice changed as he spoke. The rhythm became slower, like he was suddenly living in a different time.

"We quietly sold our possessions and saved our money, and every night I'd climb through her bedroom window and we'd lie in each other's arms, and we'd talk about the things we were going to do. We planned to go to England, and then France, and Africa. I could see my whole life in her eyes, and she could see hers in mine."

Valkyrie sat while Caelan continued.

"Her family owned a tavern. She was used to leering men and wandering hands, and she had no patience for either. And then the tavern door became darkened by the presence of a stranger. She'd tell me about him as we lay together. He'd sit at his table and he wouldn't touch the drink he'd ordered, and his eyes would never leave her face.

"Night after night he'd sit there, looking at her, always with a smile beneath his beard. One of the regular patrons was sweet on Anna, as many of them were, for she was a beautiful girl, and he took offence at this stranger. This patron, and two of his biggest friends, attempted to eject the man from the premises. Anna was fetching wine from the cellar at that moment so she didn't witness the fight, but according to the bartender it was over as quick as it had begun.

"He said the stranger had lifted one of the men over his head and thrown him the length of the room. He said he then gripped the shoulder of the second man and pulverised the bone. And the patron who was seeking to defend Anna's honour, he was dragged outside and no one saw him again.

"After that night, the stranger started talking to Anna while she served him. She said he was rough but educated, and he was charming, in his way. She found herself telling him a great many things. She told him about me. She even told him of our plans to run away. He seemed... interested.

"One night, he was waiting for me in the garden below her window. He dragged me to the willow tree and bared his fangs. But he didn't drain all of my blood, and he didn't kill me. He just threw me away."

"And that's all it took?" Valkyrie asked softly. "Just one bite?"

"That's all. I crawled through a narrow window, dropped down into the tavern cellar. I lay hidden by barrels for three days while the fevers took me.

"When my senses returned, I smelled blood, and I was starving. It was a hunger I had never experienced. I left the cellar. The tavern was dark and empty and I went up, to the living quarters. The stranger had visited only hours before, and he had torn Anna's family limb from limb. Blood painted the walls, still wet. I can't recall if there was a part of me that was horrified by the scene. All I remember was the blood, and that it was the only thing that could satisfy me."

"You... drank it?"

"I lapped it off the floor. I licked it off the walls."

Valkyrie didn't say anything.

"It was orchestrated, of course. The stranger did like his little games. In the three days I had been gone, he had convinced Anna that I had left without her. She was distraught, and he was her comfort. And he manipulated events so that when I was at my weakest, on my knees and smeared with blood, Anna would return home and see me.

"She fled to him, and he took her to his bed, and when he was finished he cut out her heart and left it for me, as a gift."

"Did you ever find him again?"

"No. I tried but he was gone. I never even knew his name."

Valkyrie looked into the darkness where Caelan sat. "I didn't know vampires could be like you," she said.

There was quiet amusement in his voice. "Known many vampires, have you?"

"Only one," she admitted. "And I gave him a scar that'll never fade, so he doesn't like me very much."

There was a moment of silence. "Dusk," said Caelan.

Valkyrie's eyes widened. "Yes. He's not a friend of yours, is he?"

"No," said Caelan softly. "No. Not a friend."

She slept badly.

She was cold and there was no padding on the ground. She was hungry and thirsty, and every time her defences lowered she thought about Skulduggery and how she was his only hope, and here she was, chained up and about to be killed. The thought that she was going to fail him brought tears to her eyes.

Sleep came in fits and starts. In the cell, time wasn't something that could be judged. Time was something that went on outside.

The door would open whenever it would open, and then time would be allowed to flood in. But until that happened, there was only the cold and the dark and the vampire across the floor.

She thought of her parents, living the rest of their lives with the reflection standing in for their daughter. She thought of her friends – of Tanith and Ghastly, and Fletcher. They'd have noticed her absence by now. They'd be worried. They'd talk to the reflection, and the reflection would tell them that Valkyrie hadn't even taken her armoured clothing when she'd gone off to do her investigating.

That's what she got. That's what she got for letting this take over her life. She made stupid mistakes. She talked to the wrong people without taking the proper precautions.

That's what she got.

Morning came. Valkyrie heard the men making their rounds. The hatch in the door opened and the light fell on her. She heard a grunt, and the hatch closed.

"They're not happy with me," said Caelan.

His voice was weak.

He didn't talk much that day. When he did, his voice was dry and thin, and there was something else behind it. A hint of anger. No, not anger. Fury. Violence. He was trying to hide it, but it was too sharp to disguise.

More hours passed, until he said, "I'm sorry."

"For what?"

"They're coming, Valkyrie. The stadium is filling up. I can hear them talking and laughing. I can hear the cars outside."

"What will they do with me?"

He didn't answer for a moment. "They'll feed you to someone else."

Outside the cell, a light switched on. The edge of the door lit up.

Valkyrie stood. The torch was in her right hand, and she gripped it tight. "I'll make a run for it," she said. "The moment that door opens..."

"You won't make it," he told her wearily. "There'll be too many of them."

"I'm not going to just wait here," she spat. "If I'm going to die, I'm going to make them *hurt*."

He managed a last laugh before the hatch rattled, and slid open. Yellow light burst through.

She pressed her back to the wall, her eyes on the light, blinking quickly to help the adjustment. The door opened and when the big man, the man Caelan had called Bruno, stepped in, she launched herself at him. The torch cracked against his head and he cursed and flung her back. She tripped over the chain and sprawled on to the ground.

"What the hell is this?" he snapped.

"I told you," said the man behind him, the one whose torch she had stolen. "I told you he wasn't drinking."

"Vampire," Bruno said, "why isn't she dead yet?"

"We talked about this last week," Caelan said calmly. "I'm on strike."

"And what makes you think that changes anything?"

"You have a crowd out there baying for blood," Caelan said, "and as much as they hate me, I'm still the biggest draw you've got. They'll be expecting a certain standard. It's not going to be a very thrilling fight when I'm as weak as I am."

Bruno laughed. "So you think we're going to let you forfeit, simply because we don't want to upset your fans?"

"That would seem to be the reasonable thing to do."

"I hate to burst your bubble, vampire, but you're really not that entertaining, and there are quite a few people out there who think you've been given too easy a time in the pit."

"That's ridiculous and you know it."

"Hey, if you don't want to take part in the scheduled fight, then so be it. We'll shake things up a little, what do you say? We're going to give them a spectacle tonight. Yes indeedy we are. Caelan, the weakened champion, going up against Victor, the eager young contender."

Caelan's voice changed immediately. "You... can't put me up against Victor."

"And yet we are."

"He won't do it. Vampires are forbidden to harm other vampires."

"That didn't stop you, now, did it? And it's not going to stop Victor, either."

Bruno stepped to the side, and two burly men came in and unlocked Caelan's shackles. They started to pull him to the door.

"You can't put me in the pit with him," Caelan protested. "He's at full strength."

"Then you should have fed when you had the chance."

Caelan looked at Valkyrie and there was something in his eyes that made her step back. "Just give me a second," he said.

Bruno shook his head. "To the pit, boys."

Caelan reached for her. "I'll just take a little sip..."

There was an electric flash and Caelan jerked and then slumped, and the men dragged him out.

Bruno smiled at Valkyrie. "I don't know how you managed to keep him away from you, girl, but you're back on the menu tonight."

He grabbed her shackles and shook the torch from her hand, then pushed her out of the cell. The men dragged Caelan on ahead, but Bruno took Valkyrie another way. Already she could hear the chanting of the crowd.

He took her through a narrow passageway that linked to a larger tunnel. She glimpsed the night sky, but she was forced in the opposite direction. The chanting got louder.

Eventually, they came to a set of large wooden doors that sealed off the tunnel. Valkyrie could hear the crowd on the other side, working itself into a frenzy. Like the cells, these doors had hatches, and Bruno opened them and pushed Valkyrie forward.

They emerged into a fenced-off area in the stands, the pit opening out below them. There were two doors opening on to the arena, both shut. Valkyrie looked at the crowd. They were wrapped up in coats and hats and a lot of them had colourful umbrellas, anticipating rain from the clouds that were blocking out the stars. They sang and chanted and laughed like they were at a football game.

This was *insane*.

The crowd grew quiet, and Valkyrie shifted her position to watch a tall man walk into the centre of the pit.

"Ladies and gentlemen," he called, his voice carrying, "welcome to the fights!"

That drew an appreciative roar from the stands. Valkyrie figured they were an easy crowd to please.

"And what a night we have in store for you," the Promoter continued. "Vicious animal against vicious animal. Inhuman killer against inhuman killer. Monster against monster. And we have a surprise or two. Oh, yes, ladies and gentlemen, we can see that you're growing complacent up there. We can see that you have your favourites, and you're betting accordingly.

"There's a lesson we have to teach you, my friends and neighbours. When it comes to monsters, you can take nothing for granted. Am I right?"

The crowd roared, and the Promoter nodded.

"They'll sneak up on you, won't they? They'll steal through the night to your open window, girls and boys, and what will they do then? They'll bite your neck and drain your blood!"

Some of the audience squealed in horrified delight.

"When it comes to vampires, especially, expect the unexpected. That's the only way we'll ever rid our lands of these parasites. And so our first fight of the evening is the rarest of the rare. There's a code that vampires live by, to never harm another one of their kind. And yet, here tonight, we have two vampires who have forsaken this code. Ladies and gentlemen – place your bets!"

The doors to Valkyrie's left opened, and a man was led through, shackled hand and foot. He wore blood-splattered tracksuit bottoms, cut off just below the knee. His body was a map of pain, criss-crossed with scars both old and new. His head was badly shaved, like he'd done it himself, in the dark, with a blunt razor. His eyes were black, his sharp teeth splitting his gums.

"Victor," the Promoter said, drawing down a chorus of booing. "Eight fights in, he's proving himself to be a capable little monster, aren't you, Victor?"

Victor didn't respond. He was trapped halfway through his transformation into full vampire. Valkyrie could see it by the pain on his face, by the way his body twitched. She'd seen it before with Dusk, when he'd been jabbed with vampire serum in the middle of a change. That time, Valkyrie herself had been responsible.

The doors to her right opened, and the Promoter swung round, pointing to the newcomer as he was led out into the light.

"And tonight, for your sporting pleasure, for your entertainment and your education, Victor will be facing... Caelan!"

The crowd roared their cheers. Caelan stumbled, and the man behind him poked him in the side with the barrel of a shotgun.

Valkyrie glimpsed the claws that tipped his fingers. He, too, was caught halfway between his two natures.

The fighters were brought to opposite sides of the pit, where their shackles were taken off as the Promoter left the pit. The men, half a dozen for each fighter, backed off warily to the doors, sealing Caelan and Victor in.

The Promoter appeared in the stands, sitting down in a chair that could only be described as a throne.

"Vampires," he shouted, "begin the slaughter!"

Caelan and Victor started circling each other, knees slightly bent, shoulders hunched. Victor bared his fangs and attacked and Caelan spun him away, keeping the space between them.

Victor moved in again, forcing Caelan to retreat and cutting off his avenues of escape. Victor was bristling with energy – every movement was sharp. Caelan's movements were tempered with a controlled wariness, and he looked positively sedate compared to the other vampire.

Valkyrie hoped this was a deception. She hoped he wasn't really as weak as he'd said. If he was, she had a feeling that this would be a very short fight.

Victor came in and this time Caelan had no room to manoeuvre, and the blow caught him across the jaw. He stepped back and Victor's claws slashed open his chest.

The crowd roared its approval.

Caelan managed to hook an arm round Victor's body, then heaved and twisted, slamming Victor to the ground. He kicked him while he was down there and Victor spun on his back and swept Caelan's feet out from under him.

Both fighters scrambled up, but Victor was noticeably faster – they collided and Caelan was thrown hard against the curved wall of the pit.

Above them, bets were being shouted, and there were people wearing bright sashes across their jackets, furiously scribbling into notebooks. Bruno was shouting, too, struggling to have his voice heard. Valkyrie tried to wriggle from his grip, but he was far too strong.

Victor pummelled Caelan, knocking him round the arena, only letting him get up just so he could have the pleasure of knocking him down again.

When they broke away from each other again, the Promoter's voice came blasting through the speakers. "How're you enjoying the spectacle, folks?"

The crowd roared.

"This is indeed a special night, isn't it? This night could not get any more special, now, could it? What's that? It could?"

The crowd went almost quiet in anticipation.

Valkyrie could hear the grin in the Promoter's voice. "Ladies and gentlemen, tonight, for our main event, we are not only giving you, for your viewing pleasure, a rare and thrilling vampire versus vampire match-up, but we're also throwing a third party into the mix! Friends, family, colleagues, you've heard about them, you've heard the stories, you've heard what they can do, but you've never seen one in action... until now! Patrons of the arena, she's young, she's beautiful, she's magical... I give to you our third and final fighter – the Sorceress!"

"What?" said Valkyrie, and then Bruno kicked her right in the ass, sending her stumbling over the lip and falling into the arena.

She landed on her knees, the sheer volume of noise from the crowd threatening to overwhelm her. She looked back at Bruno, who gave her a smile and tossed her a key. It glinted in the bright lights as it fell, and she caught it, spun immediately, making sure Victor and Caelan weren't making any moves. The two vampires stood on the opposite side of the pit, both staring straight at her.

Her hands were trembling so much the key scraped against the lock of the shackles for an eternity before it slid in. One twist to the right and both wrists were freed, and she felt the magic flood her body. But the sound of the shackles hitting the dirt-packed ground was all the signal the vampires needed.

They sprinted for her and Valkyrie pushed at the air, sending Caelan tumbling backwards. Victor dodged around, came at her, and she whipped the shadows at him, taking him off his feet. He hit the arena wall, landed in a crouch, shaking his head to clear it. His snarls were drowned out by the roar of the crowd.

Caelan burst at her. She went down, rolled, staying away from his claws and fangs. She tried to kick him off her, but it was like kicking a wall. Sharp nails dug into her leg, drawing blood, and he dragged her close. She turned over, clicking her fingers and shoving a fistful of fire into his face. Caelan lurched away, yelping like a wounded dog. Valkyrie scrambled up.

Victor thudded into her from behind. His claws raked her shoulder blade. She cried out, twisted, stumbled and fell, Victor getting tangled in her legs. He fell on top, snapping at her. She held him back. Barely. He pushed her head to one side, exposing her throat, but as his head darted in she filled his mouth with shadows. He recoiled, gagging, and she sat up, but in his blind panic he kicked out and found her jaw and the world sparked and tilted and Valkyrie was lying on her back, blinking slowly in sudden silence.

Gradually, the sounds from the arena soaked back into her hearing.

Without moving, she looked over at Caelan and Victor as they thrashed around in the dirt, snarling and biting and punching. Groaning, she rolled over, looked up.

The Promoter was leaning forward in his throne, watching the contest with an eager, greedy delight on his face. The wall of the arena was lower where he was, allowing him a better view. It wasn't low enough for a vampire to jump, but maybe if there was a sorcerer nearby willing to give a little boost...

Valkyrie got up, clutching her left arm. Blood ran freely down her back, and her leg was pretty bad. She ignored the pain, ignored the snarling, snapping vampires beside her, and limped towards the throne. When she was close enough, she turned back to the vampires, put two fingers in her mouth, and blew a short, shrill whistle.

The vampires stopped fighting and looked over. The audience stopped roaring and peered closer.

The vampires bolted for her. Valkyrie waited until they were close enough and then swept her arms in and up, lifting them off their feet so that they hurtled over her head. All she heard was the Promoter's panicked cry before all hell broke loose.

The audience stampeded. People screamed and shouted and scrambled over each other. Extra lights snapped on over the stands. Doors that should have been closed were opened, and doors that should have been opened were closed. Behind the screams of panic were screams of pain, of people getting torn apart. Valkyrie wasn't the least bit sorry.

She found a door in the arena wall, used shadows to smash the lock. She hurried through, gritting her teeth against the pain. Men with guns passed and she shrank back till they'd gone. She could hear gunshots now. A lot of them.

Ahead was the tunnel out of here, the tunnel to the outside. Two men were guarding it, arguing among themselves about what they should be doing. They had guns, too.

Valkyrie hurled a fireball at the ground between them. They cried out and jumped back, and the shadows slammed them into the walls. They collapsed. Dead or just broken, she didn't know and she didn't care. She ran out, between the rows of parked cars. Headlights swooped all around. Panicking people crashed into other panicking people. Horns blared. There were gunshots closer now – outside the arena.

Someone grabbed her, tugged her, and she was on her knees before she even realised Caelan was beside her. Up close, his fangs were ragged things that split his gums. He wasn't looking at her. He was trembling. Resisting.

They stayed low, moving quickly. Around them, excited voices and angry shouts. Accusations and orders. Valkyrie heard Bruno organising the search, telling people to get in their cars and spread out. They stayed in the dark while people ran through the rows on either side. Bruno's voice got closer.

Valkyrie shrank back as Bruno hurried to a jeep just ahead of them. Someone called to him and he called back, and as he did so he looked her way and frowned. He took a single step in their direction, and then his eyes widened. He opened his mouth to alert the others.

Caelan's hand wasn't closed round Valkyrie's wrist any more, and he wasn't by her side. Instead, he was a dark blur, rushing Bruno, dragging him down into the space between the jeep and another car. He went for the throat, and Valkyrie saw Bruno's arms spread wide in shock, and then scrabble madly against Caelan's shoulders and back. But Caelan was locked on, and there was nothing that could shift him now.

She watched in horrified fascination as he fed.

Headlights swarmed her and she rolled from her position, then the car reversed and the headlights swept away again. She was going to be seen. Any moment now, they were going to find her.

She looked back at Caelan. Bruno's arms were limp. His legs were twisted beneath him, like he'd been trying to push himself up, right until the moment his life left him. Caelan dug inside

Bruno's pockets, found what he was looking for. The serum. Without hesitating, Caelan jabbed the syringe into his skin and a moment later he straightened, his back arched, his muscles rolling beneath his moonlit skin. She saw his hands go to Bruno's head and he wrenched it to one side. She heard the pop of bone.

"We have to go," she said softly.

Caelan pulled on Bruno's coat and used the sleeve to wipe his mouth. Valkyrie was glad it was too dark to see much. He found the keys for the jeep in the jacket pocket. They got in and kept their heads low, waiting for the van in front to pull away. They followed the trail of cars to the road, and the first chance they got they broke away and sped on.

There was a phone charging on the dash, so Valkyrie called Ghastly, told him what had happened. A truckload of Cleavers and a truckload of sorcerers were on their way before she'd even hung up. Valkyrie and Caelan waited down a side road for the cavalry to arrive.

When it did, they returned to the arena. A dozen dead. Another dozen injured. The Promoter was found ripped to pieces. He had a ledger in his jacket with the names of the people who'd paid in it. Sorcerers visited each one of those people. Some were convinced to never speak of any of it. Others were taken away to places mortal lawyers couldn't help them.

The creatures, vampires and various fighters in the cells were released. There was no sign of Victor.

Caelan was human again. His scars were already beginning to

heal. Valkyrie talked to him, but got the barest of responses back. He was different, she realised. His rediscovered freedom was unnerving him. Back in that cell, with death so close it could happen at any moment, he had nothing to lose. Despite the chains, he was free. But now that the chains were off and his world had expanded, he himself was shrinking away from it. By morning, she had forgotten what his smile looked like.

"The Murder Skull," he said, breaking the silence between them. "You want it."

"Yes," she said. "I know you don't owe me anything – I got you free, but you saved my life, so we're even – but if you can help out at all, I'd be—"

"We're not even," he said. "I still owe you."

"For what?"

He didn't answer. Instead, he looked at the Cleavers and the sorcerers and then he looked back at her. "I'll be in touch," he said, and walked away.

Valkyrie watched him go. He was a dangerous one, of that she was sure. Attractive, though. There was no denying that. But she wasn't a girl to fall for the cliché. She wasn't going to be won over by brooding good looks and a tortured soul, not when the risk was so obvious.

She was a teenage girl and she made stupid decisions sometimes – but she wasn't a *complete* idiot.

MYOSOTIS
TERRA

In 2011 Derek ran a competition for German fans to come up with a new character who would feature in a one-off Skulduggery short story. The response was staggering, making it especially difficult to pick a winner – however, there was something special about Myosotis Terra that made her stand out from the rest.

Here is how Alena Metz described her character's abilities:

"… Her magical quality is more of a curse than a gift. The ability to make everyone forget her immediately after meeting her makes her feel very lonely. However, it is a very useful gift for spies and thieves, and at least it helps her to earn her bread and butter. People will only be able to remember Myosotis if they have got an item which belongs to her or if they get the chance to touch her. However, dementia sufferers are able to remember her perfectly."

MYOSOTIS TERRA

"Caves," Valkyrie Cain muttered. "I hate caves."

She reached the bottom of the stone steps, stepping into the light cast by the flame in Skulduggery Pleasant's hand.

"This isn't a cave," he told her. "At least, not a natural one. This has been carved out of the rock. Manmade. From what I can gather, we're about to enter a series of interlocking caverns that could stretch on for as much as twelve miles. Quite impressive when you think about it."

"And do I have to think about it?"

"Well, no, not really..."

"Good," she said. "It's freezing down here. Far too cold to be thinking about things."

She clicked her fingers, summoning her own flame, and started walking through the darkness. "So we're here on a rescue mission?"

He sighed as he walked after her. "Yes."

"What was that? What was that sigh? Why are you sighing?"

They walked side by side. "Do you remember who we're here to rescue?" Skulduggery asked.

"Yes," she said. "Wait. No. I mean, I do, it's on the tip of my tongue, but I can't... I just can't..."

"We're here to rescue Myosotis Terra."

She shook her head. "No, we're not. That's not the name. I'll know the name when I hear it, but that's not it. I've never heard that name before."

"That's not strictly true. She's actually a friend of yours."

"Nope. I think I'd know if I had a friend called Myo-Something Whatsit."

"Myosotis Terra. And you wouldn't know, actually. Or to be more precise, you wouldn't remember."

"You've lost me."

"I'm used to it."

Rock walls appeared in the gloom around them, signalling the narrowing of the cavern. They headed for a gap and Skulduggery went first, squeezing through.

"There is a sorcerer named Myosotis," he said, "from Germany. You first met her a few months ago, and got along very well, I have to say. You both get quite annoying when you talk, but again, I'm used to *that*, too. Myosotis is, amongst other things, a spy. What makes her so very good at her job is the fact that once she moves out of sight, you forget all about her. The human mind can't retain any information concerning Myosotis at all. We've actually had this conversation eleven times over the past few hours. You always have the same reaction."

"Bull."

"That's the one."

"You're serious?"

"Quite serious."

They emerged on the other side. Torches hung in rusted brackets on the walls, and they followed the flickering trail of light through the darkness.

"Her power doesn't work on me because of my fabulous mind – and the fact that I have no physical brain," Skulduggery continued. "And if she could turn her power off, I'm sure she would."

"You're sure who would?"

"Myosotis."

Valkyrie frowned. "Who?"

"Ah," Skulduggery said. "You're forgetting about her already."

"That's amazing," Valkyrie said. "Forgetting about who?"

"The spy, the girl who's been taken captive."

"Right," Valkyrie said, "the rescue mission. Gotcha. Who has taken her?"

"The inhabitants of this place. It was once a prison of sorts, hundreds of years ago. Now it's a refuge for sorcerers who can't bear to live on the surface. The people down here are... damaged. Some are quite dangerous."

"And what was..."

"Myosotis."

"And what was Myosotis doing down here?"

"The Sanctuary in Berlin sent her over to investigate the disappearance of one of their own. He was last seen around these parts, so the natural assumption would be that he found his way down here. And disappeared."

Valkyrie nodded. "And we're here to rescue him."

"No, we're here to rescue Myosotis, the operative sent to rescue him. If we happen to rescue him along the way, it's a bonus. But she is our main priority."

"Who is?"

"Oh dear God," Skulduggery muttered. "This is astonishingly aggravating."

He froze and she stopped, splayed her hand, felt the air move against her skin, and then she heard something, a whisper from behind.

They spun, but there was a rush of dark figures and Skulduggery went down in a tangle of arms and legs. Someone hit Valkyrie and she stumbled, couldn't do anything to stop the boot that smashed into her. She went back, rolling on the hard ground. Rough hands grabbed her, hauled her up. There was a crowd around Skulduggery, lashing in kicks, throwing down punches. Valkyrie's arms twisted and she cried out, feeling them twist almost to the point of breaking.

"What's your name?" he asked.

He looked wild, dishevelled, but otherwise harmless. "Valkyrie," she said. "Who are you?"

"I'm Baffle. How are you?"

"Not doing too well, to be honest."

He nodded, grabbed the frame and clambered up until they were at eye level. He stank of bad breath and body odour.

"I don't like eating people," he said.

"Maybe you shouldn't do it."

"Can't say no. It'd be a waste, wouldn't it? We kill you and cook and serve you – you'd want us to eat you, wouldn't you? Otherwise, what's the point?"

"Baffle, I really don't want to die. It's not fair. I never did anything to hurt any of you."

"Life isn't fair."

"You could help me."

"I could?"

"Sure. You just said you don't want to eat me, right? So you could help me, couldn't you?"

"I... I suppose."

"You'd have to be really sneaky about it."

He nodded. "That's true. If the others found out, they'd be very cross."

"So you'll do it?"

"If I do, will you be my friend?"

"Of course."

"Then, yes," he said, and smiled, "I'll help you." Then he threw his head back and started singing.

"Stop!" she hissed. "Shush!"

His eyes were closed, and he sang louder. It was 'Be My Baby', by The Ronettes. Her mum used to sing that to her all the time when she was a kid. She strained against the ropes.

"Hey! Shut up!"

Baffle stopped singing.

She glared at him. "What the hell do you think you're doing?"

"I'm... I'm helping."

"How is that helping?"

"It'll make you feel better. It might make you forget we're going to eat you."

"But you don't *want* to eat me! You want to let me go!"

He looked horrified. "No, I don't! Why would I do that?"

"Because we're *friends*, Baffle."

He shook his head. "I know friends. Friends don't shout at each other. Friends sing to each other to take their minds off bad things that are going to happen."

"Baffle!" someone shouted from inside a hut. "Are you singing to our dinner again?"

"No!" he called back.

"You better not be!"

"I'm not!"

He waited, but got no further response. Stifling a giggle, he turned back to Valkyrie. "Did I help?"

"Sure," she said, totally deflated. "You did great. You know another way you could help me? We're looking for someone. A girl. A woman. Her name is..." Valkyrie frowned. "OK, I'm not sure what her name is, but she's got... she's got... she's got hair, I think, I imagine, though I don't know what colour, but... I imagine she has hair. Or she might be bald. Or she might be a he. Do you remember anyone like that arriving down here in the last few days?"

Baffle shook his head. "No one's been down for ages. Not since the man."

"What man? Did he have an accent? Did he have a German accent?"

"Don't know what that is. He talked funny, though."

"What happened to him?"

"The Beast ate him."

"Oh. Where is the Beast now?"

"Out there," Baffle said, waving at the darkness. "Waiting. Watching. We feed it what we can. Sometimes, Owain says we must feed it our friends and families." His voice turned sad. "The Beast ate my sister."

"I'm sorry to hear that."

"I was given a bit of her leg to cheer me up."

"Right..."

There was a sound, like a growl, low and threatening, that echoed up to them.

Valkyrie raised an eyebrow at Baffle. "That's the Beast?" she asked.

"Yes," he breathed. "It doesn't come this close to the village, not usually. Not unless it's very hungry." He looked worried. "We might not get to share you after all."

There was another shout from one of the huts. "Baffle!"

"What?" he yelled back.

"Stop talking to the food!"

"I wasn't!"

"Baffle!"

"Sorry," Baffle whispered to her. Sighing grumpily, he jumped down from the frame and trudged away.

"About time," said someone from the darkness. "I thought he'd never leave."

A girl stepped into the light. She looked to be around twenty and her blonde hair hung long and wavy. She was pretty, with green eyes behind her glasses. Smaller than Valkyrie, in good shape, wearing grey jeans and a silver-grey coat.

"Myosotis," Valkyrie said, the memory of the girl flooding back into her mind, bringing with it their friendship. "Love the coat."

"Isn't it gorgeous?" Myosotis responded. "I got it a few weeks ago from a little shop in Langenfeld. It's a bit dirty now, of course, but I suppose that's what happens when you're running around somewhere like this, searching for an idiot of a man."

"Ah," Valkyrie said. "That man. I'm pretty sure he's dead."

Myosotis frowned. "So I've been searching mile after mile of dark caverns for him, and he doesn't even have the common courtesy to stay alive until I find him? That *is* irritating."

"So what are you guys doing here?"

Valkyrie hesitated. "We're here to rescue you."

"Really?"

"Really."

Myosotis nodded. "And how's that going for you?"

"I have to admit, it could be going better."

"I would agree with you. It's the thought that counts, though, isn't that what they say?"

"It is."

"In which case, thank you for coming to rescue me."

"You're welcome," said Valkyrie. "Can you get me out of these shackles now?"

"What are friends for?" Myosotis asked, then clambered up the frame, took a lock pick from her sleeve and set to work on the shackles. After a moment, she paused.

Valkyrie raised an eyebrow. "What?"

"Nothing," Myosotis said. "It's just... I'm not used to having a friend. It's a little odd, you know?"

"Yeah. You could probably work a little faster on the shackles."

"Shut up, I'm being sincere and vulnerable."

"Can't you be those things *and* work a little faster?"

"The problem with people forgetting you when you're gone is that nobody actually cares if you don't come back."

Valkyrie regarded her as the lock picks scratched and scraped. "Sounds lonely."

"It can be," Myosotis said. "But this is the life I chose. Mystery and intrigue and anonymity. There are things one must sacrifice in order to be a good spy."

"You could give it up, you know. Become a regular operative."

Myosotis smiled, her thin lips rising. "My Sanctuary values my expertise too much to allow that. But do not feel sorry for me. I never do." The shackles clicked open. "There. My rescuer is freed."

Valkyrie's magic washed over her as they jumped down from the frame. Myosotis handed her a bracelet. "Wear this, it's one of mine. So long as you keep it close to your skin, you won't forget me."

"I'm honoured."

"You should be."

"Though it's a pretty cheap bracelet."

"I buy in bulk."

"I'm still honoured."

"You still should be."

Valkyrie's grin caught on her lips as a low growl reached them. It was close. It was far too close. "The Beast," she whispered. "It's behind me."

Myosotis nodded.

Valkyrie turned slowly, ready to click her fingers and summon a fireball, ready to grab the darkness and hurl spears of shadow. Instead, she frowned.

The Beast was two feet tall, with small arms and tiny hands. It was covered in fur, everywhere except its face, where two large eyes blinked above a small snout. It had little ears that twitched, and big feet.

"Uh," Valkyrie said. "That's it?"

"That's it," said Myosotis.

"Does it grow? Is it suddenly going to expand into a giant and devour us in one bite?"

"Nope," Myosotis said. "That's the size it stays."

"Does it have razor claws that are going to pop out, or huge teeth, or...?"

"Nope."

"Is it... I mean, is it really bad-tempered?"

"It's quite good-natured, actually."

"Then I don't understand. Why is it so terrible?"

"Who said it was terrible?"

"What do you mean? Everyone's terrified of it. From the moment we got here they've been talking about feeding the Beast, how the Beast must be fed, all that kind of stuff."

"And the Beast *must* be fed," Myosotis nodded. "Otherwise it'd go hungry. But they're not scared of it. They love it. Look at it – it's adorable."

Valkyrie had to admit, it was pretty cute. It kind of wobbled when it walked.

"I think they named it the Beast because they thought it was kind of funny," Myosotis continued. "It's their pet."

"And how exactly would that little thing eat us?"

"From what I can gather, it's going to just stand there, and then the people who are sneaking up behind us are going to cut our throats, chop us into bits, and feed us to it over the next week or so in very small chunks."

Valkyrie turned, and a dozen villagers froze mid-step. Baffle was the closest. He looked embarrassed to have been caught out. "Ah," she said. "So this is where we fight."

She snapped both hands against the air and Baffle flew backwards, yelling as he crashed into his fellow villagers. She grabbed the shadows, brought them in low, knocking a big man off his feet before he could get to her. Fire flared in her hands and she lobbed it into the middle of the crowd, scattering them. She slammed her elbow into a woman's face and stomped on the knee of another man. They were everywhere, all around her, but unable to use their magic in case they hit one of their own. Valkyrie didn't have that problem.

She caught sight of Myosotis, taking on three at a time, but then more villagers were running in, joining the fight, and Myosotis was blocked from view.

Valkyrie knew there were too many of them. She knew this wasn't going to end well.

A beam of blue light flashed by her face and she jerked back. It hit the man behind her and he dropped instantly. Villagers were stumbling out of the way as one of them, a man in rags with crazy hair, swung his arms wildly, like he couldn't control the energy that was pouring from his fingertips. Valkyrie dived to the ground, and the blue beam swept over her, taking down half a dozen villagers in one go. Everyone was screaming at Crazy Hair to stop, but he looked terrified, like he'd forgotten how to turn off his power.

And then Myosotis was behind him, grabbing his arms, redirecting the beams into the crowd above Valkyrie's head. Villagers fell around her, unconscious before they hit the ground.

But then the beams sputtered and died, and Crazy Hair sagged, exhausted.

"Thanks for that," Myosotis said, and punched him. He did a little twirl and fell down.

Valkyrie scrambled up before the remaining villagers could grab her. She ran through the stone huts, Myosotis behind her, towards Skulduggery. A man crashed into her and she went down, rolled over, dropped an elbow into his face and hauled herself to her feet.

Skulduggery raised his head. "Oh, hello," he said. "I see you've found Myosotis."

"Thank you for saving me," Myosotis called as she ducked the swipe of a crude blade.

"Not a problem," Skulduggery answered happily. "So this is the exciting battle part, is it? I do so love these parts."

"You might have to stay up there just a little while longer," Valkyrie called, using the air to hurl three villagers off their feet.

A fist came in, crunched against her cheek and she stumbled against Skulduggery's legs.

"How long?" he asked.

She kicked out, brought her elbow to the hinge of the villager's jaw. "Just another few moments."

"I feel I have to ask," Skulduggery said as a woman with earrings made from other people's ears brought Valkyrie down, "do you have anything resembling an actual plan here, or are you making it up as you go along?"

"We have a plan," Myosotis said after a headbutt. "But we're also making most of it up."

"Best of both worlds," Valkyrie grunted, shoving the woman off her. She got up, turned, something swung into her face and the world exploded with light. She was aware of her body falling backwards, but couldn't feel the impact as she hit the ground. She was barely able to crack open one eye, but when she did she saw Owain standing above her, holding that club.

"You think you can invade our home?" he snarled. "Attack my people?"

"Owain," Skulduggery said, "we're not here to invade. We came looking for a friend—"

"Quiet!" Owain roared. He looked around. He was the only villager left standing. "This is what you've done. We are a peaceful village, but you come and ruin it all."

Valkyrie heard the scepticism in Skulduggery's voice. "No offence, Owain, but you're a village of cannibals. That's not, strictly speaking, peaceful."

"We will pull you apart, skeleton," Owain sneered. He looked down at Valkyrie. "And you," he said, "are dinner."

Owain raised the club in both hands, ready to bring it down on Valkyrie's head, and then a voice said from behind, "Hey! Forget about me?"

He turned and Myosotis hit him, slugged him right across the jaw and his knees wobbled. He swung wildly and she caught his arm and cracked his elbow. He howled in pain and dropped the club, but Myosotis grabbed it before it touched the ground and smashed it into the side of his head. Owain staggered and gurgled and fell down and didn't get up.

Myosotis helped Valkyrie to her feet, and then searched through Owain's clothes. She found the key to the shackles and freed Skulduggery. He jumped from the frame and looked around.

"You didn't leave any for me," he said.

"Sorry," Valkyrie said, before groaning in pain.

"You can kick him if you want," Myosotis said, nodding down at Owain.

"He's already unconscious," Skulduggery sulked. "It's not fun if they're already unconscious. Wait – what about the Beast? We've still got to fight that, don't we?"

"Uh," Valkyrie said, "no. And we're not calling it the Beast any more."

"We're naming it Fluffy," said Myosotis.

Skulduggery tilted his head. "You named the terrifying monster Fluffy?"

"It actually isn't a monster after all," said Valkyrie. "It's a cute little furry thing with big eyes. No fighting necessary."

Skulduggery looked at her. "So who do I get to punch?"

Valkyrie looked at Myosotis, who shrugged. "No one," Valkyrie said.

Skulduggery sighed. He picked up his hat and put it on, then walked over to Owain, whom he kicked. "Well," he said, straightening his tie, "it's better than nothing."

The Wonderful Adventures of Geoffrey Scrutinous

This story was written for Charlie Smith, who won a competition to create a new character to appear in *Mortal Coil*.

The character Charlie came up with was Geoffrey Scrutinous, and this is how Charlie described him in his competition entry:

"Wears khaki shirts (Indiana Jones style), short trousers and maroon socks with leather sandals. Lots of beads and chains, lots of rings on one hand. Has a small goatee and wild frizzy hair with piercing blue eyes. A frantic, disbelieving nature and is very erratic in both appearance and personality. He sorts out disturbances in the non-magical population. He has the ability to get you to agree with anything he says, without you realising it."

You'll have seen Geoffrey in *Mortal Coil*, of course. But as an added bonus, here's a little story all about him...

Thanks, Charlie!

THE WONDERFUL ADVENTURES OF GEOFFREY SCRUTINOUS

The cop frowned. "But there's a dead body in there. I have to... I can't let anyone into the house. It's my job to preserve the scene for the forensics people, to investigate and... and solve the crime..."

Geoffrey Scrutinous nodded. "And you will do a wonderful job of preserving and investigating, I know you will. But for the moment, you want to delay all this hustle and bustle."

"I do?"

Scrutinous nodded. "Oh, yes, very much so. I have some friends coming, they're special investigators, and they have to look around a bit first."

"Who are they?" asked the cop.

"Just some friends. A tall man and a teenage girl. They're very good at this kind of thing."

"I'm not sure I should be allowing this."

Scrutinous smiled, maintained eye contact and poured more magic into his words. "It's perfectly fine. You know it is. You can feel it, that reassuring feeling that everything is going to be fine. You can feel it, can't you?"

"I... I suppose... They're good, then?"

"Very good."

"You think they'll be able to crack the case?"

"If anyone can, they can."

The cop nodded. "Good. I was hoping I wouldn't have to. I have no idea how someone could be run over by a train in their own living room."

Scrutinous patted the cop's shoulder. "Don't you worry," he said. "They handle this kind of thing all the time."

"I have to confess," Skulduggery Pleasant said as he took his hat off in the dead man's living room, "I have no idea what's going on here at all."

Valkyrie Cain nodded up to the corner of the room. "What's that bit?"

"It's his head," said Skulduggery. "You can see the rest of it there, hidden behind the curtain."

"Oh, yeah. That's disgusting."

"Nobody ever said being hit by a train was a neat way to die."

Valkyrie turned to Scrutinous. "And you're sure that's what they said?"

"Oh, yes," Scrutinous answered. "Neighbours reported hearing an old-fashioned train. Like a steam engine, they said, with the 'choo choo' and everything. The walls of every house on the street rattled as it passed."

Skulduggery murmured something to himself. The living room was small and tidy, the furniture in place, the TV still on with the sound muted. It was three o'clock in the morning and the lamps gave the place a gentle, warm light. It would have been a perfectly good room in which to spend an evening were it not for the man who had been splattered across every imaginable surface.

"Well," Skulduggery said, "purely to get this out of the way, I'll just go ahead and say it. There does not seem to be any sign of a railway track on the carpet or, indeed, a train hiding behind the sofa. And I don't think one could have fitted through the door."

"Maybe it was a ghost train," Valkyrie said. "Do ghost trains exist?"

"I've seen two," Scrutinous said. "But I've never heard of a ghost train that could run over anything living. A ghost train would be able to run over a ghost, not a man."

"And yet something big killed him," Skulduggery said. "And it was powerful and fast-moving. Just like a locomotive."

Valkyrie examined a couple of framed photographs on the mantelpiece. "Who was he? He wasn't a sorcerer, was he?"

"His name was Brendan Cassidy," Scrutinous said. "From what I can gather, he was a perfectly normal mortal. He worked as an assistant manager of a local store. Nothing whatsoever to do with us or anyone in our community."

Skulduggery took a bag of powder from his jacket and threw some into the air. It fell as a light cloud, shimmering with faint colour. "Definite traces of Adept magic," he said, "but I'm not getting a read on an exact discipline. Which only proves that he didn't explode of his own volition."

Scrutinous watched the two of them work, and tried not to get in the way. He wasn't a detective, after all. He worked in Public Relations – he convinced mortals that they didn't see what they actually saw. All this looking-for-clues lark was a tad beyond him. He liked to think of himself as a simple man.

He wandered over to a lamp. It was a very nice lamp. He'd seen better, of course he had, but this was a very fine example of a perfectly nice lamp. It suited the room. He approved. Beside the lamp was a fountain pen. He picked it up. It was an old pen, a classic. He wasn't an expert on pens, but he knew an old, classic pen when he saw one. He remembered when pens like this had first gone on sale, over a hundred and fifty years ago, when they were brand new and cutting edge. He'd probably owned a few. There was a pad of paper on which the pen had been lying, and he looked at it now, at what was written across the top page.

I'm going to be hit by a train, it read.

Scrutinous frowned. "Um," he said.

"Yes?" Skulduggery asked, from somewhere behind him.

"Um, I'm not sure, but I think I may have found a clue."

Skulduggery and Valkyrie joined him, and peered down at the pad.

"Ah," said Skulduggery. "I think you're right. That is indeed a clue. I don't know what it tells us, apart from the obvious, but it definitely tells us something. Valkyrie?"

"It tells us Cassidy knew what was going to happen," Valkyrie said.

Skulduggery nodded. "Anything else?"

"Uh..."

Skulduggery hunkered down and poked the pad with his finger. "The handwriting is very clear. Very legible. When he wrote this, he was calm. That tells us one of two things. Either he had already accepted his fate, or he didn't believe it would happen. Or he wasn't aware that he was writing it."

"That's three things," Valkyrie said. "How do we know it's even his handwriting?"

"There's a half-finished crossword by the armchair. Most of it is impressively wrong, but the handwriting is a match." Skulduggery straightened up. "Out of those three possibilities, Valkyrie, which one would you dismiss first?"

Scrutinous stepped away to let them converse. It was always fascinating watching detectives work.

"I don't think he'd accepted his fate," Valkyrie said at last. "There's nothing else here to suggest that he was preparing to die. There's no note to family or friends, the dinner plate in the kitchen hasn't been put away... He wasn't expecting this."

Skulduggery nodded. "Which leaves us with options two and three – he didn't believe what he'd written, or he wasn't aware he was writing it."

Scrutinous picked up the newspaper by the armchair and glanced at the crossword. He wasn't a fan of them, to be honest. There were enough confusing things in the world without crosswords.

"If Cassidy didn't believe what he'd written," Valkyrie said, "then why not tear out the page? This should be crumpled up in a bin somewhere, as just another bit of nonsense. But he didn't tear it out."

"So he wrote it, but didn't know he was writing it," Skulduggery said. "Which means something or someone was guiding his hand."

"Someone wanted him dead?" Valkyrie asked. "A sorcerer? Why?"

"There's something we're not seeing," Skulduggery said. "Geoffrey?"

Scrutinous looked up. "Yes?"

"What are you doing? I thought you hated crosswords."

"I do, yes."

"Where did you get that pen?"

"It was on the pad."

"What are you writing?"

Scrutinous laughed. "Writing? I'm not writing anything." And even as he said it, he heard the scratching of pen on paper, and looked down. "Oh," he said. "Oh, dear." He dropped the pen to the carpet.

Skulduggery held out his hand. "Let me see."

Scrutinous handed over the newspaper.

Skulduggery read what Scrutinous had written. "*I'm going to be eaten by a shark.*"

"Oh, dear," Scrutinous said again. "This does not bode well for me."

Valkyrie waved her hand, and the pen drifted up off the ground and hovered at eye level. "Haunted pen?" she asked.

"Cursed, more likely," Skulduggery said. "Physical contact seems to be enough for the curse to pass on. Geoffrey, you had no idea what you were writing?"

"I had no idea I was writing *anything*," Scrutinous replied. "I hate to be a pain, but do you think there's anything you can do to help me? I really don't want to be eaten by a shark tonight. The next round of my bowling tournament is on Wednesday and we're not doing too badly, all things considered. I'd hate to miss it."

"If a shark does come for you, it won't be tonight," Skulduggery told him. "The ink on the pad is at the very most a day old, Cassidy died four hours ago, and these kinds of curses really like the twelve-hour rule. Any more than that and the power starts to wane."

"So I have twelve hours before a shark eats me?"

"Or you have twelve hours for us to save you, if you want to be glass-half-full about it. Cheer up, Geoffrey, you have our full attention focused on your dilemma. Wait, where's my hat?"

Valkyrie picked it up off the armchair and handed it to him.

"Perfect," he said. "*Now* you have our full attention."

Scrutinous smiled gratefully, suddenly reassured that everything was going to be all right. The skeleton detective and Valkyrie Cain were on the case, and they would stop at nothing to solve it.

"I'm hungry," Valkyrie said.

Skulduggery nodded decisively, said, "Then let's find you something to eat," and Scrutinous sagged.

They sat in the diner, Valkyrie doing her best to eat a burger that kept slipping from its bun. Skulduggery had activated one of his false faces, one which gave him a slightly bewildered look. He had placed the pen in a wooden box and was peering at it. Scrutinous sat in the booth and did his best not to worry. He had a glass of water in front of him that he didn't touch.

"This store," Skulduggery said, "where Mister Cassidy worked – where is it?"

"Donnybrook," said Scrutinous.

"Donnybrook," Skulduggery repeated. "Interesting. Do you know of any sorcerers living in Donnybrook? I don't. Thoroughly nice area, but no sorcerers."

"This burger is hard to eat," Valkyrie muttered.

"You're doing a fantastic job," Skulduggery said happily. He closed the box and put it in his pocket. "Now then, Donnybrook. No sorcerers in Donnybrook. No sorcerers around where Cassidy lived. So how did he meet the sorcerer who killed him?"

Scrutinous found it hard to know when Skulduggery was addressing him or merely thinking out loud. The eyes on his false face were slowly swivelling in every direction.

"Unless," Skulduggery said, "he never did."

Valkyrie asked a question with her mouth full.

Skulduggery's head tilted. "What I mean is, this is a curse that passes from one person to the next, yes? The pen keeps moving around. Brendan Cassidy may not have been the first victim, which means it's possible he had no contact *at all* with the sorcerer who started it. Which means that there should be more unexplained deaths that we haven't heard about. Excuse me for a moment."

Skulduggery took his phone from his pocket, then slipped out of the booth. He went away to make a phone call. Scrutinous looked back at Valkyrie. She had managed to shove half of the burger into her mouth but now froze, her eyes on his.

She mumbled something that sounded like, "Sorry."

He looked away, and she munched on.

A few minutes later Skulduggery slid back into the booth. "Excellent news," he said. "There have been four unexplained deaths in the past two weeks. The first three were all sorcerers, and the fourth was a mortal woman who *knew* the last sorcerer killed and who lived in Donnybrook. Before she died, she could have left that pen in the store in which Brendan Cassidy worked. He picked it up, took it home, and got hit by a train."

"Who was the first sorcerer killed?" Valkyrie asked.

"His name was Elwood Satchel. Low-level Elemental. If the curse did start with him, then the killer must has some connection. We find that connection, we find the killer, we save Geoffrey."

"Then let's do it," Scrutinous said. He paused. "How do we do it?"

"We talk to someone who knew Satchel well. He has a brother who's out of the country right now, and a friend who lives close by."

"So we talk to the friend," Valkyrie said. "Let's go."

They got in the Bentley, drove to the friend's house and knocked on the door. There was nobody home, so they went back to the Bentley and waited. Skulduggery didn't move for hours, and Valkyrie fell asleep. Scrutinous sat in the back seat and thought about sharks all night.

Satchel's friend returned home at ten the next morning. He was a sorcerer but, like Satchel, he wasn't a very powerful one. He worked nights as a security guard to pay the bills.

"It was a clear day," he said when Skulduggery asked him how Satchel had died. "The sun was shining. There were no clouds. But Elwood was... panicking. He kept running around, looking up at the sky. He ran into a café, ran right back out again, screaming something about how it didn't have a ceiling. And then... And then he jerked backwards, flew right off his feet. He was all twisted up, and you could smell burnt hair."

"He was electrocuted?" Skulduggery asked.

"Yeah. Apparently. The doctors said it was a massive electrical current. But I didn't see anything, and he was running across the park when it happened. There was nothing electrical around."

"Did you find a note?" asked Valkyrie.

The man frowned. "What? How did you know about that?"

"Then you *did* find a note."

"Yes. Well, we think. A few days after he died, Elwood's brother found something written on the back of a receipt. It said 'I'm going to be struck by lightning'."

Skulduggery nodded. "Did Elwood have any enemies?"

"I... suppose. I mean, doesn't everyone?"

"Any enemies he had recently made?"

"Oh. Oh, yeah. One. Davit Maybury. They were friends once."

"What happened?"

"Ah, I don't know. The usual."

"I don't quite believe you," said Skulduggery.

"Look, Maybury's a weirdo, OK? He comes out with these weird things, and he looks... odd. He's got crazy eyes, you know? But Elwood grew up with him, they were childhood friends, and then... Elwood kind of stole Maybury's girlfriend."

"Ah."

"I suppose it was kind of a sucky thing to do. Maybury found it hard to talk to girls, because of his whole weirdness thing, and he finally found one who liked him and Elwood comes in and sweeps her off her feet... You think Maybury had something to do with his death?"

"Perhaps," Skulduggery said. "Do you know where we could find him? We just want a little chat."

Davit Maybury's house was quite nondescript from the outside. Skulduggery knocked a few times, then kicked the door in. It was quite a nondescript house from the inside, too. Skulduggery went first, hand open and fingers splayed.

"The air hasn't been disturbed for weeks," he said. "It doesn't look like anybody's home."

"So what are we going to do now?" Scrutinous asked. "It's almost eleven o'clock. I have one hour before a shark eats me."

"You'll be fine," Skulduggery said, poking around. "Everyone spread out. Look for clues."

Skulduggery and Valkyrie went wandering, examining things and muttering to themselves and each other. Scrutinous bit his lip and checked his watch.

Almost three quarters of an hour later, Skulduggery found something in the main bedroom.

"It's a door," he said, rapping his knuckles against the wall. "Very well hidden. Whoever installed it knew what they were doing."

"Where does it lead?" Scrutinous asked, and shifted his weight. The carpet in here was soggy, and water spilled through his sandals to wet his socks.

"It could be a stairway leading to a tunnel, or it could be a single room." Skulduggery stood back. "Maybury isn't the strongest sorcerer out there, and by all accounts he doesn't have many friends. It is therefore entirely conceivable that the moment he released the cursed pen upon Elwood Satchel he secluded himself away until it was all over. If something went wrong with the curse, if it didn't work, then Satchel might come after him."

Valkyrie peered at the wall. "So you think he's still in there?"

"Mister Maybury," Skulduggery said loudly, "we need to talk to you. If you can hear me, please open the door. I am a detective with the Sanctuary – we're not going to hurt you."

They looked at the wall and waited, and nothing happened.

"Um," said Scrutinous. "Where's that water coming from?"

Valkyrie looked around. "What water?"

Scrutinous splashed his foot a few times.

"That's the carpet," Valkyrie told him.

"And why is it covered in water?"

She frowned at him. "What are you talking about? It's not. It's just a regular carpet."

"It's a regular carpet covered in water, Valkyrie. You're standing in it, too."

"No, Geoffrey, I'm not. My feet are perfectly dry, as are yours. Are you feeling OK?"

He stared at her. The water was rising. It was up to her ankles. It had completely covered his own sandals. It was cold and wet. "You can't see this?" he asked. "You can't hear the splashing? You can't feel it?"

She hunkered down, put her hand in the water, flat on the floor. Her eyes were on him the whole time. "Am I touching the water now?"

He nodded. She brought her hand up. It was perfectly dry. No drops fell.

"Oh, dear," Scrutinous said.

"Interesting," Skulduggery murmured. "The curse must deliver a reality that only the victim can experience."

"Which explains how a train fitted into Cassidy's living room," Valkyrie said.

Scrutinous peered into the water, and his eyes widened. "I see a fish," he said. "A small one, a tiny one, but... it's a fish." He looked up. "When there's enough water, the shark will appear, won't it?"

"I'm afraid so," Skulduggery said. "Which means we have to get through this door."

Skulduggery and Valkyrie walked through the water without disturbing it, Scrutinous splashing noisily after them. They ran their hands all over the wall, feeling for imperfections.

"There has to be a lever here somewhere," Skulduggery said. "The time and the effort was put into making this door virtually undetectable, not into making it impenetrable. At Maybury's price range, it's one or the other. So there has to be a lever somewhere nearby."

Even as he spoke, something clicked beneath his fingers. The wall shifted, the door swung open, and Skulduggery led the way in.

It was a small room, windowless, with an armchair and a side-table. On the side-table there was thick book and a scalpel. There was water in here, too. Now it was up past Scrutinous's knees. His legs were freezing, and every now and then a school of tiny fish would brush past and he'd jerk away.

"We may have a problem," Skulduggery said.

Scrutinous stopped scanning the water and glanced up, saw a corpse in the armchair. Valkyrie had her hand covering her mouth and nose, but all Scrutinous could smell was the briny sea.

"That's Maybury?" he asked. "But... he's dead. He *is* dead, isn't he?"

"He must have trapped himself inside," Skulduggery said.

"He starved to death?" Valkyrie asked.

"I'm afraid he ran out of air long before that could happen. He obviously didn't think this through too well."

"But if he's dead," said Scrutinous, "how can he lift the curse? Who's going to lift the curse?"

"The important thing to remember is not to panic," Skulduggery said.

"How can I not panic? A shark is going to eat me!"

"It's really not as bad as it sounds. I was attacked by a shark once, back when I was alive. Well, not so much a shark as a rather large fish. And not so much attacked as looked at menacingly. But it had murder in its eyes, that fish. I knew, in that instant, if our roles had been reversed and the fish had been holding the fishing pole and I had been the one to be caught, it wouldn't hesitate a moment before eating me. So I cooked it and ate before it had a chance to turn the tables."

"That," Valkyrie said, "is one of the most useless stories you've ever told me."

"I'm just trying to make Geoffrey feel better."

"You went fishing, Skulduggery. That's not the same as being eaten by a shark."

"It shares similarities."

"Like what?"

"It was wet. Also, one eats the other. When looked upon like that, the main points are practically identical."

"Um," Scrutinous said, "could we start talking about how we're going to lift the curse if the man who started it all is dead?"

"Yes," Skulduggery said, "of course. All is not lost. While it would have been easier to have Maybury simply cancel the whole thing, that is only one way to solve the problem. Davit Maybury was not an evil man. He was a weird one, by all accounts, but not evil. As such, it does not make sense that he would want many people to die, when all he was after was revenge on the one man who had stolen the woman he loved."

He took the wooden box from his jacket and opened it. Hesitating only a moment, he took the pen from the box. "Well," he said, "now we're in this together, Geoffrey." He held the pen in both hands, and twisted. The outer shell cracked and he pulled it away. He murmured something, then held up the pen for Valkyrie and Scrutinous to see. Four symbols had been cut into the inside. "The curse," he said. "I think Maybury made a mistake. Instead of the curse afflicting the first person to touch the pen, it has instead afflicted *every* person to touch the pen. Maybe he used the wrong symbol or misjudged the depth or the width... Every aspect of these sigils has to be perfectly judged."

"How does that help us?" Valkyrie asked.

"It means we don't have to lift the curse – we just have to correct his spelling."

"He carved the wrong symbol, so now we have to carve the right one?"

"In theory, once we do, it will mean the curse will have fulfilled its purpose the first time it was used, and all this will just... stop."

"In theory?" Scrutinous pressed. His teeth were chattering.

"Yes."

"That doesn't s-sound very certain."

"It's a very strong theory, Geoffrey. In much the same way that gravity is a very strong theory. It's almost certainly true. If I were you, I wouldn't worry about it."

"I have ten m-minutes left. The water has reached the ends of my shorts. There are f-f-fish swimming all around me and the floor has changed to a s-seabed. How do you expect me to not w-worry about this?"

"By taking deep, calming breaths."

"Do you know how to correct it?" Valkyrie asked.

Skulduggery picked up the scalpel from the side-table, before opening the book. "This is obviously what Maybury used to start it all, but because he got it wrong I would be disinclined to trust the same instructions he followed. We'll have to ask China."

Valkyrie raised an eyebrow. "But China isn't here."

"Your b-boyfriend," Scrutinous said. "He's a tele... porter... He can bring her."

"Fletcher's never been here," Valkyrie said. "He can't teleport anywhere he's never been."

"Well," Skulduggery said, taking out his phone, "where magic fails, technology prevails." He took a picture of the pen, then made a call.

Scrutinous glanced behind him, just in time to see a pale fin sink beneath the water's surface.

"It's here!" he screeched. "It's over there!"

Valkyrie jumped in front of him protectively.

"That won't do any good," Skulduggery said.

"I know!" she snapped. "But we can't just stand around while he gets eaten!"

Scrutinous took a deep breath and ducked his head into the water. The confines of the room did not exist down here. Down here, he was in the middle of the ocean. He saw a dark shape move out of the corner of his eye, and then it was gone. He came up for air.

"It's huge," he said. "Oh, God, it's h-huge."

"China," Skulduggery said suddenly. "We have a bit of an emergency here. I just sent you a picture, did you get it? Excellent." He waited a moment, listening to her talk. "But that's just the thing. It *is* a mistake. The gent who set the curse didn't mean it to apply to *everyone* – he meant it to apply simply to the *first* one."

Scrutinous took another breath, and ducked down for another look.

The shark, and it must have been a Great White judging by its size, was visible in the distance, turning towards him. Scrutinous broke the surface, gasping for air. "It's coming!"

"But my question," Skulduggery was saying, "is how to correct the curse so that the original intent overrides the mistake? Really? Oh, that's interesting."

"It's coming!" Scrutinous screamed.

"Geoffrey, please," Skulduggery said, "I can't hear what she's saying." He put the phone back to his head. "Carry on."

"Splash about," Valkyrie said. "Make a lot of noise. Scare it away."

Scrutinous splashed at the water and kicked his legs and screamed and yelled and hollered.

"A shark's coming for him," Skulduggery said into the phone. "Oh, have you? OK, I'll tell him." Skulduggery looked over. "China was attacked by a shark once, just like I was, except it was an actual shark and she was actually attacked. She says you're not to splash about, she says that makes you look like a seal, and sharks really like eating seals."

Scrutinous froze, and Valkyrie winced. "Oh, yeah," she said. "I saw that once on TV. Sorry."

"So it's just the upwards slash, then?" Skulduggery was saying, peering at the pen. "Is it too long or too short? How long should it be? No, shouldn't be a problem." He put the phone on loudspeaker and placed it in his top pocket, then readied Maybury's scalpel. "OK, making the cut now..."

China's voice came from the phone. "Has the shark eaten him yet?"

"Not yet," Skulduggery muttered, focusing on his task. "What happens if I do it wrong?"

"Geoffrey gets eaten," China said. "Am I on loudspeaker?"

"Yes, sorry, should have told you. Valkyrie and Geoffrey are here."

"Can they hear me?"

"Yes, they can."

"Hello, Valkyrie," China said.

"Uh, hi," Valkyrie said back. "Is this going to take long? The shark's coming for him."

China said something in response but Scrutinous didn't hear it. The shark came at him like a torpedo, its mouth open impossibly wide and all those teeth biting in at him. Scrutinous shrieked, dimly aware of Skulduggery gesturing, and then he was sent deeper into the water, tumbling head over heels, the shark missing him by inches.

Scrutinous turned, twisted, saw the shark flick its great tail and shoot back towards him, coming in for another go. In desperation, knowing it was useless but doing it anyway, he started to swim away from it. But there was nowhere to swim to, nowhere to hide, and then something snagged his right wrist.

An invisible force yanked him to the surface, the shark passing so close that its rough skin scraped like sandpaper across his leg. He broke the surface, gasping, realising that Valkyrie had grabbed his arm and pulled, and for a moment he saw the both of them, the alarm in Valkyrie's eyes, Skulduggery still working on the pen, the room around them, and then he dropped again, below the surface, and Valkyrie and Skulduggery disappeared and there was only the shark down there in the middle of the ocean.

Oxygen bubbles filled his vision and he jerked his head from side to side, trying to get his bearings, trying to work out what direction the shark would attack from. Then he saw it, that huge mouth, those huge teeth, coming in on top of him and there was no way out, not this time, and the massive jaws closed over him just as the water went away and Scrutinous fell to the floor.

"There," Skulduggery said. "I think that did it."

Scrutinous sat up, gasping, looking around in astonishment.

"Is he dead?" China asked from the phone.

"Not even remotely," Skulduggery said. "He's back on dry land. Many thanks, China."

He hung up as Valkyrie helped Scrutinous to his feet. The water was gone, the shark was gone. Scrutinous wasn't even wet any more.

"It had me," he said. "The shark had me. I was, literally, about to be torn in two. You saved me. In the nick of time, you saved me."

"You're welcome," Skulduggery said.

"I was talking to Valkyrie."

Skulduggery's head tilted. "But I'm the one who worked the whole thing out."

Valkyrie grinned. "You're very welcome, Geoffrey, although I can't take all the credit. China helped, you know."

"But I carved the right symbol," Skulduggery said.

Scrutinous clasped Valkyrie's hand in his. "If there is anything

I can do for you in the future, anything at all, do not hesitate to ask."

Skulduggery looked at him. "Can I ask, too?"

"No."

"Why not?"

"Valkyrie cared that I was being attacked. You told me to shut up."

"That's because your screaming was very annoying. How is that my fault?"

"If you'll excuse me," Scrutinous said, "I'm going to go for a walk. A nice, long walk, on solid ground."

He left them, heard them bickering behind him, and then Valkyrie was laughing and Skulduggery was acting offended. Scrutinous emerged into the midday sun, took a deep, calming breath, and headed off in search of some lunch.

Possibly seafood.

Just Another Friday Night

In December 2011 Derek launched a competition on his blog (dereklandy.blogspot.com) to find two characters for a new short story, to be published exclusively in this book. One of them had to be Australian, and one of them had to be New Zealandish... New Zealandan... um, from New Zealand.

After much deliberation over all the fantastic entries, Derek chose:

Tane Aiavao, of New Zealand, created by Josie. Tane is a laid-back Maori Elemental with zero planning skills.

Hayley Skirmish, of Australia, created by Sparky Braginski. Hayley is a strong-willed, plain-speaking Adept with the ability to jump, flip, and run along walls and ceilings.

Congratulations to Josie and Sparky! And now read on for the brand-new story featuring their amazing characters...

JUST ANOTHER FRIDAY NIGHT

"Zombies," Tane Aiavao muttered as they crept closer to the mausoleum. "I hate zombies."

The night air was filled with the stench of the dead. It wafted through the headstones and played with the long grasses of this remote Brisbane cemetery, and it was all Tane and Hayley could do to stop from gagging whenever one of the shambling, rotting things got too close. They stayed low, moving through the shadows, ready to run or fight in an instant should their luck change.

Hayley Skirmish, her brown hair tied back in a ponytail, held the axe in a two-handed grip. Tane, his own hair sticking up in a clump, followed behind her and did most of the complaining. Unlike his Australian companion, Tane didn't cherish these calm moments before the storm, and he cherished the storm even less. Tane was a New Zealander, a Kiwi, and even more than that he was a Maori, and he reckoned Hayley could learn a thing or two from him on how to relax. Not that he'd ever suggest it. Tane was a big guy, but not all of it was muscle, and there was something about Hayley that was just flat-out *intimidating* to a bloke like him. She was athletic and pretty and impressive, looked to be around seventeen, so she was a bit younger than he was – but even so, she was in charge, and that was the end of it.

Hayley moved her hand in a quick motion and they stopped where they were, within sight of the rusted iron gates of the Doherty family crypt. They could hear movement all around them. Tane peered about and caught glimpses of things that had once been people, lurching with each step. He disguised his whimper behind a terrified moan, and realised that Hayley was looking at him, like she was waiting for something.

"What?" he whispered.

"The amulet," she whispered back impatiently in that broad Aussie accent. "Hurry."

He frowned at her. "I don't have the amulet."

"What? You were meant to bring it!"

"I thought you were meant to bring it."

"I brought the axe!"

"No one told me I had to bring the amulet."

"I told you! Before we left!"

He let a moment pass. "I thought you were joking."

"Right," she whispered decisively, turning so she was facing him. "I'm going to kill you."

He flinched away from the axe. "I thought we didn't need the amulet – didn't Skulduggery say they'd be able to do this without it?"

Her grip on the axe was turning her knuckles white, and she had that look in her eye, the look that meant she was barely controlling her anger. "He did say that. And then Valkyrie said no, they *hoped* they'd be able to do this without the amulet, but that if they couldn't, they'd use the amulet as a last resort."

"A last resort?"

"To save the world."

Tane gave a feeble smile. "See? We've got nothing to worry about. I mean, when was the last time we used a last-resort-type weapon?"

"Monday."

He chewed his lip. "I'm sure we won't need to do it again so soon, though. It'll be fine."

She leaned in close, real close, close enough to bite his nose clean off. "You," she said in a whisper so coarse it was sliding off sandpaper, "are an idiot."

He shrugged and muttered something and went to retie his bootlace before he remembered gumboots don't have laces, and eventually Hayley looked back at the mausoleum. When they were sure they wouldn't be seen, they hurried to the gate. The lock had been snapped, but the hinges still creaked as they slipped through. Tane's feet crunched on pebbles, but Hayley's bare feet moved over them with barely a sound, and within moments they were passing through the heavy door into the dank confines of the final resting place (in theory, anyway) of the once great Doherty clan. Two flaming torches, held in wall brackets on either side, illuminated the ancient coffins that lay empty and broken all around them. Moving slowly, they approached the crumbling hole in the ground, a pit so impossibly dark it could have led into the infinitely fathomless depths of Hell itself.

"Looks pretty deep," Tane said.

Hayley didn't bother answering him. She did a quick check around to make sure all the coffins were indeed empty, and then moved back to the door. Hayley was good at standing guard. She was alert, and she didn't get bored as easily as Tane did, and she didn't start fidgeting or go for a wander, the way Tane tended to.

His eyes scanned the crypt, not finding a whole lot of interest. The plan was that they wait here for the sign, and then they help Skulduggery and Valkyrie close over this gaping pit, which was the reason the dead were walking. Skulduggery had explained it to them that very afternoon, how they had figured it all out, about the centuries-old family curse and the last of the Doherty bloodline and something else about how the wicked shall not rest and something about a dog. Or a bog, or something like that. Maybe a log.

"What does a log have to do with all this?" he asked Hayley.

"Nothing whatsoever."

He nodded to himself. It was definitely either dog or bog. He looked down into the pit. Could it really be called a pit? What made a hole a pit? It was about two metres in diameter and very dark, but apart from that, it was just a hole. He picked up a small piece of rubble and dropped it into the darkness. He listened for the sound of it hitting the bottom. Nothing. Either the hole was very, very deep or the piece of rubble was way too small. He picked up another piece, a heavier, chunkier piece.

"What are you doing?" Hayley asked suddenly.

He hid the chunk of rubble behind his back. "Nothing."

"You're doing something. What are you doing?"

"I'm not doing anything," he said. "I'm standing here, that's all."

Her eyes narrowed. "Stay away from the pit."

"It's more of a hole, really."

"Shut up, and stay away from it."

He didn't respond. She glared at him once more, then went back to peering out of the door. In Tane's experience, Australians were fine most of the time, but whenever they were in dangerous situations they tended to lose their sense of humour. Making sure he wouldn't be caught, Tane tossed the chunk of rubble into the hole and listened for a sound. It came almost immediately, a soft thud and a moan. Tane frowned. A moan?

The zombie pulled itself up and grabbed his ankle and Tane shrieked. He kicked out and fell back and the zombie was clambering from the hole/pit/whatever it was, its flesh rotten and disgusting. Tane was aware of Hayley dragging him away as the zombie reached for him again.

"What did you do?" she hissed.

"I just wanted to see how deep it was!"

"I told you not to go near it!"

"Who are you to be giving me orders?"

She dropped him and strode forwards. "I'm the one with the axe."

Zombies are scary and all, and there's the whole loss of identity and mindless savagery side to them, but one on one, they're not very effective. Now in an enclosed space, if you're outnumbered and there's nowhere to run, you can offer up a prayer to whichever god you believe in and prepare to have your brains eaten. In that kind of situation, you're pretty much doomed. But when there's only one of them, and they're as slow and clumsy as they usually are, and they're facing an Australian girl who's had experience wielding an axe, they don't really stand much of a chance.

The zombie had only just got to its feet when Hayley swung, and Tane had to admire her proficiency. The only way to kill a zombie is the tried and true – destroy the brain or sever the head – and where Tane would have chopped and hacked and made an unholy mess of it, one swipe was all it took for Hayley to get the job done. The head hit the ground and the body crumpled, and she glanced back at him and her eyes widened.

"Look out!"

Tane twisted just as the mausoleum door burst open and the zombies staggered in. He scrambled up as they poured through the doorway, a seemingly endless parade of decomposing corpses, moaning and snarling in that guttural way of theirs.

He pushed at the air and a few zombies went stumbling back, but he'd be the first one to admit that he wasn't the best Elemental the world had ever seen. Hayley was doing better, jumping and flipping and taking off heads, but there were just too many of them. Enclosed space. Outnumbered. Nowhere to run.

"This is bad," he said to Hayley as they backed up to the edge of the pit.

"Yes, it is..."

"OK, listen," he said. "I've got a plan. You run at them, do that jumping-around thing you like to do so much, let them eat you, and I'll try to escape."

"Good plan."

"Thank you."

"Or how about *you* run at them," said Hayley, "do that standing-around thing *you* like to do so much, let them eat *you*, and I just stay and watch?"

"I think I prefer my idea."

They were doomed. There was no way out. The zombies were closing in. Tane looked at Hayley. So much he wanted to tell her. So much he wanted to say. And then they heard a voice behind them.

"Thought I told you to stay *away* from the flesh-eating zombies from beyond the grave?"

They whirled as a skeleton in a mud-stained suit and a seventeen-year-old Irish girl with blood-matted hair climbed from the pit. Skulduggery held a wooden staff and Valkyrie threw him a headpiece carved from stone. He fixed it to the staff, then held it up for the zombies to scc.

The shuffling stopped. The moaning stopped. They stared, transfixed.

"Hear me," Skulduggery said loudly. "You are the Doherty clan, the last of the great families. You have been cursed to an un-death, cursed to never know peace because of the sins of one man, centuries ago. That man, your ancestor, has now been punished. I have seen to it myself. The curse is lifted. This staff belonged to the one who cursed you. It is yours to destroy."

Skulduggery stepped back, held the staff over the pit they had just emerged from, and let it go. A moment passed where nothing happened and then, as one, the zombies lurched forward. Skulduggery and Hayley went one way and Valkyrie and Tane went the other, parting so that they wouldn't be caught in the surging mass of bodies that started to topple into the hole. Like lemmings they went, albeit uglier and smellier, without even a murmur as the darkness swallowed them. When the last of them disappeared into the pit, the pit itself closed over, and so was neither a hole nor a pit any longer.

"Told you we wouldn't need the amulet," Tane said, wiping the dust from his combats.

"How did you do it?" Hayley asked Skulduggery as he checked his pocket watch. "What's down there? What happened?"

"Assorted things," Skulduggery said as he led the way to the door.

"We've got to kind of hurry a little bit," Valkyrie said, walking after him.

"But how did you lift the curse?" Hayley asked. "How did you punish their ancestor?"

Skulduggery was already out the door, but Valkyrie hesitated just as she was about to leave, and turned. "He lied. We didn't lift the curse. We didn't punish anyone. We stole the staff to get the zombies to go away. And if we're not out of this graveyard by the stroke of midnight, in exactly seventy seconds, we will inherit the curse. Providing the Hound doesn't kill us first."

The Hound. So it was *dog*, not bog, and certainly not log. Tane remembered it now. The Hound was the spectral guardian of the curse on the Doherty family, and it was meant to be very, very mean. Feeling pretty chuffed with himself that he had managed to remember that much, Tane spoke up.

"So how big is it, this Hound? Big as a German Shepherd?"

Skulduggery stepped back inside the mausoleum, and nodded to just over Tane's shoulder, said, "Oh, it's about as big as that one," and Tane looked back.

The Hound stood where the pit had been. It was huge and scarred and ravaged and it was sniffing at the ground and pawing at the earth. And then it looked up at them with fiery red eyes and its hackles rose and it growled, and Tane felt very strongly that they should be running away now.

They bolted from the crypt. As they sprinted over people's graves, Tane could hear Hayley hissing apologies. He felt no such remorse. He'd run across a thousand graves if it meant delaying his entry into one of them.

The Hound burst through the mausoleum door, taking it from its hinges, but it hit the gate and for a moment it stalled, unable to find a way past. It solved its dilemma by leaping clean over the rust-tipped spikes, and landed on the far side in a crouch, its muscles rippling beneath the welts and the fur.

The road outside the cemetery was ahead. They were halfway there when the Hound caught sight of them and gave chase. Tane started laughing, one of his nervous reactions when being pursued. Skulduggery and Valkyrie and Hayley were ahead – if the Hound was going to pounce on anyone, Tane knew it was going to pounce on him. He was unlucky that way, always had been.

He didn't dare look back. He didn't need to. He could hear the Hound gaining on him. It was all over. He thought it had been all over before, in the crypt, but he had been premature. Now, *now* it was all over. His life, snatched away, extinguished like a candle in the wind, like in that song, 'Candle in the Wind'. And then Tane tripped and fell on his face and the Hound passed right over him, snapping at the space where his head had been.

Strewth, bro, that was lucky, a chirpy little voice in the back of his mind piped up.

The Hound landed and skidded on the gravel but snapped its body around, eyes fixed on Tane, saliva dripping from its bared fangs. Its body tensed, coiled, prepared to spring. One lunge would be all it took to close the distance between them, and Tane, lying belly-down on the ground, was in no position to even try to escape.

The chirpy little voice wasn't saying much of anything now.

There was shouting. Valkyrie and Hayley were at the very edge of the cemetery, calling out to the Hound and hurling stones. One of the stones, probably hurled by Hayley, hit Tane, but he didn't utter a sound. The beast snarled and reluctantly shifted its stare, snapping its jaws in the direction of the other two.

And then Skulduggery came darting out, waving his arms, and the Hound took a single step towards him and Tane kept his head down, didn't move an inch, and proved to be such an uninteresting target that the Hound quickly switched focus. It leaped for Skulduggery and Tane scrambled up and ran straight at Hayley. As he ran he saw Skulduggery sprint for a large Celtic cross, made from stone and standing as a proud testament to some dead guy's life. Right before he ran straight into it, Skulduggery turned his body sideways and let his momentum carry him forwards. His shoulder collided with the cross and he spun and hit the ground, but the Hound hit it head-on.

Tane noticed something approaching from in front of him and realised it was Valkyrie, but she was standing still, and in fact it was he that was moving. He crashed into her and they tumbled back over the low wall and sprawled on to the road in a mass of flailing limbs and cursing. It was mostly Valkyrie cursing. Out of the corner of his eye he saw Skulduggery running for them, the Hound, having recovered, right behind him. Skulduggery dived out of the cemetery and the Hound leaped after him and then kind of faded into nothing, like the air had come and whipped it away. Skulduggery landed and rolled and was on his feet again, checked that the Hound was gone, and then looked down at Tane and Valkyrie.

"Having fun?"

Valkyrie hit Tane and got up.

"Is it over?" Hayley asked, looking around warily.

"It's over," said Skulduggery, straightening his tie. "Stroke of midnight, so it was in the nick of time, but when isn't it for us?"

"Always in the nick of time," Valkyrie mumbled. "Why can't we ever solve a problem *early*?"

Skulduggery tilted his head at her. "Where's the fun in that?"

Hayley peered at Tane. "You OK down there?"

"A dog tried to eat me," Tane said, not getting up.

"If it's any consolation," Skulduggery told him, "it tried to eat me, too."

"Yeah, that's no consolation at all."

"I need a shower," Valkyrie said. "I'm covered in gore and zombie guck, and I don't want to get on the plane reeking. It's a long flight back to Ireland."

"Was this your first trip to Australia?" Hayley asked her, suddenly all friendly now that the threat was averted. Bloody typical, that.

"No, but it was definitely my goriest. Are you sure your friend is OK?"

Hayley scowled down at Tane. "He's not really my friend. He's just an idiot that I know."

"She loves me," Tane whispered. The others talked a bit more, discussed this and that, but Tane stayed on the ground and didn't join in. He was alive. He was alive and he was going to stay alive, and he was going to enjoy living again. He suddenly had a mad urge for fishnchups. He poked his head up. "Anyone hungry?"

"I don't eat, I'm afraid," Skulduggery said, "and we really have to get going."

Valkyrie smiled. "Thanks for the offer, though."

Hayley looked at him and sighed. "Fine," she said, "I'll go get some grub with you. But you better not talk to me."

He grinned, and Hayley helped him up.

THE END OF THE WORLD

This story is dedicated to cover artist extraordinaire, Tom Percival.

For most people, the cover is the reason they pick up a book in the first place. The amount of correspondence I get proves this, as people go on and on about how the cover caught their eye, made them want to read about a skeleton detective, how the covers are the best things ever, how the covers blah blah blah...

I think it's a generally agreed upon fact that I could draw the covers if I really wanted to. I have the raw talent, I have the eye, and I have that one year of art college under my belt.

And I think Tom knows this, which is why he pushes himself to excel each and every time, why he pushes himself to make these books stand out from the others on the shelf. The threat I pose is important. The threat I pose is a good motivator.

Keep pushing yourself, Tom. My time is coming.

P.S. You're welcome.

THE END OF THE WORLD

ONE

The man with the unfortunate face stood in the aisle between the Science Fiction section and Crime, and he seemed to be trying to blend in with the bookshelves. He wasn't doing a particularly good job of it. When an old woman shuffled too close, he snarled at her – actually *snarled* – and the old woman yelped like an injured puppy and hurried away as fast as her little old legs would carry her. People weren't used to snarling, not in a public library. For as long as he'd been coming here, Ryan certainly hadn't witnessed any snarling. Until today, of course.

He watched the man out of the corner of his eye, watched him whispering with his companions. They were an odd bunch. The snarling man was the biggest – arms like tree trunks, black matted hair completely failing to hide a face that was in no way attractive.

The smallest one of the group was a middle-aged man who stood very still and didn't join in with the whispering. He looked like an accountant who'd wandered out of the office one day and had accidentally joined a biker gang. The woman beside him wore battered leather and had short spiky hair. She was pretty, in a sinister sort of way, but she didn't have a very nice laugh. It carried through the quiet building, unnerving all who heard it. The librarians, usually so strict about things like that, pretended not to notice.

The final member of the gang seemed to be the leader. He was lean and his arms looked strong. He had tattoos curling down from beneath his T-shirt. His jeans were black and his boots were scuffed. He had dark hair that hung over his brow. The big man and the woman would whisper to him and he'd nod. He never stopped looking around, though. Once or twice he almost caught Ryan's eye.

Ryan sat back in his chair, exited his email account on the computer. No emails. As usual. No one ever sent him emails. Not even spam. Maybe if he made more friends, like his mother was always saying, maybe then he'd at least be sent some junk every once in a while. Fifteen years old and no friends. It was kind of sad, when he thought about it. He didn't think about it much.

He got up, walked through the Children's section, running his fingers along the spines of the books he passed. He found himself in History and picked a book at random. Something about the Second World War. He didn't care. He was just here to waste time, after all – waste time and build up the courage to run away.

It wasn't his mother's fault. It wasn't even his new stepdad's fault. Ryan didn't have a problem with either of them. He just missed his father so much, and every moment spent living in that house reminded him that his father was dead and gone and never coming back, and Ryan didn't want to live like that any more. So he was going to run away to... somewhere. Somewhere else. Just for a little while. Just to get away.

He put the book back and went to take another one, but something fell from the shelf. He saw a flash of silver – what looked like a clasp, or a brooch – and without thinking he reached out and caught it, closed his fingers round it tight. It was cold to the touch, but immediately turned hot. Pain lanced up his arm and he cried out. He opened his hand to drop it, but the only thing he was holding was silver dust. The clasp, whatever it was, had crumbled away in his grip.

The pain was gone, too. Not wanting to make a mess, Ryan emptied the silver dust on to a gap in the bookshelf, then brushed at his hand. There was something smudged on his palm. He tried to wipe it away, but it wouldn't come off. Then he realised his skin wasn't smudged – it was burnt. The clasp had burned itself into his flesh.

"What you got there?"

Ryan turned at the sound of the voice. It was the leader of the gang. The other three stood behind him. They were all looking at him like he was prey.

"Nothing," Ryan mumbled, closing his hand.

"We heard you cry out," said the man. "We heard you cry out and Mercy said – that's Mercy over there – Mercy said let's see if he needs any help."

"I said that," the woman with the spiky hair confirmed, nodding her spiky head. "I was worried. Because I care."

"She does care," said the leader. "She wanted to know if you'd hurt yourself. Have you hurt yourself? She wanted to know if you'd hurt yourself and Obloquy said – Obloquy's the big lad – Obloquy said how is he going to hurt himself in a library? Is he going to paper-cut himself to death?"

The leader laughed, and Mercy laughed, and the big one grinned.

"I'm funny," he said.

"How did you hurt yourself?" the leader asked, coming down off the laugh with a friendly chuckle.

"I didn't hurt myself," said Ryan. "I'm fine."

"But we heard you cry out," said the man, suddenly frowning. "We heard you. Didn't we hear him?"

"I heard him," said Mercy.

"I heard him too, Foe," said Obloquy.

The middle-aged man, the accountant, didn't say anything.

The leader, Foe, examined Ryan curiously. "You don't have to be scared of us. Is that what's wrong? You're scared of us? You don't have to be. We're not bad people."

Obloquy laughed, and Mercy jammed an elbow into his ribs to shut him up.

"I know you're not supposed to talk to strangers," Foe continued, "but aren't you a bit old for that? Isn't that rule more for kids? You're not a kid any more, are you? What are you, fifteen or so?" He reached out, dipping a finger into the silver dust on the bookshelf, then bringing it to the tip of his tongue. He tasted it, and smiled at Ryan. "And if you don't talk to strangers, how are you going to make friends? Friends are important. We want to be friends."

"We really do," said Mercy.

"And we were standing over there," said Foe, "talking about books, because that's what we like to do, we like to talk about books, and we heard you cry out and we came over because we were worried, and we care, and now we're here, having a conversation. Having a friendly conversation with our new friend."

"I didn't hurt myself," Ryan said, really wishing he were somewhere else right now.

"Friends don't lie to each other," Foe said.

"I'm... I'm not lying."

"You're lying a little bit," Foe said, smiling. "What's your name?"

"Ryan."

"Good to meet you, Ryan."

Foe stuck out his hand. Ryan hesitated, then went to shake it. Instead, Foe grabbed his wrist and turned his palm to face upwards. The gang looked at the symbol imprinted on to his skin, and Foe released Ryan's wrist and put his hand on Ryan's shoulder. "Ryan, my friend. You're going to have to come with us now."

Ryan shook his head. "I should be going home. My dad will be here in a minute to pick me up."

"Ryan," said Foe. "If you don't come with us right this second, we're going to kill everyone in this building and then we're going to drag you out through the blood and the gore and what remains of their dead bodies." Another smile, this time with narrowed eyes. "So really, buddy, it's up to you."

Ryan wanted to scream for help and run away, but his legs wouldn't work and his chest was too tight. He looked at them. Foe, with his smile and his eyes. Mercy, an eager look on her face, like she was really hoping she'd get to kill someone today. Obloquy, standing there looking dumb and dangerous. And the accountant, whose gaze had never faltered, who was as still as a statue, completely detached from what was going on. The accountant was the scariest of them all.

And then, whistling.

TWO

hrough the gaps in the books, Ryan could see someone in the next aisle over, moving slowly. Someone in black. Someone whistling. Ryan recognised the tune. It was the theme music to *Harry Potter*.

A pretty girl appeared at the corner of the bookcase. Tall, with long dark hair. Maybe a year or two older than Ryan. Wearing a jacket that was zipped up, tight trousers and boots, and a ring on her finger. All in black. All made from materials Ryan couldn't identify.

And still, whistling. As she whistled, her dark eyes wandered from Ryan to Foe, to Mercy and Obloquy, and then to the accountant. When she got to the accountant, she stopped whistling, and looked back at Ryan.

"Hi," she said. "My name's Valkyrie. Are these people bothering you?"

Ryan wanted to tell her to run, but he knew the gang would be on her in an instant.

The girl looked at Foe. "I'm part of Library Security," she said. "We've had some reports of overdue books in this area, and I'm going to need to ask you all some questions. We can do this here or downtown – where we'd actually have more space and access to a coffee machine."

Something was wrong. Foe didn't threaten her and Mercy didn't say anything at all. In fact, Mercy and Obloquy were glancing around, like they expected someone else to show up. Even the accountant looked wary.

"You really want this to happen?" Foe asked, his voice low. "Here? In a public place? Where all these innocent people might get caught in the crossfire?"

The pretty girl, Valkyrie, gave him a shrug. "I'm just looking for a way to spoil your day, Vincent. The choice is yours. Stick around and get beaten up and thrown in a cell, or leave, now. Immediately."

"Sure," said Foe. "We'll just take Ryan here with us."

Valkyrie shook her head. "Ryan stays, I'm afraid."

"Ah. Well, see, now we have a problem."

"That's too bad."

"That's just what I was thinking."

Valkyrie moved, snapping her palm against the air and the air shimmered and Foe shot back off his feet, colliding with Mercy.

Before Ryan could even wonder what had just happened, she grabbed him and then they were running through the aisles. A stream of red energy sizzled by his ear and Ryan shrieked, tried to throw himself to the ground but Valkyrie wouldn't let him.

"Keep moving," she snapped.

He stumbled after her.

There was a roar, and the crash of a bookcase being toppled. Ryan glanced back, saw Obloquy go hurtling through the air, and a man stepped into view – a tall man, thin, wearing a dark blue suit and hat, like one of those old-fashioned private eyes.

Another stream of red energy burst through the bookshelf to his left and Ryan forgot all about the thin man and focused all his attention on not dying. Mercy smashed into him and he went sprawling across the floor, the wind knocked out of him. Then Valkyrie was there, running straight for Mercy who turned to her, opened her mouth wide, and let loose another stream of energy. From her mouth. *From her mouth.*

Ryan blinked.

Valkyrie dived, rolled, came up and threw herself into Mercy. Mercy grunted, the stream cut off, and they went down. They grappled, throwing elbows and pulling hair. Mercy grabbed a handful of Valkyrie's hair and yanked, and Valkyrie slammed her forehead into Mercy's face. Mercy screamed with pain and rage and Valkyrie was on top now, Mercy trying to push her off. Valkyrie trapped one of Mercy's arms and moved up, too fast for Ryan to work out what was happening, but somehow she swung her leg over Mercy and was now leaning back sharply. She snapped Mercy's elbow and Mercy howled, and then Valkyrie was scrambling towards Ryan, pulling him to his feet.

Ryan wished he could have said something intelligent to her at that moment, but all he could manage was "Muh". It was not very impressive.

Around them, the good people of the library cowered behind cover or ran for the exits. Ryan would have given anything to be allowed to cower. His entire body ached to find a dark corner and collapse into it like some kind of jelly. But the pretty girl who was gripping his hand kept pulling him on through the stacks, and Ryan was suddenly determined not to embarrass himself in front of her. So he forced his legs to stay strong and when Valkyrie hesitated, he overtook her.

"This way," he said, and now he was pulling her through the stacks, and she was probably thinking what a great guy he was, and look how take-charge he is, and even though he's a year or two younger than I am he'd probably make a great boyfriend and when all this is over, I'll probably want to kiss him or something. Ryan nodded to himself. Yeah, she was probably thinking all that as he led her through the aisles and the stacks, and then they came to a wall with a nice picture on it.

"Moron," Valkyrie snapped, turning and yanking him after her.

"Sorry," he said.

"I thought you knew where you were going!"

"I thought there was a door here."

She stopped suddenly and he ran into the back of her. He was halfway through apologising when he saw the accountant standing ahead of them.

Elsewhere in the library, the thin man was still battling the others. There were a lot of crashes and yells and screams and grunts. But here, with Ryan and Valkyrie and the accountant, it somehow seemed really, really quiet.

The accountant took a step forward. Valkyrie took a step back. She stepped on Ryan's foot and he said "Ow" and then apologised. She didn't hear him.

She snapped her hand against the air. The space rippled and a bookcase was blasted back, but the accountant was already moving. Then Valkyrie clicked her fingers and Ryan yelped when fire suddenly flared in her palm. He tore off his jacket and flung it over her forearm, batting out the flames.

"What the hell are you doing?" she raged, trying to push him back.

"You're on fire!" he squealed manfully.

She pulled away from him, her hand still ablaze, and then she flung the fire, but the accountant twisted, impossibly fast, and the fireball missed him, exploded against the side of another bookcase. The accountant darted out of sight.

"Oh," Ryan said.

Valkyrie backed up against him. "If you see an exit," she whispered, "you run to it. Understand?"

He nodded.

Something moved above them and the accountant dropped down on to Valkyrie. She cried out and Ryan stumbled back, watched as the accountant grabbed her and threw her like she was nothing. Valkyrie disappeared among the stacks.

Ryan spun, and ran. He didn't know where he was going, but anywhere was better than where he'd just been. The accountant was following, but he had leaped back up so he was off the ground, gliding from bookcase to bookcase, like a hawk chasing a terrified field mouse.

Then Ryan saw it – a green EXIT sign over a fire door. He changed direction, almost tripped over a cowering man who was hiding in the Reference section, and ran on. He was almost at the door when he glanced back over his shoulder, saw the accountant leaping for him. Valkyrie emerged from the stacks and something was happening to her right hand – it was covered in writhing, moving shadows. She whipped her hand and a trail of darkness reached for the accountant, wrapped around his leg. Valkyrie pulled back, hard, and the accountant crunched to the ground.

He snarled, sprang up and turned, and Valkyrie sent a wave of shadows crashing into him. He hit the far wall and that's all Ryan saw, because Valkyrie was pushing him out through the fire door. The alarm wailed as they emerged into the narrow alley behind the library. With Valkyrie's hand pressing into his back, Ryan sprinted towards the road. A gleaming black car was parked illegally, like it was waiting for them. It looked old, but a brand-new kind of old.

Valkyrie opened the door, bundled him in the back. She got behind the wheel, leaving the door open. She started the car and the engine roared, and she slipped into the passenger seat and buckled her belt.

"Seatbelt," she ordered.

Ryan buckled his seatbelt. He looked at the empty driver's seat. "Does it drive itself?" he asked.

"Don't be thick," she replied, looking back at the library. "He just hates it when I drive the Bentley, that's all."

The thin man came sprinting out of the library, clutching his hat in one gloved hand. Ryan blinked. The way the sun caught his bald head made it seem almost white, almost like...

Ryan swallowed. It wasn't the sun. The thin man wasn't bald.

The thin man was a skeleton.

Ryan screamed as the skeleton jumped in behind the wheel.

"Shut him up, please," the skeleton said as the car shot forward.

"Shut up, Ryan," said Valkyrie.

Foe came charging out of the library but the car, the Bentley, was already slicing through traffic. And still Ryan screamed.

"Ryan," Valkyrie said, "stop that."

"He's a skeleton!" Ryan yelled. "Look at him! They killed your friend!"

"No, they didn't," said the skeleton. "But they punched me. A lot. And one of them hit me with a desk. Have you ever been hit with a desk, Ryan? It's sore."

"I was hit with a desk once," Valkyrie said.

"Oh, that's right," said the skeleton. "It really hurts, doesn't it?"

"It does."

Ryan sat in the back seat, petrified. Valkyrie turned to him, sighed, and then gave him the kind of smile usually reserved for idiots, or toddlers, or idiot toddlers.

"Hi," she said. "I'm Valkyrie Cain. My partner here is Skulduggery Pleasant. We just saved your life. The least you can do is not throw up in our car."

THREE

The skeleton's jaw moved when he talked, but he had no tongue. He had no lungs, or vocal cords. There was nothing at all to give him a voice, and yet Skulduggery still talked. Good God, did he talk.

"The short version," he said as they drove, "is that magic exists. Monsters exist. Sorcerers, like myself and Valkyrie, fight to stop other sorcerers, like Foe and his friends, from doing bad things. We're the heroes, if you really must give us a title. They're the villains. We try to stay out of the public eye as much as possible. It's really quite straightforward if you don't think about it too hard."

"But I don't understand," Ryan whispered.

"That's the spirit," Skulduggery said. "We don't have an awful lot of time, so there are some things you're just going to have to accept."

"You're a skeleton."

"Like that."

"But how can you move?"

Valkyrie undid her seatbelt and climbed into the back. "Ryan," she said when she was settled, "the world is an amazing place. It's full of wonderful things and fascinating people and deep mysteries just waiting to be uncovered. In order to not annoy me, though, you've really got to put all of that to one side and concentrate on what we tell you. He's a walking skeleton. I wear tight trousers. Do you have any questions so far?"

"Uh, no."

"Excellent."

"You can feel safe with us," Skulduggery said. "We've saved the world a few times and we've become quite good at it. Really, if I were you, there's no one else I'd rather be with at a time like this."

"Skulduggery," Valkyrie said, "your façade."

"Oh, yes," he said, and his gloved fingers tapped his collarbones. A face flowed up, covering his skull with skin and hair and features. He smiled at a lady in a car they passed and she frowned at him.

"He can only wear a face for half an hour every day," Valkyrie whispered to Ryan. "So he tends to overdo it on the sociable front."

"But all that went on in a library," Ryan said, finally confident enough to form a complete sentence without gibbering. "It's going to be all over the news."

"Actually," Valkyrie responded, "it's not. We have people for that sort of thing. Sometime within the next hour a very nice man called Geoffrey is going to convince everyone who witnessed that fight that they didn't see what they thought they saw. He's kind of a Public Relations officer, in a way – making sure the civilian world doesn't notice the rest of us as we go about our business."

Skulduggery glanced at Ryan over his shoulder. The face he wore was dark-haired and sallow-skinned. "Some people, like Geoffrey, find they are suited to non-combative roles. He's what we call a Sensitive – someone with psychic abilities. Some Sensitives read minds, some see the future – Geoffrey just makes you believe whatever he tells you. Another Sensitive was a man called Deacon Maybury. Which is where you come in."

"I've never heard of him," Ryan said.

"Of course not," said Valkyrie. "I hadn't, either, up until a few days ago. I'd heard of his brother, Davit, who died. There were sextuplets, apparently. Six identical Mayburys. Only four now, though."

"This Deacon Maybury, he's dead, too?"

Skulduggery turned the Bentley off the busy road, down a quieter street. "Deacon was a Sensitive who worked for the Sanctuary – where we work. Sometimes we arrest criminals for whom there is no redemption. If they're susceptible, it's possible to enter their mind and insert a new personality. It's always been a controversial procedure, and it only works if the criminal's will is weak, but the old personality would be subdued, the new one would have a life and a history and memories, and the criminal would get a chance at a normal life. Inserting new personalities was Deacon's job."

"But he got bored," Valkyrie said. "We spoke to people who knew him. He wanted adventure and excitement. He wanted money and power. So he fell in with the wrong crowd – Foe and his gang."

Skulduggery nodded. "A very bad lot. Vincent Foe was a mercenary during the war. I won't tell you what war, I don't want to complicate things. Mercy Charient is, for all intents and purposes, a serial killer. Obloquy, I doubt you'll disagree, is something of a moron – but a savage moron. And then there's Samuel."

Valkyrie made a face. "Bloody vampires."

Ryan sat forward. "That was a vampire? That guy who looked like an accountant?"

"We don't talk about vampires," Skulduggery warned.

"But it was daytime. How could he have been out during the—"

"We don't talk about vampires!" Valkyrie said sharply.

Ryan shrank back. "Sorry," he said.

"Don't worry about it," Skulduggery told him. "Valkyrie used to date a vampire, that's all."

"We didn't *date*," Valkyrie said immediately.

Skulduggery held up a hand. "I'm not judging."

Valkyrie scowled, and looked back at Ryan. "Anyway, Deacon Maybury fell in with Foe's gang, and Foe's gang are nuts. Some people want to take over the world. Some people want to change the world. Foe and his mates want to destroy the world." She shook her head. "They're idiots."

"Nihilists," Skulduggery corrected.

"Idiots," Valkyrie repeated. "There's something called a Doomsday Machine, Ryan. Yes, I know how that sounds. And, yes, it is as stupid as it appears. Some genius went ahead and built a bomb that could blow up the planet. He said he built it so that if the Faceless Ones ever returned, we could kill ourselves and kill them at the same time so that they could never travel to and infect other realities."

Ryan frowned. "Faceless Ones?"

"Don't complicate things," Skulduggery said.

"Yeah, sorry Ryan," said Valkyrie. "Anyway, that's why it exists. So it was sitting there, existing, not harming anyone, and then a few years ago it was stolen. Foe and his gang stole it and hid it – which wouldn't be an easy thing to do because the Machine is bigger than a house."

"Why did they hide it?" Ryan asked. "Why not just set if off?"

"Because they didn't have the key," Skulduggery said. "They spent the next few years searching for it. That's when Deacon joined them. They finally found it, nine days ago. But Deacon had no intention of activating the Machine. He hid the key, shaped like a clasp, to sell to the highest bidder."

"But Foe's gang caught up with him before the auction could take place," Valkyrie said. "They chased him and he accidentally fell into a wood chipper."

Ryan winced.

"Yeah," said Valkyrie.

"So now Foe is hunting for the key," Skulduggery said. "Their hunt led them to the library, and our hunt led us to them. And both hunts have led to you, Ryan."

Ryan looked at his hand. "But the key's gone. It crumbled when I held it. It's just dust now."

"The key wasn't what you held," Skulduggery said. "It's the imprint it left on your skin. I've got good news and bad news for you, Ryan. The bad news is that you're the only one in the world who can activate the Doomsday Machine, and Foe and his gang are never going to stop coming after you. The good news is that with myself and Valkyrie protecting you, you stand a very good chance of emerging from this relatively unscathed."

Valkyrie looked at the back of Skulduggery's head. "You said they'd probably try to cut his hand off."

"I said relatively," Skulduggery reminded her.

FOUR

Deacon Maybury's apartment was trashed.

Skulduggery and Valkyrie went first, to check if it was safe, and Ryan crept in after them. Papers littered the bad carpet. The ugly couch had been slashed open and its stuffing had been pulled out like fluffy intestines. Chairs were overturned, picture frames smashed and every drawer taken from its slot, the contents dumped and scattered.

"What exactly are we looking for in this mess?" Valkyrie asked.

"Foe secured the Doomsday Machine somewhere," Skulduggery said, picking through the debris. "We need to find out where. Maybe we'll get lucky and discover that Deacon was an avid journal keeper. But if we can't find a solid lead to take us to the Machine, there might be something else here, a clue or a name, something that will take us a step further."

Valkyrie sighed. "I hate looking for clues."

Ryan smiled at the cuteness of Valkyrie's sulk.

"Looking for clues is an integral part of detective work," Skulduggery told her.

"I prefer the part where we hit people."

"That's just because you have a violent nature. You should endeavour to be more peace-loving, like Ryan."

Ryan stopped admiring Valkyrie and frowned. "Why am I peace-loving?"

"Hmm?" Skulduggery said, looking up. "Oh, I meant nothing by it. I just assumed you were peace-loving because you seem to be terrible at violence. Plus, you scream a lot."

"Just because I don't go around getting into fights every day doesn't mean I can't fight," Ryan said, his face growing warm.

"Not being good at violence is nothing to be ashamed of," Skulduggery said, standing a filing cabinet upright and sifting through it. "If there were more people like you in the world, there'd be less need for people like us."

"I don't have a violent nature," Valkyrie growled.

"And I'm not peace-loving," Ryan insisted.

"But you do scream a lot," Skulduggery said.

"How can you know that?" Ryan asked. "You've known me for, like, two hours."

"And in those two hours, you have spent most of your time

screaming." Skulduggery shrugged. "I really can't see how my logic can be faulted."

"I don't have a violent nature," Valkyrie repeated.

"Of course you don't," Skulduggery said as he continued to sift the files in the cabinet. "Entirely my mistake."

Valkyrie scowled and started sorting through the papers on the floor. She hadn't been too interested in Ryan's defence of his manliness. He couldn't say he blamed her. She was a sorcerer who battled evil villains every other day. He was a chubby loser who needed girls to fight his battles for him. The only way he was going to change how she thought of him was to do something so brave and noble that she couldn't fail to be impressed. He turned and screamed at a middle-aged woman who stood in the doorway.

The middle-aged woman was startled by the scream, but not half as startled as Ryan himself. It had been a surprisingly high-pitched scream this time, and to make matters worse, it resulted in Valkyrie leaping in front of him protectively.

"Oh," said the middle-aged woman. She wore a floral dress and a cardigan. As middle-aged women went, she wasn't particularly frightening.

Skulduggery walked forward, a new false face smiling broadly. "Hello there," he said. "How are you on this fine day? Come in, come in. And you are...?"

"Francine," the woman said, a little flustered. "I live down the hall... What are you doing in Deacon Maybury's apartment?"

"You know Deacon?" Skulduggery asked. Valkyrie walked behind her, checked the corridor for anyone else, then stepped back in and closed the door.

"Well, yes," said Francine, frowning at Valkyrie and then looking at Skulduggery. "He's my neighbour and he's a good man. If you're robbing him, I must warn you – we don't take kindly to that sort of thing here."

"We're not robbing him," Skulduggery said. "But I'm afraid I have some bad news."

"Is it Deacon?" Francine asked, her eyes wide.

"It is."

"Is he sick?"

"It's a little worse than that."

She gasped. "He's dying?"

"He was briefly dying," said Skulduggery. "Now he's dead."

Francine's mouth dropped open. "What? Deacon... Deacon is *dead*?"

"I'm afraid so."

"Oh, no. Oh, no, no, no." She sagged, and Valkyrie caught her before she collapsed. "My Deacon... My poor Deacon..."

Valkyrie staggered over to the only upright chair, and dumped Francine into it.

"He was so strong," Francine sobbed. "So proud. So much dignity. How did he die?"

"Wood chipper," said Valkyrie.

Francine wailed again, pounding the table with her little fists. "Why?" she cried. "Why did you take him, Lord?"

Valkyrie looked at Skulduggery, and Skulduggery shrugged.

"Uh," Valkyrie said. "I'm sorry for your, you know, your loss. I'm sure he was a great... I'm sure..." She faltered, and gave a shrug of her own. Ryan looked at Skulduggery, but he showed no signs of offering any real comfort to the poor woman.

"You obviously loved him very much," Ryan said, surprising himself by stepping forward.

"I did," Francine sobbed.

"I'm sure he loved you back."

Francine looked up, her eyes red and puffy and pleading. "Did he ever mention me?"

Ryan hesitated, and Valkyrie smirked at him from behind Francine. "All the time," he said. "Yes. God, every time I spoke to him he was all, Francine this and Francine that and... ohh, how I love Francine."

"He said that?"

"Uh, something along those lines, definitely..."

Francine clasped her hands to her chest. "I knew it," she said. "I knew he loved me. All those long silences. All those awkward moments. I should have told him I felt the same way. Then we could have... Then we could have..."

She broke off into a fit of sobbing. Behind her, Valkyrie gave Ryan the thumbs up. He had a feeling she meant it sarcastically.

"Did you talk to Deacon much?" Skulduggery asked, leaning down to gently pat her hand. "Did you tell each other about your days? Did you confide in each other...?"

"With a love like ours," Francine warbled, "we didn't need words."

"How inconvenient," Skulduggery muttered, straightening up immediately and walking away.

"Francine," Ryan said, "we're looking for something that Deacon was keeping for us. Do you know where it is? It'd be big, now, as big as a house."

Francine blinked away tears. "What could he have had that was as big as a house?"

Ryan frowned. He really had no answer to that.

"A house," Valkyrie said quickly. "He had a house. He was keeping it for us. One of those mobile houses, you know the kind."

"A mobile home?" Francine asked.

"Something like that. A little bigger. Do you remember if he ever mentioned a warehouse, or some kind of big storage facility that he visited?"

Francine frowned. "Well, I... I heard him on the phone once. I remember him saying something about having the paperwork for a warehouse that was cluttering up his files."

"It has to be here somewhere," Skulduggery said, going back to the filing cabinet. Valkyrie went into the bedroom, and started pulling the place apart.

"Did I say something wrong?" Francine asked.

"No," Ryan said. "Actually, you've been a big help. Would you like something? A cup of tea or...?"

"I should get back to my apartment," Francine said, standing slowly. "I need a lie-down. This is all... this is all a big shock to me."

"I'm really sorry," Ryan said.

She smiled weakly, took a step and swayed. Ryan jumped for her, wrapping one of her arms round his neck.

"I'll help you," he said.

"Thank you," she replied. A tear rolled down her cheek. "You're very nice."

While Skulduggery and Valkyrie searched, Ryan hobbled along with Francine out of the apartment and down the corridor. She was light but awkward.

"Your friends are a little odd," Francine said.

"I know."

"The girl's pretty, though. Is she your girlfriend?"

Ryan gave a laugh, realised he was blushing. "No, she's not. We've just met, actually."

"My apartment's around the corner," Francine said, gesturing ahead of them and sniffling. "Do you want my advice? Don't make the same mistake I made with Deacon. Tell her how you feel."

"I really just met her."

"But you like her, don't you?"

"I, yeah, I suppose."

He helped her round the corner.

"Seize the moment," Francine said. "You never know when you might get another chance at happiness."

"I'll think about it," he promised, hoping that she'd change the subject before anyone overheard them.

"My apartment's just up ahead," Francine said, standing a little straighter. "You really are very nice. Such good manners, helping me all the way to my door."

"It's no trouble at all."

"Unfortunately," Francine said, "it will be."

"Sorry? It will be what?"

"Trouble," Francine said. "It will be a lot of trouble."

Vincent Foe walked out of the apartment ahead of them.

FIVE

Ryan spun, grabbed Francine, tried to drag her with him, but she laughed. She got an arm round his throat before he could call for help and hauled him backwards. He kicked and struggled, but she was much too strong, and then he was in the apartment and Foe was closing the door behind them.

Francine released him, and Ryan jumped away, almost colliding with Obloquy. Samuel watched him from the corner of the room.

"If you shout or scream," Foe said, "we'll kill you."

"And then we'll kill Valkyrie," said Francine. She looked at Foe, and grinned. "He's got a little crush on her."

Foe raised an eyebrow. "Is that right? Well, can't say I blame you, Ryan – she is a fine-looking girl. If I were a few hundred years younger, I'd be in there like a shot, believe you me. I'm not altogether sure what she'd ever see in *you*, though. You don't seem quite up to her standard. No offence, but you're kind of... unexceptional."

"Maybe he's hoping she'll like him for his sense of humour," Obloquy chuckled.

"Young love," Foe said, almost wistfully. "If you're lucky, you might have a chance to confess to her your eternal devotion, so long as you do exactly what I tell you."

Ryan's mouth was so dry his voice was a croak. "I'm not going to help you destroy the world."

"Yes, you are."

"It doesn't make any sense. If you want to die, why don't you just kill yourselves and leave everyone else out of it?"

"Where's the drama in that?" asked Francine.

Foe glanced at her. "That's getting really disconcerting, you know."

"Ain't that something?" she murmured, and Ryan watched as Francine flickered, and he glimpsed someone underneath, someone slimmer, wearing black, with a bandaged arm... And then Francine was gone, and Mercy stood there. "That better?"

"Much," Foe said, turning his attention back to Ryan. "We're going to destroy the world because there is absolutely no point to its continued existence."

There were a hundred things Ryan wanted to say. *That's it? That's the reason? You want to kill everyone because you can't see the point? What kind of stupid, pathetic, selfish reason is that?* But he didn't say any of it, because he was too scared. Because he wasn't the hero. Because he was the one who was waiting for someone to rescue him.

There was a knock on the door.

"Francine?"

It was Valkyrie's voice. Mercy stepped up to Ryan, pressing a blade against his belly.

"Francine," Valkyrie called, "is Ryan in there with you?"

Foe looked at Ryan, and held his finger to his lips as Obloquy went to the door. The knife dug into Ryan's skin painfully. He had to warn her. He had to. He couldn't just stand here and keep quiet.

"I know what you're thinking," Mercy whispered. "I can see it all over your face. Just know that if you make a sound, I'll kill you and cut off your hand."

Valkyrie knocked again, and Mercy looked towards the door, and a sudden pressure built up inside Ryan until he shoved her away from him. And then Samuel was there, a hand closing round his throat and Ryan was moving with his feet off the ground, slamming back into the wall. Samuel's fingers were like steel and Ryan's vision clouded, dimmed, and a distant part of him knew he was about to pass out.

The window exploded. Ryan dropped. He sucked in air and his head pounded. There was movement all around him. Foe flew backwards over the couch. Skulduggery was there, flipping Mercy over his hip. The door came down, on top of Obloquy. Valkyrie, clambering over it, shouting at Ryan to run. Ryan's legs, like concrete. Around him shouts and curses and the sound of breaking things. Samuel, hitting Valkyrie so hard she folded in mid-air. Foe diving at Skulduggery.

The floor moved and Ryan realised he was stumbling. He didn't even remember ordering his legs to do it. He climbed over the door, slid down it, rolled out into the corridor. Got to his hands and knees, trying to get his brain back in gear.

"Oh, God, oh, God," he muttered, and stood, walked and ran, ran down to the corner, through the corridor, running for the stairs, leaving Skulduggery and Valkyrie to fight behind him. He got to the stairs and stopped. He couldn't. He couldn't leave them. They'd saved his life. He had this stupid key imprinted on to his hand and they were fighting to protect him. He couldn't abandon them. He had to help. There was nothing he could do, but he had to help. He had to try. He had to do something. They would want him to run, he knew that. They would want him to run to safety, to leave the fighting to the professionals. They didn't expect him to turn back and help. But he had no choice.

Ryan turned, ran back the way he had come. An old man was in the corridor, blinking.

"I've phoned the police," he said.

"Get back inside," Ryan told him. "Lock the door."

The old man nodded, shuffled out of the corridor, and then Valkyrie came crashing through the wall of his apartment in a shower of broken plaster and chipboard. The old man howled in shock, ran past Ryan, sprinting round the corner with surprising agility. Valkyrie was on the floor in a cloud of dust, groaning and trying to get up. Obloquy climbed through the broken wall after her and saw Ryan.

"Run!" Valkyrie shouted.

Ryan ran.

He got to the corner before he heard Obloquy's voice in his head – *pain, feel pain, too much pain to move* – and Ryan staggered, doubled up, sweat breaking out on his forehead. He looked back, saw Obloquy, and now he dropped to his knees, trying not to cry out. The pain was building, intensifying, the closer Obloquy got to him, and then Valkyrie was there, covered in dust and swinging both arms, and the pain went away as Obloquy hurtled into the wall.

Mercy stepped out behind her and Ryan shouted a warning, but even as Valkyrie spun, Mercy was opening her mouth, and that red stream of energy slammed straight into Valkyrie's chest, throwing her back. Skulduggery leaped from nowhere, barging into Mercy, and Ryan scrambled over to Valkyrie, his eyes wide, expecting to see a gaping, bloody hole. But when she came to a groaning stop, there was no injury – just trails of steam that rose from her jacket. He grabbed her, pulled her up.

There were gunshots, and with every deafening bang, Ryan yelped and flinched, but he managed to drag Valkyrie round the corner before either of them was horribly killed. She straightened up, taking a deep breath and rubbing her chest.

He had to ask. "Why aren't you dead?"

"Protective clothing," she said, eyes scanning the corridor. "You don't think I wear this outfit just because it's tight, do you?"

She ran to the window at the end of the corridor, flattened both hands against the air. The glass exploded outwards and the frame splintered. "Come on," she said, climbing on to the narrow sill.

"Uh," Ryan said.

She looked back in. "Move!"

He swallowed, and did what she ordered. As he searched for the securest position possible, fingers curling round the edge of the wall, he tried not to look at the concrete courtyard below them. "We're... we're not going to jump, are we?"

She took hold of his arm, and said gently, "Not if you don't want to."

He relaxed, his grip on the edge of the wall loosening slightly, and that's when she stepped off the sill and yanked him after her.

Ryan screamed as they plummeted to the ground, the wind rushing into his mouth and up his nose and through his hair and suddenly it was buffeting them both, slowing their descent. He saw Valkyrie's hand move, like she was orchestrating the air. They landed heavily, but at least they didn't go splat.

Ryan staggered away from her. "Oh my God. Oh my God."

Skulduggery dropped down in front of him and Ryan screamed again.

"Well said," Skulduggery muttered, reloading his revolver. "We'd better hurry, now. Come along."

They ran through the tunnel connecting the courtyard to the street on the other side of the apartment buildings. Skulduggery put his gun away and let his façade flow over his skull. They got in the Bentley and the car roared and shot forward.

"Everyone OK?" Skulduggery asked.

"I'm in pain," Valkyrie groaned. "Ryan?"

Ryan nodded quickly. "I'm fine. I'm OK. I'm not hurt."

"Are you shaking yet?"

Ryan looked at his hand. "No."

"It'll start any minute now."

Ryan's hand began to tremble violently. "Oh, wow, yeah. I'm definitely shaking now." He laughed. It was a weird sound.

"Geoffrey's going to have his hands full explaining this one," Valkyrie said as she brushed the dust off her jacket. It rose from her in small clouds.

"Please don't do that in the car," Skulduggery said.

"You didn't say Mercy could do that," Ryan said. "She changed shape. She's a shape-changer."

"Actually," Skulduggery said, "she's not. Francine was a psychic image. Basically, an illusion. Physically, there *was* no disguise. That was Mercy sitting at the table, talking to us, in her normal form. But our minds reinterpreted Mercy as Francine. We heard Francine's voice."

"I smelled her perfume," Ryan said.

"All an illusion. The only person in Dublin, in all of Ireland really, capable of disguising her like that is a man called Robert Crasis. In wartime, his skills were invaluable. We might have twenty people ready to storm an enemy position, but thanks to Crasis it would look like we had a thousand."

"So he's a good guy?" Valkyrie asked. "Then why did he help Foe?"

"I don't know," Skulduggery said. "I suppose we'll have to ask him."

SIX

On the way to see Crasis, they stopped off so Ryan and Valkyrie could get something to eat. They each bought a Coke and a sandwich, but Skulduggery made them eat with their heads sticking out of the window to avoid crumbs being dropped. Ryan didn't dare open his Coke in case it fizzed out over the seats, and by the time the Bentley pulled over, his throat was parched.

Skulduggery led the way to an old workshop in a quiet part of town. He knocked on the door and waited. When Robert Crasis opened the door, he looked at Skulduggery and Valkyrie, but barely glanced at Ryan. He was a man in his sixties. He was tall, broad-shouldered. His hair was grey, his jaw coated in stubble.

"Can I help you?"

"Hello, Robert," said Skulduggery. "Mind if we come in?"

"Skulduggery?" Crasis frowned, peering at him. "Since when do you have a face?"

"It's a relatively new addition. We'd like a word, if that's OK."

Crasis hesitated, then stepped back to allow them through the door.

They walked into a carpenter's workshop, to the smell of wood shavings and varnish. It was a big space, no windows, lit in spots that allowed the darkness to soak in around the edges.

Skulduggery let his face melt away, and he took off his hat and looked around. "This reminds me of your place in Venice."

"Before it was burned down," Crasis responded. "Skulduggery, I don't mean to be rude, but I was really hoping never to see you again."

"You know why we're here."

Crasis shook his head. The muscles in his jaw tightened. "All I want is to be left alone. I'm out of that game, but people... people keep pulling me back in. After years of not being involved in any craziness, suddenly there's one after another, when all I want to do is be a carpenter and grow old."

"You *want* to get old?" Valkyrie asked, sounding surprised.

"Staying young isn't all it's cracked up to be," Crasis said. "I've been young and strong and healthy for two hundred years. I've had to leave my home countless times to stop my mortal friends from wondering why I never seem to age. Then I met Sarah, and she became my wife, and suddenly I had someone I wanted to grow old with. So I stopped doing magic. Up until two weeks ago, I hadn't done magic in nearly fifteen years. I went grey. Last month I noticed a bald spot. It was working. I was ageing again. But now? Now it'll take years for me to age a *day*."

"This last job you did," Skulduggery said, "it was for Mercy Charient, wasn't it?"

Crasis nodded. "They came in the back, the whole lot of them. Deacon Maybury, the idiot, had mentioned what I used to do for the Sanctuary, and they remembered. Of course they remembered. So they came in, threatened me, threatened my wife, my kids... What could I do?"

"We're not blaming you," Skulduggery said.

"So I did it. I made her into a frumpy little woman. It wasn't my best work, but it would do for a few hours, which is all they wanted it for. Sorry if any of you were hurt, but I have a family to protect."

"We weren't hurt," Valkyrie said. "But Deacon Maybury... he was killed a few days ago."

Crasis looked at her for a moment, saying nothing. He swallowed, and nodded. "That's a shame," he said, his eyes drifting down. "He was... I'd like to say he was a good man, but he was... Deacon. I owed him, though. He's the one who actually introduced me to Sarah. He'd asked her out the previous week and she'd laughed so hard she fell over. It was love at first sight for Sarah and me. So I owed him, I did. It's a... it's a real pity I'll never get to repay him."

Ryan tried opening his Coke quietly. It fizzed and they all looked at him. He blushed.

"Maybe you can repay him," Skulduggery said, looking back at

Crasis. "When you were working on Mercy, did any of them say anything? They have the Doomsday Machine hidden away somewhere and we need to find it."

"Foe has the Doomsday Machine?" Crasis said, his eyes widening. "And Deacon was working with those guys?"

"He planned to sell the key to whoever paid him enough," Valkyrie said.

Crasis stared at her, stared at Skulduggery, stared at Ryan, then stared at his hands. "It's a good thing he's dead," he said. "Because if I had the chance, I'd kill him myself. I did hear something, actually. I heard Obloquy complain that there were always people around whenever they'd check on 'it'. They never said what it was, but obviously it was the Machine. Mercy was supposed to stay still and quiet while I worked, but she kept moving and joining in with the conversation. She was joking that if their car broke down, they'd all have to get the Luas. She said they'd be riding the tram to the end of the world. I told her to shut up or I'd have to start again. I should have let her keep talking."

"You wouldn't happen to have a street map of Dublin, would you?" Skulduggery asked.

"Uh, yeah," Crasis said. "I think I have one somewhere around here."

He went off to search, and Skulduggery picked up a thick felt pen off a desk that was littered with paperwork. "They've hidden the Machine in a public place," he said, "and it's somewhere on or near a tram line."

Crasis came back with a tattered map and laid it out on a large, freshly carved table. Skulduggery started drawing lines down streets, drawing in the routes the Luas tram went down. Crasis and Valkyrie pored over the map and Ryan, not wanting to feel left out, did the same. He put his Coke on the table and did his best to appear as smart as the other people in the room.

When Skulduggery had marked all the routes they examined the map anew.

"Lot of public places," Valkyrie murmured.

"A very large amount," Ryan said, nodding like he was contributing.

"Ryan," Skulduggery said, and for a moment Ryan thought that he'd accidentally solved the mystery.

"Yes?" he said eagerly.

"Could you take your Coke off the map, please?"

"Oh," Ryan said. "Sorry." He lifted his bottle. There was now a wet circle around Dundrum. To hide his blush he took a long swig from his drink.

"The heaviest population centres would be here, here and here," Skulduggery said, marking the map with Xs. "If the Machine is hidden outdoors, we should be looking for areas that have had extensive construction work in the last few years. If it's indoors, then we're looking for new public buildings or shopping areas."

The Coke went down the wrong way and Ryan choked, gagged, and spat a mouthful all over the map.

Skulduggery, Crasis and Valkyrie looked at him.

"Sorry," he wheezed, before doubling over into a coughing fit.

"Maybe you should get some air," Skulduggery suggested.

Ryan nodded, coughing too much to respond, and staggered out of the door. His eyes were streaming and he knew his face was glowing an attractive shade of red. He went to the Bentley and leaned against it, finally getting the coughing under control. Not his finest moment.

"How're you doing, Ryan?"

He looked around as Valkyrie walked up.

"I'm OK," he said. "Just choking a bit. Sorry about that. I hope I didn't spit any on you."

"Don't worry about it."

He became aware of her looking at him and he looked away.

"Why do you do that?" she asked.

"Why do I do what?"

"Why do you look away whenever I look at you?"

"Um," Ryan said, "I don't know. I think, once I realise that I'm looking someone in the eye, I forget how long I'm supposed to do it. So I don't know, I suppose I look away before it gets weird."

She smiled. "You're an oddball."

"Yeah," he said, sagging.

Valkyrie didn't notice the sag. She was looking up the street, watching the people pass. "But that's OK. We're all oddballs here."

Now that she wasn't paying attention, he could look at her. He liked her face. She was very pretty, had a cute nose and a single dimple when she smiled. He'd always wanted a girlfriend like her – someone impressive, someone confident. He'd like to go back to school once the summer was over and have her beside him. Then everyone would stop and stare, and they'd think to themselves that there must be more to this Ryan guy after all.

But he'd never get a girlfriend like her. He knew that. Girls like Valkyrie saw him as a friend only. They went off with the good-looking guys or the cool guys or the guys who didn't make fools of themselves at regular intervals. A girl like Valkyrie would never be impressed with someone like Ryan.

He looked away before she looked back. He didn't want her to catch him watching.

"You're coping pretty well, you know," she said, facing him again. "When I first saw Skulduggery and all this stuff, I freaked. I actually blacked out."

"You fainted?"

"No," she said, her good humour fading. "I blacked out. There's a difference."

He grinned. "You fainted."

"Shut up. You're handling this well, that's all I'm saying. You haven't once asked to go home."

His grin went away. "Why would I? You're not that much older than me, you know."

She frowned. "What's that got to do with anything?"

"I'm fifteen. You're, I don't know, seventeen?"

"So?"

"That's only two years' difference," Ryan said hotly. "We're practically the same age and you're treating me like I'm a child. Fine, OK? You have no interest in me. I'm used to that. But don't stand there and talk down to me like you're so much better than I am."

Valkyrie looked at him and didn't say anything. He started to feel stupid.

Then she folded her arms and tilted her hips and it only got worse. "First of all," she said, "I'm not talking down to you *or* treating you like a child."

"But you expect me to want to go home."

"Of course I do. You were attacked. You're in danger. You're hanging around with people who can do magic. You've had what we call in the business a shock. Usually, when people get a shock they want to retreat to a safe place so that they can process what they've seen. Most people would want to go home right now. But not you. You haven't mentioned home, haven't mentioned your family, haven't tried to run off or call the cops. You are coping well, Ryan. That's all I said. That's all I meant. I have no idea what our ages have to do with anything or what you're talking about when you say I have no interest."

"Oh," he said.

"And the only time you have actually acted like a child," she said, "is right now. I don't like petulance, Ryan. I don't respond well to it."

"Right."

"When it comes to this kind of stuff, I'm the only one who is allowed to sulk. Skulduggery understands that. Do you?"

"Yes," he said, nodding quickly. "I'm sorry."

"You better be."

"I really am."

"I gave you a compliment and you jumped down my throat." She narrowed her eyes at him. "And what was all that about having no interest? Having no interest in what?"

"Uh, nothing."

"Don't make me hit you, Ryan."

He winced. "I don't know, I was just... I thought you saw me as a, you know, as a kid and... I was just saying that while, obviously, you'd never, like, go out with someone like me, that's still no reason to talk down to me. Which you weren't doing, and I apologise again for thinking you were."

"But what does me going out or not going out with someone like you have to do with anything?"

Ryan tried a smile. "I really don't know any more. It made sense when I said it."

She shook her head, looked about to say something else, then stopped. "Oh," she said. She was looking at him now like Andrea from school had looked at him when he'd asked her to the movies. She was looking at him with a kind of gentle pity.

"It's OK," he said. "You don't have to worry about it."

"Ryan, we only just met."

He nodded. "Absolutely."

"It's not that I never would," Valkyrie said, "but I generally go for guys... older than me, you know?"

Ryan tried a laugh. "Like vampires."

Her tone turned sharp. "We don't joke about vampires, Ryan."

"Right. Sorry."

"I think you're nice," Valkyrie said, softening again. "But let's concentrate on being friends for the time being, all right?"

"Sure. Yep. Don't worry."

The workshop door opened and Skulduggery emerged. "Ryan," he said, "stop leaning against my car."

"Sorry," Ryan mumbled, straightening up.

Skulduggery stopped in front of them. He was wearing a different face, and he put his hat on. "I have solved the mystery," he announced. "Before I take you to where the Doomsday Machine is located, I would like you both to acknowledge how brilliant I am."

"Uh," said Ryan, "you're brilliant."

"You're OK," said Valkyrie.

"That's good enough for me," Skulduggery nodded. "Get in the car. We've got a world to save."

SEVEN

They drove into Dundrum town centre and parked in the multi-storey. Along the way, Skulduggery had pulled over three times to allow Ryan to pee. If Ryan had wanted Valkyrie to start thinking of him as older and more mature than he was, he knew he was not going about it the right way.

Once the Bentley found a place to park, they got out.

"How did you know it was here?" Valkyrie asked.

Skulduggery checked his façade in the wing mirror, then straightened up. "Simple detective work," he said. "We're going to need somewhere quiet to wait until everyone's gone. We'll search for the Machine tonight, dismantle it and then it'll all be over."

They started walking. "Shouldn't we call in the Cleavers?"

Valkyrie asked. "We'll find it faster with a hundred people looking for it."

"I'd prefer to approach this with a little more delicacy," Skulduggery said. "The three of us should be fine." He looked at Ryan. "Nervous?"

"A little," Ryan admitted. "What if Foe and the others are waiting for us?"

"They might pay a visit to the Machine," Skulduggery conceded, "but they're not going to be lying in wait. They have no idea that we know it's here."

They passed from the car park into the mall. Valkyrie appeared to trust Skulduggery without hesitation, but Ryan was more cautious. Every time someone walked too close, he'd hop away, waiting for their image to flicker and drop, revealing Mercy or Obloquy or Foe. But the people in the mall seemed to be actual people, focused on their conversations or their shopping, and the only time they glanced at Ryan was when he stumbled awkwardly away from them.

Valkyrie raised an eyebrow at him. "You're not very good at acting casual."

"I forget how," Ryan confessed, skipping away from a suspicious-looking two-year-old holding a balloon.

Skulduggery and Valkyrie walked up the travelator and Ryan followed, flinching away from an elderly woman with a wrinkled prune-face. They approached a stocky security guard.

"Excuse me, good sir," Skulduggery began.

The security guard turned to them. "I'm a woman," she said.

"And a fetching one you are, too," Skulduggery continued, smiling. "Which way to the security control room?"

The security guard frowned. "Why? What business do you have there? Who are you?"

"All good questions," Skulduggery said, nodding, "and all questions I would love to answer. Unfortunately, we only have time for *one* answer, and since my question was the *first* and, let's be honest, the most *important* question, I feel that it is the question that deserves an answer. So, your security control room?"

The security guard folded her arms. "Do you have the authority to be there?"

Skulduggery's false face fixed her with a glare. "Do I have the authority?" he repeated. "Do *I* have the *authority*? Tell me, my dear, do I not *look* like I have the authority? Do I not *look* like the type of person who goes wherever he sees fit to go? Or do I look like the kind of person who needs *permission* to do the things that need to be done?"

"Uh," said the security guard, her arms no longer folded.

Skulduggery loomed over her. "There are things in this world that would turn your hair *white*. Threats and dangers to your very way of life that would send you shrieking into the corner to tremble and sob. Someone needs to protect the world from these dangers and threats. Is that someone going to be you? Is it? Because if it is, my companions and I will leave, right now, and entrust to you our continued survival. But if you have doubts, if you think you might falter right when you are needed to make the ultimate sacrifice, then tell us now and step back, for saving the world is what we do, and we're really very good at it."

The security guard's lip trembled, and she pointed to a door. "That way," she said. "Turn left."

Skulduggery clamped a hand on to her shoulder. "You are doing fine work," he told her, and led the way to the door. When they were through he walked past the left turn, to a room at the end of the concrete corridor. Inside was a table and two chairs. Ryan reckoned this must be where they kept shoplifters while they waited for the cops to arrive.

"We shouldn't be bothered in here," Skulduggery said, closing the door behind them. His false face melted away as he looked at his pocket watch. "Three hours until closing. Make yourselves comfortable."

He sat at the table and took off his hat. Ryan and Valkyrie remained standing.

"I still don't understand why they want to destroy the world," said Ryan. "Foe said he couldn't see the point of life but, I mean, that's a really *silly* reason..."

"They're bad guys," Valkyrie told him. "Villains. Some villains have proper plans. Others don't. They've just been around for a few hundred years. Given enough time, a stray thought can become an obsession, and then a purpose. They're nuts, Ryan. They're actually insane people who all agree with one another."

"Insanity fuels insanity," Skulduggery said, nodding, "just as stupidity fuels stupidity."

"Speaking of stupidity," Valkyrie said, "I'm just going to ask this one more time and you better give me an answer, because I haven't a clue how you worked it out. How do we know the Machine is here?"

A moment passed before Skulduggery spoke again. "Ryan told me," he said.

Ryan looked at him. "I told you what?"

Skulduggery raised his head, and he looked at Ryan with those hollow eye sockets. "You told me the Machine was hidden in Dundrum. Completely unconsciously, of course. You tried to hide Dundrum on the map with your bottle of Coke, then you tried to distract us with a coughing fit."

"Uh," Ryan said, "what?"

"The drive over confirmed it. Stopping three times to relieve yourself? You were only delaying the inevitable."

"No, I wasn't," Ryan said. "What are you talking about? How would I know where the Machine was hidden?"

"And why would Ryan be trying to stop us from finding it?" Valkyrie asked.

Skulduggery hesitated. "Ryan, why haven't you asked to go home?"

Ryan frowned, genuinely and completely puzzled. "What?"

"You haven't asked to go home," Skulduggery said. "You haven't tried to *call* home to tell them you're OK, even though they must be worried about you by now."

Ryan glowered, angry at having to admit this in front of Valkyrie. "I'm... I'm running away."

Valkyrie's eyes widened. "What? Why?"

"It's a long story."

"No, it isn't," said Skulduggery.

Valkyrie swatted the skeleton's arm. "Skulduggery, shut up. Ryan, what's wrong?"

"My... my dad died. My mum remarried. He's an OK guy but... I don't like being in that house. It reminds me—"

"No, it doesn't," Skulduggery said.

"Stop interrupting!" Ryan shouted. "You don't know what it's like! You don't know!"

"You don't know, either," Skulduggery said. "I'm really sorry to have to tell you this, Ryan, but the reason you don't want to go home is because there is no home to go to. Ryan, you're not real. You don't exist."

Ryan stared at him. "What?"

"You're Deacon Maybury," Skulduggery said. "You're a hiding place who thinks it's a boy."

EIGHT

Ryan backed away. "You're crazy."

"I am," Skulduggery said. "I'm also right. Deacon planned this whole thing – as much as he could, anyway. He hid the key, faked his own death and then went to Crasis – called in that old favour. He told Crasis to make him look inconspicuous – someone Foe would never suspect of having anything to do with any of this."

"Skulduggery," Valkyrie said softly. "Are you sure?"

"Crasis only looked at Ryan twice in the whole time we were there. He wanted to tell us, but I expect he'd made a promise to stay quiet. Once his new image was in place, Deacon went to work on his own mind. He couldn't take the chance that Obloquy would be able to read his thoughts. He had to disappear completely. He subdued his personality and replaced it with Ryan – a good boy. A decent person."

"You're wrong," Ryan said. "I don't know what you're talking about, but you're wrong."

"I wish I was," Skulduggery said, "but I rarely am. Deacon planned to hide away until Foe lost his trail. Ryan, can you remember what you did this morning?"

"I got up," Ryan said. "Had breakfast with my mum."

"Again, I'm sorry to tell you, but that's a false memory. The person you think is your mother doesn't exist."

Ryan had an ache, somewhere in his chest. "No. She's my mum. She's my mum and I love her."

"I know you do," Skulduggery said. "Deacon is very thorough. But there's only so much a Sensitive can do to suppress a personality, especially when he works on himself. Cracks start to show much earlier. That's why you were at the library today. Somewhere in your subconscious, you knew it was important. You knew exactly where to find that key."

Ryan realised he was crying. He wiped away tears.

"When we were looking at the map, you knew we wanted to dismantle the Machine. Your subconscious didn't want that. So it tried to block our way here."

"You're wrong," Ryan said.

"I'm right. You know I'm right."

"No. No, you're not. I know who I am."

"Which is why you're crying."

"No," Ryan said. "Shut up. Stop it. I know who I am. I'm me. What you're saying is stupid. It's ridiculous. I'd know if I wasn't me. I'd know it."

"No, you wouldn't. And I'm very sorry."

They hadn't spoken to him in three hours. They sat over there, at the table. Occasionally, he'd hear them talking softly. They were giving him space.

From somewhere outside, he could hear the announcements, alerting shoppers that the mall was closing. He imagined all the friends and families hurrying out, chatting and laughing and mothers dragging kids and kids wailing and crying...

Ryan remembered being a kid. He remembered his mum. And his dad. He remembered how much he loved his mum, and how much he missed his dad. He didn't want to run away any more. He wanted to go home. But the more he thought about going home, the less real it became.

It was dark in the room when Valkyrie came over. She sat on the ground beside him, her back against the wall.

"Hey, Ryan," she said, her voice quiet.

"That's not my name," he told her. His own voice shook like it always did when he was emotional. At least, that's what he remembered.

"I'm going to call you Ryan until I can't call you Ryan any more," Valkyrie said. "I don't care about Deacon. I've never met him. I don't know him. I know you, Ryan. And I like you."

He nodded. Didn't answer.

"We're going to go looking for the Machine now," she said. "We have a few hours before the cleaning crews get here. Skulduggery thinks dismantling the bomb won't be a problem. Do you still want to do it?"

Ryan tried to see her pretty face in the gloom. "What would you do if I didn't? Would you cut off my hand and dismantle it yourself? How do you know you can trust me? I'm Deacon, after all."

"You're still you."

"There *is* no me."

Her hand found his. Despite himself, Ryan's heartbeat quickened. "We all have a side to ourselves that we don't like," she said. "Skulduggery has one. I have one. Now you have one. But you don't have to be ruled by it. You can make your own choices, Ryan. Deacon wants to sell the Machine – to make some money and then leave the mess for someone else to deal with. You want to take it apart so that nobody can ever use it. You can choose to help us. You can choose to help *me*."

"And me," Skulduggery said from the other side of the room.

"Shut up," Valkyrie said, not turning away from Ryan.

"Right," said Skulduggery.

The ghost of a smile found its way on to Ryan's lips. "If I do help you," he said, "that would really annoy Deacon, wouldn't it?"

"Oh," said Valkyrie, "it would."

Ryan liked that idea. It was the only way he could think of to have his revenge on a man who had snatched away a family and a life that were never real in the first place. But Ryan's hurt was real. His pain was real. And for the next few hours, at least, Ryan himself was determined that he himself would be real.

"I have one condition," Ryan said.

He saw the outline of Valkyrie's head tilting to one side. "OK," she said cautiously.

"If I do this, and I dismantle the bomb, can I kiss you?"

He felt her slow, slow smile. "We'll have to see about that," she said, and got up. She pulled him to his feet.

Skulduggery led the way out into the mall. The shops themselves were dark and shuttered, but the main strip of the mall was still lit. It was odd, being in a space designed for crowds and seeing it empty. It didn't fit. It wasn't right. It was, all of a sudden, incredibly lonely.

They walked down the deactivated travelator, no one talking. They reached the ground floor and Ryan wandered around, his hand held open in front of him. Skulduggery had insisted that once he got close to the Machine, he'd start to feel something. A buzzing, maybe. A tingle. Ryan had asked if it would be sore. Skulduggery couldn't promise anything.

Valkyrie walked behind him. She pitied him. He knew she did. Of course she did. Who wouldn't? He was a pitiful person who wasn't even a person. He didn't even know what he looked like, not really. He knew he wasn't fifteen. He knew he was older. He wondered what colour hair he had. He wondered what his face was like. How his voice sounded. He wondered what his thoughts were like. The only thing he knew was that he wasn't a very nice person – not really. Not truly. A nice person wouldn't do something like this.

His hand tingled. Slight pins and needles. "I think we're close," he said. His words sounded weird in this place.

"It's below us," said Skulduggery, "built into the foundations. There's an activation panel somewhere around here. Follow the buzzing."

Ryan did as he was told, and led them to a section of the wall. Skulduggery tapped it with his knuckle. It sounded normal to Ryan, but Skulduggery obviously heard something that he didn't. It must have been great to be Skulduggery – to always know what to do, to always know what needed to be done. Even in the false life Deacon Maybury had given him, Ryan had never known that kind of certainty.

"Why didn't he make me better?" he asked as Skulduggery continued to tap.

Valkyrie looked at him. "What do you mean?"

Ryan's laugh came out of nowhere and didn't last long. "I mean, look at me. Why didn't he make me cooler, or smarter, or better-looking? He was creating a whole new person, right? So why did he make him as rubbish as me?"

"You're... you're not rubbish, Ryan."

"Yes, I am. I'm fat and ugly and useless."

"Skulduggery," Valkyrie said, "tell him."

Skulduggery stopped tapping the wall, and looked at Ryan. "Deacon made someone who would blend in with the background, someone too unexceptional to notice."

Valkyrie shook her head. "You're meant to make him feel better."

"I'm about to," Skulduggery said. "He made you unexceptional, Ryan. He made you normal. As normal as he could. And in doing so, he has single-handedly proven how exceptional normal people can be. When we were at Deacon's apartment, you could have run and left Valkyrie and myself to fight them off ourselves. But you turned back. You turned back to help. You stood up to terrifying people who want to kill the world, who would snap you in two and tear you apart and not lose one wink of sleep over it, and you did so without training or magic. You did so because you are a good person, and you have true courage. You have the kind of courage Deacon Maybury himself never had. He made you the most normal boy he could, and inadvertently he made you so much better than he could ever hope to be."

"Oh," Valkyrie said, "well... OK, that's better than I thought it was going to be. How are you feeling now, Ryan?"

Ryan looked at her. "I'm feeling pretty special, actually," he said, and she laughed.

Skulduggery pressed his thumbs into the wall, and a large section slid to one side. Instead of the mass of wires that Ryan expected, however, there was a carving of the key in the centre of what looked like a complicated metal maze.

"Oh, good," Skulduggery said.

Valkyrie peered closer. "Is it going to be easy to dismantle?"

"Not in the slightest."

"Do you think you can manage it?"

Skulduggery tapped his chin. "Only with an inordinate amount of luck."

"So we should probably wait for an expert."

"Good God, no," Skulduggery said, jerking his head around. "Where's the fun in that?"

"But... but if you get it wrong, we might all die."

"Yes, that is true, but I probably won't get it wrong."

Valkyrie's eyes flickered to Ryan, then back to Skulduggery. "You *probably* won't?"

"The odds are in my favour."

"Really?"

"Almost."

"I vote we wait for an expert."

"But that might take twenty minutes or *longer*, Valkyrie."

"So? It's not like it's counting down or anything. We have all the time in the world."

"And there's no time like the present. Ryan, I'm going to need you to press your hand against the carving. I'll guide you every step of the way from then on."

Valkyrie's tone was firm. "Skulduggery. We are calling this in and then we're waiting for a bomb-disposal expert."

"What will he know that I don't?"

"About the disposal of bombs? Lots."

Skulduggery waved a hand dismissively. "Bombs are simple things. They're designed to go off. What we have to do in order to thwart the bomb is to *stop* it from going off. What could be more straightforward?"

Valkyrie's fingers closed round Ryan's wrist and she pulled him away. "We are waiting for an expert."

"I think we should let him try," said a voice from behind them. They spun, saw Foe and his gang walking up. Foe was grinning. "It might save us the bother of destroying the world ourselves."

NINE

Valkyrie stepped in front of Ryan, and Skulduggery straightened his tie. "Excellent," he said. "You've fallen right into our trap."

Foe looked around at the otherwise empty mall, eyebrow raised. "This is a trap, is it? So this is the bit where all the Cleavers appear? This is the part where we surrender due to being completely outnumbered and you cart us off to our cells?"

"Roughly, yes."

Foe's grin grew wider. "Has the trap been sprung yet?"

"I'm simply not going to dignify that with an answer," said Skulduggery.

Standing behind Obloquy, Samuel was sweating badly. Ryan could see the lines of tension on his face. He looked to be in pain.

"Your pet doesn't look too good," Valkyrie said.

Foe glanced back, then shrugged. "When the sun goes down, all a vampire wants to do is rip off his skin and kill everything in sight. Right now, the only thing keeping all of us safe is the last drop of a serum he took. Your boyfriend took something similar, didn't he? What was his name? Caelan?"

Valkyrie's shoulders stiffened and her voice grew harder. "He was *not* my boyfriend."

"Bad break-up, was it? Actually, don't answer that. I heard it was. Bad for him more than you, though, wasn't it?"

"We don't talk about vampires," Ryan muttered.

Foe smiled and Mercy laughed. "See?" she said. "Told you he fancies her."

"So what if he does?" Valkyrie snapped back. "He's a nice guy. After we've smacked you lot around, we may as well give it a go. What's the matter, Mercy – jealous that two people can like each other when nobody in their right mind would ever like you?"

Mercy glared. "Plenty have liked me."

"Yeah," Valkyrie said, "I've heard."

The glare turned to a scowl. "Not like that."

"You don't have to justify yourself to me."

"Says the girl who dated a vampire."

"Says the psycho who dated everyone."

"Detective Pleasant," Foe said, interrupting the conversation just when it was getting interesting, "you've gone suspiciously quiet. It's not like you to miss an argument."

"Carry on," Skulduggery said, his head down. "Don't mind me..."

Foe frowned. "What are you doing?"

Skulduggery waited a moment, then looked up, and showed them his phone. "Just sending a message. Reinforcements should be here soon."

Obloquy sagged. "I told you we should have just attacked them," he rumbled. "But, no, you wanted to talk and trade witty banter."

"Shut up, Obloquy," Foe said. "Fine, Detective. You want to skip straight to business? Fine with me. Kill them."

Valkyrie pushed Ryan back slightly as Obloquy headed for her and Mercy zeroed in on Skulduggery.

"Oh, sure," Valkyrie said, "I'll take the big one, no problem."

Foe stayed where he was, his eyes on Ryan. Behind him, Samuel sweated.

Mercy opened her mouth and Skulduggery ducked the stream of energy that carved a furrow across the wall behind him. He dodged behind a pillar, but the stream intensified, melting right through the pillar and taking Skulduggery's hat off his head.

Obloquy pressed his hands to his temples and he squeezed, like he wanted to pop his own head open. Valkyrie staggered. She fell to one knee, bringing up her own hands like she was trying to shield herself. Ryan wanted to run and help, but now Foe was walking towards him.

"This doesn't have to hurt," Foe said.

Ryan turned, ran up the still travelator, swung around at the top and ran up the next one. He was halfway up when he started to seriously regret his choice. His legs were already screaming at him and his lungs were burning. He'd never been able to run for any length of time – not even in the school that he remembered but had never actually attended.

He glanced down, saw Skulduggery waving a hand and Mercy flying backwards. Valkyrie was on both knees now, with Obloquy standing directly over her. Darkness pulsed from the ring on her finger and Obloquy jerked back in shock. His psychic attack must have faltered, because Valkyrie immediately wrapped an arm around each leg. She pressed her shoulder against his belly and as she lifted she launched herself forward. Obloquy yelled as he hit the ground, Valkyrie on top, and Ryan saw her first headbutt go in before he reached the top floor and lost her to sight.

Staggering slightly, Ryan ran on, no idea where he was going or what he would do when he got there. The mall was terrifying at night. The few lights that were on cast the deepest shadows. Anyone could be hiding in those shadows.

Foe stepped out ahead of him and Ryan yelled and changed course and ran into a potted plant, tripped over it and sprawled on to the floor.

"I'd ask you to activate the Machine," Foe said, walking up, "but I don't have the time for an argument. So I'm going to be rude. I hope you don't mind, me being rude. It's nothing personal. I'm not going to kill you. Don't think I'm going to kill you. I'm just going to cut off your hand a little bit. You might die from blood loss or trauma or shock – let's not kid ourselves – but you will not die from me cutting off your hand. When you think about it like that, you have nothing to fear from me or my giant knife."

Foe took a machete from his jacket.

Ryan crawled away on his hands and knees, panting too hard to get up.

"I know some people say they like the thrill of the chase," Foe said, stepping on Ryan's ankle and pinning it there, "but I'm not one of those people. The only thing I care about is ending this world."

Ryan collapsed, and rolled over on to his back. "Why?" he gasped. "Why do you want to... want to kill everyone?"

Foe looked down at him, and shrugged. "Because it's Wednesday."

The machete swung down and Ryan screamed and Skulduggery crashed into Foe from behind. They both went stumbling off. Ryan sat up, looking at his hand, making sure it was still there. He realised he was still screaming so he stopped that and looked around. Skulduggery kicked at Foe's knee, grabbed his head when he bent forward and cracked it against a narrow pillar. Foe staggered and swung a fist, but Skulduggery stepped inside the swing, latched on and started hitting him with elbows. It was all very violent. Ryan's mother, if she'd existed, would not have approved.

"Skulduggery!" Valkyrie shouted from below them.

"Ryan," Skulduggery muttered, as Foe grabbed him round the waist and slammed him back against the wall, "could you take a look and see what she's shouting about now?"

Ryan got up, hurried to the railing, looked over. Mercy and

Obloquy were down and not moving, but Valkyrie was backing away from Samuel, who was lurching towards her, bent over like he had stomach cramps.

Ryan looked back. Foe had his arm wrapped around Skulduggery's neck from behind, and he was dragging him like he wanted to pull Skulduggery's head from his spinal column. Skulduggery twisted but Foe adapted, turning his hold into a headlock. Skulduggery reached up, his gloved fingers digging into Foe's eyes. Foe jerked away and lost his grip and Skulduggery pushed against him, tripping him with a sneaky sweep to the ankle. Foe went down and Skulduggery landed on top of him.

"Well?" Skulduggery asked as he pounded Foe with punches.

"Uh, I don't know," said Ryan. "Samuel looks like he's about to throw up."

Surprisingly, Skulduggery and Foe stopped fighting and they both looked over.

"He's doubled over?" Foe asked, panting for breath.

"Yeah," said Ryan.

Foe looked at Skulduggery, and they both stood up.

"You're on your own," Foe said, and ran.

Ryan frowned, looked down at Samuel again. Samuel's moan of pain drifted up, and then suddenly it turned to a growl. Samuel straightened, digging his fingers into his shirt and ripping it open. No, not just his shirt. His skin, too. Samuel ripped his flesh and his clothes from his body, from the bone-white body that lay beneath. His hands, and even from where he stood, Ryan could see the claws on those hands, tore Samuel's face off and threw it to one side, revealing the smooth head and big black eyes and jagged, jagged teeth.

Valkyrie turned and ran, and the vampire bounded after her. Something blurred out of the corner of Ryan's eye and suddenly Skulduggery was vaulting over the railing and dropping to the ground far below.

Ryan ran for the travelator, heading down, heading down to help Valkyrie. He heard her cry out and nearly tripped, nearly went head first. There was a crash of breaking glass and Ryan glimpsed Skulduggery disappearing through a shop window. He was almost at the ground floor when he saw her, saw Valkyrie, hurling fireballs and whipping shadows at the vampire that came at her like a wild animal. It twisted in mid-air, avoiding the slash of darkness Valkyrie sent its way. It landed on her, took her down, its claws raking across her body. She gasped and it raked again, and again, trying to get through her protective clothing, trying to rend flesh and puncture skin, trying to draw blood.

"Hey!" Ryan screamed, running into full view of the monster. "Hey, you! Hey! Come and get me! Come on!"

The vampire snapped its head up, snarling.

"I've got what you want!" Ryan shouted, holding up his imprinted palm. If Samuel the man was still in there somewhere, maybe he'd remember why all this was going on in the first place. Maybe he'd remember that Ryan was the real target. Or maybe the vampire would just see an easy kill and—

The vampire leaped off Valkyrie. Ryan howled in terror and started running again. He glanced back in time to see its claws and its teeth and feel the rush of air as it swooped up and over him.

Ryan's feet got mixed up and he tripped over himself. He sat on the ground, looking up. The vampire hung in the air, looking down. It writhed and snarled, slashed at him with its claws.

Skulduggery walked over, hands open, fingers flexing slightly as he held the creature in place. His suit was torn and his tie was crooked. Valkyrie limped over, holding his hat. She showed it to him, and he groaned. There was a large hole burned through the top.

The vampire snarled at them all.

Skulduggery raised his arms, and the vampire rose in the air. Higher and higher it went, up past every floor. Valkyrie took Ryan's arm, escorted him to the benches. When the vampire couldn't rise any higher, Skulduggery dropped his hands quickly, and the vampire plunged downwards.

"This won't kill it," Valkyrie told Ryan as the vampire fell. "But it'll break enough bones to stop it from bothering us."

The vampire hit the ground with a satisfying *thwack*, and didn't get up.

Skulduggery examined his poor hat, and laid it to one side. "Ryan," he said, "I know you've been through a lot, but there is the small matter of dismantling a bomb to get through, and then I'll let you rest. I promise."

TEN

With Skulduggery's guidance, Ryan dismantled the Doomsday Machine. He rendered each and every part of it inert. When it was done, when the last piece was made useless, his hand started to burn. He hissed, looked at his palm, and the imprint faded to nothing.

"Well done, Ryan," Skulduggery said. "You saved the world."

"You knew exactly what to do," Ryan said. "You *did* know how to dismantle it after all."

"I'm glad you got that impression," Skulduggery said kindly. "But really I could have just as easily killed us all. Still, it's better than waiting around for the experts, isn't it?"

He took a set of handcuffs from his belt and went to shackle the unconscious prisoners, leaving Ryan and Valkyrie alone.

"How long do I have?" Ryan asked.

Valkyrie hesitated. "Skulduggery said... he said that as soon as this was over, one way or the other, Deacon's personality would start to reassert itself."

"So I don't have long," Ryan said quietly.

"I'm... I'm afraid not."

Ryan nodded. He didn't say anything. He didn't trust his voice not to break.

"You probably saved my life back there," Valkyrie said. "That was a very brave thing you did."

Ryan managed a smile. "Maybe it's something you'll remember me for."

"I definitely think so."

"I don't feel very brave right now. To be honest, I kind of feel like crying."

Valkyrie's hand rested on his shoulder.

"I really don't want to die," Ryan said. He was crying now. He didn't care. The only thing he cared about was that in a few moments he wouldn't be here any more. He wouldn't exist. They'd stopped Foe and the others from destroying the world, but Ryan's world was ending just the same. "It's not fair. How come Deacon gets to live and I don't?"

"I don't know," Valkyrie said softly.

"Isn't there anything you can do? Maybe Skulduggery can do something? Maybe he knows someone who can, who can block Deacon from coming back or..."

"I'm sorry, Ryan," Valkyrie said. She was crying, too. This pretty girl with the single dimple when she smiled, she was crying for him. This pretty girl who would never go out with a guy like Ryan, not in a million years, was sitting here with her arm round him, and they were crying together.

He fought to control his sobs. When he could speak, he spoke quietly. "Could I have that kiss now?"

She looked at him. "Definitely," she said, and leaned in. He turned his head slightly, didn't know if he should close his eyes or keep them open, but when their lips met his eyes closed. His first kiss in fifteen years of false memories. His only kiss in fifteen hours of real life.

They parted. His head was clouded. His thoughts were fuzzy.

"I really like you, Valkyrie," he managed to mumble.

"I really like you, Ryan," she said back to him.

Ryan smiled and tried to kiss her again, this pretty girl with the dimple, what was her name again, Valkyrie, that was it, seventeen years old and cute as a button, the kind of girl who had never even noticed Deacon when he was that age. He grinned and leaned in and felt her hand against his chest, keeping him back, and then her eyes were narrowing.

"Ryan?"

"I'll be whoever you want me to be," Deacon said, and she hit him so hard the whole world spun.

She stood over him. "Get rid of that face," she said. "Stop using Ryan's face right now or I swear to God I'll batter you."

"OK!" he cried. "Just don't hit me again!"

Deacon got to his feet, his jaw aching. "Ain't that something?" he muttered, and at those words, the image around him flickered and withdrew, and suddenly he was back to his old self again.

Valkyrie's eyes sparkled with tears. She was looking at him like she was going to hit him again anyway.

"I just want to thank you," he said before she did. "I was in a serious bind and you, you came in and you really helped me. I was in over my head, I don't mind admitting it. If it makes any difference, I never intended for the Machine to end up in enemy hands. The moment I sold the key, I was going to alert the Sanctuary and get an army of Cleavers in here to—"

"You risked the lives of everyone on the *planet*," Valkyrie said, her voice tight.

"I did," he said, nodding sadly, "and I truly regret that. It was stupid. It was short-sighted, and selfish. If I knew then what I know now, I would never have tried it. But we all make mistakes, isn't that right? And I made a mistake. A terrible, terrible mistake that could have had untold consequences for—"

He didn't even see the punch. He saw her shoulder shift and then he was toppling backwards. He hit the ground and his face felt three sizes too big. Good *God*, she hit hard.

"You better get up," she said, standing over him. "The Cleavers are coming, and if you're here when they arrive, you'll get arrested, too."

He blinked. "You're letting me go?"

"We're letting *Ryan* go," Skulduggery Pleasant said, walking up behind her. "Ryan was a friend of ours. He deserved better than to be you, Deacon."

"I know he did," Deacon said, rising slowly to his feet for the second time in the last sixty seconds. "I only hope I can make it up to him somehow, maybe by being a better person, by treating people with the same kind of—"

"If you want me to hit you again, you'll keep talking like that," Valkyrie said.

Deacon shut up. If looks could kill, he'd be skewered. "I know I did wrong," he said, hanging his head. "I know I did. And I've already paid for it. My brother. My poor brother Dafydd. Foe thought Dafydd was me. He chased him and Dafydd... Dafydd fell into that wood chipper. He was always the clumsy one, was Dafydd. So, so clumsy..."

Valkyrie shoved him to get his attention, and when he looked up she leaned in. "If we ever hear of you doing something like that again, creating an innocent person just so you can hide behind them..."

Deacon held up his hands. "I won't, I swear. I've learned my lesson. I was greedy, and selfish. But now I see that it was wrong to—"

"We don't care," Skulduggery said. "Run away before I shoot you."

Deacon nodded, and started walking.

"He said *run*," Valkyrie snarled, and Deacon did just that.

TRICK OR TREAT

TRICK OR TREAT

Tanith wiped the blood off the carving knife and, ignoring the body of the man she had just stabbed to death, went back to carving her jack-o'-lantern.

Her skill with a blade always came in useful this time of year. While other people would be satisfied with triangular eyes and jagged teeth, Tanith transformed her Halloween pumpkins into works of slowly rotting art. Tonight she was carving a portrait of her dear friend and object of worship Valkyrie Cain. By all accounts, poor Valkyrie still refused to embrace her destiny as destroyer of the world, but Tanith could forgive her this little moment of self-doubt. After all, if Tanith herself hadn't been corrupted by a Remnant, then she would have been *helping* Val run from the inevitable.

It was the Remnant inside her, the thing of cruelty and nastiness, that had shared with Tanith this vision of the future, when Valkyrie would become Darquesse and burn all life to a cinder. It had been a glorious revelation, one that had spurred Tanith on to schemes and plans she had never before thought herself capable of. But the fact was there were no more Remnants out there. Her kith and kin were all trapped and locked away and hidden from her – so Tanith was on her own. More or less. She had a Texan psychopath who was besotted with her, and there were times when he certainly did come in useful. But she didn't love him. Her love was reserved for Darquesse, and Darquesse alone.

She put down the carving knife and picked up a candle, placed it carefully inside the jack-o'-lantern. She lit it and stepped back. It was a good likeness. No, it was a *great* likeness. Valkyrie was such a pretty girl, and Tanith had to resist the urge to take a picture and send it to her. But she knew that Valkyrie would only tell Skulduggery, and Skulduggery would trace the picture back here to this small town in Ohio, and suddenly there'd be Cleavers, Cleavers everywhere. It was all so unfair. All Tanith wanted to do was protect Darquesse from the people who were planning on harming her, after all. She was on Valkyrie's side, in a way. Why couldn't Val see that?

Headlights looped in around the room, and Tanith went to the window, looked out. A battered old car lurched to a stop outside the house next door, and a shabby, middle-aged man climbed out. As she watched him hitch his trousers higher round his waist, Tanith made sure to keep her mind calm and free of violent thoughts. There were Sensitives who could pick up feelings of hostility and, while she didn't know if Jerry Ordain was one of them, she couldn't take the chance. There was too much riding on tonight to risk a stray thought at the wrong time. The fact that he came home at all meant that he hadn't foreseen tonight's events, and that was a promising start.

Of course, it was entirely possible that Jerry knew full well she was there, and he had a trap waiting for her the moment she made a move. That was the trouble with Sensitives – it was very hard to sneak up on them.

She took her sword from the table and left through the back door. She sprang lightly over the fence, landed without a sound in Jerry's yard as lights flicked on in the house. She crept to the window. No sign of an ambush. She saw Jerry ambling into the kitchenette. If he sensed her watching him, he gave no sign.

Taking a breath, Tanith moved to the door and rested her hand against the lock. It clicked open and she moved in silently. Jerry was a bachelor and lived like it. The house smelled of dust and old socks. She slid her sword from its scabbard and walked up the wall. Those floorboards were old and she didn't trust them not to creak. She crept upside down along the ceiling, careful not to disturb the bulb as she passed it or cast her shadow on to her target. Jerry had his back to her, and was making himself a massive sandwich. She reached the far wall and walked down until she was standing normally again. He still didn't turn round. She took out her phone, sent a text. A few moments later, Billy-Ray Sanguine rose up from the floor beside her.

They waited for Jerry to sense the hostility that only a psychopath of Sanguine's stature could radiate – the kind of hostility that he could never conceal, no matter how hard he tried. Instead, Jerry continued making his sandwich. Tanith was impressed at how cool and collected he was. It was almost as if he wasn't even aware of their presence. Jerry started humming to himself, and Sanguine looked at her. She frowned back. Now it *really* seemed like he wasn't aware of their presence.

Once he had piled every conceivable type of meat on to his sandwich, Jerry cut off the crusts and then sliced it down the middle. He picked up one half, raised it slowly to his mouth and bit into it as he turned. He saw them and shrieked, spitting it all out again as he stumbled back against the fridge. A bit of lettuce hung wetly off his chin.

"Hi," said Tanith. "Just checking – you *are* Jerry Ordain, right?"

The man stood there, eyes bulging. "Whuh," he said.

"Jerry Ordain? You *are* Jerry the psychic, aren't you?"

He shook his head. The piece of lettuce fell away. "No. Not me. No. Wrong person."

"Then who are you?" Sanguine asked.

The man gaped at him. "Me?"

It was Jerry. It was obviously Jerry, from the look on his face as his fear-frozen mind tried coming up with a false name. "I'm... I'm..."

Sanguine added an edge to his voice. "What's your damn name?"

"Jerry!" Jerry blurted. "But not the Jerry you're looking for! I'm a different Jerry!"

Jerry had to be the worst liar Tanith had ever met.

"I'll get him, though," Jerry said, stepping sideways. "If you stay right there, I'll get him. Just stay there. I'll be right back, with Jerry. The Jerry you're looking for."

Sanguine strolled over to intercept him, and Jerry reversed direction, started heading for the window.

"Make yourselves at home," he was saying. "Want a sandwich? I just made a sandwich. You can have my sandwich. I won't be long. Thirty seconds, tops."

"Jerry," Tanith said, "we've come a long way to talk to you."

He shook his head. "You've come a long way to talk to the *other* Jerry..."

Tanith showed him her sword. Jerry stared. And then he bolted for the window.

In his haste, however, he completely forgot about the coffee table and, when his shin smacked into it, he barely had time to howl before his face hit the floor. Tanith watched him contort in pain, one hand over his shin, the other covering his mouth. He'd bitten his tongue. She winced. She hated that.

Tears in his eyes, Jerry launched himself up and ran into the wall. He rebounded impressively, gave a little whirl and staggered to the window. Clumsy hands fumbled at the latch. He finally raised it, glanced behind him to make sure he still had time, and in that moment the window closed. Jerry turned back and dived into the glass, cracking it and careering backwards. He collapsed on to the rug and curled up into a sobbing, moaning ball.

"Pleathe," he lisped, "shtop hurting me."

Tanith sighed. "We haven't touched you, Jerry."

"I seen a lot of things in my time," Sanguine said, "but I ain't never seen a man beat himself up before. That was highly entertainin'."

Tanith walked over to Jerry as he continued to sob.

"Pleathe don't kill me."

"Don't worry," Tanith said, her voice soothing. "We weren't planning on it."

Sanguine looked at her, surprised. "We weren't? Why not? He's clearly an idiot."

She glared. "We're not here to hurt anyone. We're here to ask some questions and leave."

"But we'll be killin' him before we go, won't we?"

Jerry squealed softly.

"No, we won't," Tanith insisted. "Violence is not always the answer, Billy-Ray. This time, Jerry here gets to live out the rest of his life in peace – understand?"

"Barely."

She hunkered down and patted Jerry on the shoulder. "Don't mind him, Jerry. He's cranky. He's used to being the only American in my life, but now there's you. Jealousy is a terrible thing in a grown man, isn't it?"

"I ain't jealous."

"Of course not, dear. Jerry, what do you say you answer our questions and then we leave you alone? Does that sound good to you?"

Jerry nodded.

"Good man. How's your tongue?"

"I bith it."

"I can see that."

"Ith bleeding."

"I can see that, too."

He stuck his tongue out at her. "Ith it bad?"

His tongue was bloody and horrible. She took a small leaf from her coat and placed it delicately into his mouth. "Don't say anything for a few seconds. Let that heal."

Jerry blinked at her. His eyes were wet. He wasn't an impressive human being.

"Show me," she said, and he stuck his tongue out again. She nodded. "It's healing. It was only a small bite. Now you can answer our questions, can't you?"

He nodded, and she stood.

"You're involved with a group of people, aren't you? A group of sorcerers from different Sanctuaries around the world."

"How... how did you know that?"

"I've spent the last few months asking a lot of people a lot of questions. See, I figured there'd be someone out there who would be trying to do something about Darquesse before she even turned up. That's when I heard your name for the first time. You're a psychic, aren't you, Jerry?"

"I... I prefer the term clairvoyant."

Tanith did her best not to roll her eyes. "Clairvoyant, of course. And, as a clairvoyant, you would have seen visions of Darquesse."

"Of course," Jerry said, nodding. He was still on the floor, but he was sitting a little straighter now. His chest puffed out slightly. "Even low-level Sensitives picked up something. For a clairvoyant of my ability, it was a veritable tsunami of images and sensations and emotions. Very powerful."

"What did you see?"

"I saw death."

Sanguine gave a barely suppressed sigh.

"What do you mean?" Tanith asked, smiling at Jerry.

"I saw a city destroyed. Streets cracked and broken. Buildings burning. And I saw her. I saw Darquesse."

"Did you see her face?"

"Alas, no, I did not," said Jerry, and Tanith resisted smacking him for using the word *alas* in an irony-free context. "But there is no doubt in my mind that it was her. Ten foot tall, she was. A terrible sight to behold."

"Ten foot tall?" Sanguine asked.

Jerry nodded. "Oh, yes. Easily. And the way she moved... like a cat."

Sanguine frowned behind his sunglasses. "What, on all fours?"

"Pardon me?"

Sanguine continued. "I heard from another psychic – sorry, *clairvoyant* – that Darquesse had long black fingernails that she used to cut off people's heads. Did you see that?"

Jerry nodded. "It was awful."

"And she shot laser beams out of her eyes."

"Well," Jerry said with a shrug, "I don't know if they were laser beams, but yes. Devastating blasts, they were."

"This clairvoyant friend of ours," Sanguine continued, "he also caught a glimpse of red hair beneath her hood. Did you see that? Don't worry if you didn't. Our friend is probably the most powerful Sensitive in the world. I wouldn't be surprised if you didn't see as much as him."

"Red hair?" Jerry said. "Yes. Yes, I saw that too, now that you mention it. Long tousled red hair."

"He said it was straight."

"Long straight red hair, yes."

"He said it was short."

"Short straight red hair, that's what I meant to say."

Sanguine looked at Tanith, who glowered and poked Jerry. He screamed. She had poked him with her sword.

"You're lying to us," she said. He screamed again. "We don't have a psychic friend. Billy-Ray made all that stuff up. You didn't see a vision, did you?"

She twisted the sword and his screams reached a new pitch. "No! No, I didn't! I'm sorry! Please stop stabbing me!"

She withdrew the sword and wiped the tip of the blade on his shirt. "Are you even a Sensitive, Jerry?"

"I am," he whimpered, cradling his wound, "but I'm not a very good one. Sometimes... sometimes I can predict the weather, if it's a nice day."

"Is it going to rain tomorrow?" Sanguine asked.

"I don't know," Jerry confessed. "I can only predict a few minutes into the future. Most of the time I have to watch the forecast like everyone else."

"You," Sanguine said, "are the worst psychic I've ever met."

"Does anyone else know that you're a fraud?" asked Tanith.

"No," Jerry said, sobbing. "I've managed to keep them fooled. It hasn't been easy, but whenever they ask me to look into the future I always try to be as vague as possible. I talk about shadows and death and ominous feelings, and they generally infer their own meanings into that and then leave me alone."

"So when this group of sorcerers asked you to find out more about Darquesse," Tanith said, "you basically just copied what every other Sensitive was saying?"

"Essentially, yes," Jerry said. "Can I have a bandage? I'm bleeding quite badly here."

"First you tell us what they're planning, and then we'll see about bandages."

"I'm losing a lot of blood."

Tanith let the veins rise beneath her skin, and her black lips curled into a smile. "Tell us what they're planning."

Jerry paled, his face going slack. "Yes. Yes, of course. They're going after weapons. Four God-Killer weapons that they think could hurt Darquesse."

"Where are these weapons?"

"Scattered," said Jerry. "All over the world. They're going to go after them."

"And you know where they're goin'?" Sanguine asked.

"I have a list of the possible locations." Jerry took out his wallet, rifled through it, came out with a crumpled piece of paper.

Tanith took it from him, examined it and nodded. "Looks like we won't be needing you any more."

He brightened. "So that's it? I can go?"

She pulled him to his feet. "You can go," she smiled, and her sword flashed and she took off his head.

"You," Sanguine said, "are delicious when you're vicious."

She gave him a smirk, and led the way to the front door. She opened it and froze.

Six little children in Halloween outfits looked up at her.

"Trick or treat," said the little witch. Surrounding the witch was a pirate, a zombie, a vampire, a Mad Hatter and a rabbit. They rattled their buckets.

"Uh," said Tanith.

Sanguine appeared at her elbow and grinned at the kids. "Look," he said, "there's a little zombie. Smells a darn sight better than the real thing, doesn't he? And a vampire! Doesn't she look cute? And a rabbit!" He faltered. "A rabbit. That... that ain't exactly scary, though, is it?"

The rabbit looked up at him. "It is if you're scared of rabbits."

Tanith nodded. "You've got to admit he makes a good point."

"You talk funny," said the witch. "Where are you from?"

Tanith smiled. "I'm from London."

The pirate frowned. "Is that in France?"

The Mad Hatter scowled. "It's in England, dummy." He looked at Tanith. "You're English. Why do you have a sword?"

"Because I'm an English ninja," Tanith replied. "We're just like regular ninjas, except we wear leather and flirt more."

The kids nodded, satisfied with the definition, and then rattled their buckets again. "Trick or treat," they chorused.

"This isn't actually our house," Tanith told them, "but whatever you find in there is yours to keep."

The pirate perked up. "Even the TV?"

"Especially the TV."

The kids glanced at each other, then stormed the house. Tanith waited a moment, watching them approach Jerry's headless corpse warily. The rabbit hesitated, then nudged Jerry's head with his fluffy foot. The head rolled in its own blood, and the rabbit shrugged. "That's so fake," he said, and turned to help the pirate with the TV.

GET THEE BEHIND ME, BUBBA MOON

GET THEE BEHIND ME, BUBBA MOON

1

Every town has a haunted house, I guess, and Bredon, small as it was, was no different. My older brother and his friends used to go up there, dare each other to knock on the door. He told me once that when his time came, he accepted the dare like there was nothing else he'd rather be doing. He'd mocked others for being scared and he wasn't about to turn around and show anything like that kind of fear in his own eyes.

He said one Wednesday night, at the height of summer, they sneaked out and cycled over by the light of the full moon. Full moons were important for this kind of thing, he said. We were kids, and we knew this stuff. They reached the house a little before midnight and waited until Ryan Sanderson's brand-new digital watch beeped 11:59. My brother now had one minute to open that gate, walk up that weed-cracked path, and knock on that door. Midnight was important for this kind of thing. That was something else we knew.

So my brother pushed open the iron gate that creaked with rust and age, and he laughed at how creepy it was. Behind him, his friends laughed, too. He pretended the path was one big hopscotch game, and he jumped and hopped the whole way up to the sound of laughter and cheers. But my brother wasn't laughing any more. He told me he'd nailed that grin to his face when he felt it starting to slide off. He told me the closer he got to that door, the more real it all became. All the stories. All the rumours. All the scary, scary dreams.

He reached the three steps that led up to the front door. This close, he could see how old the wood was. He could see the broken doorbell with the wires hanging out. This part of town was all dark. No streetlights. Behind the house were the woods, and the trees there never seemed to grow any leaves. They stood against the dark sky and didn't move, like they were waiting for something bad to happen.

All these thoughts, my brother said, flickered through his mind. Them and more. The biggest and darkest thought, and the heaviest, the one that pressed down on all the others, was the feeling that he was being watched by someone with no goodness in them. He felt eyes on him that were mean and greedy and so full of hate, and he felt like the house would swallow him up if he got too close.

So he stood on the first step, leaned in as far as he could get, and knocked three times on the door.

Three loud knocks, so loud they could have woken the dead and, even though he was one who made it, the noise broke something within him and he turned tail and bolted, back to the hooting and hollering of his friends, and they grabbed their bikes and cycled away from there like the devil himself was on their tails.

All this he told me one Saturday night years later, right before he went out with his college buddies. This was his version of a pep talk, because tonight it was my turn to knock on that door and my brother knew it, and he went away laughing at how white my face had gotten.

I told my parents I was going to bed early, and my dad grunted like he'd barely heard me and didn't lift his head from the book he was reading. My mom didn't drag her gaze away from the TV. She was watching some game show. Her favourite was *Wheel of Fortune*. Dad said he hated game shows, but I caught him enough times glued to *Jeopardy!* that we ended up watching it in secret, just us. That's one of my fondest memories of my dad, even now.

I went to my room and turned out the light and got into bed fully dressed. I don't know why I did that. My parents never checked on me, anyway.

At 11:20 pm, I got up. I could still hear the sounds of the TV from the living room. I put my flashlight in my pocket and climbed out the window, scuttled across the garage roof, and dropped down to where my bicycle lay. I cycled over to Pete Green's house, and together we cycled over to the school. Pete had been my friend since we were little kids. We liked the same things. We liked skateboards and comic books and *Star Wars* movies and arcade games. Haven't had a friend like him since, and I doubt I'll find one now.

When we got to the school, Benny and Tyler were already there, waiting for us, and so was Chrissy. I hadn't expected Chrissy to be there, and neither had Pete. She was something else we both liked.

Pete braked and brought the rear wheel of his bike around in an impressive skid. If I tried that, I'd have ended up on my face, so I slowed and stopped normally. I looked at the guys, pretending not to notice Chrissy or else I'd start blushing.

"Ready for this?" Benny asked, his grin in place.

I gave him a shrug, doing my best to act cool.

"He's peeing his pants," Pete said, laughing, and I laughed along with them just to show what a joke it was. As much as we were friends, I'd found it best to laugh along with Pete. He had a sharp tongue that'd turn on you if you weren't careful.

We rode up along Mulgarvey Street, got to the edge of town where the Streets started becoming Roads, and ended up on King Road. We turned off that before the junkyard, cycled on for another few minutes, and we came to the house at the very top of King Hill.

It stood on its own like a bad idea. It was dark and ramshackle, with some boarded-up windows and a boarded-up door. No graffiti, though. I didn't know of any kid brave enough to tag the yellowing sides of this house.

We left our bikes on their kickstands, and I went to the gate. Going to the gate was the easy part. Looking brave doing it wasn't much of an effort, either. It was the passing through the gate that was the problem. The house had a feeling about it. The closer you got, the more you felt it. It was a sick feeling, made you queasy and light-headed while your arms rippled with gooseflesh. It was a bad house. Everyone knew it.

But I guess I had a secret weapon. I had Chrissy Brennan watching me, and I knew there was no way, there was just no way, that I was going to chicken out in front of her. My hand went to the gate, pushed it open.

It creaked, just like in a horror movie.

I didn't look back. They'd see how white I was. How scared. I took my first step on to the garden path – though there'd never been much of a garden and there wasn't much left of a path. A few paving stones, islands in a sea of long grass. I stepped from island to island, focusing on that, letting my mind slip away from the house that suddenly seemed to loom over me. Island to island. Step to step. I was dimly aware of how much time I was taking, and when I looked up I was dismayed to find out I was only halfway there.

Something in me faltered.

"You OK, buddy?" Pete called.

I nodded, and looked back. Chrissy stood surrounded by the others, clasping her hands at her throat.

"He's too scared!" Benny cried.

"No, he isn't," said Pete, and to my horror he kicked the gate open and strode up the path after me, waving his hands in the air. "Ooooh, Bubba Moon! We're so scared of you! We're so scared of you, Bubba Moon!"

And then he was striding past me, and I stood there like the paving stones had latched on to my feet, and there was nothing I could do as he bounded up those steps and slammed his fist against the door.

"Yoo-hoo!" he called. "Anybody home?"

The cold feeling in my chest was gone, and in its place was a dreadful hollowness. He'd robbed me of my moment. I didn't have the words back then and I didn't have the frame of reference, but walking up that path and knocking on that door was a rite of passage for kids like me, and my friend Pete had denied me that one small foothold into adulthood and, I suppose, manliness. And he hadn't done it for me. He hadn't done it as a show of solidarity. He'd done it simply to show off to Chrissy, who hadn't come along the first time he'd knocked on that door, three months earlier.

"Come on, buddy," he said, grabbing my sleeve and pulling me forward. "Show Mr Moon we're not scared of him!"

I didn't want to, there was no point in it, but I knocked, anyway. It was a feeble effort. I couldn't believe Pete had done that to me.

He wrapped an arm round my shoulders and turned me to face the others.

"See?" he said. "He did it! Happy now?"

"Yeah, big deal," said Benny. "Bet you wouldn't break in, though."

I was a good kid. I never shoplifted, I never spoke back to teachers, I never even carved my name into my desk at school. I obeyed the rules and I never got the feeling I was missing out on too much by doing so. Obeying the rules meant a smoother life, all things considered. But when I saw the look on Pete's face, when I saw how truly scared that idea made him, I saw a chance to prove myself.

"Sure I would," I said, and I started round the house, testing the windows, seeing if any would open. When I got round the corner, I lost the confident smile and started praying that I wouldn't be able to find a way in. It was dark round here, so I took out my flashlight, which glared back at me from the grimy window panes as I looked in.

Pete and the others came after me and I ignored them, adopting an air of casual indifference. They weren't speaking. Not even Pete. Chrissy was wide-eyed. Three windows in a row were boarded up, so I could skip them, but I made a big show of trying to force open the ones on either side. Sadly, my burglary skills were not up to the task, and I stood back and exhaled in exasperation.

"Hey, look," said Tyler. "You can get in here."

He stood by the wall, lightly nudging open the narrow window at his foot. The basement window.

Everyone knew the story of Bubba Moon. When he died, they found all kinds of black magic stuff in his house. There were books and scrolls and all sorts of daggers and things, and there were jars of preserved human remains. That's what my brother said, anyway. He said Bubba Moon used these human remains in his satanic rituals. I didn't know how much of that was true, but what I did know for sure, what everyone knew for sure, was that when Bubba Moon's dead body was found, it was found in the basement.

"Don't," said Chrissy.

"He said he'd do it," said Benny. "Let him do it."

"Will I be able to fit?" I asked, struggling to keep the tremor from my voice as I wandered over. It was pretty obvious I'd fit, but all I needed was for one of them to say something like I was too fat, or I'd get stuck, and that'd give me reason enough to back out.

"You'll fit no problem," said Pete. It had to be Pete.

I crouched, lifted the window, and shone my light in. There was a load of junk piled up, just like in any other basement.

"If there are rats in there, I'm not going," I said. "I hate rats. No way am I going in if there are rats."

The others crouched down beside me. More flashlights flicked on.

"Can't see any rats," said Benny.

"They'd hardly come out to see what the fuss was about," Tyler said. "They're probably scampering off into the corners or something. You'll be fine."

"This is stupid," Chrissy said. "You might cut yourself on a rusty nail and need a tetanus shot. And we don't know if there's anybody in there. There might be homeless people living here."

"Or the ghost of Bubba Moon," Pete said in a scary voice.

"Shut up," Chrissy said sharply, and Pete laughed, but I could tell the laugh was forced. He wanted her to like him as much as I wanted her to like me.

"Hold it open," I said, and I lay down on my belly. Tyler did the honours, and I slithered forward, my flashlight in my lead hand. There were a load of cobwebs that I had to brush aside, and I forced myself not to cry out when I saw the huge spider scurrying away from the destruction of its home and dinner plate. I got my head through, shone the light on the floor below, making sure it was clear. All I saw were small piles of dead, dried leaves. No one waiting to grab me.

I brought my legs up and turned, lifting my hips slightly to avoid the latch, and let my feet go first. I was looking back at my friends as I lowered myself down. There could be anyone sneaking towards me now, any number of gnarled hands reaching for my ankles.

When my legs were down as far as they could go and I was halfway in, I glanced up and for the first time looked Chrissy right in the eyes. She had such beautiful blue eyes. Her dark hair fell in slight waves to the middle of her back. She was as tall as me and so pretty. She was the prettiest girl in school, but she refused to act like it, and here she was, out with a bunch of guys at a haunted house at a little past midnight on the weekend, and she was looking at me like she was scared she was going to lose me. I'd never felt braver.

I let myself go, and dropped into the basement.

I turned quickly, adding my beam to the shaking lights held by my friends. I wished they wouldn't shake like that – it threw moving shadows across the far wall. I took three small steps, making sure there was nothing waiting for me in my immediate vicinity, and then broadened the sweep of my flashlight. My fleeting moment of bravery was gone, replaced by a flesh-rippling fear that was creeping up behind me no matter which direction I faced.

"See anything?" Tyler asked.

"Junk," I managed to say. My voice sounded weird. Strangled.

"Any black magic stuff?"

I shook my head. My shadow, which was the biggest and starkest of them all, replicated the movement right in front of me. It occurred to me that someone could literally be hiding in my shadow and I'd never see him. "Just old lamps and furniture," I said. "A table. Sofa."

It was a big basement. My light couldn't even reach the side walls.

"If you see a Ouija board, grab it," said Benny.

"Don't you dare," said Chrissy. "My aunt did the Ouija board once and she doesn't believe in any of that stuff, but she said that Ouija boards are actually dangerous."

"Can't see any," I said, taking a single step to my left. Twenty more seconds and then I was done. Twenty more seconds.

"Can you see the circle?" Pete asked.

I knew what circle he meant. We all did. Bubba Moon had been found lying on a blanket in a circle he'd painted on the floor.

"Can't see it," I said.

"Go in further."

I took another step, sighed, and shifted my weight, did my best to look energised. "Nope," I said. "Just junk. It was years ago, anyway. It's probably faded away to—"

One of the lights jiggled fiercely, and before I even looked back I knew what was happening. Pete was crawling through the window. He was taking my moment away from me again, and I was too weak to stop him.

He dropped down. "Right," he said, walking past me like he didn't have a care in the world, "where is it?"

The others came after him. I don't know how. Didn't they feel the same cold, sickly dread that I did? Didn't they feel that something in this house, something down here in this basement with us, was just fundamentally wrong, and out of step with how the world was supposed to be?

I could feel the unnatural malevolence that hung heavy in the air, but I'd forced myself to come down here because I needed to do it. I needed to do it to prove to myself, and to Chrissy, that I could. That I wasn't about to let my fear beat me. Pete was probably the same, but Benny and Tyler and Chrissy herself? Why they came down I will never know. They regretted it, though. Later, they regretted it.

We spread out. The basement wasn't that big, not really, but there were moments when it looked big. There were moments, glimpses out of the corner of my eye, when the walls disappeared and the basement went on forever.

"Found it," said Chrissy.

Nobody rushed to her side. We all walked like condemned men, each step like wading through treacle. We joined our light to hers. On the floor before us was a circle that had maybe once been red. Time and dust and air and whatever had turned it dark, almost black. It was a wide circle, big enough for a tall man to lie down and die in. There were symbols on the outside. Black magic stuff. Satanic stuff. Not that any of us knew what satanic stuff looked like.

Not back then.

"I didn't think that part was true," said Benny. He sounded quiet. He sounded young.

We stood there and looked at this circle. Later, I asked the others if they felt what I felt, that electric tingle of panic beginning to crackle at the back of the neck. They all had. None of us let on, though. It was just an empty circle, after all. There was nothing in there that could hurt us.

"Big bad Bubba Moon," Pete said in a soft voice.

"Don't tease him," said Chrissy.

The softness left Pete's voice, and he laughed. "Tease him? He's dead, Chrissy! He's not around any more!"

"I didn't mean it like that," Chrissy said, defensive, her face flushing in the light.

"Don't tease him!" Pete cried, laughing again. "Don't make fun of the poor dead guy! We'll hurt his little dead feelings!"

"Pete," I said, "stop."

"Don't tease him, she says!" Pete continued, howling with laughter.

I knew what he was doing. I'd gone into the basement first, I'd gotten her attention, so this was his clumsy way of pulling her pigtails, of getting her to notice him again. That probably made him do what he did next. He was just showing off. He didn't deserve what happened. He was just showing off.

"Don't tease the big bad Bubba Moon!" he called, and jumped into the circle.

"Pete!" Tyler cried.

Benny tried to snatch him back, almost toppled, almost stepped over the painted line himself, but Chrissy grabbed him, pulled him to her side. She said later she didn't know why she did that – she'd had no way of knowing how important that had been – but her hands had moved and they'd probably saved Benny's life. He's still alive today because of her.

Pete spun and danced in the circle and he laughed and howled Bubba Moon's name like a wolf. We stared, horrified. It took me a few seconds to realise how cold it had gotten. At first I thought it was just me, but in the light I could see little puffs of vapour leaving Chrissy's mouth.

"We should go," Tyler said.

"Run away!" Pete shouted. "Run away all you like! You'll never get away from big bad Bubba Moon!"

He stopped singing and dancing and suddenly dropped to the ground, crossed his hands over his chest and said, "Hey, guys, who am I?" He laid his head back and closed his eyes and pretended to be dead.

And then all our flashlights went out.

Chrissy cursed and Tyler cried out and Benny stumbled back and someone stumbled into me and Chrissy was beside me and I grabbed her and she grabbed me and we hit a pile of junk behind us and it all came crashing down, and then we were running for the window. Tyler was first, trying to haul himself out of there. I shoved a chair into him and he got a foot up on that and boosted himself up. I wanted Chrissy to go next, but Benny was shrieking too loud to reason with, so when he was halfway out I pushed Chrissy forward and she didn't object. Tyler took hold of her left arm and helped her out, and her long legs vanished like spaghetti being sucked into a hungry mouth.

I got one foot on the chair, reached up, looked over my shoulder into the darkness and called Pete's name, and there was sudden silence.

The world beyond the window was dull. I could hear the others scrambling, their faint voices. There was light now, their flashlights active once again, flooding my little patch of basement. I existed in a cocoon of yellow and white that kept the darkness back.

"Pete!" I said again.

Pete was silent.

I couldn't go without him. I'd never be able to face him if I ran out on him. The panic was fading. I was starting to think rationally again.

In the shaking light of my cocoon, I saw the tips of Pete's shoes. Chrissy saw them, too, and shifted her flashlight. I could see Pete's legs now. He stood on the very edge of the darkness, his hands by his sides, his upper body in shadow. Not moving. Not speaking.

Every last bit of moisture left my mouth. I tried to say his name, but my heart was thudding so loudly that I couldn't even hear how it sounded. Pete's arms rose and he stood like that for a moment.

And then he ran at me, teeth bared, face frozen in a mask of hatred.

I screamed and Chrissy screamed and Benny and Tyler probably screamed as well, and Pete had almost reached me when he fell sideways, laughing so hard I thought he was crying.

"Your face!" he gasped. "Oh my God, your face!"

And he collapsed again with laughter.

"You're such a tool," I said, turning my back on him and climbing out. Chrissy helped me to my feet, but I shook off her hands and walked away, my whole body trembling. Tyler helped Pete out of the basement, which wasn't an easy task due to how much Pete was laughing.

"Your face!" was all he could say. I left him there, left all of them, and I got on my bike and cycled home.

2

I didn't see any of them the next day, but the day after that school started again and we were back together, all of us except Chrissy, who I passed a few times in the hall, but didn't say anything to. What happened at Bubba Moon's house was quickly forgotten about amid the hustle of a new school year. Pete didn't come in the next day, though, or the day after that, and on the third day in a row when he didn't come in Chrissy Brennan tracked me down at my locker.

"Have you heard from Pete?" she asked, without even saying hello first. Her hair, a rich brown that always shone so healthily, was tied back off her face. I may have only been a kid, but I knew enough to know that she probably wasn't as beautiful as I thought she was. My brother had once talked about a girl he'd liked, the prettiest girl he'd ever known, and then I met her and she was OK, but nothing special. She had a nice smile, but her eyes were too close together. My brother couldn't see it, though. He was blinded by his own infatuation, and I reckoned I was, too.

What I saw when I looked at Chrissy Brennan was pretty blue eyes and an amazing smile and a face I could gaze at for hours. She was lean and athletic and she wore ripped jeans and T-shirts, and even though her friends thought we were dorks she still hung out with us whenever she felt like it. I knew she liked *Moonlighting* and *Knight Rider* and I thought she was beautiful, but I was fully aware that I probably couldn't trust my own judgement.

It was only years later when I was looking back through old photographs that I realised that yeah, Chrissy Brennan really was as beautiful as I'd always thought, and that realisation made me smile a little.

"He hasn't been in for a few days," I said, but of course she already knew that. That's why she was asking.

"I was going to call by his place after school," she said, "to see if he's OK. Do you want to come?"

She probably didn't want to go there alone, that was all, and yet there was a small flicker of hope that lit inside me that maybe, perhaps, she wanted to spend some time with me without the other guys getting in the way.

"Sure," I said. "Straight after?"

"Yeah. Were you doing anything?"

I shook my head and kept my mouth shut so I wouldn't ask any more questions. Pressing for insignificant details was something I did when I was excited, and it was a dead giveaway. We arranged to meet at the school gates and then Chrissy walked off, her books under her arm, and I went to double history and served my time until the bell rang. I grabbed my bag, hurried to the gates, waited there for Chrissy. She walked up and we went off together in full view of everyone on the bus. It was a good moment for me.

"What do you know about Bubba Moon?" she asked, breaking the silence that followed immediately after.

I suddenly suspected that this time together was going to be all business. "When he was alive? He was a Satanist. He had a black magic cult that met at his house. My brother says you used to be able to hear chanting if you passed late at night and the wind was coming from the right direction, and sometimes screams. He says."

"Did you know the police were investigating him?"

I didn't know that. "What for?"

Chrissy looked at me. "Murder. Kids were going missing and they thought Bubba Moon and his cult were doing it."

"I didn't hear anything about any kids going missing."

"Not here, not in this town. Not even in this state. But in areas where his cult members lived, a kid would go missing before each one of his meetings. It started years ago, way back in the sixties. Why do you think they dug up his yard after he died?"

"I didn't know they had."

"Well, they did," said Chrissy. "Dug it all up, looking for the bodies. They never found any."

"Jeez," I said. "Where did you hear all this?"

"My housekeeper. She says everyone knows, but they don't like to talk about it."

"That's creepy," I said. "Someone like that, living in our town... Any one of us could have disappeared."

"My housekeeper says Bubba Moon was an evil man. Like real, actual evil. Not just bad. You know?"

I nodded.

"Did you feel it?" she asked. "You did, right? In the basement? You felt how evil he was, didn't you?"

That feeling, that dreadful feeling of malevolence that had made the hairs on my neck stand up. "I guess."

Chrissy's eyes flashed. "You *guess*? That's it? You *guess* you felt something?"

"No," I said quickly, "I mean I did. I felt it."

Satisfied by my answer, Chrissy nodded. "I think he was so evil he infected his house, that's what I think. That's why the place felt like that. The basement especially. It's probably strongest in the basement because that's where he died. And that circle, the circle Pete lay down in..."

She was scared. She was actually scared as we walked along on that beautiful warm afternoon.

"You think that's why he hasn't been in?" I asked, not sure I wanted an answer.

Chrissy blushed, and didn't look at me. "I don't know. Maybe. If Bubba Moon's evil can infect a house, why not a person?"

"Because he was living in that house for years," I said, as if it was a scientific principle. "It's like a bad smell that's been around for ages. It doesn't just go when you take the rotten thing out the room. It takes a while. You have to open windows and stuff. If it's been there for long enough, the smell lingers. Pete was only in that circle for a few seconds. He was lying down for less than that."

"Did you see how sick he looked on the first day back, though? He was all pale, and he had bags under his eyes."

I hadn't noticed that. But I did notice that Chrissy had led the way to Pete's neighbourhood without once having to ask me for directions.

Pete's house stood on a quiet street, and like all the other houses it had a sectioned-off front lawn and a back yard closed off by a wooden fence. We passed a man waiting for a bus and crossed to the other side of the road where a woman stood leaning against a lamp post, reading a paper. There were a few other people standing around, everyone doing their best to mind their own business. Chrissy glanced at me, frowning slightly.

We walked up the path and I knocked on Pete's front door.

"They're looking at us," Chrissy whispered.

I kept my eyes forward. Seeing a whole bunch of random people on the street all with their heads turned, staring at me and Chrissy, would have been more than I could have handled. It would have been like something out of *Invasion of the Bodysnatchers*, a film I'd caught on TV the previous year that had given me nightmares. I shivered. My mouth was dry. No one was coming to the door.

I tugged Chrissy's sleeve and she followed me round the side of the house. We paused at the living-room window. Pete's mom and dad sat sleeping on the couch. The TV was on and so were all the lights, even though there were still hours to go before the sun dipped. We moved on without saying anything, all the way round the house to the back, to Pete's window. We peered in.

Pete sat in the middle of the floor, legs splayed in front of him and shoulders hunched. His head was down. Eyes closed. There was something above him. Something that flickered, like heat rising off asphalt. It made my head hurt to look at it. Every few seconds, it became almost solid, and that solid form was a man, leaning down with his hands grasping Pete's head.

Chrissy made a sound, halfway between a gasp and a whimper, and the next time the form flickered into view the man was looking straight at us.

We both cried out, stumbled back from the window, and bolted for the street. We had just reached the path when Pete's front door opened and his mom stepped out.

"Well, hello there," she said brightly.

We faltered in our escape, came to an awkward, stilted stop.

"Pete's in his room," Pete's mom said, standing aside. "Come on in. I'll tell him you're here."

We should have run. I knew we should have run. Every instinct in my body was telling me to run, to get out of there. But instead we bowed our heads, the both of us, and walked dutifully into the house. The door shut behind us.

"Pete," Pete's mom called, "your friends are here!" She smiled at us. "You're so good to come by," she said. "He hasn't been feeling well lately."

Then she turned, went to the couch, and sat down beside her husband. Instantly, her chin dropped to her chest, and she was back asleep.

"Hey, guys," Pete said as he passed us on his way to the kitchen.

Chrissy and I looked at each other, then we followed him in. He stood with his back to us, looking at the fridge.

"Come to see how I'm doing, eh?" he asked.

"You haven't been in school," said Chrissy. Her voice sounded weirdly thick.

"No, I haven't," said Pete. After another moment, he opened the fridge door. "I've been feeling under the weather. I'm getting better now, though. Would either of you like a juice box?"

"No thank you," said Chrissy.

"No thanks," I said.

"I'm going to have one," said Pete, and he took out a juice box, closed the fridge, and turned. "Have you been getting much homework?"

Chrissy didn't answer. She probably figured it was my turn.

"Not really," I said. "What's been wrong with you?"

"I've been under the weather."

"The flu?"

"Just under the weather."

"Pete," said Chrissy, "does it have anything to do with what happened at Bubba Moon's house?"

Pete looked at her, looked at us both, and then down at his juice box. A moment passed. His right hand trembled. I was reminded of my grandpa, who'd had Parkinson's, which made his hands shake constantly. It got so bad he couldn't even take his own pills without spilling them all over the floor.

Then Pete's tremble passed, and he opened the juice box with ease and took a long, slow drink. When he was done, he wiped his mouth with his sleeve, burped, and grinned like a little kid. "Sorry, Chrissy, what did you say?"

"Nothing," I said before Chrissy could repeat her question. "We just called by, to make sure you're OK. So you're OK, you're doing fine, and that's good. We have to go now."

Pete's face fell, almost comically. "Already? But you just got here!"

"We have to go," I said again.

"Yeah," said Chrissy. "My mom's waiting in the car outside."

Pete frowned. "But you walked here."

Chrissy was moving back, but I froze. "How did you know?" I asked, and he looked at me. When he locked eyes with me, I could see that haze again, just over his head, and the flickering image of the man looming over his shoulder.

My thoughts slowed and a weight pressed down on my mind like a thick, heavy blanket, smothering the sharp edges, deadening the sharp voices, darkening everything and bringing it all to a slow and

329

lethargic crawl. My eyelids lowered. My strength drained. My energy sank from my body, to my feet, and out across the floor. A yearning for rest filled me, like too much food at Thanksgiving, and I yawned, such a big yawn, and my head nodded forward with such a slow and gentle—

Chrissy yanked on my arm, pulling me out from under that blanket, and strength and fright surged through me, and before I knew it I was following her out of the house, up the path. The people on the street swung their heads towards us.

I pushed Chrissy and we ran.

There was a shout and I glanced back and they were chasing, all those people, running after us. They were bigger and stronger and faster, they were full-grown adults, and in a flat-out race they were going to catch us. I grabbed Chrissy's hand, pulled her off the street again, trampling the flowers in some nice old lady's front lawn. We ran into her back yard, jumped and scrambled over the fence, landed in a garden, and sprinted for the street beyond the house. There was a loud crack and we both looked back to see the wooden fence explode, a man running through the gap.

Still gripping Chrissy's hand, I took a short cut through the narrow alley that led to the rear of the parking lot at the Green Fields Mall. We hopped over the low wall, dropped the two metres to the ground on the other side, and ran on across the sparse lot. This time of day, most people would be parking out front. We needed to get to a populated area. They wouldn't do anything in a populated area. I hoped.

Chrissy looked back, gave a cry. I didn't need to look. I knew they were behind us. I knew they were gaining. I also knew we only needed a few more moments and then we'd be safe.

We ran up to the rear doors of the mall, which slid open much too slowly for my liking. I squeezed through the gap, dragging Chrissy after me, ran up the steps, and we burst through an invisible barrier into a bubble of safety. Suddenly we were surrounded by people – mothers and kids and teenagers and fathers and businessmen and working women and shops and stalls and muzak and people handing out pamphlets and people collecting for charities – and we slowed to a fast walk and got into the middle of them all.

Only then did I turn, only then did I look back at the ones chasing us. They stood at the edge of this imagined bubble of mine, their eyes on me and Chrissy, cheated out of their prey. Slowly, they drifted back, until we lost them in the crowd.

I was still trying to get my breathing under control, but Chrissy was fitter than me, and already looking around for help. She spotted a mall cop and squeezed my arm. We hurried over. He stood on the periphery of the Food Court, thumbs hooked into his belt. He looked bored and unimpressive, but he was a mall cop with a walkie-talkie, and a mall cop with a walkie-talkie could get real cops over here in two minutes flat.

Right before we left the forest of people, literally two steps before we emerged into the empty space in front of the mall cop, Chrissy pulled me to a sudden stop.

The mall cop said something into his walkie-talkie. He chuckled at the response. A thought, completely unconnected to the danger we'd found ourselves in, floated to the surface of my mind like a stray balloon that had lost its tether. I wondered if mall cops, or anyone who used a walkie-talkie for that matter, had to undergo specialised training in order to understand what anyone else was saying on those walkie-talkies. Every time I passed one and it gurgled to life, all I heard was a confusing mess of abrupt sounds and crackle.

The thought went away when I caught sight of the man standing behind the mall cop. He looked straight at us and smiled. To his left stood a woman, also with her eyes fixed on us. Another man walked by, nodded good-naturedly to the mall cop, who nodded back, and then he smiled at us and lifted his shirt slightly. We saw the knife in his waistband, and backed off.

At the very centre of the Green Fields Mall there was an area of recessed seating. Chrissy and I sat there for an hour, huddled together but not speaking. A neighbour of Chrissy's passed, saw us sitting there and made a teasing comment about me being Chrissy's new boyfriend. Despite everything, I blushed. Chrissy's neighbour asked her if she'd like a lift home. Chrissy looked at me, desperate to say yes, but reluctant to leave me. I told her to go on, I'd be fine.

And I was fine. I walked home quickly, leaving the mall amid a mass exodus of shoppers. I didn't see any of the people who'd been chasing us. Nobody followed me – at least that I was aware of. I got home and everything was normal, and my dad got back from work and we had dinner and I watched *Airwolf* and then *Knight Rider*, and I didn't say a single word about what had happened.

The threat was clear. *You talk to the mall cop, and he dies.* And it hadn't just been a threat to mall cops. Somehow I knew it was a threat to anyone I might go to for help.

I didn't sleep that night. Chrissy told me later that she didn't, either.

I spent the weekend in my house, refusing to leave my bedroom for the most part. I tried doing my homework, I tried reading. I dreaded Monday morning. What if Pete was back in school? What if I walked into class and he was there, sitting in his usual seat, with the flickering image of that man looming over him?

Monday came, though, and Pete's seat remained empty. It was empty for the rest of that week, and the week after. Then came the news that Pete's folks had pulled him out of school. Everyone came to me and asked what had happened, what was wrong with my friend, but I just shrugged and told them I hadn't been speaking to him. Eventually, they stopped asking.

Four months after that, I woke up one night to my name being called outside my window. I got out of bed, parted the curtains. There was a sliver of moon in the cloudy sky that barely lit anything in my backyard, but I could see Pete's face, pale and smiling up at me.

He called my name softly, and I heard him giggle. Then the clouds covered the moon, and when the moon came back Pete was gone.

I went back to bed and I didn't sleep that night, either.

3

I left home when I was eighteen, glad to see the back of the place, glad to leave all those bad memories behind. By then, of course, my selective memory had long since sorted through it all and thrown out the more outlandish elements of what had happened. The version of the truth it left me with was a lot more palatable to a reasonable mind such as mine.

In this new version, elegant in its simplicity and carefully censored to protect the innocent, me and my friends had broken into this creepy old house when we were kids and we'd scared each other witless. A few days later, I went for a walk with a pretty girl to see my sick buddy, then ended up getting chased over fences by irate neighbours after we trampled some flowers. This revised version of events didn't feature the flickering figure or the subtle threats and it made absolutely no mention of Bubba Moon, and that was OK by me.

I went to college in NYU and studied hard. I guess I knew that dropping out or failing would mean an inevitable return to my hometown, and I had no intention of going back there any time soon.

In my second year in New York, I met a girl in the library. She was surrounded by coursework and weighty tomes, and I glimpsed the lurid cover of a Gordon Edgley paperback peeking out from behind a textbook. I sat opposite, threatened to expose her for the fraud she was if she didn't agree to have a coffee with me. I'd never been that forward before, but there was something about her, something about the way her attention was completely and utterly focused on the horror story in her hands, that made her irresistible to a bookworm like me.

She gave me a smile that only hinted at her mischievous nature, and five years later we were married. Two years after that we had our first kid. Three years after that, our second. I got a good job in a bank and Felicity stayed at home and took care of the kids, and for a nice long while life was sweet.

Then the subprime crisis came along and the bank I was working for went under, and I lost my job and most of our savings in the same month. We'd invested heavily in rock-solid shares built on shaky foundations, and when the tremors began it all came crashing down. We were surviving, barely keeping our heads above water, holding on to our home with the tips of our fingers.

Felicity and I started arguing. A little at first, a cross word or a snapped comment, and those icy silences that grew into cold nights. We kept the edge from our voices when the kids were around, or at least we thought we did. I guess kids notice a lot more than we want them to.

Then, in February of the next year, my brother called, told me our dad had died. This odd kind of numbness crept over me as I talked to him, as I listened to his voice, leaden with grief, and when the call was done I put down the phone and sat in my study, surrounded by bills and notices and demands for payment, and cried.

We packed our bags and drove home. I did most of the driving. I thought about my dad a lot, of course, but also my childhood, my old friends. I thought about Tyler and Benny and the girl, the pretty one, what was her name? Chrissy, that was it. Chrissy Brennan. Man, I had such a crush on her. It was all coming back to me, like the miles were bricks in a wall that blocked me from my memories, and each mile we ticked off was one less brick.

I remembered Pete Green, too, my earliest childhood friend. I'd lost touch with him. Couldn't really remember why.

The town had grown since I was there last. Bits and pieces were the same, but mostly it looked like a large alien city had been superimposed over it. The old cinema was gone, but around the next corner there was a giant sprawling mall that had a multi-screen cinema of its very own. Chapters Second-hand Bookstore, a store that had once been like a church to me, was now a tanning salon. They did nails, too, announced the sign in the window. My eleven-year-old self would have been horrified. I mentioned this to my kids in the back seat. My son grunted. My daughter ignored me.

We arrived at my old house. Mom started fussing over us immediately. She didn't know about the problems Felicity and I were having, but I think she suspected. My brother was there. He said Mom had been trying to keep busy, like she was determined to work so hard that the sadness never had a chance to settle. We let her. Everyone grieves in their own way.

I was tired after the long drive, but that evening I went with my brother to a local bar, and we sat and talked. He told me about his life and I gave him an edited version of mine. I hadn't seen him in over seven years. He'd put on weight and he'd lost some more hair. He looked like a real grown-up now. I told him this and he laughed ruefully, and went to get us another drink.

When he was gone, a pretty girl at the table beside me gave me a smile. She couldn't have been much more than seventeen, but I smiled back, anyway, out of politeness more than anything. A woman approached my table. She was a few years older than me, pretty but strained, with grey in her hair, and a little too thin to be healthy.

"I was sorry to hear about your father," she said.

I looked at her and fished for a name, but it wouldn't come. Not at first. Someone laughed at the bar and she glanced over, and I caught an angle and the realisation hit me like a wrecking ball.

"Chrissy Brennan," I said, like I had no breath in my lungs.

She smiled, sat opposite me, setting her glass neatly on a coaster. I remembered the smile. It used to be such a beautiful smile. It still had echoes of that beauty, but now it threw up all those lines around her mouth. She looked old. She was my age, but she looked old. "Didn't think you'd recognise me," she said, brushing a strand of hair back over her ear, the way she used to.

"You're looking well," I said.

She smiled again. "How long are you here for?"

"Funeral's tomorrow. We'll stick around for a few days after that, to keep my mom busy. It's good to see you. I was just thinking about you, actually, on the drive over."

"I've been thinking about you, too," she said, in a way that nagged at me slightly.

My brother caught my eye, gestured over his shoulder to a few friends of his, and I nodded as he left me and Chrissy alone.

"So what have you been up to?" I asked. "How've you been?"

"I've been better," she said, and then laughed. "Sorry. Didn't mean to be a buzzkill quite so early on in the conversation. I saw you half an hour ago and I was sitting over there, debating whether or not to come and talk to you. Now I'm here and suddenly the mood goes way down."

She was blushing, and I leaned forward. "Hey, don't worry about it. Things have been better for me, too. My marriage, for one. I lost my job a few months ago. Before we see the summer, we'll probably lose the house as well." I hadn't even told my brother that part. "And that's not even mentioning my dad, OK? So don't feel bad about bringing down the mood. The mood is pretty low to begin with."

I'd wanted to make her feel better, but it hadn't even raised a sympathetic smile.

"I got married," she said. "I have a son, Scott, who'll be fourteen in May. I'm not with my husband any more. He's not a very nice man. I have two jobs, neither of which pays me enough to give up the other. And I'm scared."

I nodded. "These are scary times."

She looked up at me, frowning. "No. I'm scared of *him*."

I answered her frown with one of my own. "Your husband?"

Now it was her turn to lean forward. "*Pete*," she said in a whisper. "Pete Green?"

"Who else? What's wrong with you?"

"I'm sorry, Chrissy, I'm not really sure what you're talking about."

She stared at me.

She stared at me for so long I thought something brittle had snapped off in her mind.

"Don't do this," she said. "Don't you dare do this to me. You're the only other one who was there. You're the only other one who knows what happened."

"What happened when? I'm really not—"

"Bubba Moon," she said sharply, and the edge of a migraine stabbed at me behind my eyes.

"Bubba Moon," I repeated. "Yeah, OK. The town bogeyman. We broke into his house when we were kids. But we weren't the only ones there. Tyler McCormick and Benny Alverez were with us, and Pete."

Chrissy nodded. "And then a few days later we went to see if Pete was all right. We went to his house, you and me. Do you remember that?"

I smiled. "I remember us running from some particularly angry neighbours. I do remember that much."

"Angry neighbours? What are you talking about? They weren't angry neighbours. They were his followers."

"Whose followers? Pete's? Pete was an eleven-year-old boy."

"*Bubba Moon's* followers," Chrissy said, with a vehemence that made me sit back warily. "They were outside his house. Remember? You told me later it reminded you of a movie. That one with Donald Sutherland and Jeff Goldblum."

"*Invasion of the Bodysnatchers*," I said automatically, and something loosened in my mind. More bricks fell, enough to let an old feeling seep out. Fear.

I shifted in my seat. "Chrissy, it was a long time ago. Obviously I remember it differently than you do."

"You left," she said, like she was accusing me of treason. "Looks like you blocked it out. You didn't want to think of it any more. But I stayed. I remember everything, exactly the way it happened. You know those people who chased us into the Green Fields Mall? I see them practically every day. They haven't changed. They have not aged one little bit since that time we saw them. And there are more of them now. Over a dozen, I think, all living on the same street as Pete."

"I don't remember their faces, Chrissy, so I wouldn't be able to tell if they'd aged or not. But before we go any further, I want you to take a moment and think about the things you're saying."

She chewed her lip and nodded, then she looked down at the table, and I let out a breath. My hands were clenched, though I didn't know why. I drained the last dregs from my beer and was about to cut our encounter short by standing up, when she raised her eyes. She was calmer.

"I understand that it sounds insane," she said. "And I apologise for that. I also apologise for all this... anger. I suppose... I suppose I've been angry with you for leaving, and angry with you for the way our friendship ended, but neither of those things are your fault."

I didn't remember how our friendship ended, but I wanted this conversation to be over so I didn't ask.

"Here are the facts as I know them," Chrissy said. "Please bear with me. Some of them might jog some memories. A lot won't. Please don't walk out until I'm done."

I hesitated, but there was still enough of the beautiful girl I had once known in her face that I couldn't deny her this one request. "OK. Say what you have to."

"Thank you," she said. "Bubba Moon was a serial killer. Just because he was never called one by the police or the papers doesn't make this simple fact any less true. He was a serial killer, and he had his followers. As far as I know, they called themselves the People. They were a black magic cult. Maybe Satanists or devil worshippers."

"Satanists," I repeated, raising an eyebrow.

"It's not uncommon. Or it wasn't, anyway. People like Bubba Moon and Charles Manson, they attract people who live on the fringes of society – Satanists, fascists, convicted felons."

"OK," I said. "Go on."

"Moon's People would meet every month here in town, at his house. They'd take it in turns to bring an offering."

"What kind of offering?"

Chrissy looked me in the eye and said, in that same calm tone, "Kids. Fourteen-year-old kids. Girls or boys, it didn't matter, they just had to be fourteen years old. I don't know why. From what I've worked out, they were brought down to the basement and ritually murdered while the People chanted around them."

"Uh-huh. And what proof do you have of this?"

"No proof. Just stories."

"Right."

"Can I continue?"

I sighed. "Sure."

"Bubba Moon was also a psychic. He didn't read palms or tell fortunes, but he was clairvoyant. I've spoken to police officers who swear that he knew things about them during interrogations that he couldn't possibly have known."

"And the officers in question admitted this to you, did they?"

"Some of them did, yes. Though of course they'd never admit it in public."

"Oh, of course," I said.

"They'd been bringing him in for questioning for years, all related to various murders. They could get nothing to stick, until one of his People slipped up and got himself arrested. He told the cops everything. He told them more than everything. He told them about stuff so bizarre and insane that he had to be making it up, but within all that craziness he knew enough details about open murder cases that they were forced to take him seriously."

"So did they have enough to arrest Moon?"

Chrissy took a moment to sip her drink. "It didn't make any difference. Their key witness, who had agreed to testify and name Moon as the one who'd done all the killing, died in his cell the same night they went to search Moon's house. He hanged himself with a sheet."

"How inconvenient," I said, but Chrissy ignored me and continued.

"You should know this part," she said. "The cops have their warrant, knock on the door, don't get an answer, and they break the door down. They find Bubba Moon's body in the basement, lying in the middle of a circle, surrounded by occult symbols."

The circle. I remembered it now.

"They put him in a body bag, take him away, and search the house. They find a lot of old bloodstains, but tests are inconclusive. They dig up the back yard, looking for bodies. They don't find any.

They find no evidence at all, actually. Bubba Moon is buried in some crappy little grave, his house is boarded up and never sold, and that's the end of the story."

"OK, then."

"Until a bunch of stupid kids break into that old house eighteen years later, and one of them, showing off to the others, jumps into that circle, and lies down where Bubba Moon had been lying down when they found him."

I needed another drink. My mouth was dry. "Pete," I said.

"That's right. Pete. He was perfectly fine for a couple of days, and then he didn't turn up at school. That Thursday afternoon, you and me paid him a visit. We wanted to see if he was OK. We walked there."

"There were people looking at us," I said softly.

Chrissy nodded. "We knocked on his door, then went round the back of the house. We saw Pete sitting on the floor and there was someone standing over him, only we couldn't see him properly because he kept flickering—"

"Like a heat haze," I said.

"Yes. Just like that. We tried to run, but Pete's mom called us in. Do you remember she went right back to the couch?"

"And fell asleep," I said. "Then Pete came out. There was something weird about the way he moved sometimes. He had a drink or something..."

"A juice box," said Chrissy.

"A juice box, yeah. It was like he wanted to open it, but it took a while for the message to reach his hands. Then... then something happened to me."

"He looked at you and all of a sudden you were falling asleep," said Chrissy. "He was doing the same thing to you as he'd done to his parents."

"But you saved me," I said. "We ran. They chased us. Into the mall. The security guard..."

"They were going to kill him," said Chrissy. "I'm certain of it. If we'd even tried to alert him, they'd have killed him there and then. They'd have killed anyone we told. Our parents. Teachers. Cops. Anyone."

"My God. I remember."

"Pete was taken out of school. We didn't really see him much after that. I'd come across him occasionally on the street, but I'd always hide until he was gone. His People were around him at all times. It should have been funny seeing all these grown-ups trailing after a kid, obeying his every command... but it wasn't funny. It wasn't funny one little bit."

Chrissy took another drink. "We stopped talking. You and me. We were too scared to talk, to be honest. We were too scared to remain friends. It was my fault as much as it was yours, but I blamed you for as long as I could. So you went away, all the way to New York City. And I met Toby, and I fell in what I thought was love, and I got a fantastic kid out of it, and then I realised Toby wasn't worth much as a human being, and I kicked him out. I took on another job, raised Scott myself."

"Must have been hard."

She shrugged. "People do it every day. But I did my best to live my life, to put the past behind me."

"Where it belongs," I said.

A thin smile. "If only we were that lucky. A few years ago, I started searching, just out of pure curiosity."

"Searching for what?"

"Disappearances," she said. "Fourteen-year-old kids going missing. I figured, if it was still happening, it'd be easy to spot. All of Moon's People are living in the same town now, after all. Their victims wouldn't be spread out halfway across America like last time."

"And... and did you find anything? Were they doing it again?"

Chrissy held her glass, but didn't raise it to her lips. She just smiled, a smile that was the furthest thing from peaceful I had ever seen. "They'd never stopped," she said. "Every month, a fourteen-year-old goes missing. People go missing all the time, of course they do, everyone knows that, but these kids get lost in the statistics. They're classed as *lost teenagers* instead of *lost fourteen-year-olds*. No one has made the connection. And they're local, but this town isn't as small as it used to be. Neither are the towns around us. Moon's People are choosing targets close to home."

"OK... OK, if that's true—"

"I've got the numbers, I can show you—"

"I don't want to see them," I said, a little more sharply than I'd intended. "Sorry. I mean I don't need to see them. I believe you

346

that there does seem to be a... trend. But let's say you're right... I still don't know what this has to do with Pete Green."

"Yes, you do," said Chrissy.

"No, I don't."

"You saw the flickering man. That wasn't a hallucination. We both saw it."

"Yeah. I admit it. I saw it. It was real. But what *was* it?"

That strand of hair had come loose again. Chrissy tucked it behind her ear with her left hand. There was a band of lighter skin around her ring finger. "You know what it was," she said. "I told you, Moon was a psychic."

"I don't believe in psychics."

"You don't believe in the fakes and the frauds and the shysters who con grieving widows out of their life savings... But that's not what we're talking about here. Bubba Moon was a psychic. He died in that circle doing black magic. Pete lay down in the same circle, and when he got up we started seeing a figure hunched over him."

"You think... you think the figure was Bubba Moon?"

"Yes."

"And... what do you think Moon was doing with Pete?"

"Controlling him. That's what it looked like, right?"

I nodded. "You think he's still controlling him, even now?"

"More than that," said Chrissy. "I think Bubba Moon is possessing him."

"This is crazy."

"I know. And I've been living with it for most of my life, too afraid to talk about it, or tell anyone, or do anything... But now you're back. I'm not alone any more."

Her eyes were filled with such hope that it killed a little part of me. "Chrissy," I said slowly, "what do think is going to happen now? If this is all true and Moon is that powerful and there are that many of them... what can the two of us do about it?"

She smiled, a sweet, trusting smile. "We can stop them."

"No, we can't," I said. "These are dangerous people. They're killers. What good would we be against a bunch of murderers?"

The smile faltered. "I... we'd come up with a plan."

"What kind of plan? Have you ever had to come up with any kind of plan like this before? Would you even know where to begin? I wouldn't. Here's our plan, Chrissy. We go to the police. They won't believe us, but we tell them everything we know. We have a responsibility to do that, but that's as far as it goes."

She shook her head. "The police can't stop them."

"We don't know that."

"They'll kill the police."

"Back when we were kids, sure," I said. "Back when they were a handful of small-town cops. But this isn't a small town any more. The cops are better trained and better equipped. We'll tell them Moon's People are planning a mass shooting. They'll get a SWAT team in, they'll get helicopters..."

"That won't work."

"We have to try."

"If we try and it doesn't work, it'll make things worse."

"What do you mean worse?"

Chrissy took a drink, drained her glass. "His People know me. When I see them in the street, they look at me. They smile. A few of them have tapped their watches."

"I don't get it."

Tears brimmed. "Scott is turning fourteen next month. They're going to take my son. I know they are."

I didn't have anything to say to that, so she continued. "I was going to move. A few weeks ago, I was all set to quit my jobs, take Scott out of school, and just run. I'd made some calls, managed to get an interview for a job in Utah, of all places. And then I get a postcard. A big bright 'Welcome to Utah' postcard, and on the back someone had written 'Can't wait for you to get here!' They knew. He knew. Moon knew I was planning to run. He was telling me there's nowhere I can go where Scott will be safe."

"Chrissy, I—"

"Please," she said, tears welling. "I can't lose my son. Please, help me."

4

The cemetery was on Bredon's southernmost hill. When I was a kid, we used to cycle up there on a summer's day and have picnics of peanut butter and jelly sandwiches and Dr Peppers. Back then, you could see practically the whole town from up here. Not any more. Now the town's sprawl was too wide and the buildings too high. Whole neighbourhoods were hidden from view and locked away, like old secrets.

Benny Alverez came to the funeral. When it was done, he walked up to me and we shook hands.

"I always liked your dad," Benny said. "He'd make those stupid jokes, then act surprised when we laughed *at* him rather than w*ith* him."

"That was no act," I said, feigning a lighter kind of sadness. "You're looking well. Middle age must agree with you."

He blanched. "Is that what we are now? Middle-aged? I thought being in your fifties was middle-aged. I read that somewhere. In a science magazine."

I nodded. "Oh, that's right, I read that, too. Middle age is always the decade ahead of the one you're in now."

"That's it," he said, grinning. "Yeah, I'm doing OK. Married a woman ten years younger than me, had our first kid last year."

"You dog."

He shrugged. "It is what it is." He nodded to my kids. "They yours?"

"They are," I said, my eyes on my wife for a moment. She looked tired. Even Chrissy Brennan hadn't looked so tired. "Wait till your bouncing baby becomes a temperamental teen," I said. "That'll put some grey hairs on your chest."

"Looking forward to it," Benny said, smiling. "So how's life in the big city?"

I looked away, pretending to scan the crowd. "Chaotic. Uncertain. All the words you don't want to hear with a family to support." I looked back at him. "This place has changed a lot."

"Hasn't it?"

"I could barely recognise some of the streets," I said. "The Palladium is gone."

"Replaced with a twenty-screen behemoth on the next block over. Which, to be honest, is so much better than the Palladium ever was. Remember the sticky floors and the tattered seats and the dreadful sound system? Most of the movies we saw there started off as silent films before the projectionist heard the booing."

I laughed. "I'd forgotten that. Rose-tinted glasses, I suppose."

Benny's smile faded. "Yeah. Nostalgia's a killer. In town for long?"

"Don't know," I said. "After this, we'll be taking it day by day. All depends on what Mom needs."

"Tell her I was asking after her. I'd offer her my condolences, but she wouldn't know who the hell I was. Last time she saw me I was, what, twelve?"

"Eleven or twelve, yeah. You and Tyler, pulling wheelies on the street outside, showing off. Ever hear anything about him?"

Benny looked at me, his eyes narrow. "What do you mean?"

"After he ran away. Did he ever come back?"

"Man, Tyler didn't run away. He was snatched."

I frowned. "What?"

"He disappeared one afternoon on his way home from school. I can't believe you don't remember this."

"I remember him running away."

"Why do you keep saying that? They said he ran away for the first few days he was gone, then they found his bike and his bag and evidence of a struggle. It was all anyone talked about in school for months."

"So what happened to him?"

"He was murdered, most likely. His remains are probably still lying in some shallow grave in the woods even now. You seriously don't remember that?"

"It... it's coming back to me..."

"Last day of April, it was. I remember it vividly." Benny put his hands in his pockets and turned slightly, looking out over the town. "Poor kid. He was only fourteen."

"I can't believe I missed it," Chrissy said on the phone later. "I suppose... I suppose when it happened I didn't know what was going on, and when I started to look back a few years ago it was a cursory glance. Just enough to convince myself the murders were still taking place. I'd never even considered that Tyler's disappearance had anything to do with Bubba Moon."

"Well, don't feel too bad," I said, speaking softly as I stood in the back yard behind my old house. "All I'd remembered about it was those first few days when everyone said he'd run away because of his dad. I'd convinced myself that's what happened, even though I was here when the cops decided he'd been murdered. What the hell is wrong with me?"

"You wanted to leave it all behind, and I can't blame you," Chrissy said. "But do you believe me? If Moon went after Tyler, one of Pete's best friends, then he won't think twice about going after the kids of Pete's other friends now."

"But why Tyler?" I asked. "Why just him? We all turned fourteen the same year. If Moon kills one kid every month, why didn't he snatch all four of us?"

"That would have been way too suspicious," Chrissy said. "The cops would be investigating everyone we'd ever spoken to, and that would have led straight to Pete Green's door."

"So Moon just took one of us," I said, my voice dull. "Snatched him away like he was playing a game."

"I think that's exactly what this is," Chrissy said. "With all the People smiling at me, tapping their watches... it's a game. He wants to scare me. He has to be stopped."

"How? If Pete's possessed... what do we do? Call an exorcist? Hold a prayer meeting? I don't even know what the first step is. The best thing we can do, and I know you've already objected to this, is go to the police. At the very least they'll put Scott into protective custody or something."

"Are you sure about that? Are you absolutely, one hundred per cent sure about that? Because if we tell the police, and the police don't believe us, or they can't do anything, then Bubba Moon will make us pay. I know he will, and so do you. He'll make us pay for ruining this game of his, and that means Scott or someone or..."

"What? Chrissy, what?"

"How... how old is your son?"

I looked at the phone like it was an odd thing, like it was a foreign object that did not belong in my hand. On stiff legs, I walked back inside. I hadn't seen my son all evening. He'd been in my old bedroom. That's where he was now. Probably sitting in my old room, watching TV on his laptop or something. Not bothering to come up for air, or say hi, and definitely not feeling the urge to communicate. I knew this behaviour well. It had started last year. It had started when he turned thirteen.

I knocked on the bedroom door and opened it. My daughter passed me. "Where is he?" I asked.

She knew who I meant. She just shrugged, walked on.

On stiff legs, with a dry mouth, I went to the living room, where Felicity was sitting with Mom and my aunt. "Anyone seen Sammy?" I asked.

Shaking of heads all round. I nodded. My keys were in my pocket. I walked out the front door, closed it gently behind me, and bolted to my car. I jumped in, slid the key into the ignition. The engine came to life and I snapped it into gear and the passenger-side doors opened, two of them at the same time. A slender black man in a good suit slid in beside me. On the back seat, a girl in black.

"I wouldn't do that if I were you," the man said.

"Where's my son?" I screamed, making a grab for him. My hands were pushed down with unsettling ease and the man reached over and smacked my head painfully against the steering wheel.

"We don't know," he said, "but I'm sure we'll figure it out easily enough. How's your nose? Sorry about that, but we can't afford to let you drive to Pete Green's house and get yourself killed."

"Where is my son?" I repeated, through gritted teeth.

"He could be in one of three places," the man said, "or he could be in a fourth that we don't yet know about. We didn't take him, if that's what you're thinking."

"That's what he's thinking," said the girl in the back seat.

"That's what I thought," said the man. "But we didn't. Take him, that is."

I looked at the man in the seat beside me. He was well-groomed. Clean-shaven. He wore gloves and had a hat sitting on his lap. He didn't strike me as a Satanist. I turned to peer at the girl. I'd seen her before. She smiled at me and I recognised her from the bar the previous night – she'd been sitting at the next table when Chrissy came over.

"You're Moon's People," I said.

"We're not," she told me.

"You've been spying on me."

"Only a little." She gave another smile. "And we've been listening to your phone calls slightly."

They both spoke with an accent. Irish, though his was a little less distinct that hers. Maybe he travelled a lot.

"What do you want?" I asked.

"We're here to help," the man said. "We're your exorcists."

"My name's Valkyrie," said the girl.

"And you can call me Mr Pleasant," said the man.

5

They made me drive to the bottom of King Hill, and left me in the car with the engine still running. I could have driven away right there and then. Instead, I turned the engine off, killed the lights, and got out.

Mr Pleasant stood looking up at Bubba Moon's old house on the top of the hill. He had his hat on now, which made him look like an old-time private eye, the kind I used to watch on TV when I was a kid. A black Humphrey Bogart. The girl sat on the bonnet of my car and swung her legs.

"Why did you bring me here?" I asked.

Pleasant looked round. "We didn't," he said. "You drove us."

"You made me drive you."

"We asked you to and you did. We didn't force you to do anything."

Valkyrie looked at me. "I heard what your friend said last night about Bubba Moon. She got it right. Well, most of it. Moon isn't a Satanist, though."

"That's right," Pleasant murmured. "He's just sick."

He started walking up the hill. Valkyrie hopped off the bonnet and followed. I didn't know what was expected of me, so I followed, too.

"Where's my son?" I asked, for what felt like the hundredth time.

"I should have thought it was obvious," said Pleasant. "The People have him."

"Then we call the police. We have to call the police."

"We don't know where he is," Valkyrie interjected, and it struck me that she was playing the good cop role in this partnership. He was allowed to be as rude as he liked, as long as she was there to smooth things over.

"If you call the police, they'll rush in and whoever's holding Sammy will kill him immediately and dump the body. He's not in any danger right now. They do their killings on the fourteenth of each month. That's tomorrow night. He's safe for now."

"Is he here?" I asked, my eyes flicking ahead of us. The house loomed, a dark thing in the darkness, its faded paint peeling like burst blisters, its windows blanked out by rotten wood, its roof patchy with old tiles.

"This is the most obvious place," Pleasant said, "so I doubt it.

But before we go charging in to the rescue, first we eliminate all the places we shouldn't be charging."

I frowned. "Rescue? You're going to rescue Sammy? You're going to help me?"

"Of course," said Pleasant. "You're only just getting that? We announced ourselves as the exorcists. How much clearer can we make it?"

"Don't mind him," said Valkyrie, patting my arm. "He's just cranky. He didn't even want to come here in the first place."

Pleasant looked around sharply. "We are in the middle of a very important investigation. Very important. Things are happening."

"We were in Chicago," Valkyrie said, "doing a thing. About to go home. Then we're asked to come here, to do a little digging if we had the time."

"Which of course we don't," said Pleasant. "But your Sanctuary asked, and our Sanctuary said sure, let's put our investigation on hold, let's ignore the possibility of a disease that turns ordinary people into ticking time bombs and send our two best detectives to Bredon. Even though you have your own."

I frowned. "Sorry?"

"Detectives," he said. "America. America has its own detectives. Some good ones, too. None as good as me, of course."

"And that's the burden you bear with such humility," Valkyrie said, but her voice was softer now as we neared the house.

Pleasant led the way around the full circumference. The place looked even deader than it had when I was a kid. It also looked infinitely creepier. If I had thought that adulthood meant I wasn't going to find my flesh crawling, I was about as wrong as I could possibly be.

"You feel that?" Valkyrie said, pulling back the sleeve of her jacket and examining her arm. "Goosebumps. Skulduggery, I have goosebumps."

Pleasant looked round. "Interesting," he said.

"Your name is Skulduggery Pleasant?" I asked.

"Yes," he said. "Have you heard of me?"

"No. What kind of name is Skulduggery Pleasant? It sounds made up."

"It is made up. All names are made up. Why are we talking about this? The basement, wasn't it? That's where you broke in? Through this window, I take it?"

He pointed to the narrow window close to the ground, and I realised I was standing exactly where I had been all those years ago. I nodded.

Pleasant handed his hat to Valkyrie. "Do not wear it," he said, then crouched, prising the window open with his fingers. When it was open, he lay flat and slid through easily. It was like his body momentarily deflated, his clothes sinking to allow him access. A moment later, the window was lit from inside by a warm, flickering orange light.

Valkyrie put the hat on and looked at me. "Your friend was right. Bubba Moon is a psychic, or what we call a Sensitive. His followers have similar gifts. The same way Skulduggery and I have gifts. Some of his followers are Sensitives, some are... other things. You don't have to worry about any of that."

Her phone buzzed. She held it to her ear. She wore a big clunky black ring. She listened for a moment, then hung up. "They're not there," she said. "He'll be out in a sec. He's just looking around."

"Who *are* you?" I asked.

She hesitated. "We take care of things like this. Like Skulduggery said, we're exorcists. Of a sort. Except instead of praying and waving a crucifix we, y'know... punch. And shoot. There's a bit of stabbing, too. Lots of screaming. Some running."

A gust of wind snatched the hat from her head, took it up to one of the windows, and Skulduggery Pleasant reached through the wooden boards and grabbed it.

Valkyrie glared. "He never lets me wear it."

I wanted to drive right up to Pete's house and hammer on the door, but Pleasant made me park a block away, and we got out and walked.

"You said Sammy is at one of three places," I said. "Bubba Moon's house was the first, this is the second. What's the third?"

"A warehouse on the edge of town," said Pleasant. "We followed one of his People there yesterday. It's owned by a business that doesn't exist. Fudged paperwork, not done with any degree of style or finesse, but enough to pass routine inspection. High level of security, though, for a building that, as far as we can see, doesn't actually contain anything."

"That sounds like it's where they do their... killings," I said, then frowned. "Doesn't it?"

"It does," Pleasant agreed. "But it may not necessarily be where they keep their offerings."

"Shouldn't we get back-up? Do you *have* back-up? Chrissy said Pete has over a dozen followers."

"I wouldn't worry about that," said Pleasant. "Valkyrie and I have faced worse odds than this."

"You have?"

"We have," said Valkyrie, and then her reassuring smile slipped. "We've never actually *won* against those odds, but..."

"But we've come close," Pleasant said, "and trying is the main thing when it comes to life-and-death situations. Or one of the main things, anyway. It's in the top three. Well, top five. You need to stop thinking of him as Pete Green, by the way. He's Bubba Moon now. By this stage there'll be no trace of your old friend left in there at all, and any assumption otherwise could prove fatal."

"But can you get rid of him? Get rid of Moon?"

"Not if he doesn't want to go," said Pleasant, "and not without a powerful Sensitive of our own."

"So how are you going to exorcise him? Do you say prayers or...?"

Pleasant glanced at Valkyrie, then looked at me. "I'm going to have to kill him. Do you have a problem with that?"

I went cold, but my legs didn't stop moving. "Pete's innocent," I said. "But Bubba Moon is a serial killer and... I just want my son back."

"And even if they worked, prayers wouldn't do any good," said

Valkyrie. "It wasn't Moon's spirit that possessed your friend – it was his disembodied consciousness. Apparently, there's a difference. Bubba Moon wasn't dead when the cops found him. He was doing some astral projection. You know what that is?"

"I think so," I said. "Didn't the CIA try that in the seventies? They'd have their agents go into a trance and send their minds out to spy on the Russians or something."

"Very much like that," said Valkyrie. "Although Moon could do a lot more than spy."

We got to the corner. A hundred yards down the block lay Pete Green's house. The lights were on.

"Moon knew the cops had one of his People," she continued, "and he knew this guy was talking. So he sent out his astral self and killed his follower in his jail cell. Made it look like a suicide. It all would have worked out fine if the cops hadn't burst in with that search warrant. When they found him, he wasn't dead, he was comatose. The circle was keeping his body alive."

"So when they moved him out of the circle," I said, "his body died."

Valkyrie nodded. "And his consciousness had nowhere to return to. It was drawn back to that circle where it stayed, trapped, until you kids came along."

"Eighteen years of Bubba Moon seething in that circle," Pleasant said. "He infected the whole house with his foul thoughts. That's why you felt uneasy. That's why the both of you had goosebumps."

"What about you?" I asked. "Did you have goosebumps?"

Pleasant looked at me, and Valkyrie grinned. Neither of them said anything, and then Pleasant moved off. Valkyrie stayed where she was, and I stayed beside her.

"Where's he going?"

"He's just checking out the house," she said.

I looked back, but Pleasant was gone. The suddenness of his disappearance alarmed me. I scanned the area. It was dark, but it wasn't that dark. There was nowhere for him to hide, and he couldn't possibly have jumped one of the fences in the three seconds I was looking away. I was going to ask Valkyrie where he'd gone, but I was struck by the quiet knowledge that she wasn't going to tell me. So I stayed beside her, and we both looked at Pete Green's house.

The street wasn't much different than I remembered. The houses were the same. Some of them, Pete's included, may have had an extension added on, but they were basically unchanged. There were a few tall walls where there had once been only fences. The lawns were neater.

I was suddenly struck by the insanity of the situation. Here I was, sneaking around the town I grew up in with two Irish exorcists who planned to kill my childhood friend because he was possessed by the consciousness of a serial killer.

But just as that wave of insanity hit me, another one followed, and this brought with it a cold determination to do whatever I had to do, to believe whatever I had to believe, in order to get my son back. Because behind all this madness was the reality, the only reality that mattered. I had carried my son in my arms and on my back, administered more Band-Aids than I could remember, held him when he cried, made up bedtime stories every night for ten years, and laughed with him at a thousand dumb things.

With him gone, it was like a piece of me had been sliced away – stolen. Once Sammy was back, once my family was safe, I could afford to allow plain, boring, run-of-the-mill reality to creep back into my world view. Until then, sneaking around with Irish exorcists was the place for me.

"Your son's not in there," Skulduggery Pleasant said from behind us. I turned sharply, stifling a curse, but he was already walking away. Valkyrie's reaction was much calmer, like she knew he was there. How he had snuck up on us, though, I had no idea.

"How do you know?" I asked, hurrying after him.

"Because I looked."

"You can't have looked. You were only gone a few minutes."

"A few minutes are all I need," Pleasant said. He touched his face, kneading the skin, and I saw him frown. "We'll have to hurry to the warehouse. We don't have much time."

The warehouse was empty. It was obviously empty. Somehow I just knew it. The others did, too, but Pleasant had to make sure. Like before, I stayed outside with Valkyrie while he vanished into the shadows. He came back a few minutes later, shaking his head.

"It's set up, ready for a ritual sacrifice, but there's no sign of your son," he said. He was touching his face again. "They could be keeping him anywhere. We're going to have to wait until tomorrow."

"What?" I said. "No. No, we can't leave Sammy with them overnight."

"Of course we can," Pleasant said, "and we'll catch them red-handed tomorrow. It'll all be very dramatic. You'll love it, believe me."

"No," I said. "We have to keep searching."

"It's pointless. Even if you knew this town, which you don't, not any more, it'd be a waste of time. Go home, get some sleep. We'll pick you up at three in the afternoon. I'll tell you the plan then."

"You're... you're sure? You're sure this is the best course of action?"

"This is the only course of action. Be ready at three."

I nodded, sagging against my car. I suddenly realised how tired I was. How utterly exhausted. "Can I give you a lift anywhere? To your hotel?"

"We're fine," Valkyrie said. "And try not to worry, OK? Saving people is what we do."

I gave another nod, then got in the car. I swung round, pointing the nose back the way I'd come. I glanced in the rear-view mirror, saw Pleasant and Valkyrie standing close to each other. His arm was round her waist. My eyes flickered to the road ahead, then back to the rear-view. The road behind me was empty.

6

I got no sleep. My son was in the hands of a madman. Every ten minutes, I grabbed the phone, ready to dial for the cops. But I didn't. I don't know why I was trusting these strangers, but trusting them I was, and so I didn't dial. I just thought about it a lot.

Three o'clock the following day I was sitting in my car outside my old home, waiting for Skulduggery Pleasant and Valkyrie to suddenly open the doors and get in.

At four o'clock, I was standing in the kitchen, a mug of cold coffee in my hand, my eyes on the street outside.

"You seen Sammy?" Felicity asked, passing behind me.

"He's checking out the places I used to go as a kid," I said. The words came out quickly, spilled out like a lie I'd been waiting to tell. "I drew him a map."

She came up, put her hand on my arm. "How're you doing?"

I stiffened, and she took her hand away. Then left.

At ten minutes to five, my phone rang.

"Hi," said Chrissy.

"Oh," I said, "hey."

"You sound disappointed."

"I'm just waiting for someone. They're late."

"Oh. OK. Listen, I'm sorry if I upset you last night."

"You didn't," I said, making sure no one was around before I continued in a softer voice. "They have him. They have Sammy. You were right, Chrissy. About all of it."

"They have Sammy? Oh, God."

"Chrissy, I met some people last night. A man called Pleasant and a girl called Valkyrie. They knew everything. They said they could help."

There was a pause. "Be careful," Chrissy said. "This sounds like something Pete would do."

"No, it's not him. They're genuine. I really think they're genuine. They knew everything. They knew stuff we don't know. They do this kind of thing for a living."

"I don't like it. I don't—"

"Dammit, Chrissy, yesterday we said we needed exorcists, didn't we? Well, now we have them. They took me to the warehouse where they think Moon kills the kids. They can help. Only... only they were supposed to meet me here two hours ago and they haven't shown."

"And you trust them?"

I hesitated. "Yeah. Yes, I do."

"Do you think they're in trouble?"

My heart became something heavy, weighing down on my lungs. "Yes."

I stood there in the kitchen, the phone pressed to my ear, as helpless and useless in the face of true evil as any child.

"Then do you want to go help them?" Chrissy asked.

"Yes," I said.

I picked Chrissy up outside her house, a small Cape Cod on what used to be called Dearson Street, but which now went by the rather more grander-sounding Eastview Drive. If they'd thought renaming the street would elevate the neighbourhood, they must surely have been disappointed. The houses stood forlorn, the spaces between them filled with coarse grasses and the rusted detritus of modern living – flat-wheeled bicycles, broken-down dishwashers, and old cars run on nothing but hope, spit and desperation.

Chrissy was waiting for me outside the neatest of these houses, and she got in quickly, her purse in her lap. Even now, with the lines on her face and the grey in her hair, I felt a little buzz in my stomach when I met those blue eyes of hers. A buzz that I hadn't felt with my wife for a long time.

I felt guilty about that.

We didn't meet much traffic as we drove to the warehouse, but it was already getting dark as I pulled over.

"Is this it?" Chrissy asked.

"No, it's further up," I said, having learned from the experts. "We'll walk the rest of the way."

She nodded. "OK, yeah. I brought something. For us. For protection."

Glancing at me nervously, she pulled a nickel-plated revolver from her purse.

"It was my husband's," she said. "I kept it when he left. It's loaded, I checked. This little lever here is the safety."

I looked at it. "I've never fired a gun in my life."

"Me, either. But I thought we might need it."

She held it out to me. I took it, felt how heavy it was. I kept my finger away from the trigger. "OK," I said. "OK, this is probably... probably a good idea."

She gave me a smile, a thin, brittle smile, and got out. I hesitated only a moment before joining her.

I tried sticking the gun into the waistband of my trousers, but it didn't feel secure, so I just put it in my jacket pocket as we walked. I kept an eye out for cameras. Pleasant had said something about the security being impressive, but I didn't see any, not even when we were peering through the chain-link fence. There were lights on in the warehouse and a few cars parked outside that hadn't been there the day before. But I couldn't see any guards, and still no sign of cameras.

The gate was heavy and closed and the fence was twice my height. I realised that our first hurdle might also be our last.

"How the hell do we get in?" I murmured.

Chrissy hugged herself. It was cold out here. "Bruce Willis would just drive through the gate," she said. "Or if he wanted to be sneaky he'd drop down from a neighbouring roof." She craned her neck. "But how would he get up there?"

"This is ridiculous," I said. "We're intelligent people. We should be able to get past a fence."

"We could climb it."

We were going to have to. Even though I hadn't indulged in any strenuous physical activity for over six years, I was going to have to climb a fence in front of my childhood crush. I offered up a silent prayer that I wouldn't make too much of a fool of myself, then extended my arm, my fingers curling into the chain-link. Once I had a good grip, I rattled it a little, just to get an idea of what I had to work with, and then I jumped, grabbing a handhold further up. It wouldn't take much for my fingers to start burning, so I wasted no time. I dug my feet in against the fence, tried to get the toes of my shoes through the links. I hung there, scrabbling for purchase mere inches off the sidewalk.

"You have never stopped being sexy," Chrissy said in a quiet voice, and, despite the danger to ourselves and the threat to my son, I couldn't help it, I laughed, and I laughed so hard I had to let go and stagger away from my failed attempt at being impressive.

Chrissy covered her laugh with her hands, eyes glittering with mirth. We both knew what it was, of course. The laughter was a nervous reaction to a scary situation. It didn't make it any less funny.

"Boost me up," she said. "If I can reach the top, I'll try to pull you up after me."

I went back to the fence, interlaced my fingers and bent my knees, keeping my back straight. Chrissy put her right foot in the cradle my hands formed. Her hands rested lightly on my shoulders. She was taking deep breaths.

"One," I said, rocking slightly, "two... three."

On *three*, I straightened and lifted and she sprang, catapulting upwards. She got a hand round the bar on the top of the fence and hauled herself up quickly till she was resting on her belly. Steadying herself with her hands, she lifted her right leg up and over and sat up, straddling the bar and looking down at me.

"I'm not going to be able to pull you up," she said. Her words were fast and clipped. She was up high and she was scared. She leaned forward, her knees tight and her right hand curled into the links. With her free left hand, she reached down to me. "That's as far as I can go."

"I can't reach that high, Chrissy."

"Then find something to step on. If I lean down any more, I'll fall."

I looked around for something to stand on, but the street was empty. "I'll be right back."

"Where're you going?"

"I'll have to get the car."

"Hurry."

I ran back to the car, not liking this one bit. I turned the key gently, like that would make the engine quieter, and drove very slowly up to the warehouse with the lights off. I mounted the sidewalk, slowing down even more until the wing mirror scraped against the fence just below Chrissy. I turned off the ignition, got out, and clambered up on to the hood. Using the fence to steady me, I lunged up on to the roof. It clunked dully under my weight. I got into position, bent my knees, took a breath, and sprang. I hit the fence and clung on and Chrissy grabbed me with her free hand, then, after lots of grunting and exertion, I was straddling the fence, facing her. We held on to each other.

"We're going to have to jump down," I said.

She smiled without a whole lot of humour. "You first."

She let go of me and I gripped the bar with both hands, swinging my other leg over the side. I lowered myself down as far as I could go, then dropped. My heels slammed painfully to the ground and the fence rattled and I bit my tongue.

"You OK?" Chrissy whispered. "Are you all right?"

I nodded up to her, one hand over my mouth, blinking away tears of pain as I hobbled around in a small circle. She swung her other leg over, lowered herself down just like I had done.

"Catch me," she whispered and let go. She fell into my arms. She was heavier than I'd expected, but I didn't drop her. I set her back on her feet and she looked at me, frowning. "You sure you're OK?"

"Bit my tongue," I said, a little shamefacedly.

"Maybe I'll kiss it better for you later," she said, a grin on her face. "Providing we live through the—"

She grabbed me, pulled me down behind one of the parked cars. We stayed there for a few seconds, frozen. I peeked up. There was a sentry. He walked like he had walked this route a hundred times tonight already. He was watchful, but not wary – otherwise he'd have noticed my car on the other side of the fence. It was pure luck he missed us.

He glanced at his watch, then put his hands back in his coat. When he passed through the side door of the warehouse, a blue light in an obscure pattern glowed briefly on the doorframe. I was reminded of the security pads I'd seen in movies – where a green light would mean authorised, and red would mean intruder. I got the feeling that the light would glow red if we tried going in. When he was gone, when we were sure we weren't going to be discovered, we jogged to the door, slowing as we approached.

I had expected an electronic pad fitted to the wall. Instead, the pattern, some kind of obscure symbol, was simply painted on. I ran my finger against the surface. No sign of any electronics at all. Maybe it wasn't an alarm. Maybe it had been a trick of the light. Even so, I was wary of passing it before testing its—

Chrissy took a giant step through the doorway and I sucked in a breath... but the symbol stayed dark. No alarms sounded. She shrugged at me while I got my heart back under control. I took the gun from my pocket and joined her.

We moved quietly by a small office, got to the corner that led to the main warehouse. There were two tables set up. One, in the centre of the cavernous space, was broad and heavy and covered in a white sheet. The other, over by the wall, held a coffee pot and two trays of sandwiches. Five of Bubba Moon's People stood here, chatting in soft voices.

Skulduggery Pleasant and Valkyrie sat with their backs to a steel pillar. Chains kept them in place. Pleasant was facing away from the door, but Valkyrie was looking right at us. Her left eye was swollen almost shut and she had dried blood on her chin. When she saw me, she turned slightly, whispered something. I could see Pleasant's shoulder move as he nodded. I showed her the gun and she immediately shook her head. I looked over at the People. None of them appeared to be armed.

The door rattled suddenly and opened. A blue van drove in, killing its lights once inside. The sentry pulled the door closed and the van trundled to the left side of the warehouse, leaving the centre clear but for the cloth-covered table. It stopped and the engine was cut off.

Bubba Moon got out. He looked like Pete Green all grown up, but he wasn't. There was something extra about him, something extra in the way he moved – like he still, even after all these years, hadn't fully figured out how to work his new body. Like he didn't quite fit into it. He was tall and lean and still had all his hair. He wore ripped jeans and cowboy boots, and as he sauntered forward he took off his shirt, let it drop to the ground.

Underneath he was scarred.

Someone, years ago, had gone to work on him with a blade. Bizarre symbols, like the one on the warehouse door, like the ones we'd found in the basement when we were kids, had been meticulously cut into his flesh like savage tattoos. The way he was showing off to his People made me realise he'd probably commissioned the work himself – and something about his grin made me think he'd been fully conscious the entire time.

"Brothers and sisters," he announced, his voice echoing in the great expanse, "I thank you for coming on what is truly a special day."

Bubba Moon spoke with a Southern accent, an accent that Pete Green had never had.

"We are blessed, we are truly blessed, to have two witnesses to this month's offering. Two valued guests, over from the Emerald Isle, here for one night only. Ladies and gentlemen, I give you Skulduggery Pleasant and Valkyrie Cain!"

The People applauded. Now that I was focusing on them, I could see the cuts and bruises they sported. One of them had his arm in a cast. They each looked like they'd gone twelve rounds with a prizefighter.

"Pleasant and Cain," Moon continued, wandering over to his captives, "we have heard tales of your exploits and adventures. I am truly honoured. Never in my life did I expect that our modest little operation here would warrant your attention. We are but simple folk."

He grinned. Some of his People laughed. The grin didn't stay on for long. "Of course, you did put six of my people in hospital this morning. We did what we could with our limited knowledge of medical procedures, but our friends, our very good friends, are now languishing in hospital wards being seen to by clumsy mortal doctors, and that's... that's just not cool."

He lashed a kick into Pleasant's side.

"But I'm not one to hold grudges," he said. "I have a simple philosophy in life. Do unto others as they do unto you. You have honoured me by coming to this nowhere little town. You have honoured me by taking an interest in me, in us, and in the work we do here. So allow me to repay you in kind. I will honour you, sir, you and your partner."

He smiled down at her. "Valkyrie, Valkyrie, Valkyrie... what age are you, Valkyrie? Seventeen, aren't you? A little old to be an offering, strictly speaking... but tonight is a night for exceptions, is it not?"

Two of his People hurried forward. They undid the chains holding Valkyrie to the pillar, and pulled her to her feet. She lunged at one of them, but her hands were cuffed behind her back and Moon stepped forward, slapped her so hard she almost fell.

"Play nice," said Moon, "or you don't get to play at all."

The two men dragged her to the table, and Moon's attention returned to Pleasant as Pleasant spoke.

"An offering?" Pleasant said as the two men dragged Valkyrie to the table. "A blood sacrifice? You people are still doing that?"

I wished I could catch a glimpse of his face, just to see if he looked as cool as he sounded.

Moon shrugged. "It's a little retro, sure, but we've been doing it for decades and we've received no complaints so far."

"What about the sacrifices?"

"Oh, well, yes, *they* complain, but they're always in a bad mood, anyway."

"And do you mind me asking who you're making the offerings to? Just for my own personal amusement, you understand."

Moon laughed. "That's just the thing, Detective Pleasant, I don't even know myself. All I know is that a being of wonderment and awe came to me in a particularly vivid dream, and he told me that I was an integral part of the anti-Sanctuary. He told me I was to gather around me like-minded individuals and every time we met we were to offer him the blood of a mortal."

"There is no anti-Sanctuary," Pleasant responded.

"Well, the only thing I can say to that is there *is*, and I am an integral part of it."

"Because you had a dream."

Moon smiled. "Doubt all you want, Detective Cynic, Detective Sceptic, but I know the truth and so do my People. We have seen what lurks on the other side. And within minutes you will see, too."

I was running through things to say in my head – *Freeze! Nobody move!* – when another of Moon's People went to the back of the van and pulled out Sammy. His mouth was gagged, his hands tied. He'd been crying. He looked terrified as he was pushed towards the table, which had become a sacrificial altar in my mind, and I stepped out and raised the gun.

"Stop!" I shrieked. "Just stop! Let my son go! Let them all go!"

Bubba Moon and his People looked at me with nothing more than surprise in their eyes. Chrissy hurried out beside me, sticking close.

Moon began to smile. "Look at this. Look at this situation we currently find ourselves in. Why, this is nothing less than a class reunion! My oldest friend and my oldest crush. And there was I thinking this night could not get any more special..."

"You're not Pete," I said. The gun was shaking badly in my hand, so I brought my left in to steady it. "You're Bubba Moon. I know all about you."

"I doubt it," said Moon, and gave another smile. "Chrissy. The years have not been good to you, now, have they? Probably down to that thug of a man you married. Yes, I know all about that. Your life has never quite taken flight, has it? You had your wings clipped young."

"Sammy," I said. "Come over here."

Sammy looked around, making sure no one was going to try and stop him, then he ran over. Moon chuckled.

I pointed the gun at the man holding Valkyrie down. "Release her. Take off the handcuffs."

The man looked over at Moon, who glanced at his watch. For some reason that made his smile grow wider. "Do what my friend says."

A few seconds later, Valkyrie was free. The moment the cuffs were off, she sighed, like freedom hadn't been the only thing that had been kept from her. She grabbed the key from the man and threw it to Chrissy.

"Help my friend," she said.

Chrissy immediately went to the pillar where Pleasant sat.

Moon didn't seem to care about any of this. He was looking straight at me. "How've you been, old buddy? Done any skateboarding lately? Sammy, you might not know this about your old man, but he was quite the skateboarder when we were kids, just a few years younger than you are now. He was cool back then. We used to skate in the park, even though we weren't allowed. We frightened the pigeons and the old people. Good times, were they not?"

Things were going according to plan. The gun trembled less as I pointed it at him. "You're not Pete."

"But I'm in here with Pete," said Moon. "I know everything he knows. I know you and me were both in love with Chrissy Brennan. I know she preferred me."

"I'm pretty sure she's changed her mind about that now," I said, and Moon laughed.

I looked over when the chain fell, and saw Pleasant getting to his feet. Before he came round the pillar, his hand went to his collar, like he was fixing his tie. He stepped into view and I frowned. It wasn't Pleasant. He was as tall and as slender, he was dressed in a similar suit, but this man was white, handsome but unshaven, his brown hair tousled.

It wasn't the man I'd met the previous night, but when he spoke, he spoke with Skulduggery Pleasant's voice. "I must admit, this is disconcerting. You could have disarmed my gun-toting friend here without a second thought, but you didn't."

"No, we didn't," said Moon, and then gestured to the man's face. "I like this, by the way. Inspires trust."

This man – Pleasant in disguise? – observed Moon through narrowed eyes. "All of which leads me to suspect you have something up your sleeve. Which is not a nice thought, to be honest."

Moon smiled. "I wouldn't say it is."

"You looked at your watch before you allowed Valkyrie to be released. Time is not on our side, is it? It's on yours, but not ours. Are we expecting company?"

"We are."

"Someone who will cancel out the threat posed by Valkyrie and myself?"

"Indeed."

Skulduggery Pleasant, for I had come to the conclusion now that it was definitely him, wearing a disguise of some kind, nodded. "I really don't like the way this is going. Still, at least I'm no longer in shackles. That's something, at least."

"I'm glad you think so."

Chrissy came over, standing beside me with Sammy behind us. Sammy was pale, frightened, still bound and gagged, but his eyes were fixed on Pleasant, not Moon.

Moon looked at his watch again, and a brand-new smile broke out.

"Here we—" was all he had time to say before a hole tore open in empty space and a light poured through and I glimpsed something, something within that light, which I somehow knew to be a portal to somewhere else, somewhere terrible, and I saw a monster's face in that light and the light grew and grew and burst and—

7

uncovered my eyes, blinking rapidly, and found myself in a dark room that smelled of settled dust and moth-balls.

I was alone. It was cold. There was a bed in the corner without a mattress. I crossed to the window, peered out through the grime-streaked glass at Bredon. The warehouse was on the east side, but I was on the west, looking down on to King Road and the junkyard. From here I could see the church and the lights of the gas station, and if there hadn't been that line of trees on Hyland Street I'd have been able to see my school.

I was in Bubba Moon's old house. Only... I'd passed Hyland

Street a few times since I'd been home, and those trees weren't there any more. They hadn't been there since I was a kid.

There was a sound, somewhere below me.

I wiped the perspiration from my right hand, then gripped the gun tighter. I opened the door and immediately stepped away, expecting something to rush in at me. My back rippled with gooseflesh as I stood there, looking out into the gloom, waiting for horror. Finally, I started moving again, the floorboards creaking gently under my weight.

The landing was empty. There were no lights on in the house. The usual smells one would expect in an abandoned house – smells resulting from drunk teenagers breaking in or passing vagrants spending the night – were absent. No teenager had ever been drunk enough to break in here, and no vagrant had ever been cold enough to seek shelter under this roof. The only smell, apart from the dust, was a damp, unhealthy rot that seeped through the walls. It was like the house was sick, riddled with some wasting disease.

I reached the stairs and looked over the banisters. I had to go down there. I didn't know how I had got here, but I knew I had to go down there.

I started down the stairs.

Whether this was illusion or madness or magic, or if I had died in that warehouse and this was the hell I was to spend eternity in, mattered little to me at this point. For all I knew, I was still in the warehouse and this was all happening in my mind. Maybe it had affected everyone there. Maybe that bright flash of light had hypnotised me, hypnotised all of us.

Or maybe I was really here. And that thing I had glimpsed, that thing coming through the portal, maybe it was here, too.

I got to the bottom of the stairs without a clawed hand reaching through the banisters and grabbing my ankle. The front door was just ahead of me. I could have run straight to it, pulled it open, and fled. But what would I be fleeing into? Or when? Whatever had happened to bring me here had not only sent me across town, it had sent me across time. I knew, with no doubt in my mind, that this was the night we had snuck into Bubba Moon's house, all those years ago.

And that meant I had to go down, into the basement.

The basement door was under the stairs. The doorknob was black and loose and rattled when I turned it. I had to give it an extra turn it was fitted so badly. When it opened, the darkness from the basement spread upwards, passing me, darkening the hall, turning everything colder still, and then it settled, my eyes adjusted, and I started down the wooden steps.

There were more steps than there should have been. They descended into a gaping mouth of pitch-black. Twice on my way down I almost lost my nerve – but if I was here, then Sammy might be down here, too, and I wasn't going to abandon my son.

Gradually, the gloom began to lift, ever so slightly, and I saw the concrete floor below. When I reached the bottom, I looked back, unsurprised to find that there were, at most, maybe ten steps in all leading up to the open door.

The house was playing tricks on me.

Navigating my way round the stacks of piled-up junk was like being caught in a maze. I didn't remember there being this many stacks, and I didn't remember them being this high. It was the house again, growing and widening, adding more twists and turns to the journey. Playing its games.

There were shouts in among the stacks, but shouts from far away. Something else, too. Like distant gunfire.

I entered a clearing of sorts, getting my first real impression of just how big the basement had grown. It was massive, as big as the warehouse. Maybe it *was* the warehouse. Maybe the bright light had hypnotised me into confusing the two. But the warehouse hadn't had all this junk, and along the walls it didn't have all those wooden steps leading upwards.

Someone emerged from the stacks on my right.

"Chrissy!" I hissed.

She jumped, covering her mouth with both hands, stifling a yell. Then she hurried over, clinging to my right arm.

"We're in his house," she whispered.

"I know," I said. "Stay close to me."

We moved onwards, through the clearing and back into the stacks. We approached a low table on which sat a dollhouse. As we passed, a light switched on in one of the small windows.

"That's mine," Chrissy said softly. "I used to have that. That exact one."

We stared at it for a few more moments. Another light turned on. Chrissy let go of my arm and stepped towards it.

"What are you doing? Chrissy, don't."

She looked back at me, her face strained. "I have to," she said, and reached out, fingers hooking into the exterior wall of the dollhouse. She pulled it open and all the lights came on and she stepped back with a cry of disgust. Cockroaches skittered over the toy furniture, burrowing under the thin blankets on the beds to get out of the sudden light and pushing over the plastic plates on the kitchen table. Some of them had got on to her hand and Chrissy cursed, swiping at them as they tried to scuttle up her sleeve.

I pulled her away and the lights in the dollhouse went out, though we could still hear the cockroaches spilling over the edge of the table and hitting the ground.

Chrissy pushed against me and we moved on quickly. My foot nudged something so solid I almost tripped. I looked down, cursed, stepped back right into Chrissy. Together, we looked down at the still form, half-hidden by the stacks. When the figure didn't move, I inched forward, nudged it again. Then I got my foot under it and pushed the shoulder back far enough to reveal the face of the warehouse sentry. Blood leaked from a gash over his eye. He was either asleep or dead. I took my foot away, let the body slump back, and we stepped over it and carried on.

Ahead of us, around the next corner, another light flickered, and I heard the sound of a helicopter's rotor blades before it was replaced by synthesiser music. I recognised it immediately as the theme tune to *Airwolf*. Keeping the gun out in front, I led the way to an old TV with rabbit ears and terrible reception, the same TV that I had sat in front of, cross-legged in my living room, when I was a kid. We'd had that TV until the day my brother and I were throwing around the baseball indoors, and the ball bounced off the wall and hit the screen and cracked it. Our mom was not happy that day. Our dad was furious.

Even as this memory swam through my head, the crack appeared on the TV in front of us. The screen bulged slightly and retracted, like it was breathing. Every time it bulged, the crack would widen a little, and then it stopped retracting, it kept bulging, and black liquid (*blood*) started to drip from the screen, and then flow like an open wound. Then the screen burst open and the black liquid gushed out in a torrent that hit me square in the chest, forced me back, splashed into my mouth as I cried out.

Chrissy slipped and I fell over her and the black liquid covered us, drenched us, and then the torrent weakened, and went back to being a trickle, and then it stopped altogether and there was nothing except the busted TV.

I went to wipe my eyes clear, but I was dry. I was clean. I looked at Chrissy. There'd been no black liquid. No gushing blood.

"Playing games," I said.

We got up. Ahead, we heard voices. Children's voices.

We reached another clearing in time to watch myself, aged eleven, drop down from the narrow window into the basement.

"Oh my God," Chrissy whispered.

I was so small. So tiny. So young. I stared.

"See anything?" a voice asked from the window. Tyler's voice.

"Junk," my younger self said.

"Any black magic stuff?"

My younger self shone his flashlight right into my face and then moved it on without seeing me.

"Just old lamps and furniture. A table. Sofa."

We heard Benny telling me to grab a Ouija board if I saw one, and then Chrissy's voice came through loud and clear.

"Don't you dare. My aunt did the Ouija board once and she doesn't believe in any of that stuff, but she said that Ouija boards are actually dangerous."

Chrissy's fingers dug into my arm.

We watched history repeat itself until there were five eleven-year-olds down in the basement with us, the beams of their flashlights cutting through the murk.

Chrissy yanked on my shirt and I looked round. From behind a distant stack there came a fast-moving, flickering light, like someone going crazy with a flame-thrower. Then it cut off. No light, no flames, no smoke. The kids hadn't noticed it.

"Found it," Chrissy's younger self said. We walked after Tyler, joined the kids at the circle. Standing inside the circle was Bubba Moon.

Not the Pete Green Bubba Moon, but the original. A bald man, once heavily muscled, but with all that going to seed now. His gut was expanding, stretching the scars, distorting the symbols on his bare torso. He watched the kids crowd round him. They couldn't see him and he couldn't see us.

"Big bad Bubba Moon," Pete said in a soft voice.

Chrissy shrieked as the stacks beside us exploded, sending junk flying and old magazines fluttering like dying bats. A man hurtled through the air, bursting from one stack and disappearing into another. All this went unnoticed by the kids, unnoticed by Moon, but Chrissy and I ran over and I lunged into the stacks, gun at the ready, but of the man there was no sign.

We looked back at the circle. Pete was lying down in it while Bubba Moon stood over him. "Hey, guys, who am I?" he said, and laid his head back and pretended to be dead.

Grinning, Moon lay down with him, on top of him and over him, and all the flashlights went out.

The kids screamed, panicked, ran for the window, but Chrissy and I stayed and watched with mounting horror as Bubba Moon slowly got up, Pete moving within him, aping every movement. When they were both on their feet, Moon stepped back slightly, allowed Pete to stand on his own. Then Moon's hands went to Pete's shoulders, fingers digging into his shirt. When he lifted one shoulder, Pete lifted his foot, and together they lurched back towards the window.

I turned away from the unfolding scene, towards the sound of shouting. Gun in one hand, Chrissy's hand in another, I stepped cautiously towards a tall pile of shoeboxes. There was sudden movement, and one of Moon's People staggered out of the darkness. His shoulder hit the pile and he hit the ground and the shoeboxes toppled, spilling out hundreds of cassette tapes that clattered across the floor.

There was something else now, a sound like the snarl that thing had made as it passed through the portal. It was above us, and around us, moving through the stacks, and with it were more shouts and more gunshots. I heard Valkyrie Cain's voice.

When we looked back to the kids, they were gone. All but one.

Pete Green remained. He stood in the circle, looking at us, an eleven-year-old boy. At his feet, my son, unconscious.

I fought the urge to rush forward. "Why?" I asked.

Pete shrugged. "It likes the taste. The thing you saw. It likes the taste of mortal children. Fourteen years old, that's when they taste best, that's when it gets all the nutrients it needs. Who am I to disagree?"

"But why Sammy? Why our children?"

"Because I couldn't take *you*," said Pete. "I wanted all of you. You two and Benny. We all went down here, but I was the only one who stayed. How is that fair?"

"You killed Tyler," I said.

He grew up before our eyes. He grew taller and older and his clothes changed and his shirt disappeared and he was bare-chested and tattooed with scars again, just like he had been in the warehouse.

"Tyler was the only one I could take," he said. "But I made plans. Contingency plans. I was too late to stop you from leaving, my buddy, my pal, but I made sure Chrissy never got beyond the town limits, didn't I, sweetheart? I saddled her with a husband who was going to drain the fight right out of her. I left her with nowhere to turn. I left her with one option, and one option only."

Chrissy stiffened, and Bubba Moon looked at me and laughed. "All part of the game, you understand. I needed a way to get you to bring your family back to the old homestead for a few days, and really, what choice did she have? It was either your kid... or hers."

I frowned, raising the gun. "What?"

"I'm sorry," Chrissy said. She stepped away from me. She went to stand beside Moon.

I stared at them both. My hand started to tremble.

"You want to shoot me?" said Moon. "Or do you want to shoot the person who broke in and suffocated your dear old dad?"

He took one single step to the side, distancing himself from Chrissy.

"No..." I whispered. "Chrissy... what...?"

"He made me do it," she said, tears running down her face. "He said he'd take Scott next. He wouldn't let me leave—"

"Excuses, excuses," said Moon. "The point is, she killed your daddy, betrayed you to me, and now she wants me to kill your son instead of hers. You can't go home again, isn't that what they say?"

"I'll kill you," I said, pointing the gun at him.

"Go ahead."

The gun shook. He deserved it. For everything he'd done, he deserved it. He wasn't my friend. He was a killer. He was a killer and he was going to kill my son.

I pulled the trigger. Nothing happened.

Moon laughed. "You really think she'd give you a loaded gun?"

A scream pierced the air, and Moon grinned. "That would be your friends, I imagine," he said. "What, you thought they were going to come save you? They've never gone up against anything like this before. You have no one to..."

He faltered. The scream twisted and undulated and screeched. No human being could ever make anything close to that kind of sound.

Then there was silence.

Darkness swarmed my vision and dissipated like smoke...

...and then we were back in the warehouse with Moon's People sprawled unconscious around us. Sammy stood beside me, his hands still tied and his mouth still gagged. Next to the cloth-covered table, Moon stood with Chrissy, shaking his head, trying to clear it. Skulduggery Pleasant and Valkyrie Cain stood behind them both.

Valkyrie pushed Chrissy aside and Moon spun, too startled to do anything more than curse, just before Pleasant stepped into him and flipped him over his hip. Moon crashed to the ground and Valkyrie moved in. The handcuffs that had been used to bind her snapped over his wrists.

Moon got to his knees, shaking his head. "You can't stand up to it, you'll never defeat it—"

"We already have," said Valkyrie.

Moon screamed in abject rage as I dropped the gun and turned, untied Sammy. His hands free, he pulled the gag from his mouth, too startled, too shocked to speak.

I looked at Chrissy as she ran from the warehouse, then at Moon, tears streaming down his face, and finally I turned to Pleasant. "Are you going to kill him?"

"I thought we'd have to," he said. "We didn't think we'd be able to capture him. But now that we have..."

Valkyrie held Moon as well as she could while Pleasant picked the knife up off the table and cut a new symbol into Moon's forehead. When it was done, Pleasant stood over him, his gloved hand splayed against his bloody wound. He looked at me.

"Before I begin," he said, "I need you to understand that the words I am about to recite in no way indicate the presence, or indeed the existence, of a Divine Being of any sort. Words are words, and they have power, and arranged in a particular way they can have a particular effect. Is that understood?"

I nodded.

Pleasant looked down at his prisoner. "I command you, unclean spirit, in the name of whichever god you believe in, I command you to depart. Depart, then, transgressor. Depart, seducer, full of lies and cunning, foe of virtue, persecutor of the innocent."

"Get away from me," said Moon. "Get away!"

Pleasant ignored him. "Give place, abominable creature, give way, you monster. Depart, then, depart, accursed one, depart with all your deceits."

Valkyrie grinned. "Say it."

"I'm not saying it," said Pleasant.

"Go on," said Valkyrie. "Say it for me. Please."

Pleasant sighed, and returned his attention to the exorcism, and then, in a loud voice, he commanded, "*Get thee behind me, Bubba Moon!*" and Valkyrie cheered.

We went home. Felicity had tried to stay up, but she'd fallen asleep on the couch. I helped Sammy to bed, and he hugged me before I turned out the light. For a moment he was a little kid again, a little kid who needed me.

I stayed with him until he was asleep, and then I sat on the couch and waited for Felicity to wake. When she did, we talked. I didn't tell her about Bubba Moon. We didn't talk about what I had just been through. Instead, we talked about us, and our great kids, and our life together. We talked for hours, until the sun bled into the night and turned the sky orange.

Bubba Moon's van pulled up and I went outside. Valkyrie Cain got out, and so did a tall man with dark hair. Skulduggery Pleasant in yet another astonishing disguise.

Valkyrie told us that the exorcism had lasted three hours. When Pete Green's body finally slumped into unconsciousness, she'd dragged him out of the circle, leaving only the flickering image of the original Bubba Moon trapped within. By that stage, she said, a team of Sensitives had arrived to drain him of his power. Pleasant told us that Moon would never again get the chance to infect anyone. He would stay there, in that warehouse, in that circle, too weak to possess even a passing pigeon, and that's where he would remain until the end of days.

I thanked them. Not only for saving my life, not only for saving the life of my son, but also for saving the lives of all the other children who would otherwise have been sacrificed to whatever creature had lived in that light. Valkyrie smiled, thanked *me* for rescuing *them*, and ignored Pleasant when he insisted that he'd had the situation under control. He made a joke about not telling anyone what had happened, or he'd have to send in his friends who'd wipe our memories.

I'm pretty sure it was a joke.

They left without saying much else. They didn't tell me who they were, who they worked for, or what all this meant. Pleasant didn't explain why he wore so many disguises, although Sammy told me later that he'd caught a glimpse of him when he was handcuffed to the pillar, and he could have sworn Pleasant had a skull for a head. At this point, nothing would have surprised me.

Bubba Moon's People were scooped up by whoever scoops people like that up, and Chrissy left town with her son. I asked Pleasant not to send anyone after her. She'd suffered enough, I reckoned.

Pete Green was introduced to a team of psychiatrists who were very curious to find out what trauma had led a grown man with all those unusual scars to revert to his eleven-year-old self overnight. They told me they didn't dare reunite him with any old friends for fear it would traumatise him further – but maybe at some stage in the future...

That suits me fine. Pete's my best friend, and I'm not going anywhere. This is my home, after all.

THE BUTTON

THE BUTTON

Somewhere in the distance, a train rattled on its tracks.

Conor sat in his kitchen with the curtains drawn, the lamp on the table casting its searing eye over his handiwork. It was the size of a shoebox, and wooden. Heavy. Inside were things he did not, could not, understand. There were gears and levers and finely balanced cogs and symbols painstakingly etched into it all. He didn't know what they meant, didn't know what they were for, but he had seen them in his head for as long as he could remember. Transferring those symbols to metal and wood, after all these years, was... well, it was wonderful. It was a relief. It was like he'd been tense his whole life, every muscle knotted and his teeth gritted and his eyes screwed shut, and now suddenly he was relaxing, and a strange sort of euphoric calm spread through him.

He took a screwdriver from the junkyard of tools on the table and fixed the lid in place. His hands were covered in nicks and cuts. He had run out of plasters days ago. Some of the cuts still stung. There were particular gears and symbols that required blood. He didn't know why – he just knew that they did. He saw it in his head. He always had. This device, this box, these designs, these gears and levers and symbols – they had always been a part of who he was. This was all he thought about. It was why he didn't finish school. It was why he couldn't hold a job. It was why Cathy had left him. This device had ruined any chance he'd ever had at happiness – but here it was, finished. A wooden box with a big red button on its lid.

Conor straightened his back. Vertebrae cracked. How long had he been sitting hunched over like that? How long had he been sitting here? He became suddenly aware of how full his bladder was, and how empty his stomach. He needed to go for a walk. He needed fresh air. Was it even daytime? The curtains were closed and everywhere but the table was in darkness. It was night. But what night? Was it still the weekend?

There was something over by the door, a shape in the gloom. Like a man, standing very still. Conor squinted at it, then turned his head, looked at it out of the corner of his eye. No matter how he viewed the thing, this coat or this shadow or whatever it was, it still looked like a man. A tall man. In a hat.

Conor frowned at it.

"Hello, Conor," said the man.

A bolt of fear and fright shot from Conor's belly to his chest, but his body remained still. Would his legs even work if he tried to jump up? He'd been sitting here for so long he doubted it.

Conor's mouth was dry. How long had it been since he'd taken a drink of water? His voice cracked. The question he asked was not *Who are you?* or *What do you want?*, two questions he felt needed answers, but rather, "How long have you been standing there?"

"Just a few minutes," said the man. He had a reassuring voice. It was smooth. "You didn't hear me come in. You were otherwise occupied. What is that you've got there?"

"You can't have it," said Conor. "If you want to rob me, rob me. I have a little money somewhere. But you can't have this."

"I'm not here to rob you," said the man. "What happens if you press that button, Conor?"

The pressure on his bladder, the dryness of his mouth, the emptiness of his belly, and now a headache, rising slowly from the heat that was stinging his skin and making him sweat. He felt sick. He *was* sick. He needed to lie down.

"I don't know," said Conor.

The tall man in the hat moved his head ever so slightly. "You don't know what it does? But you made it, didn't you?"

Conor nodded.

"How did you know what to do?"

"I've always known," said Conor. "My whole life I've known. I had these images in my head. But I couldn't see them clear enough until... sorry, what date is it?"

"The twenty-first," said the tall man. "Four days before Christmas."

Conor frowned. "That can't be right. It was the eighth just... just a few days ago."

"Time got away from you," said another voice in the gloom, somewhere over by the window. It was a girl's voice.

"Who are you?" Conor asked at last.

"No one in particular," said the man. "We have a job to do, that's all. We help people."

"I don't need your help."

"You may not," said the girl, "but everyone else does." She walked forward a bit, until the peripheral glow from the lamp could pick out her features. She was pretty, with dark hair. Wearing black. Seventeen or eighteen, no older. "What does the button do?" she asked.

"I told you," said Conor. "I don't know."

"Then why is your finger on it?"

He looked down. There it was, his finger, resting on the big red button like it had no intention of ever moving. He frowned. He couldn't remember putting it there and yet... yet it seemed there was no other possible place he could put it. His finger belonged on that button.

"I'm sorry," Conor said. "I'm not feeling well."

"Conor Delaney," said the man, "take your finger off the button."

And Conor almost did it. Without thinking, his finger rose a fraction before the weight of his obligation forced it back down again.

Obligation? What obligation? What the hell was going on?

"How did you do that?" he asked the man. "How did you make me do that?"

The man made a sound, like a dissatisfied grunt, and it was the girl who spoke. "How did you disobey? Did you take a name?"

"What?" said Conor. "What do you mean?"

"How did you disobey?"

"I don't know what you're talking about, do you understand? I don't know who you are or what you're doing here."

"They're saying the world will end," said the girl.

This stopped Conor for a moment. "What?"

"They're saying the world will end," the girl repeated. "Did you hear that?"

"Are you... are you talking about that Mayan thing? What about it? The Mayan calendar ends on the twenty-first of December. So what? It's a calendar. They ran out of room, or they stopped calculating, or a new cycle begins again or something... I'm sorry, what does that have to do with anything? It's nonsense."

"Do you know what a Sensitive is, Conor?" the girl asked. "It's a psychic. You believe in psychics?"

"No," said Conor. "I don't believe in astrology, either, or tarot cards, or palm reading."

The girl nodded. "Palm reading is silly. So is astrology. Most tarot-card readers haven't a clue what they're doing. I met one once who assured me I had a happy life ahead of me – so she's pretty obviously an idiot. But psychics have been predicting the

403

end of the world, Conor, to coincide with the end of the Mayan calendar."

"So?"

"So we think the end of the world starts here," said the man.

Conor frowned. "In Ireland? You think the end of the world starts here in this country?"

"Actually, I think it starts here in this kitchen."

Conor blinked. "You can't be serious."

"I can be, but rarely am."

"And what? You think this button kicks it all off?" Conor said, almost laughing. "You think that's what I've been making? This is a box of gears and junk and things that don't make sense! There's not a single computer chip or piece of technology in it. It's not connected to anything. I don't know what will happen when I push the button, but whatever it is will happen in this box and this box alone. It's not going to set off a chain reaction, or explode, or detonate nuclear warheads, or... It's just a silly box."

"A silly box that has been in your head for your entire life," said the man.

"But now it's out," said Conor. "It's not in my head any more. It's gone. I don't have to... I don't have to think about it any more."

"How's your mother, Conor?"

The smile faded from Conor's face.

"She's doing well, from what I gather," the man continued.

"Responding to the treatment. She still draws on the wall, of course. Strange symbols. Strange designs. Gears and levers and a big red button."

"My mother is ill."

The man nodded his head in the shadows. "Like her father before her. And his father before him. Stretching back through the generations. And all of you with this design in your minds. This box. That button. But you, Conor, you're the only one who saw it clearly enough to construct it."

"I've broken the cycle," said Conor. "I'm not going to end up in an asylum like the rest of them. I've done it. I've made it. Now I get to have a normal life. Now that my duty is almost done, I get to be free of it."

"What duty?" asked the girl.

The headache was getting worse. He was getting hotter. He probably had a fever. "Did I say duty? I don't know. That's not the word I meant to use."

"But it's the one you did use," said the man. "Do you have a duty, Conor? Is that what it feels like?"

"I'm not sure I... I..."

"That box has cursed your bloodline for hundreds of years," the man said. "Maybe more. You were compelled to construct it, weren't you? You didn't have a choice. You may not even have been fully aware of what you were doing. You have a duty to that box, don't you, Conor?"

Conor nodded. "An obligation," he whispered.

"An obligation to that box. Why is your finger on the button, Conor? Is that part of your obligation? Once you build it, you set it off?"

Something broke in Conor's heart, and tears came to his eyes. "I have to press it," he said, his face crumpling. "I just have to press it once and it'll all be over. I'll be able to walk away and never think about it again."

"Pressing that button will hurt a lot of people."

"It's just a box," Conor sobbed.

"It's more than a box."

"It's just a box, I'm telling you. It doesn't do anything. I'm not a scientist or an engineer. I'm just a man. I'm just ordinary. I wouldn't know how to build anything that would hurt people. I don't want to hurt anyone. I just want to be able to walk away."

There was a sound outside. A car pulling up. A line of light swept in through the crack in the curtains and brushed by the man's jaw. It looked like his skin was white as chalk, or he was wearing a mask or something.

"Be right back," said the man, and slipped through the door.

"Who's out there?" Conor asked.

"Some people," said the girl. "There's been a race to find you. We got here first."

"What do they want?"

There was a cry from outside, and a sudden light like a bursting flame, and then it was gone again.

"They want the box," said the girl. "They want to sell it, or use it, or worship it. I don't know. Some of these people just don't make any sense to me. You look tired."

"I feel sick."

Outside there was another sound. Loud. Abrupt.

"Was that a gunshot?" asked Conor.

"It was," said the girl.

"Aren't you scared?"

"You've got your finger on a button that will end the world," the girl said. "Why should I be scared of guns that aren't even aimed at me?"

"I'm not going to end the world."

"You've got your finger on the button."

"I can barely work out how to make calls on my own phone – why do you think I know how to destroy the planet? This is ridiculous. Please leave me alone."

"I wish we could. But if we do, you'll press that button, and you'll kill us all. You'll kill my friends and my parents and my little sister. I can't let you do that, Conor."

"I won't be hurting anyone. The box doesn't do anything. It's just a stupid box with a stupid button, but it's been in my head for my entire life, like a constant whine in my ear. All I have to do to be rid of it is just press the thing. That's all. Easy as that. I'll press it, no one will get hurt, the world won't end, and I won't have to listen to that whine any more. I won't have to dream about gears and symbols. I'll be able to close my eyes and not see how one cog fits into the other. I'll be able to live in the kind of peace that my mother never could.

"You don't... you don't know. You don't know what it was like, seeing her... seeing what happened to her. Seeing how bad it got. When I was ten years old, she sat me down and told me these dreams I had would only get worse. She told me they'd consume my life, like they were consuming hers. This is my chance to escape that madness. Please, just leave me alone. This is the only chance I'll ever have."

"It isn't madness you're suffering from," said the girl. "My friend, the one that's out there right now fighting on your front lawn, told me what you are. You're a conduit for an idea, an idea that was planted centuries ago. It's grown inside the minds of your ancestors, been added to, been improved... and here, tonight, it's finally ready. You're not mad, Conor. Your mother isn't mad. You're just open to a stream of information that the rest of us aren't."

"So who planted it?" Conor asked. "This idea you're talking about. Whose idea was it? The Mayans?"

"The Mayan people just foresaw the end," said the man from beside the door. Conor hadn't even heard him come back in. "They had nothing to do with this. We don't know who started it. We don't even know if ending the world was what was originally intended. All we know is that our Sensitives had visions of a man in a dark room, building a box, and when he pressed the button everything just... ended."

"Then how did you know it was me?"

"They heard a train in the distance."

"That's it? That's all?"

"That narrowed it down," said the man. "A few other hints. A few other clues. Why haven't you pushed the button?"

"Why haven't I...? But you don't want me to."

"That's not why you haven't pushed it. Your finger's on it. There's nothing stopping you. Why haven't you?"

"I don't... I'm not sure."

"It's because you know that it isn't just a silly box and that isn't just a silly button. You believe us, don't you?"

"No, I... Oh, God. I don't know."

"Will you give us the box, Conor?"

"What will happen then?"

"We'll take it somewhere safe," said the girl. "We can't dismantle it and we can't destroy it – something might go wrong. But we'll take care of it. We'll hide it away where no one will ever find it."

"It won't be used to hurt anyone," the man said. "I promise."

"And me?" said Conor. "What will happen to me?"

The man hesitated. "I won't lie to you. You'll probably always feel that urge to push the button. That won't go away. You'll have to live with it for the rest of your life."

"But I'm so close. I'm so close to leaving it behind."

"We're asking you to make a sacrifice," the girl said. "We're asking you to continue living with this so that the rest of the world can continue living. Please, Conor."

More tears now, but they came silently. Conor lifted his finger from the button, and with his other hand he pushed the box slowly across the table. The girl came forward to take it. She wore a black ring, Conor noticed. For a moment it seemed to play with the shadows, and then the girl was lifting the box and stepping back, taking great care.

The last remaining dregs of strength drained from Conor's body. He was exhausted, confused, scared, and all he wanted to do was lunge across the table and push that big red button before the girl took it away.

"Thank you," said the man, and Conor just nodded.

The man looked down at something – a pocket watch? – and opened the door. "Two hours until midnight," he said. "Should be loads of time."

"Loads of time for what?" Conor asked, even though he knew the man hadn't been speaking to him.

The girl walked slowly out, taking the box with her. Conor forced himself to remain where he was.

"There's a woman who believes the souls of all her dead lovers are trapped in the centre of the earth," said the man. "She wants to crack the world open to free them."

Conor frowned. "Can she do it?"

"Yes. So we have to stop her before she kills us all."

"But... but didn't your psychics say that *I'd* be responsible for the end of the world?"

"Some of them did, yes. And some others said that she would. We've averted eight potential apocalypses already today, and she'll be our last. Once midnight comes, we can relax. Then we just have to hope the Americans don't mess up."

"The Americans?"

"A day can last forty-nine hours around the world," said the man, walking out and leaving Conor sitting there at his kitchen table. "A lot can happen in a day."

EXCLUSIVE PEEK AT

The Dying
of the
Light

I'm writing this little introduction on March 17th, 2014, and I'm taking a break from *The Dying of the Light* to do it. This here is the second chapter of the ninth book, and there really isn't a whole lot for me to say about it except, y'know, if you like this, the rest is just as good!

Or if you don't like this, the rest is better. I swear.

Um.

LIVING IN THE SHADOW

The flickering lights of the trashed supermarket threw deep shadows from dark places, and Stephanie stepped through it all with one hand wrapped tightly round the golden Sceptre. Rows of shelves lay toppled against each other in a domino-sprawl of scattered food tins and ketchup bottles. She caught the scent of a small ocean of spilled vinegar and glanced to her right in time to catch a flash of pinstripe. Then she was alone again in this half-collapsed maze, the only sound the gentle hum from the freezers.

She edged into the darkness and out again into the light. Slow steps and quiet ones and once more the darkness swallowed her in its cold hunger. Ahead of her, a man hovered, a metre off the ground, as if he were lying on an invisible bed. His hands were clasped on his belly, and his eyes were closed.

Stephanie raised the Sceptre.

One thought would be all it'd take for a bolt of black lightning to turn him to dust. One simple command that, less than a year ago, she wouldn't have even hesitated to give. Davos Rhadaman was a threat. He was a danger to her and to others. He had stepped into the Accelerator and the boost to his powers had turned him violent. Unstable. He was now the enemy. The enemy deserved to die.

And yet... she hesitated.

She was not one to second-guess herself. She was not prone to introspection. For the majority of her existence, Stephanie had been all surface. She was the reflection, the stand-in, the copy. While Valkyrie Cain was out playing hero, Stephanie went to school, sat at the dinner table, carried on with normal life. People viewed her as an unfeeling object. She had been an *it*.

But now that she was a *she*, things were murkier. Less clean. Now that she was a person, now that she was actually alive, she found that she didn't want to deprive any other living thing of that same opportunity – not if she could at all help it. Which was, she openly admitted, hugely inconvenient.

Wearing a scowl as dark as her hair, she stepped out from cover and advanced on Rhadaman slowly. She took a pair of shackles from her bag, made sure the chain didn't jingle. She kept the Sceptre pointed at him – she didn't want to kill anyone if she could help it, but she wasn't stupid – and chose her steps carefully. The floor was littered with supermarket debris. She was halfway there and still Rhadaman hadn't opened his eyes.

The closer she got, the louder her pulse sounded in her head. She felt sure he was going to hear her heartbeat. If not her heartbeat then at the very least her ridiculously loud breathing. When had she started breathing so loud? Had she always breathed this loud? She would have thought someone would have mentioned it.

She was three steps away and she paused, looked around, watching for pinstripes. Nothing. Why hadn't she waited? Why did she have to do this on her own? Did she really have that much to prove? Probably, now that she thought of it. So would capturing Rhadaman single-handedly make her a worthy partner? Would that justify her continued existence?

She wasn't used to all these conflicting thoughts, ricocheting around in her head.

Three more steps and she reached out, shackles ready.

Rhadaman's eyes snapped open.

He stared at her. She stared at him.

"This is a dream?" she tried, and a wave of energy threw her back.

She went tumbling, realised in some dim part of her mind that her hands were empty, and when she came to a stop she looked up and Rhadaman was standing there, holding the Sceptre.

"I've seen this in books," he said. He was American. "It's the real thing, isn't it? The Ancients actually used this to kill the Faceless

Ones, to drive them out of this reality. The original God-Killer."
He pointed it at her as she stood, then frowned. "It doesn't work."

"Must be broken," said Stephanie. "Could I have it back?"

She held out her hand. He looked at her a moment longer, and
his eyes widened. "You're her."

"No," she said.

He dropped the Sceptre and his hands started glowing. "You're
her!"

"I am not!" she said, before he could attack. "You think I'm
Darquesse, but I'm not! I'm her reflection! I'm perfectly normal!"

"You killed my friends!"

"Stop!" she said, pointing at him. "Stop right there! If I were
Darquesse, I could kill you right now, right? I wouldn't need shackles
to restrain you. Listen to me. Valkyrie Cain had a reflection. That's
me. Valkyrie Cain went off and turned evil and became Darquesse,
but I'm still here. So I am not Darquesse and I did not kill your
friends."

Rhadaman's bottom lip trembled. "You're not a reflection."

"I am. Or I was. I evolved. My name is Stephanie. How do you
do?"

"This is a trick."

"No," said Stephanie. "A trick would be much cleverer than
this."

"I should... I should kill you."

"Why would you want to do that? I'm working with the Sanctuary.
The war is over, right? You do remember that? We're all back on

the same side, although you guys kind of lost and we're in charge. So if I tell you to surrender, you have to surrender. Agreed?"

"No one gives me orders any more," said Rhadaman.

"Davos, you don't want to do something you'll regret. The Accelerator boosted your magic, but it made you unstable. You're not thinking clearly."

"I'm thinking very clearly. Killing you may not bring my friends back, but it'll sure as hell make me smile."

"Now that," Skulduggery Pleasant said, pressing the barrel of his gun into Rhadaman's temple, "is just disturbingly unhealthy."

Rhadaman froze, his eyes wide. Skulduggery stood there in all his pinstriped glory, his hat at a rakish angle, his skull catching the light.

"I don't want you getting any ideas," Skulduggery said. "You're powerful, but not powerful enough to walk away from a bullet to the head. You're under arrest."

"You'll never take me alive."

"I really think you should examine what you say before you say it. You're not sounding altogether sane. Stephanie, you seem to have dropped your shackles. Would you mind picking them up and placing them on—"

Rhadaman moved faster than Stephanie was expecting. Faster even than Skulduggery was expecting. In the blink of an eye, Skulduggery's gun was sliding along the floor and Skulduggery himself was leaping away from Rhadaman's grasping hands.

"You can't stop me!" Rhadaman screeched.

Skulduggery's tie was crooked. He straightened it, his movements short and sharp. He was annoyed. "We wanted to take you in without violence, Davos. Do not make this any harder than it has to be."

"You have no idea what it's like to have this kind of power," Rhadaman said, anger flashing in his eyes. "And you want me to give it up? To go back to being how I was before?"

"This power level isn't going to last," Skulduggery said. "You know that. It's already starting to dip, isn't it? In fifteen days, there'll be more dips than peaks, and by the end of the month you'll be back to normal. It's inevitable, Davos. So do yourself a favour. Give up before you do any serious damage. We'll get you the help you need, and when it's all over, you'll return to your old life. The alternative is to keep going until you hurt someone. If you do that, your future will be a prison cell."

"You're scared of my power."

"As you should be."

"Why should I be scared? This is the greatest thing that has ever happened to me."

"This?" Skulduggery said. "Really? Look around, Davos. We're in the middle of a supermarket. The greatest thing that has ever happened to you and you choose to trash a supermarket? Are you really that limited?"

"I didn't do this."

"No? Who did?"

"My friends."

Stephanie couldn't help herself – she had to look round.

"And where are your friends now?" Skulduggery asked.

Rhadaman shrugged. "Close by. They don't wander off too far. There were loads of them around after the various battles, and I found a group and adopted them. They don't say a whole lot."

Stephanie picked up a faint whiff in the air. "Hollow Men?"

"I've given them names," Rhadaman told her. "I've given them names and I've dressed them in clothes. I've called them after my friends, the ones Darquesse killed. I think they like having names, not that they'd ever show it."

"Hollow Men don't like anything," Stephanie responded. "They don't think. They don't feel."

"Reflections aren't supposed to feel, either," Rhadaman said. "But you say you do. What makes you any different to them?"

"Because I'm a real person."

"Or you just think you are."

"If you surrender," Skulduggery said, "I promise we'll take your friends in and treat them well. Once the effects of the Accelerator wear off, they'll be returned to you. Do we have a deal?"

"You know what they *do* enjoy?" Rhadaman asked, as if he hadn't even heard Skulduggery. "They enjoy beating people to a pulp. They enjoy watching the blood splatter. They love the feel of bones breaking beneath their fists. That's what my friends enjoy. That's what will make them happy."

"You don't want to do this," Skulduggery said.

Rhadaman smiled, curled his lip and gave a short shriek of a whistle.

Skulduggery ran at him, and with a flick of the wrist he sent the Sceptre flying into Stephanie's hands. Rhadaman caught him and threw him and leaped after him, and before she could run to help the Hollow Men came at her, stumbling through a mountain of cereal boxes. Hollow Men dressed in clothes, ridiculous in badly fitting suits, ludicrous in flowing floral dresses.

Black lightning flashed from the crystal set into the Sceptre, turning three of them to dust without even a sound. Lightning flashed again, and again, but they kept coming, and there were more Hollow Men behind her, and they were closing in. They had that knack. They were slow and clumsy and stupid, but it was when they were underestimated that they were at their most dangerous.

Stephanie darted right, clearing a path for herself, ducking under the heavy hands that reached for her. She led them down a narrow aisle, big heavy freezers on both sides, turned to them and backed away as they gave lurching chase. Numbers mean nothing if the enemy can be corralled, Skulduggery had taught her. It's all about choosing where to fight.

The black crystal spat crackling energy. The Ancients had used it to kill the Faceless Ones, to drive them from this reality eons before. If it was powerful enough to kill insane gods whose very appearance could drive people mad, then artificial beings with skin of leathery paper and not one brain cell between them didn't stand much of a chance. They exploded into dust that drifted to the floor and was trodden on by their unthinking brethren. They didn't stop. Of course they didn't. They didn't know fear. They had no sense of self. They were poor imitations of life, much like Stephanie herself had once been. Once upon a time.

But now Valkyrie Cain was gone, and Stephanie Edgley was all that was left.

From elsewhere in the supermarket, she heard a crash as Skulduggery fought Rhadaman. She wasn't worried. He could take care of himself.

The shadows moved beside her and a fist came down on her arm. Her fingers sprang open and the Sceptre went spinning beneath a toppled shelf. She ducked back, cursing. Her only other weapon was the carved stick across her back, which had a limited charge and was useless against anything without a nervous system.

She ran by a shelf of microwaves and blenders, past pots and pans. She grabbed a stainless-steel ladle that felt unsurprisingly unsatisfying in her hand, and immediately dropped it when she saw the one remaining box of kitchen knives. She dragged it from the shelf, threw it straight into the face of the nearest Hollow Man. The box fell, knives scattering across the floor.

Stephanie snatched up the two biggest ones and swung, the blades slicing through the Hollow Man's neck. Green gas billowed like air from a punctured tyre. Even as she ran on she could taste the sting of the gas in the back of her throat.

Two Hollow Men ahead of her, one in a shirt and tie and no trousers and the other in a silk dressing gown. She dropped to her knees, sliding between them, cutting into their legs as she passed, and even as they were starting to deflate she was already on her feet again, stabbing the filleting knife into the chest of a Hollow Man wearing pyjamas. She spun away from the blast of gas, coughing, her eyes filling with tears. Something blurred and she hacked at it, shoved it away, her vision worsening, her lungs burning. Her stomach roiled. She tasted bile. She slipped on something. Fell. Lost one of the knives.

A hand grabbed Stephanie's hair, pulled her back and she cried out. She tried slashing at it with the second knife, but it got tangled in her jacket and then it too was lost. She reached up, felt the rough skin, dug her nails in, tried to tear through. Her hair was released. Something crunched into her face. The blurred world flashed and spun. She was hit again. She covered up, her arm doing its best to soak up the heavy punches, her head rattling with each impact.

If she'd had magic, she'd have set the Hollow Man on fire by now or sent her shadows in to tear it apart. But she didn't have magic. She didn't have such a luxury to fall back on, to get her out of trouble. She wasn't Valkyrie Cain. She didn't *need* magic.

Stephanie brought her knees in and spun on her back. The Hollow Man loomed over her, a black shape through her blurred eyes. Its fist came down on to her belly like a wrecking ball, would have emptied her lungs were it not for her armoured clothes. She braced her feet against its legs and pushed herself back out of range, rolling backwards into a crouch, the Hollow Man stumbling slightly. She plunged her hand into the display stand next to her, grabbing for a weapon, fingers curling round a mop. The Hollow Man came at her and she rose, swinging the mop like a baseball bat.

She missed wooden mops. Wooden mops would have a little bit of weight to them – whereas the plastic one in her hands merely bounced lightly off the Hollow Man's head.

She flipped it, drove the other end into the Hollow Man's mouth, pushed until she'd sent it staggering and then she let go, turned and ran back the way she'd come. Her eyes were clearing. She no longer wanted to puke. A Hollow Man turned to her and she dodged round it, tripped and fell and saw the Sceptre. She threw herself forward, plunged her hand under the fallen shelf, her fingers closing round its reassuring weight. The Hollow Man reached for her. She turned it to dust.

She got up, disintegrated the next one, and the one after that. Three more trundled into view and she dispatched them with equal ease. Then the only sounds in the place were coming from Skulduggery.

Stephanie hurried back in time to see Rhadaman pull Skulduggery's arm from its socket.

Skulduggery screamed as his bones clattered to the floor. A blast of energy took him off his feet, and Rhadaman closed in, ready to deliver the killing blow.

"Freeze!" Stephanie yelled, the Sceptre aimed right at his chest.

He looked at her and laughed. "That doesn't work, remember?"

She shifted her aim, turned the door behind him to dust. "It only works for its owner, moron. Now unless you want your remains to be swept into a dustpan, you'll shackle yourself." With her free hand, she lobbed the shackles at him. They hit the ground at his feet, but he didn't move.

"I know what you're thinking," she said. "You're thinking, 'Can I kill this girl before she fires?' Well, seeing as how this is the Sceptre of the Ancients, the most powerful God-Killer in the world, and it can turn you to dust in a single thought, you've got to ask yourself—"

Skulduggery swung the butt of his gun into Rhadaman's jaw and Rhadaman spun in a semicircle and collapsed.

Stephanie stared. "Seriously?"

Skulduggery nudged Rhadaman with his foot, making sure he was unconscious.

"I was in the middle of something," Stephanie said. "I had him, and I was in the middle of something. I was doing a bit. You don't interrupt someone when they're doing a bit."

"Cuff him," Skulduggery said. He holstered the gun and picked up his arm, started to thread it through his sleeve.

"I'd almost got to the best line and you... fine." Stephanie shoved the Sceptre into the bag on her back, walked over and cuffed Rhadaman's hands tight. She stood as Skulduggery's arm clicked back into its socket.

"Ouch," he muttered, then looked at her. "Sorry? You were saying something?"

"I was being cool," she said.

"I doubt that."

"I was being really cool and I was quoting from a really cool movie and you totally ruined it for me."

"Oh," he said. "Sorry."

"No, you're not. You just can't stand it when other people get to say cool stuff while you're too busy screaming, can you?"

"He did pull my arm off."

"Your arms get pulled off all the time. I rarely get to say anything cool, and usually there's no one else around to hear it, anyway."

"I apologise," Skulduggery said. "Please, continue."

"Well, I'm not going to say it *now*."

"Why not? It obviously means a lot to you."

"No. There's no point. He's already in shackles. Also, he's unconscious."

"It might make you feel better."

"I'd feel stupid," said Stephanie. "I can't say cool things to an unconscious person."

"This isn't about him. It's about you."

"No. Forget it. You'd just laugh at me."

"I promise I won't."

"Forget it, I said."

He shrugged. "OK. If you don't want to finish it, you don't have to. But it might make you feel better."

"No."

"OK, then."

He stood there, looking at her. She glared back, opened her

mouth to continue the conversation, but he suddenly turned, walked away, like he'd just remembered that she may look and sound and talk like Valkyrie Cain, but she *wasn't* Valkyrie Cain.

And she never would be.